STOUT

Taylor Small

Published by Taylor Small – www.taylorjsmall.com

Printed by Biddles Books Ltd

Printed in Great Britain

Cover art by Pasi Leinonen – www.pasilion.com

For Dan and Terry

'Its gates were fire, its walls the mountain. Most would have turned back long ago, but not this brave hero. He had come so far since that chance meeting in the tavern, nine moons ago. Further than he ever thought he could come. He knew his good heart would shield him from the flames, so he was not afraid when he stepped over that burning threshold. When he emerged, not a single hair on his chin had been singed. Imagine that! He unsheathed his swords and crept down the dark tunnel, but it was not long before he heard approaching footsteps. Twenty green-skinned foes with sharp, pointy teeth came rushing towards him: minions of the dragon!'

'Wassa min-yon?'

'It's like a little person.'

'Are we min-yons, papa?'

'No, son, we're dwarves.' He chuckled, and rubbed his son's shaggy head.

'One by one,' papa continued, 'the hero dispatched the minions, until there was but one left. "Lead me through this labyrinth to your master's lair, and I will spare your life," said the hero. The goblin, cowardly now that it no longer outnumbered the hero, agreed to the terms. Back and forth, round and round they went, until the hero reached the mouth of a glowing cavern. There, on a pile of stolen riches, lay the dragon.'

'Rhev, it's time for bed,' said a kindly voice.

'Please mama, we jus' got to the bit wi' the daggon!'

'Your father can finish the story when he gets back.' Mama's voice was sterner now.

'We better listen to your mother, Rhev. She knows best.'

1

'But I wanna know if the hero kills the daggon an' gets the treasure back!'

Papa smiled and fished something out of his pocket.

'Does this answer your question?'

He held in front of him a silver ring inlaid with verdigris bronze. The engraved patterns were so intricate it made little Rhev go cross-eyed just to look at it.

'For me?' Rhev exclaimed.

'You shouldn't,' began mama.

'Come now, it's just a ring. Let the boy have his story.' He leant his forehead against his son's. 'A good heart is all a hero needs, Rhev. Remember that.' He caught his wife's eye, and smiled. 'And they always listen to their mamas.'

Mama snuffed out the candle as papa left the tiny bedroom. Rhev could hear them arguing in hushed tones next door, but he was too transfixed by the ring to care. He had heard arguments lots of times, but this was the first real treasure he had ever seen.

***

Rhev left the pub through a window on the second floor. His broad frame made an undignified sound as it hit the mud below.

'Crap', spat Rhev, both figuratively and literally. *At least I won't be paying for the broken window again,* he thought.

Indeed, the proprietors of The Salty Wench had long given up replacing the glass in the windows of their less than respectable establishment. More often than not they were broken by people like Rhev who couldn't keep down their ale, their fists, or both. The dwarf patted his leather jerkin to check that his ducats were still safely tucked away, and then made to get up. To his surprise, somebody helped him to his feet: somebody with very large hands and a very, very loose understanding of personal hygiene.

'Ello, Rhev', growled the filthy goliath, his face resembling

2

a rather disgruntled potato. 'Dat li'l disappearin' act o' yours usually works better when we're on da bottom floor, dun it?'

'Ah, Grint, my old pal,' Rhev beamed. 'My good, old pal. *Best pal?* Maybe, in time, who knows? Thanks for the pick-me-up, very kind of you. I was just looking for the lavvy actually, must have taken a wrong turn. Better put me down before I wet myself.'

The goliath released the dwarf, who had been dangling a good five feet above the ground. He lost his footing in the mud and landed on his arse yet again. A diminutive figure sauntered between the goliath's legs towards him. He held something in his hands.

'Care to explain these?' said the halfling, the threat of violence dripping from his voice.

'They're dice, Sleedo. You roll them, and they show numbers. I can help you count them if you like.'

'I know how to count, you worm!' Sleedo sneered. 'I was referring to *these.*' A pudgy finger pointed to something wiggling on the dice. Rhev grimaced.

'They're, erm, legs,' he admitted.

'They do appear to be, don't they, Rhev? Now humour me, why have your dice got legs?'

'A naturally occurring phenomenon? Or maybe there are very little people inside the dice, and they just worked out how to cut some leg holes.'

His insolence was met with a surprisingly swift jab to the chops from the halfling. Considering the size of the fist, it didn't half hurt.

'You know that magickal trinkets of any kind are banned at my table. I mean, come on Rhev, *dice with legs.* Where's your respect? Where's the subtlety? Where's the craft in the grift?'

'You're right, it was very disrespectful of me. A thousand apologies. I'll never darken your doorway again. Now, if I could just get my property back-'

'You ain't getting dese dice, *or* our gold, runt!' Grint interrupted, his slobber leaving sticky dark patches on Rhev's auburn beard.

'Well, in that case, up yours.'

Rhev unhitched the heavy iron tankard he kept on his belt and chucked it at Grint's vegetable of a face. The sound of metal on stodgy flesh made a satisfying *thwack,* distracting the halfling for just a second. Without hesitation Rhev leapt up and took the opportunity to deliver a powerful kick to Sleedo's nether regions. With a poetic symmetry, the halfling's face crumpled into something resembling an angry scrotum.

With his two adversaries momentarily immobilised, Rhev bolted across the square towards the nearest goods lift. It began to descend out of sight mere moments after he had landed on a sack of turnips. As the lift was lowered into the Underport, Rhev saw two sour faces lean over the railings surrounding the surface opening.

'Too easy,' he chuckled to himself.

Wham. Grint landed on the platform next to Rhev. The ropes suspending them creaked pitifully.

'You dropped dis,' said the goliath, as he hurled the tankard back at the dwarf. It hit Rhev squarely in his nascent beer gut and pushed him backwards, bringing him within an inch of plummeting to his death. His eyes flicked to a sign next to him. In crude letters it read 'no bigs!'. Either Grint was going to have to go on one of those fashionable plague diets, or somebody had to leave.

Rhev surveyed the forest of ropes and pulleys hanging from the roof of the vast underground cove they were now entering, each set suspending a lift. Years of hitching rides where he wasn't wanted had left him with an instinct for when each lift rose and fell, at what speed, and for how long. After a split second of calculation, he leapt.

He landed among a flock of sheep. Bleats of annoyance

4

rang in his ears, and he was overcome by the j
lumps. As his platform went upwards, Grint
view. *Time to go.* Rhev clambered onto the bε
indignant ewes and used the rest as steppin
the next lift, this one going downwards.

A sheep fell onto the platform behind him, followed by
Grint. Sacks of potatoes were mashed underfoot by the
goliath's giant boots, accompanied by faint, starchy profanities
from the vegetables themselves. *Can't be cautious if I'm going to
outrun this bastard.* Rhev took note of his position and counted
in his head. Then, without stopping to look, he sprinted
forward. Each time his foot stepped out over the abyss it was
met by a new platform. A perfect run. He glanced behind him.
Somehow, Grint was still on his tail. Recklessly, the dwarf
made a sharp right turn and blindly leapt for what he was
more or less certain would be a downward bound lift not far
below him.

Rhev's heart moved up to his throat. He was falling now.
Falling, falling, falling. Too much falling. He hadn't expected
this. The brazen recklessness that had given him the edge all
these years had finally pushed him over it.

Oof. A wagon of hay saved him from an untimely death.
He didn't bother getting up. Instead, he caught his breath as
the lift descended, away from the scowling Grint. By now the
goliath was too far away for even the biggest wagon of hay to
break his fall. He was resigned to send a globule of spit after
Rhev instead. The dwarf rolled off the wagon at the last
moment and denied his pursuer even that small victory. Then,
brushing the hay from his jerkin, he surveyed the view below
him.

Velheim's massive subterranean harbour was even more
dilapidated than the town above. Many of the old buildings
clung to the wet rock like barnacles, covering the walls of the
cove in a wave of rotting timber. The docks below undulated

orkers moved to and fro like a tide, unloading cargo from .e galleys and cogs anchored there. A few members of the Cliff Guard ambled around the workers, every now and then tripping up the younger lads or trying desperately to light a cigar in the damp air. The lift thudded down onto the cobbles, and Rhev became part of the throng.

As he passed some of the guards he acknowledged them with a tug of his beard. A few returned the sentiment by tapping their helms.

'Hope you've been behaving yerself, Rhev. We wouldn't want a strike on your *spotless* record, eh?' called out one of the guards, a pimply orc with an unfortunate crease in his forehead.

'Aye, and we wouldn't want my knuckles imprinted on your *spotless* mug, would we Buttmug?' grinned Rhev.

'Why you good-fer-nuthin', greasy-bearded-' Rhev ducked underneath a crate one of the dockworkers was carrying, and was soon out of sight. Rhev and 'Buttmug' did not have the best of relationships, as was well known amongst the guards. The wily dwarf was responsible for popularising the orc's *nom de guerre*, and Buttmug himself was not best pleased. In all fairness, the orc's birth name translated into the common tongue as Feculent Buggerhat, so he wasn't going to be best pleased either way.

After a few minutes of traversing unconscious drunkards, fighting drunkards, and a local cat known as Steve who seemed to have the uncanny ability of being under everyone's feet *all the time*, Rhev arrived home. The rotten door creaked perilously on its hinges as he opened it. He knew he should get it fixed, but he had other, more important matters to attend to.

He hadn't slept in the room for a while now, but Rhev still kept his lockbox under his childhood bed. He slid it out and took it into the kitchen, carelessly brushing dirty pots and

6

pans off the table to make room for the box. He retrieved the key from his mama's snuff box on the mantle, and revealed his hoard. Ninety ducats. One hundred once he added the contents of the purse. Not bad for a barely adult dwarf who spent the majority of his free time in Velheim's myriad watering holes. He took a moment to admire the treasure he had earned. Collected. Gathered? *Semantics*. All that mattered was that it was his, and he wasn't going to spend it on drink this time. Well, technically he only needed ninety five ducats, so that left five for a little celebratory booze up. After all, he deserved it.

He scooped the shimmering pile into a small sack, slung it over his shoulder, and hefted the front door back into place behind him. A happy whistling tune sprang forth from his lips. He'd been waiting months for this day, and nothing was about to bring him down.

'Off to the pits, are ya?'

The whistling had caught some unwanted attention.

'What pits would those be, Josephine?' said Rhev. He looked up at the window belonging to the hovel stacked on top of his own home.

'The carnal pits, of course! Isn't that where all you criminals go to spend your ill-gotten coin?' replied Josephine, emphasising her question with a well-timed raise of a shaggy eyebrow.

'What exactly *is* a carnal pit, Josephine?'

Josephine scoffed, and then spat with gusto onto the dirt below.

'A pit where your kind goes to fornicate and fight, of course. Bodily sins, committed out of Almighty Mother Ava's sight.'

'Which is it then?'

'Which is what?'

'Is the pit for fornicating, or for fighting? It doesn't sound

7

like we should be mixing the two, it could get very messy. Are there partitions in the pit? Different coloured wristbands for participants?'

'I don't know, do I! I've never been. I'm not a filthy degenerate.' Josephine scratched at a worryingly green armpit. 'If only your mother knew what you were up to.'

'Well she doesn't, does she!' Rhev had been quite enjoying the badinage until then. Now, he began to lose his composure. 'I earned everything... *almost* everything in this sack from defending this stinking city on behalf of equally stinking people like you!'

Josephine sneered, revealing a row of worryingly black teeth.

'Tell yourself what you need to, if it helps you sleep at night. All I'm saying is that you're still a young'un. There's time for you to see Ava's light yet. Blessings be to you, arsehole.'

Josephine retreated into the darkness of her hovel, coughing violently. Almighty Mother Ava clearly hadn't been kind to her. Still bristling from Josephine's inquisition, Rhev adjusted the sack over his shoulder and continued on his way.

The smithy's workshop was a small affair attached to the husk of an old ship that had been taken ashore and converted into affordable housing. The owner, a bald man with one arm the size of a cow and the other the size of a pig, looked up from his work as Rhev approached.

'Aha! Rhev! You're just in the time to see the legumes of my labour,' said the blacksmith, smiling broadly. He had immigrated to the Peninsula quite late in life and had since been doing his best to learn the language, especially the colloquialisms, with varying levels of success. Among many of his customers this had led to the belief that he was fundamentally stupid. This was, in fact, largely untrue; in his own words, he was as bright as a cucumber.

'Afternoon, Hoskin,' hailed Rhev. 'That's a good looking weapon you've got there.'

The blade in Hoskin's beefy hands caught the half-light of the Underport with a violent keenness.

'Aye, it'll cut through a dragon like a spoon through butters,' said Hoskin gleefully.

'Glad to hear it, that's what I'm paying for after all.' Rhev couldn't wait to get his hands on the sword. He had ordered it over a month ago, something to finally replace the pitted guard-issue shortsword he'd been carrying around. With a sword like this, he was certain that he'd finally command the respect of his colleagues, as well as buzzkills like Sleedo and Grint. 'So, if you could just pass it over, I've got the money right here-'

'No,' replied Hoskin, a smile still on his face.

'No?'

'Can't do that.'

'Why?' Rhev blurted, his good spirits crushed.

'*Yours* is in the back. Hang on, I shall be returning in a jiffy-tick.'

Hoskin, along with the masterwork blade he had been holding, disappeared into the smithy. After what seemed like a few minutes but could have equally been a 'jiffy-tick', he returned holding a greatsword that looked infinitely worse than the one he had walked in with. Its strangely mottled blade seemed to consist of an unhealthy amalgamation of different metals, each catching the light differently. Hoskin held the sword by a grip consisting of crudely wound leather straps, topped off at either end by a simple blocky pommel and a solid, but uninspiring, crossguard.

'I had to recycle some of the scrap swords to get the metal for it, but that is what you get for the ducats you were offering me. You robbed me deaf, yes you did', Hoskin grumbled. 'But see here, I did the engraving that you asked for.'

Hoskin handed over the mongrel sword to Rhev, who turned it over to inspect the fuller. Near the hilt end, in terrible handwriting, flashed the word 'Onur'. Hoskin hadn't quite got the hang of spelling either. Rhev cursed himself for not writing the word on a piece of paper for Hoskin to copy. He cursed himself again for thinking it was a good idea to have 'Honour' written on his sword in the first place.

'That's some bloody… grand work you've done here, mate' said Rhev, patting Hoskin on his hairy back while looking down dejectedly at his new sword. 'Here's the coin. I'll see you later for a drink.'

He tossed the sack up in the air, and it landed in Hoskin's calloused palm. Hoskin said his goodbyes, butchering another slang phrase that heavily implied he was off to punch a wizard in the face, and Rhev hurried away with the greatsword strapped to his back, wishing he had brought a cloak to cover it.

***

The old man creaked. He was, undoubtedly, falling apart. It was a wonder that he had managed to last this long at all. A groan escaped his lips as he hoisted himself from the chair. In truth, he longed for the day when he could cast off this cursed body. It took him considerable time to reach the door. During his journey, he considered that it might be more efficient to simply move his chair to the hallway, but that would remove most of the excitement from his very dull life.

He opened the door just in time to see the postman sprinting away down the empty road. The old man chuckled, and bent down to pick up the letter. It had a seal on it signifying that it had come all the way from Heptamil. Carefully, he opened the envelope and retrieved the parchment. His pale eyes scanned the words before him, and he nodded to himself. As planned, it had begun. Finally, some excitement. The day was coming.

10

**

Her entire wardrobe was full of earthy colours: browns, greens, the odd ochre or lavender. It had always suited her aesthetic, but now she was struggling. *'More people-oriented,' they had said. What are good 'people' colours,* Erin wondered. *I suppose a sort of pink. With a bit of brown on top? Sounds a little bit gross. Maybe I should dress more like how the people dress. Perhaps something bright, like a cherry red, or an aquamarine. I wonder what's at the back here…*

Erin hacked her way through the forest of clothes in front of her, gathered what she could, and withdrew. Her freckled face crinkled. *I suppose you could say it's a look of sorts.* She took a deep breath. *'Embrace the change,'* that's what they had said. *'Move with the times…'*

'You look like a jester,' said the god who met Erin at the entrance some time later. He was dressed in crisp white.

Erin's freckles disappeared into the red blush rushing across her cheeks. 'I wasn't sure what the dress code was.'

'Clearly,' he replied.

The crisp white god turned on his heel and motioned for Erin to follow. She was led through a pale pastel corridor, the light of the firmament that surrounded them filtering through the nebulous walls of the New Pantheon. The buzz of activity was incessant. A large group of workers dressed in grey sorted through reams of paperwork, periodically pausing to write on index cards. These cards were then slid into position onto one of an untold number of racks lining the walls. As new cards were moved on, a thousand others were shuffled to accommodate. Now and again a card was taken from the racks and moved to another room.

'That looks very complicated,' Erin piped up, desperate to draw attention away from her garb.

'Hardly,' replied the crisp god. 'It all makes perfect sense. Perfect, logical sense. Prayers come in, they're stratified, prioritised, indexed, stamped, filed, stamped again, and taken to the appropriate department for answering.' The god spoke as one who operates in one of two modes: annoyance and indifference.

'I never used a filing system at my old job, it wasn't really needed. You don't get many prayers when your congregation can't talk!'

Erin smiled, in the vain hope of making some sort of connection with the other god. She didn't get to speak with many other deities usually. Most of her existence so far had been spent astrally projecting into burrows and shrubs. The god stopped walking.

'What were you *of* exactly?'

'Hedgehogs,' she replied, a slight inflection of uncertainty slipping in at the end.

Although 'hedgehogs' was the truthful answer, there was something in the god's tone that made her think it wasn't the *right* answer.

'I see.'

He paused for a long time, staring at a point on the ground just to the right of Erin's feet. The pause lingered long enough for Erin to worry that something more was expected of her, although she couldn't think what. Thankfully, the god snapped back to reality.

'I suppose it takes all sorts to keep a pantheon running. Now hurry up, or you'll be late.'

He started walking again as quickly as he had stopped. He moved at an uncomfortable speed that had the effect of making one's own pace somehow inadequate, no matter how fast one was going. As Erin struggled to keep pace, she couldn't help feeling that she had already blown it. If all her colleagues were like this god, she knew she was done for.

Eventually they came to a threshold, and the man stopped again. 'This is you,' he said without ceremony, and left Erin standing there alone. She watched his crisp white form disappear around a corner.

'Are you Erin?'

Erin hadn't noticed the new god appear. Turning around, she found that they were standing very close to her. She took a step back.

'Hello! Yes, that's me,' she smiled, trying to match the welcome enthusiasm in this newcomer's voice.

'Brilliant! I'm Mercatrus, but call me Merky. Come on in, I'll introduce you to the team.'

Merky ushered Erin into the space beyond. He was a short god, probably around Erin's age, although it seemed that he had already raced through his youth in a bid to get to the receding hairline first.

'Right, everyone. This is Erin, our new starter.' Three faces turned to Erin. None were quite as enthusiastic as Merky's, but they were polite enough. 'So, we have Cal, Aed, and Dermis.'

'Hi, everyone.'

A chorus of greetings wafted over Erin in response. She had already forgotten their names.

'So, Erin, I think the best thing for you to do is just get familiar with the Table for the moment. Have a look, and if you have any questions just let us know. I won't waste your time by walking you through it, I'm sure you've used something similar in your old position! I assumed that's why you've been put here, after all.'

Merky beamed. Erin beamed back, but inside she was screaming. She had never used a Table before. Of course, she had used a *table*, but this sounded like a Table with a capital 'T'. Somewhere down the line someone had made a huge mistake. This was not where she should be, but she had a feeling the crisp white god wouldn't take kindly to her kicking up a fuss. Too embarrassed to go against the flow, she

13

approached the apparatus in the middle of the chamber. The rictus grin was still plastered across her face, her only shield against the scrutiny of her new peers.

The Table before her was large enough to comfortably seat eight for a pleasant evening meal. It was clearly not, however, designed for that. For starters, it wasn't very flat. It also had bits of wet all over it, especially near the edges where you would probably want to put your plate. Other things would have got in the way of the cutlery and the gravy boat, such as forests, mountains, and the odd castle. This is because the Table was a scale replica of the world below, although 'scale replica' is not entirely accurate. Usually, when something is scaled down it loses much of its detail in the manufacturing process. However, this replica had not lost any detail whatsoever in its production. In fact, it had retained so much detail in such a tiny space that it was really quite unnerving. Looking at the world on the Table was like being able to see all the atoms of an apple, every single one of them jostling for position, whilst at the same time seeing a generally spherical, palm sized red-green fruit. The act of seeing the big picture and small picture at exactly the same time was enough to send almost anyone mad, except perhaps for some particularly successful stockbrokers.

The overwhelming stimuli of the Table brought Erin into a nauseated stupor, which was only broken by the sound of Merky's voice.

'You'll probably be wanting these, of course.'

He offered her a pair of large spectacles, their lenses flawlessly circular and rimmed with rose gold covered in intricate runes. Erin took them and nodded in thanks. Assuming it was the right thing to do, she put them on, the slender wire arms wrapping around the back of her ears securely. Merky's image swam in front of her.

'You're the first person I've met who actually suits them'

14

he said, a subtle blush creeping across his pudgy cheeks.

Erin didn't hear this. She didn't hear anything in fact. Confused and frightened, she obeyed instinct and reached up to take the spectacles off. Her fingers brushed against the runed frame.

She flew through Merky at tremendous speed. The Table loomed in front of her. Its surface filled her vision. A forest, then branches, then leaves, a woodland floor. The woodlouse now in front of her nose didn't seem to notice her. She could see its little legs trundle over the uneven terrain, the bindle over its shoulder swinging with the rise and fall of the land. After a moment of adjustment, her ears could make out the merry tune it was whistling. Then, everything was a blur.

She blinked her eyes and saw Merky's concerned face. He was holding the spectacles in both hands as one does with an offending object.

'Are you alright, Erin?' he asked.

Erin looked around the room and caught a sideways glance from Dermis. The others didn't look up from their work, quite deliberately. A potent embarrassment filled her stomach.

'I'm... fine.'

She picked herself up off the floor and brushed herself down. In doing so she was reminded of the garish trousers and tunic that she was wearing, and her embarrassment moved from her stomach to her heart.

'I'm just going to-'

Before finishing her sentence she had already left the room on shaky legs. In a quiet corner of the New Pantheon, she breathed deep, ragged breaths, and thought of hedgehogs.

***

The training grounds in the barracks were quiet. None of the Cliff Guard bothered much with martial practice nowadays. There just wasn't much call for it. Velheim was

15

notoriously difficult for external forces to besiege, protected by the formidable Grippen Mountains to the west and the sea on the remaining three sides. Even folks of a piratical nature had mutually agreed that, with Velheim's loose interpretation of customs laws, they were better off leaving the booming trading port standing. As such, the Cliff Guard had devolved from a standing army to a police militia. Better a beat guardsman practice repairing his boots than swinging a sword.

Rhev, however, had different ideas. He swung his new greatsword in wide, lazy arcs, warming up his muscles. He had spent the last week getting the feel for its weight. Despite its unhealthy, mottled appearance, Hoskin had done an excellent job balancing the blade. It was a difficult task making a long sword for a short swordsman, and Hoskin had been the only blacksmith Rhev had trusted with the task.

Suddenly, a bloodthirsty werewolf leapt from the shadows. *Whoomph* sang the blade. *Choonk* said the straw training dummy in reply as the sword embedded itself in its torso.

'Take that, you bastard monster!'

Rhev chuckled to himself. He was glad the yard was empty. It was a silly game, something he had played by himself as a child. He knew if one of his less friendly colleagues had seen him, his reputation as a no-nonsense brawler would be gone in a flash, but he couldn't help it. The feel of this *proper* sword in his hands was as electrifying as the first time his father had chucked him a wooden soup ladle and challenged him to a duel.

Whoomph. Choonk. A goblin lay defeated, straw bursting from its head.

Whoomph, whoomph. Choonk. There went an evil wizard, his hessian robes in tatters.

He was pleased with his handiwork, but it was a

bittersweet feeling. As impressive as his weapon and his swordsmanship was, he knew that it would never be used for anything other than intimidating street thugs and knocking the stuffing out of dummies. His attention turned to his calloused hands, covered in old scars and scabs. They were the only weapons that living in this city really required. Useful for decking the bloke that just nicked your pint, but hardly the stuff of legends. His ring caught the light of the sun. Unlike his hands, it had never tarnished. It still shined as brightly as the day it was given to him. A memory of a more exciting future.

That's what Velheim did to people. Lowered expectations. Dissolved hopes. Bred cynical acceptance like the ever present mould of the Underport. It was difficult to keep a flame alive when you lived in a damp cave, and when everyone is stumbling around in the dark with shivs in their hands, you're forgiven for throwing ethics out the window. That's what Rhev often told himself anyway, after each grift or brawl.

In his youth, he had spent a lot of time having his own meager wealth reallocated. It was only in the last five years or so that he had started to turn the tide, picking up the necessary skills from Velheim's highly vocational school of life. The way he saw it, if your treasure gets stolen, you're well within your rights to get it back, even if it's from the dragon's minions rather than the dragon itself. Or perhaps the minion's cousin. Or someone who looks like a bit of a minion and had it coming anyway because they looked at you funny. For sure, there was a time when Rhev thought about taking on Velheim's dragons himself, but although he thought of himself as a bit tasty, he was still just one dwarf.

The bell for shift change rang out. Rhev sheathed his sword and made his way back into the barracks. To his surprise a few other guards were in there, doffing armour. As soon as Rhev walked in they looked away, whispering under their breath. Then, of all people, Buttmug appeared from the shadows beside him.

'Finished playing at dragonslayer, have we?' he said with a sneer.

Rhev froze. *Had he been watching me?*

'Just keeping my arm in. Maybe you should try it yourself, you're looking a bit flabby,' he replied.

In this situation, the best defence was a good offence.

'I would, but it looks like you've already killed all the goblins and ghouls plaguing the city, and with such rousin' commentary to boot.'

He had *been watching me.*

'What are you saying, Buttmug?'

'I'm saying,' the orc leaned towards Rhev, his breath stinking, 'that it would be a shame if the rest of Velheim found out that 'hard as nails' Rhev Culluggan liked to pretend that he was an *ickle adventurer* in his spare time.'

Rhev clenched his fists and squared his shoulders. 'That's big talk from someone who's just put their face within range of my fist…'

'Culluggan! Buggerhat!'

· Captain Ardein strode into the barracks, and the two quarrelling guardsmen snapped to attention.

'I thought we had talked about this, you two,' he said, disappointed. 'No more bust ups on city property. I was expecting better behaviour, especially from you, Rhev. You're already on two strikes. One more and I'll have to put you back where I found you, and trust me, that's a place I don't like visiting. Now get your armour on and over to the Keep with you.' He turned to the orc. 'Buggerhat, *bugger off.*'

The commander of the Cliff Guard stayed to make sure the two guardsmen went their separate ways without any further violence. Rhev fumed as he strapped his armour on overly tight, and kicked the dirt as he headed along the path towards the Keep. The stronghold atop the sea stack came into view like the prow of a tall ship, its lofty towers hanging precariously over the long drop towards the roaring sea. The dwarf called to the guard standing watch in the gatehouse, and a rotting drawbridge was lowered across the gap between the cliff and the tower of rock. Rhev marched across before the entire structure collapsed, and made his way to his regular post on the far side of the castle.

As night drew in and the sea and sky melded into an indistinguishable blanket of darkness, Rhev considered his course of action. He couldn't believe he'd let himself get so caught up in his little game of make believe that he had actually uttered the words 'back whence ye came, scourge of Velheim', not just once but several times. He knew it wouldn't take long for Buttmug to spread the word to every guard in the barracks that Rhev Cullugan, bare knuckle brawler and sly swindler, was actually a wannabe hero with delusions of grandeur. If there was one thing Rhev knew about Velheim, it was that the people of the city did a good job of dragging down anyone who thought they were above the muck. This could be anything from a couple of swift jabs to the chops, a permanent hole in your pocket or, gods forbid, an unflattering nickname *that stuck*.

In an effort to get his mind straight, Rhev removed a brick from the wall behind him and retrieved his spare tankard and stash of ale. He sloshed some of the naturally refrigerated beverage into the tankard and took a long draught. One of the great benefits of his regular post was that it was seaward facing and rarely patrolled, meaning that he was free to imbibe as he wished, and so, he did. It was mostly to keep the chill away, of course, but it had some other benefits. Alcohol had a way of helping him think through his problems, usually monetary in nature. He'd thought up some of his best grifts in this very spot, ten pints deep and pleasantly warm.

It only took him eight pints that night for him to have an epiphany. *Eight pints in and I'm as sharp as ever,* he thought, only a slight numbness creeping into his toes. *I've probably got more practice drinking than eating at this point.* He rubbed his paunch with pride. *I reckon I'm the best drunk... drinker... drinksman in the whole of Velheim. Better than stupid old Buttmug, that's for sure. I bet he'd keel over as soon as he even uncorked a bottle of Dankvyrian Dragonfire No. 12. Not this dwarf though. I'd guzzle that Dragonfire down and recite the alphabet widdershins all night long. Then they'd all see I'm not some daydreaming goody goody two boots. I've got the blood of Velheim running through these veins! And not the plagued kind! The kind that catches light near a naked flame!*

Rhev, you bloody genius. If you just bust up Buttmug the captain will have you out on your ear, but you can *put him in his place* and *regain the mob's respect another way. A way that you're very well suited for. A way that you've been training for all this time without even realising it.*

***

'Where are the ledgers Hampton? Get me the damn ledgers!'

'Don't you worry Mister Beckett, I'll get them right away sir. Just one moment, sir. They're here somewhere, sir.'

Mister Hampton burrowed furiously into his paperwork, which was filed away on the floor in a pile. A large brass paperweight in the shape of a mallard duck sat on top of the pile not really doing much at all. The paper far outnumbered the paperweight and seemed to be rebelling against its tyrannous rule by systematically floating away sheet by sheet in ever more audacious arcs, despite the oppressing stillness of the air. Mister Hampton finally came up for a gulp of it, a bundle of large leather bound books in his hands. Having had its precarious paper kingdom disturbed, the mallard promptly abdicated from its pulpy throne and slid into the side of the accountant's head. As the clerk fell to the ground, Mister Beckett leant over and took the ledgers without even a glance.

He leafed back and forth through the heavy books. Each time he landed on the page he was looking for he would scrutinise it with the look of disgust a teacher gives when going through a particularly troublesome student's rough work book. Whenever he finished going through a ledger, he threw it at Hampton. By this point in their relationship Hampton was quite skilled at catching the ledgers, even though they were invariably thrown at his head, rather than his hands. On this occasion however, his failure to duck the duck had left his accuracy wanting.

'Is there something-oof...amiss sir?' Hampton took another heavy tome to the head.

'Amiss? Amiss! I'll tell you what's a-missing, Hampton! Revenue! Dividends! Profit! When I sink money into something, I expect it to resurface sooner or later with all its limbs intact holding countless treasures. Instead I find that my money has disappeared into the murky abyss!'

'Ah, you're talking about the shares in that expedition to the bottom of the Unending Depths, sir?'

'What? No! Well, *in a way*, but I was speaking in metaphors, Hampton. Seeing as we're on the subject though, has there been any progress reports on the expedition?'

'I'm afraid not, sir.'

'But it's been five years!'

'Perhaps they haven't reached the bottom yet, sir...'

Another ledger flew at Hampton. He shielded himself with a previously thrown ledger.

Mister Beckett crossed the room and put on his heavy overcoat. As he checked the contents of his inside pocket out of habit, a finger poked through a hole in the bottom. He let out a quiet growl. *I can't even keep a few pennies from disappearing.* He slammed the door of the office behind him.

On it, in fading gilt, read 'Beckett & Beckett Investments: Your Wealth In Good Hands'.

Beckett's boots clapped loudly on the cobblestones as he began his trudge through the city. It was early evening, and the light surrounding the city of Dankvyr had turned a special shade of pink that only summer skies can produce. The beautiful quality of light found on the southern tip of the Peninsula was sought after by artists, poets, and anyone who appreciated the joys of colour. Mister Beckett looked up at the myriad hues and remained resolutely miserable. He had decided that absolutely nothing could lift him from the funk that he was in, and that the only sensible decision was to go to the local pub and add fuel to the fire. He really knew how to savour a good sulk, in the only way someone who deliberately nourishes complaints and grumbles can.

He turned a corner onto Fence Street, and the smell of money hit him immediately. Money, not wealth. Wealth smells like daily cleaned porcelain and heritage musk. Money smells like the bloody metallic tint of coins changing hands rapidly, the sweat of a stockbroker as he reads the daily lists, the effluence from the dray horses that whisk bankers around the city to sign predatory contracts.

Fence Street was the place where only those who were making money spent the majority of their time, because only those making money could afford to stay there for any significant duration. Mister Beckett's office was, for obvious reasons, not on Fence Street. At one point in time though, it had been. A long time ago.

Although times had changed, Beckett was a man of habit. He traced a familiar route through the crowds of men brandishing papers in the air and the young, earnest contract carriers, and entered through the doorway of The Bartering Knave. The polished, dark wood that now surrounded him seemed to be an impenetrable barrier between the inside of the tavern and the world outside. The effect was heightened by the lack of any windows bar one in the roof, casting a beam of dusty light through the gallery and down to the bar in the centre of the room. All along the edges of the taproom men were seated in a brown sort of darkness, either alone with their lists or with other comparable gentlemen. Beckett sighed, sucked up the still air, and made his way towards the bar.

'A pint of the house draught,' he asked, not bothering with platitudes. People on Fence Street hadn't time for them.

'I need to grab a fresh keg,' explained the barkeep.

Beckett nodded and waved his hand, as if he was giving the man his permission. While he waited, his ears became attuned to the murmurous conversation being had around him.

'… in more than fifty years. Apparently old Boswell almost refused, said he doesn't do those any more. It would seem though, as ever, that the coin won out.'

Boswell was a name Beckett recognised. Boswell wrote contracts. In his prime, Boswell had specialised in particularly *binding* contracts. Contracts that one does not sign in a hurry, or create for that matter. Contracts that bind with more than ink and paper and words. So steeped in eldritch mystery were these contracts that they had been banned throughout most of the civilised world, and those who specialised in their creation had slowly died out or were forgotten. Boswell was the last of them.

That conversation ended with a grumble and the sound of papers being folded. Beckett's ear found another.

'Now look at that coat. I know we're not a fashionable lot but since when were frayed hems and moth holes acceptable in our circles?'

Beckett looked around the tavern with a sneer, trying to find this raggedy outsider so he could better appreciate the man's jibe. His stomach dropped as he realised they were

23

talking about him.

'Seems like the rumours are true then. Beckett & Beckett must be going under. Speaking of going under, did you hear what his last venture was? An expedition,' the portly gossiper began to chuckle, 'to the Unending Depths! The Unending Depths! What were they expecting to bring back? Saltwater? For Ava's sake, the depths are *unending*.'

The gossipers, both the dictionary definition of portly in fact, had a large belly laugh at Beckett's expense. They were either supremely confident in the dampening acoustics of the tavern, or had simply decided that Beckett was the sort of man with whom one could laugh both behind and in front of his back. Beckett bristled, tapping his fingers impatiently on the bar top. *How long does it take to change a keg*, he thought, trying to distract himself from the banter behind him. The laughing eventually died down.

'You know', said the other gentleman, 'now that the other Beckett isn't around it has become quite clear which one was the brains of the outfit back when they were on Fence Street. I remember a time when the name Beckett wasn't something to scoff at! Ah, but times change, eh?'

'Here's your pint of bitter, sir.' The barkeep slid the mug across with one hand, silently took the coin that had been placed there by Beckett with the other, and withdrew to the other end of the bar. The Bartering Knave was generally frequented by moneymen who were *up*, and moneymen who were very much *down*, and he knew not to be in the way when the two inevitably met.

Beckett's hand gripped the mug firmly. Very firmly. His knuckles turned white. He slowly moved away from the bar over to a table.

'Good afternoon gentlemen. Walter. Matlock.' The portly gossipers stared at Beckett like two freshly caught fish. 'May I sit?'

The two men looked at each other with their fishy eyes, both thinking of something to bluster. Before they could, Beckett had drawn the seat back, and settled down into its worn red leather upholstery. He smiled thinly at his drinking partners.

Regaining some composure after Beckett's unexpected acknowledgement of their presence, one of the portly men found his tongue and, to his credit, a soupcon of his former bravado.

'We were just talking about you Beckett. You've been missed on Fence Street, you know. How's business nowadays?'

'It's nice to hear I've been missed, Walter. I had almost begun to think that I had been forgotten about after all this time. But business? Yes, business. Admittedly, not as good as one would hope for.' He took a long draught from his mug. 'But heavenly Mercatrus does like to play his games, doesn't he gentlemen?'

Beckett let out a single, sharp laugh. An unhinged laugh. One that is not supposed to be reciprocated. Matlock chirped up.

'It's a dangerous game mixing religious beliefs and finance, Beckett. Money moves by the predictable hand of man, not the hand of absent gods.'

'Blasphemy, is it?' exclaimed Beckett, a little too loudly.

Walter and Matlock's heads both receded a little more than usual into their upper torso. Beckett let out another singular laugh.

'A joke, gentlemen, a joke. I don't believe in that sort of thing any more. Why should I?' He took another long draught. 'Then again, no need. I have a sure fire plan. The predictable hand of man, you say. Indeed. Beckett & Beckett will be back on Fence Street by the end of the year.'

'Oh?' Walter looked to Matlock and raised a bushy

eyebrow. 'So certain Beckett? If this plan is so sure fire, I must ask why you didn't implement it *before* you were moved from… ahem… *left* Fence Street?'

'A valid question, dear Walter.'

There was a pause. Walter and Matlock both raised both eyebrows. They bushed furiously in anticipation. The pause continued.

'A very valid question,' murmured Beckett.

His knuckles had gone past white, his hand locked in a rictus grip around his mug. For a moment it looked like he was going to crack the ceramic, weak man that he was. Then, a release.

'Oh you swine! You absolute knaves!' Another uncomfortable bark of laughter. 'I haven't been off Fence Street for *that* long you know. I can't be goaded that easily into tipping you two rogues off. The plan stays in here I'm afraid, you know the game!'

He tapped his head with a long finger, and smiled.

'Of course!' Matlock bellowed, chuckling.

'Of course…' replied Walter, looking at Matlock knowingly. They met eyes for a moment.

'Another one for the rumour mill, eh, Beckett?' Walter continued. 'You've let loose the fox, and the hounds won't be able to resist the scent! Matlock and I obviously won't be taking part in this particular hunt though. Our current investments are doing very well and we have no need for the sport. But be assured, Beckett, all eyes will be on you. This will surely be your triumphant return to the financial community that we've *all* been expecting. Either that or-', he let out a jovial guffaw laced with menace, 'accountancy!'

Beckett seethed. *Accountancy?* How dare he suggest such a thing. He was a capitalist, an investor, at the very least a broker. But an accountant? Never. He would rather jump into the Unending Depths than sink to the lows of *accountancy*.

26

Why would someone count money when they can make it?

'Accountancy, indeed,' Beckett said to himself. Walter and Matlock were overcome with a bad case of the chortles. 'You shall see gentlemen. Within the year Becket & Beckett will be back on Fence Street.' He scraped his chair back over the well-worn floor of the inn. 'And by the way! This isn't my coat. I picked my assistant's off the rack by accident.'

He could see there was no point waiting around for a response; the two men were too far in their cups to bring their laughter to an end any time soon.

The adrenaline wore off by the time he had left the bustle of Fence Street. He wandered aimlessly through Dankvyr, his thoughts racing. *You fool, you bloody fool. You let them play you, the two biggest gossips on the Street, and you know they're right; if you lose one more penny you'll have to close the firm, and then... accountancy. Gah!* He kicked a pebble across the cobbles. It made a horrible scraping noise. *You know who* would *have a sure fire plan?* His fists clenched. *But he isn't here, and all you have is Hampton, and all* he *is good at is dodging ledgers.*

***

Rhev's walk through the streets of the Underport the night following his epiphany was not a happy one. Not only had word spread like wildfire through the Cliff Guard, it had also reached the more gossip prone and loud mouthed civilians.

'Look out Dignan! It's the stout knight of Velheim!'

'I've got a ghoul you can sort out, happens to live at my mother-in-law's house.'

'Have at ye, tosser!'

A couple of merry lads put on a little performance of 'ogre steals damsel' for Rhev's benefit, inviting him to rescue the fair maiden from a terrible and smelly fate, much to the delight of passersby. Rhev just kept his head down and quickened his pace. He didn't need these wise guys to distract him. They would change their tune soon enough. All he had to do was get to The Belly of the Beast.

The lanterns hanging from the tavern's exterior swung gently, not from the breeze, but from the rocking motion of the tavern itself. The Belly of the Beast was not a normal pub. Originally a pirate ship under the command of the infamous Wobbly Roger, it arrived in Velheim fifty years ago with a cargo of stolen rum. Unlike most stolen rum that's liberated from legitimate trading vessels, *this* rum was stolen from another pirate ship, and not just any pirate ship, but a *ghost pirate ship*.

Roger had been incredibly happy with his haul, despite the unnerving green glow emanating from the kegs and the accompanying noise of someone slowly exhaling with their mouth wide open. It gave the crew the willies, and all but Roger himself was convinced there was a curse on the boosted booze. Unfortunately, Wobbly Roger hadn't got his name for nothing: he was loathed to see any rum, cursed or not, go overboard. To safeguard it from his crew he moved the entire cargo into his personal cabin. This proved to be a poor move. On one particularly wobbly night, Roger returned from playing Stacks with his first mate to his cabin, where he was busting for a nightcap. Unable to locate his usual stash underneath the pile of glowing, hissing kegs, he decided to have a little nip of his loot instead. With a practice flourish, he pierced a hole one of the ghostly barrels and released a small stream of rum into his favourite drinking skull.

If it wasn't for Roger's incredibly high tolerance to spirits, incidentally explaining how he was able to pillage a ghost ship in the first place, he would have died just from inhaling the fumes of the beverage before him. As it happened, his tolerance only stretched so far, and he actually died from drinking it. It was a painless death, and left quite a pleasant burn on the tongue. In fact, Roger wouldn't have realised he was dead if it weren't for the fact that he turned translucent and green, and the rum started talking to him.

'Wobbly Roger,' it said in a breathy voice, 'you are dead, and you bloody well deserve it. You stole the one thing that gave the dead an iota of respite in their eternal voyage. For this crime, you must pay a debt. You are forever bound to serve the spirits of the dead.'

'Avast,' mumbled Roger, who took another sip from the cup his ethereal hands were somehow still holding.

'Truly, you are a monster, Wobbly Roger,' continued the rum.

'So they say,' Roger agreed, as he lowered himself into his plush captain's chair.

'How are you doing that? Why are you not floating!' wailed the rum with the screeches of a hundred damned souls.

'I've built up a tolerance,' Roger replied.

The rum gurgled angrily. 'It matters not! You are still bound to serve the spirits of the dead!'

'Uhuh,' replied Roger, draining the skull as he thought deeply about his predicament.

The next morning The Belly of the Beast docked in the Underport, where a rather translucent but worryingly solid ship captain immediately alighted and purchased a large quantity of high quality rum, absinthe, and whisky, and a licence in his name to serve the aforementioned spirits from his own ship. For the last fifty years Wobbly Rogers has lived quite comfortably with his curse, fulfilling his debt to serve the spirits of the dead to the letter. His tavern grew in popularity overnight, thanks mostly to the novelty of Roger being the only poltergeist proprietor on the Peninsula. For the next fifty years Roger ran a fantastically profitable business, built four extra stories onto his ship to accommodate the influx of customers, and continued to fund his constant thirst for grog with change to spare. If anything he was very much happier than he once was, as ghosts can't get hangovers.

Rhev climbed the steep gangplank into The Belly of the Beast now. Rabble rousers who had been too unsteady on their feet bobbed below him in the cool and refreshing water. A wall of sound and heat hit him as he opened the front door that had been cut into the side of the hull.

'Another round of Smuggler's Cider 'ere matey!' called a man who was all peg and no leg.

'Hands off me booty, blaggard! Only the husband gets to touch the goods,' yelled a blue bearded captain.

Rhev squeezed himself between some interesting smelling people towards the stairs leading to the lower deck. He knew that Buttmug was obsessed with playing, some would say *losing*, the card game known as Stacks. The lower deck was reserved for such games of chance, and being slightly below the water level meant it was legal to play for pretty much anything, from shots to souls.

He'd just about managed to make it to the top of the steps when he found something slippery under his feet. He had no idea why there was a squid in the pub, or why it was on a leash, but he did know that even with the low center of gravity innate to dwarves, there was nothing more counter to remaining upright than a landbound squid underfoot. Even a banana peel.

The Stacks table nearest the bottom of the stairs exploded with cards as Rhev barrelled into it. The modest three piece shanty crew in the corner stopped singing. All eyes turned towards the ruckus.

'Oh no, I appeared to have misplaced my winning hand,' said a man who had been sitting at the table and who had quite obviously been about to lose a lot of money.

''Ello 'ello,' chuckled a familiar voice. 'Is that the hero of Velheim I see before me? Had trouble with the kraken upstairs did ya?'

30

Buttmug's two cronies sniggered along with him. They were seated at one of the high roller tables near the back of the room.

"Ey lads, that's the fella I was telling you about. Likes to play make-believe in his spare time with that big boy sword on his back.'

One of the other players, a sharp faced orc woman with a wonky tusk turned to get a better look at Rhev.

'He looks pathetic,' she sneered. 'Go back to one of the taverns on the surface, boy. They suit more gentle folk like you.'

Boy? Gentle folk? Just last week he'd nutted three bastards in a row without breaking a sweat, and now he was *gentle folk?* This wouldn't do at all. He dragged himself up, gave the toppled Stacks table a passing kick so that everyone there knew he meant business, and walked purposefully towards his nemesis.

'Sounds like you've been spreading rumours, Buttmug,' he growled. 'I won't allow that.'

The orc woman sat across from Buttmug snorted.

'I wasn't talking to you,' snapped Rhev, not quite sure how to deal with this kind of disrespect. The woman put her hands up in mock fright. With every ounce of his willpower he ignored her, and turned back to Buttmug.

'You think I'm a soft touch, aye? And you've got everyone else thinking it too? Bravo, Buttmug, bravo. Honestly mate, it's impressive that you managed to get anyone to listen to you with breath like yours.'

The orc's lip twitched. The best jibes were always the ones that rang true, after all. Rhev felt himself regain some of his confidence.

'Funny thing is, I reckon you're a bit of a soft touch as well. That seems to put us at an impasse, doesn't it?'

'I dunno know about that, dwarf. I'm feeling pretty good

31

from where I'm sitting.' Buttmug winked at the cronies next to him. 'You're the one with his reputation down the john. I ain't got nothing to prove. Everyone knows I'm the real deal.'

A quiet voice floated over from the other side of the room. 'Who *are* these guys?'

Both the orc and the dwarf glared daggers in their general direction, and a flurry of shushes followed. The standoff continued.

'Something tells me,' said Rhev, 'that the good people of Velheim will change their minds about the both of us after... *the Trial of the Brews.*'

Shocked gasps filled the lower deck. Even Rhev's heart stopped for a moment when the words finally crossed his lips. There was no taking this back.

Buttmug blustered. 'Very funny Culluggan, *very funny,* but the jester's club is down the street.'

The sharp faced woman interjected. 'The Trial of the Brews is no laughing matter.'

'Yes I bloody know that!' bellowed Buttmug.

'Then you must also know that to refuse such a challenge is shameful and... weak,' she continued.

'You heard the lady, Buttmug,' Rhev said, as if addressing the entire room. 'Refuse, and all of Velheim will know that Rhev Culluggan proved once and for all that Feculent 'Buttmug' Buggerhat is a liar, and a right proper *soft touch.*'

This was going better than expected. With any luck, Buttmug would crumble and Rhev would have proved he still had his bottle without ever having to take part in the Trial.

The orc was sweating. All eyes were on him. One of his cronies, a skinny man full of snot, whispered: 'Well go on then boss, go on. It's like you said, he ain't nuthin', is he?'

An almost imperceptible grunt came from Buttmug. 'Alright then.'

More gasps. For a fraction of a second Rhev's face

dropped, but he picked it up before anyone noticed. The orc woman nodded solemnly.

'I'll get Roger,' she said, and got up from her chair. On her way past she leant down to Rhev. 'I'll admit I'm impressed, dwarf. You're either very brave or very, *very* stupid.'

Rhev and Buttmug sat at the table opposite each, doing their best to explode the other's head just by staring at them. Unfortunately for both, it wasn't working. The cronies and the rest of the Stacks players at the table had respectfully relinquished their seats and joined the crowd that was now forming around the pair. A tense five minutes passed. Then a hush swept through those present as they formed an opening. A man stepped up to the table. He was see-through, faintly green, and had the swaying swagger of the most self-assured person in the world: Wobbly Roger himself.

'Good evening, mateys,' he said, his voice layered with hollow echoes. 'I have been summoned to conduct the Trial of the Brews. Can you confirm that it is the two of ye that will be participating?'

'Aye', said Rhev and Buttmug in unison.

'Oo-arr,' the ghostly pirate replied with a grin of golden-green teeth. 'This does shiver me timbers, to be sure. Now, maties, it's been three long years since the last Trial.'

Several people in the crowd removed their hats and bowed their heads out of respect. Rhev couldn't remember what had happened to the previous challengers, but it clearly didn't bode well. Wobbly Roger continued.

'Since it has been so long, I'll be refreshing ye of the rules. There will be fifteen brews that you will have to consume in order. If ye don't finish your brew, or spill it, you're out. If ye are unable or unwilling to drink the next brew for whatever reason, you're out. You spew, you lose. Last challenger standing wins. Of course, the Trial is not like any other drinking competition in the Peninsula, or I daresay, the world.

Some of these brews are not simply drunk to wet your whistle before a couple of rousing shanties, no! They're drunk to test the mettle of those maties who are fixing to mutiny on each other, to settle their differences without violence. Although, I may add, it can end up being far *messier*. With that in mind, I remind you that the final brew is a skullful of my own stolen grog. I hope you've built up a tolerance…'

Although Rhev was aware of the rudiments of the Trial, he hadn't heard about that last part. *What have I gotten myself into?* Something told him that even *he* didn't have the tolerance to handle that cursed brew. On the other hand, he was almost certain that Buttmug wouldn't be able to take it that far either. Then again, they did *really* hate each other.

A tray was brought through the crowd by a man who must have been the first of all mates: rippling musculature, tight stripy shirt, a variety of nautical tattoos, and a bandana that was actually embroidered with the words 'No. 1 Mate'. It was a good thing that he was so muscular, as the tray held all manner of conceivable vessels.

'Yarr, here we are gentlemen,' announced Roger. 'Your poisons for the evening. We'll start off with something cheap. I don't want to be wasting my top shelf stuff before we be knowing if you're worthy hearties.'

He grasped two tankards with his translucent hands and plonked them on the table in front of the two challengers.

'A pint of Hoist The Mains-ale. Hoppy, with a dash of salty seawater. You may begin when ready, but take your time. We've got a long way to go.'

The dwarf and the orc slipped their fingers around the tankard handles like two duellists preparing to draw swords. There was a pause, at which point Rhev realised that this wasn't just about the steel of his belly, it was about mental fortitude as well. It was a mind game as much as a drinking game. Quick as a flash he brought the tankard to his lips and

34

began chugging ferociously. A second later Buttmug did the same, but he was clearly unprepared. His chugging speed matched Rhev's, but being caught off guard led him to splutter between mouthfuls. As Rhev smacked the tankard on the table upside down, he knew that he was well on his way to regaining his reputation. He'd not only beat Buttmug, but he'd do it in style.

There was genial clamour from the gathered crowd, but nothing outrageous. Downing a pint of ale like that was common for the majority of them, but they respected the attitude nonetheless.

'I see that we're meaning business, eh lads?' said Roger with a grin. 'Very well. Let's continue.'

Another pair of pints were set on the table. They were both gone within seconds. Another pair followed. Both combatants were getting into their stride. The crowd steadily got rowdier. Five pints in and neither had broken a sweat, much to Rhev's chagrin.

'Let's be moving onto something a little more robust, shall we?' Roger announced. 'Dankvyrian Dragonfire No.12. A most valued export from our friends to the south. An apt name I find: smokey in the mouth, fire in the belly. But can ye take the heat?'

Rhev couldn't help smirking. This was his hard liquor of choice, mostly because he knew that most people couldn't handle it, and there was a certain pride in that. He was hoping this would be the point where Buttmug would tap out. Generously sized mugs were placed on the table, much larger than the thimbles Dragonfire was usually served in. Determined to keep his opponent on his toes, Rhev leant back in his chair, and waited. It would be much sweeter for Buttmug to give up now, only for Rhev to happily down both their drinks.

It was, however, not to be. Buttmug narrowed his heavy

brows and knocked the Dankvyrian export back in one. Rhev's eye twitched in surprise, but he regained his composure and downed his own cup with a cheeky 'cheers', hoping to save face. The crowd was getting more lively now. They could see they were dealing with some serious challengers.

'Next on the menu we have an independent label. I can't tell you where it's from because the cowled woman who delivers it won't tell me. Suffice to say it is certainly a *brew*.'

The first mate handed Roger a ladle that he kept on his belt. The poltergeist then proceeded to spoon out a mysterious black liquid a miniature cauldron on the first mate's tray. He presented the concoction to the competitors wooden drinking bowls. The smell crept up Rhev's nose and settled snugly in the back of his throat, where it congealed. Barely able to breath, he peered into the murky depths of the softly bubbling potion in front of him.

'What is this, exactly?' he gagged.

Roger shrugged. 'All I know is that it has booze in it, and if it's got booze in it, I serve it.'

'To who, ghouls?' Rhev choked.

'Careful what you say, landlubber,' replied Roger coldly. 'Ghouls and poltergeists are cousins, you know.'

'Having trouble there, dwarf? The aroma too pungent for ya?' sneered Buttmug. 'No shame in dropping out now. You'd just have to move to another city.'

'No problem with the aroma, matey. I've managed to get by working alongside you, haven't I?' The last couple of words tasted sour and acidic in Rhev's mouth. The longer this drink sat in front of him, uncontained, the more likely he was to spew.

Rather than rise to the insult, Buttmug just smiled to himself and tapped his nose. Then he began sucking up the foul liquid. Rhev watched aghast as he realised something incredibly vital: Buttmug couldn't smell. He *did* smell, of course, awfully in fact, but he had no *sense* of it, the former likely being the result of the latter. Rhev hadn't ever considered this, and now he was beginning to wonder if there were any other vital factors that he hadn't considered. It was starting to dawn on him that this whole thing might, *just might*, be a rather ill-conceived plan. However, there was too much on the line. He swallowed his pride and pinched his nose. It was the only way he could get this vile brew down his throat. It slid rather than poured, and he could feel it settle in his belly, a little puddle of regret.

'I am impressed laddies, brew number seven is a mighty foul one,' said Roger. 'I'll just give you a minute to catch your breath.'

As much as Rhev didn't want to let the pressure off Buttmug, he was secretly welcome for the respite. The last brew was not sitting well with him. In fact, it felt quite like it was coming up. Like his whole stomach was coming up. Everything was coming up. He was coming up! The reassuring pressure of his bottom on the chair had been replaced with... nothing. And then the rotations started.

The crowd hooted and hollered as Rhev and Buttmug began slowly turning upside down and floating towards the ceiling. Neither of their bodies seemed particularly well suited to weightlessness. The orc floundered as one of his chins threatened to suffocate him. Rhev, on the other hand, couldn't stop rotating, and if there's one thing all drunks fear, it's the spins. Both began making 'hurk' noises.

'That's a bit more interesting,' said Roger calmly. 'Last time they just combusted for a few seconds.'

Both competitors were now lying on the ceiling, moaning gently.

'You'll be cheered to know the eighth brew is an antidote of sorts. That is, of course, if you can drink it. Remember: no

37

spills!'

Two thimbles of a pink, custard-like substance were placed on the table. Rhev and Buttmug got to their feet. Blood rushed to their heads. Consumed liquid threatened to take the easy way out. Without hesitation Buttmug reached down, or up from his perspective, and took the tiny cup between his warty fingers.

'Looks like the end of the road for you, little dwarf,' he spat.

The orc tipped the shot awkwardly into his mouth, and then fell to the floor with a loud bang, breaking his chair in the process. Rhev cursed himself. The gloating orc was right: he was too little to reach the eighth brew from where he stood on the ceiling. *This can't be how I lose,* he thought. *I don't even feel that drunk.* He tried a standing jump, and immediately regretted it. His thick but short arms flailed pathetically, eliciting a laugh from the crowd.

'Rhev, what are you doing upwise on the ceilings?' A friendly voice.

'Hoskin? What are you doing here?' asked Rhev in surprise.

'Weekly expats meeting,' Hoskin explained. 'We like the multicultural atmosphere. Do you need a foot?'

Rhev paused. He certainly did need a foot, or even better, a hand, but in front of this crowd? Was outside help even allowed? He had nothing to lose; if he couldn't reach this next drink, he was out.

'Pass me up that drink there, mate.'

'Wos this? Das against the rules innit?' slurred Buttmug, much more inebriated than he was a second ago.

Roger smiled wickedly. 'Yarr, but I do love a good loophole.'

Hoskin stepped in and lifted the custardy drink up to Rhev, but just when it was nearing the dwarf's reach, he

38

stopped.

'Hang off Rhev, this isn't one of those Challenges of the Tipples, is it?' he asked dubiously.

'Maybe,' said Rhev dismissively.

'My friend, you could end up dead as a doorman!'

'Aww, wook everybody,' Buttmug said, waving a wobbly finger in his opponents direction. 'Culluggan's mummy is worried *hic* about him. Better go home dwarf, before she *hic* gives you a slap on the arse with that massive arm of hers.'

Anger rose in Rhev's throat, along with all his blood and a little bit of bile.

'Give me the bloody drink Hoskin,' he growled. 'If I go out now I either die of shame or die of a knife in the gut when everyone knows I can't handle myself.'

'And drinking will solve this problem?' his friend asked innocently.

'Yes!'

Hoskin handed him the drink. Rhev quickly downed it and fell from the ceiling, his fall broken by his friend.

'Thanks *hic* mate.'

Rhev's head span, and it wasn't just because his personal gravity had switched. The custardy drink had been sickly sweet, without a trace of alcohol burn, but the way it was starting to affect him was like he'd drank concentrated lamp oil.

'I can't feel ma toes,' grumbled Buttmug, who still hadn't bothered to get up. He burped the sort of burp that was on the verge of condensing from gas to liquid at any moment. 'Bloody 'ell.'

Rhev would have echoed the sentiments if he had been able to form words, but at the moment he was having trouble getting them from his brain to his mouth.

'It looks like you're enjoying that last one,' said Roger. 'It's called 'Gnomes Just Want To Have Fun'. As with all the most brightly coloured and embarrassing beverages, it's disregarded by most patrons, but this little concoction hides one of the highest grog contents of them all! Enough concentrated alcohol to be burning away any lingering magickal nasties in the bloodstream, which I'm sure you're appreciatin'. Now, here's four more shots each.'

'These... oh by Ava... *hic*... these count as brews nine to-' Rhev paused as he tried to chase down the brain cells responsible for arithmetic. 'Nine to twelve, right? Then we're almost done, right...please.'

Buttmug echoed the 'please' quietly.

'Yarr, is that a tone of defeat I'm detecting in you lubbers? No, these all count as one brew. I just thought I would spread this one out into smaller portions, for I be a merciful captain!'

Both Rhev and Buttmug groaned and dragged themselves back up to the table, leaning heavily on their elbows as they began necking each thimble of poison nectar. After the last one both their legs buckled simultaneously. The orc appeared to steam slightly.

'Brew number eight is down the hatch, and they're still alive!' roared Roger. The crowd hollered in response, banging hooks on tankards and stamping their peg legs. 'Let's give them a little break, shall we?'

Two more tankards arrived. 'The ninth brew! Everyone's favourite stout: Dwarven Fury!'

Rhev could smell that beautiful toasted aroma even from his position on the floor, cutting through his rapidly solidifying drunken haze. Dwarven Fury was one of his favourites, something that he could drink all night long. A favourable omen, to be sure. If only he could lift his inebriated carcass off the floor.

'Hoskin, you gots ta pass me the drink again,' he slurred, waving his hand at the table.

40

'You must be having jokes Rhev!' his friend replied. 'Not being able to drink because you're on the ceiling is one thing. If you can't get the tankard yourself because you're too buzzle-guzzled, you need to stop.'

As he said this, Buttmug beckoned a crony over so they could get him the tankard. They did so without question. Through the table legs, Buttmug gave Rhev a cheeky wink as he began to drink.

'Look Hoskin,' Rhev yelled. 'He's getting *hic* ahead! Even if he doesn't finish the brew, if I can't get to mine, he's won! I've come *hic* so far…'

For a moment it seemed that Rhev had passed out, and Hoskin was glad.

'This is my one chance to clear my name,' continued Rhev, his eyes closed. 'To be a legend. The ultimate quaffer…chugman… groggateur. I still haven't *hic* got the word.'

'Why are your eyes closed?' asked Hoskin with concern.

'Conserving energy, innit! Don't betray me now my old friend. People will tell *hic* stories of this night, and you'll go down in history with me! But more importantly, that orc is a proper twonk and I need to beat him!'

'I'm not sure this is the story you want to be telling, my friend. But you ask for my help, so I will help you. A tooth for a tooth, eh?'

The blacksmith lowered the tankard into the dwarf's shaky hands and stepped back. Rhev lifted the tankard to his lips and began to drain it. The draining lasted a very long time, too long in fact. Rhev opened his eyes to see that the tankard was still full. *Impossible!* Buttmug was panting heavily. He had come to the same terrible realisation.

'I assure you, gents,' said Roger, 'that the vessel in your hands is not bottomless. It is, on the other hand, deceptively deep. The ninth brew is not a test of tolerance, or gag reflex, or

41

courage. It's all about the depth of your belly, yarr!'

With pained expressions, the two opponents continued to drink, and did so for over a quarter of an hour. The onlookers were stunned into silence. The Trial had become a war of attrition. Each time either of them put their tankard aside to breathe, the same question murmured across everyone's lips: would they continue? Finally, both competitors stopped with their tankards still half full.

'You… done… dwarf?' wheezed the orc.

'Not… on… your… life,' replied the dwarf. 'You?'

The orc shook his head with the uncontrolled jerks of someone on the verge of alcohol poisoning. Rhev sighed. He had no more room. His belly, once thought bottomless, was full. It was a stalemate though, and that wouldn't do. He needed to humiliate Buttmug, destroy his credibility. He needed to win, so he did the only reasonable thing he could think of in his current state.

'Rhev. Rhev!' whispered Hoskin urgently. 'Your breeches are getting wet. What is going on? Oh… oh I see. Oh dear.'

The release of pressure was almost orgasmic, but the dwarf couldn't forget his goal. With a sense of divine purpose, he drained the tankard, for good. He slammed it down on the planks. The crowd burst into a chaotic uproar, followed by mumblings of displeasure as the smell coming from Rhev's trousers reached their noses.

'He's won, but at what cost?' said the sharp-faced orc woman.

Before anyone could answer, a sound akin to an enormous toad echoed around the lower deck, a belch louder than any had ever heard.

'Dats better,' said Buttmug, before he too drained his tankard.

Rhev groaned softly, and became acutely more aware of the wet patch below him: a wet patch of shame.

42

'The Trial has not ended!' announced Roger, waving his hands to quieten the crowd. 'Both challengers have finished their brews, and must now decide if they want to move onto the next one.'

'What is it now?' mumbled Rhev, suffering mightily from the sudden withdrawal of his victory.

'Your tenth brew comes all the way from across the Bay of Larendor. I give you: water!'

'What?' said Rhev and Buttmug together.

'Holy water from the temple of Blurm, to be exact.'

'Jus' water then?' asked Buttmug, scratching his sandpaper chin.

Roger grinned. 'Well, we're two thirds of the way through. Seems like the time for a palate cleanser, wouldn't ye agree?' He placed two corked bottles on the table, each with a label depicting a man with a third eye in his forehead. 'In your own time.'

Rhev didn't need to ask Hoskin this time. His friend gladly fetched the water for him. 'I really hope this sobers you up, Rhev. No more accidentally draining the gecko, eh?'

Rhev took the bottle's cork in his teeth and pulled, then spat it out. The cork hit someone in the eye. A ruckus tried to break out before Roger calmly explained that they should have known the risks of standing in the front row of a Trial, and he had a spare eyepatch in the back somewhere if they really wanted it.

Together, the two challengers began to guzzle like they had been stranded in a desert for months. It was, as Roger had said, water. Rhev couldn't help feeling cheated. How was he supposed to show how much a better boozer he was if all they had to drink was water?

'I met a priest of Blurm once on my travels,' Roger recalled to the crowd, quite casually. 'Said he had come within a hair's breadth of finding transcendence. Then someone shooed him

43

away with a stick and told me all the Blurmites are quite mad. Not surprising really, considering they drink their own bathwater...'

Rhev gagged and lowered the bottle, still half full. He blinked. In front of him, rather than an uglier-than-average orc, was a bear wearing a toupee. To his even greater surprise, he found that he didn't seem to think this was unusual.

'Why do you need to wear a toupee? You're a bear, you're covered in fur,' he asked, quite soberly.

'I find it gives me confidence,' the bear replied.

Rhev nodded sagely, fully in control of his body's actions now. *Blimey, this water is doing wonders,* he thought. 'Would you mind if I have a go?' he asked.

'Certainly, but you'll have to catch me first,' said the bear with a grin.

'Naturally,' Rhev replied.

The bear made a break for the stairs, floating over the group of squid people on a cloud of purple gas. Rhev got to his feet, which were now twice as big as he remembered them, and began hopping after his prey.

'What are you doing Rhev? Rhev!' shouted one of the squid people.

'I've got to get that bear's toupee to regain my confidence, you stupid squid!' Rhev replied in haste. He continued hopping, making slow progress due to his mysterious lack of gas propulsion. When he finally got out of the lower deck, he spotted the bear by the exit smoking a cigar quite nonchalantly, in no hurry to get away. *Such confidence.*

Just as Rhev was about to swipe the toupee from the bear's head, his furry quarry slipped out of a porthole and onto the deck of an adjacent boat. Rhev followed, slipping wildly on a pile of haddock heads below.

'You're a wily one, bear, but I'll get you yet!' he bellowed. The bear was half bounding, half floating from ship to ship,

44

making its way towards the far side of the port where a red ship with a prancing stag figurehead was moored. It was the Staghart, a ship belonging to the baron of the same name.

Rhev continued to hop and skip in pursuit, until he had the bear cornered at the prow of the baron's ship. He paid no heed to the talking rock and the giant seagull that had just walked out onto the deck behind him, even though the rock seemed very keen on getting him to stop whatever he was doing.

'Nowhere to go now, Mister Bear,' said Rhev, a wild grin plastered on his face. 'Now you just hand over that toupee and give ol' Rhev Culluggan here a taste of that confidence you got yourself.'

'The thing about this toupee,' said the bear quite placidly, 'is that it can also make you invisible.' The bear disappeared from sight. Rhev wailed and, out of manic frustration, threw the half drunk bottle he found in his hands right at the spot where the bear had been. It smashed on the deck, its contents slowly dribbling through the cracks in the planks.

'Blast! If only I had been quicker,' Rhev mused. 'But of course, these soggy things were weighing me down! Stupid dwarf!'

He removed his sodden trousers with difficulty, and looked for a place to dry them.

'Ah, this will do nicely,' he declared as he hung his laundry across the antlers of the Staghart's figurehead.

'Villainy! Treason!' screeched the giant seagull, which was now sporting a little black moustache and a heavy gold medallion. 'Sedition! Gross... gross grossness! Make him put his trousers back on!'

'Guardsman Culluggan!' boomed the talking rock. 'Cease this behaviour immediately and put your bloody trousers back on!' The rock looked uncannily like Captain Ardein of the Velheim Cliff Guard. 'Third strike!'

Rhev desperately tried to undo the effects of the Trial of the Brews in the twenty minutes it took to be escorted to the throne room, but it was no use.

'Rhev Culluggan, I hereby strip you of your rank as Guardsman of the Velheim Cliff Guard,' declared the captain solemnly.

Baron Staghart did not look pleased. His pursed lips and sour expression suggested that he had been sucking on a particularly large lemon. In his inebriated state, all Rhev could think about was how wasteful it would be to use such an expensive fruit for sucking purposes.

'Captain Ardein, remind me why we ever hired this wretched oaf? I can't see how a man of his ineptitude could have possibly joined the ranks of our esteemed Cliff Guard.'

'You mean guards like Buttmug? *Esteemed*? More like effluent- *burp*... '

'Quiet Culluggan! Sire, we hired the dwarf after we observed his fighting prowess in an, *ahem...* an impromptu combat situation.'

'Tavern brawl,' interrupted Rhev, 'really good one too. Lots of *wham, bap, blammo*.' He punctuated each word with a clumsy shadow box. He stopped when he caught Ardein's steel eye.

'He really is very proficient with his fists... and chairs... *haddock,* even. But I can see now that we made a mistake. Despite my best hopes, it seems he has proven himself a liability. Shame, really.' The captain sighed heavily. 'Hand over your badge, Rhev.'

Rhev reluctantly patted himself down and explored the many pockets sewn into his jerkin. Unsatisfied with the speed of badge finding, the dwarf turned all his pockets inside out in the hope that it would come up somewhere. What came out was an unruly assortment of fluff, sharp objects, brass knuckles, a small unspecified rodent, and a little bronze disc.

'*Aha!*' Rhev chucked the tarnished badge petulantly at the feet of the captain. It landed face up, the Cliff Guard's motto 'Crime Doesn't Pay' catching the light. Rhev had never been certain if it was a reminder for the criminals or the guardsmen, the latter comprising people much like himself. Ardein scowled at the badge on the floor, every muscle straining against the instinct to pick it up. Instead, he just shook his head. 'Get your things Culluggan, I want you out of the barracks in an hour.'

Unsure of what else to do, and fearing the hangover he would experience if he allowed himself to fully sober up, Rhev spent the next few days in the pub. The Jolly Foreigner, so named because it was full of a lot of them, was the last drinking hole in Velheim whose patrons hadn't yet heard of Rhev's embarrassing hobby, his failure in the Trial of the Brews, and the events surrounding his dismissal from the Cliff Guard, because most of them couldn't speak the language.

As an expat, Hoskin spent a lot of his time in The Jolly Foreigner, and it didn't take long for him to find his friend.

'I will not say "I told you so", because I'm not very sure what it means,' said the blacksmith as he brought over another round.

'But I was close, wasn't I? Tell me I was close at least,' Rhev replied forlornly, already in the process of emptying his fresh pint.'

'You were close,' Hoskin admitted. 'But Buggerhat drank the whole bottle in the end. Although, you will be cheered to know, afterwards he could not do anything except dribble and talk about the people who lived under his toenails.'

'Aye, but I'm not cheered. He won. I lost. That's old Wobbly Roger's ruling. It's official, *I'm a loser*. I've got nothing.'

'Keep your nose up, eh Rhev?' said Hoskin, nudging Rhev with a meaty elbow. 'It is not all lost, yes? You still have your wits, a good pair of feet, and a new sword! You will come up smelling of cabbages, mark my words.'

Rhev grimaced and took a long draught from his tankard, all the way down to the dregs.

'All I'm good for is drinking, fighting, and grifting,' he sighed. 'And now I can't show my face in any of my favourite boozers without being laughed at, I've lost my licence to legally rough people up, and I just heard earlier today that bloody Sleedo has rubbished my name at all the high roller tables. I'm telling you Hoskin, I've got nothing.'

'No, no, my friend, do not think like Danny Downer. Maybe you can follow in your papa's shoes? You are always telling me how you are wishing you were like him. And now that you have nothing keeping you here...'

Rhev twitched. 'I'm getting another drink.'

Hoskin bit his tongue. He was too deep in his cups already and had let it run loose.

'Another flagon, Rhev?' asked Bensen, the proprietor of The Jolly Foreigner. After a brief nod from Rhev, Bensen hobbled over to the kegs on his peg leg, and poured a drink with difficulty, using one hand and one hook that didn't screw in properly. The tale behind the publican's injuries was often told around Velheim, not as an inspiring tale of heroism, but more as a public safety warning concerning the folly of single-handedly fighting a kraken with nothing but a head full of narcotics and your fists. Bensen returned, sloshing much of the ale out of the cup as he staggered over to Rhev. 'So what course are you setting sail on now, my boy? Not planning on returning to your less than legitimate ways, I hope?'

Rhev shrugged lazily. 'I dunno. I've tried both sides of the law, neither of them have worked out for me particularly well.'

'Sounds like you need to do something slap bang in the middle: a bit of good old fashioned merceneering!

Caravaneers are always in dire need of some hardened lads like yourself for security', replied Bensen.

'Mercenary work, eh? I suppose that's an option, but I've never set foot outside Velheim.'

'And? What's a ship if it never leaves port?'

Rhev wrinkled his nose and paused. 'Am I the ship in this analogy?'

'Alright, maybe I shoehorned that in a little, but you get where my wind is blowing. Listen, there's a group out back in the den. I sent a fella to them earlier who was looking for a group to take on a courier contract. He came out a bag o' gold lighter, so I'm guessing they took the job. Why don't you go over and introduce yourself? Tell them I sent you. Although, fair warning Rhev, they've been in there a while, so you might have some trouble talking straight business with them.'

Rhev nodded his thanks and downed the fresh tankard in one. He hopped off the stool with a thump and shimmied between the sticky tables towards a grimy red velvet curtain.

As the curtain pulled back, the smoke from the pub and a dense purple smog on the other side met, looked at each other for a moment, and decided to go their separate ways. Rhev stepped into the mist, letting the heavy curtain waft down behind him. A light beckoned to him, flickering through the purple and creating new colours indescribable to the human mind. The smoke parted as Rhev neared the light to reveal a towering silver and bronze contraption covered in valves, pipes, and other miscellanea that could have just been ornamentation. It was from the top of this metallic monolith that the purple cloud was emanating from, and it was from its base that the fire was burning. Around the pipe-to-end-all-pipes sat four figures, looking like pilgrims at the altar of some really far out god.

Rhev coughed. Somebody giggled in reply, which he found immediately disconcerting.

'My name's Rhev Culluggan. Bensen said you might be looking to hire security, and such like', he tried.

The statement was met with a 'woah' from one of the hidden figures. Rhev's patience was waning. He waved away the mist that was descending about him and finally started to get a good look at the figures he was trying to address. The first was a short man in late middle-age, sporting a jet black moustache that entirely dominated his otherwise greying head. A battered top hat was fighting to maintain balance on his crown.

'You've your own sword' he said, in a matter of fact tone. 'That's a good start. Do you know how to use it?'

Rhev shrugged. He was trying to act nonchalant, but he was also becoming very aware of how the room was starting to sway.

'Stick 'em, slash 'em, smack 'em, it's all good.'

The man grunted and said, 'Experience?'

'Guard work, erm, ad hoc crowd control, um...wealth transportation and reallocation.'

The man raised an eyebrow. 'Wash weekly or yearly?'

Rhev considered for a moment. He was hoping for a third option, but thought it wise to not discuss the topic in detail.

'Weekly.'

The man grunted again, betraying nothing. He turned and spoke into the smoke beside him. 'What do we reckon then?'

He was met with a giggle. 'I think it would be lovely for Sterling to have someone to talk to without the need to strain his neck.' The laughter, far too abundant for this particular jape, displaced the smoke around the speaker. He appeared to be an elf, but very unlike the muscle bound lot Rhev was used to seeing on the docks. This one was young, not much older than Rhev, and very slim, with long dark hair framing a clean shaved pointy face. He wore fine silk travelling clothes adorned with green and purple patterns that seemed to shift ever so slightly when caught in the corner of the eye. His laughter was interrupted when a small elbow jabbed him in the ribs.

'Don't be an arse, Kev, he doesn't even look that short. If anything, he looks pretty bloody massive from my perspective.'

The elf's hand displaced more smoke as it cuffed this fellow around the head. 'That's because you're lying down.'

'No I'm not,' insisted the now revealed halfling. He sat up. '*Now* I am. Wait, no, that's not right.' His eyes crossed and he blinked in confusion. Despite his temporary slackjaw, he was handsome, with a blond goatee and hair tied up into a short ponytail by a black ribbon. Rhev guessed he was a similar age to his elven companion, but his garb made him look like a child playing dress-up as a swashbuckler. He would have laughed at the halfling if it hadn't been for the bandolier of small throwing knives around his torso, each encrusted with tiny jewels in the handles. 'Alright, yeah, definitely dwarf sized,' he said as he squinted at Rhev. 'Take him on I say, always up for bringing the average height of the group down a foot or two.'

The moustachioed man glared at both of them. 'I wasn't talking to you two idiots. Lay off the pipe for a while before you throw your guts up again. Now, Mercy, what do you say?'

At the edge of the room someone let out a long, controlled breath. It was followed by a wave of a hand. A woman with a heavy red plait emerged. Judging by the collection of scars and weatherbeaten skin, she was at least a decade older than Rhev. She was sitting on a cushion like the rest of her companions, but she maintained a perfect upright posture that suggested strength, discipline, and most of all, an inability to relax.

'He's certainly got the look of a... fighter,' she said dryly, 'good active stance.' Rhev suddenly became very aware of how he was holding his body. In his drunken state he'd been rocking on the balls of his feet to keep his balance, and now he wasn't sure if this woman was mistaking it for battle readiness, or simply mocking him. Her dark-skinned face remained enigmatic.

Out of nowhere a sequined cushion flew at Rhev's head. He had time to notice it, but not to avoid it. Had he been sober he might have had a chance, but he was definitely not. It hit him with incredible force. If it hadn't been for his low centre of gravity, he would have been taken clean off his feet.

The woman smiled. There was a jingle of chainmail as she lowered her arm. The way she moved betrayed a taut musculature. 'Perhaps not so active, but he knows how to take a hit. On balance, this is probably better. I say we give him a go.'

'Not really sure what all that proved, but I assume it's a soldier thing. Regardless, if Bensen sent him, that's good enough for me.' The man took out a scroll of heavy vellum from behind him, and unfurled it on a small table. The writing was elaborately cursive, with more than one illumination and curious runes dotted here and there. It was so intricate, in fact, that Rhev realised he couldn't actually read it. Whether it was because his vision was swimming or it was beyond his comprehension, he wasn't sure.

'Right lad, sign your name here. It's the contract for our next job. Standard procedure for longer deliveries, just paperwork the client gives us for their records. After this job is done, we can discuss bringing you on for the next one. Call it a probation period. You've come at the right time, mind; this job is a right little earner. You'll be on three ducats a week, plus expenses paid...'

Rhev's mind was reeling from trying to read the contract while the man talked at him, but the phrase 'expenses paid' shined brightly in his head. In his current state all he could think of was 'more booze', and immediately began signing his name beneath the others with a quill that was offered to him.

'All that sound good to you lad?'

Rhev realised that he had blocked out at least half of what the man had told him, but he didn't want to let on to his new employer that he hadn't been listening.

'Aye, sir, it does,' he replied, and tried his best to straighten up. For a moment he considered doing a salute, forgetting that he was no longer in the Cliff Guard.

'No 'sirs', thank you. You can call me by my name: Steem Vennts. This here is Kevin, our... elf.'

The elf paused in the middle of a hefty draw on the pipe, exhaled awkwardly and objected.

'Wizard. *Wizard*. Wielder of the magick of Pingle, forty-seventh... no, forty-sixth mightiest of all the gods of magick, and bastion of arcane knowledge. Not Pingle, me, Kevin. Kevin of Yedforth.'

Both Rhev and Steem looked less than impressed. 'Anyway,' Steem continued, 'this here shortarse is Sterling Panthelios. I've forgotten why I hired him.'

'To give a sense of flair to the outfit of course,' said the halfling. 'To provide entertainment and boost morale. To be the handsome face of the operation. It's the only reason you get any business, Steem. You don't think they come for your ugly mug do you?'

'And this,' said Steem, ignoring the halfling entirely, 'is Mercy Nazaar, the brawn of our crew.'

Mercy flicked a stray lock of hair that had loosened from her plait. 'And probably the brains too,' she said with a wry smile.

'You're right. It's a wonder that I haven't fired myself, seeing as I clearly have no role to play in my own business,' Steem said, sarcasm dripping from his every word.

53

'Nonetheless, it is *my* caravan that you'll be riding, living in, and most importantly, protecting. Welcome aboard, Rhev.'

He smiled and stuck out his hand. The smile surprised Rhev. After the confusing gauntlet of banter and interrogation, he was disarmed by how genuine it was. Rhev took Steem's hand and shook as firmly as he could.

'As long you don't back-talk me like these sorry bastards, we'll be as thick as thieves.' He winked. 'Meet us at the end of Mudditch Street tomorrow at dawn. Big red wagon, you can't miss it.'

'So, that's it? I've... got a job?' Rhev asked cautiously.

'What were you expecting?' Steem replied. 'Some sort of ritual? A series of heroic tests? No need to overcomplicate things. I don't like complications. Listen, Rhev, we move things from point 'A' to point 'B'. I see that you have already moved your own arse from your home to the tavern, so I daren't say this job will be too much of a problem for you. Mudditch Street, dawn, big red wagon.'

Steem took a long puff on the strange pipe and relaxed into the cushions. It appeared that the interview, hiring, and onboarding process, was over. Rhev stumbled back to the table where Hoskin sat nursing a pint.

'Where have you been?' he asked. 'Chatting up the ladies, showing them your big sword, eh?'

'I got a job.'

'Doing what? Bensen say you can clean his lavvies?'

'Hired security for a wagon, a courier...type...thing...' Rhev realised that he wasn't entirely sure what he had signed on for.

'Where is this wagon going?' Hoskin asked, leaning forward in interest.

'I'm not sure.' He was sobering up quickly now.

'Ha ha! This is just like the Rhev I know. Jumping in arse first, no thinking, reckless-feckless. But this sounds good, yes?

This sounds like the adventure you are always telling me you want.'

Rhev didn't reply. Instead, he grabbed what was left of Hoskin's pint and sucked it dry.

***

It took half an hour for Merky to find Erin in the sprawling halls of firmament. Her face was sticky with dried tears, and her gaudy jacket lay in a crumpled heap beside her.

'I thought you had run off for good,' Merky said, a comforting smile on his face. 'I would hate to think we'd scared you away.' He sat down on the floor next to her, and let his presence settle in. 'I hadn't used a Table either, before I started here.'

'How… how did you know I hadn't used it before?' Erin's voice was still shaky.

'Well, usually if you've used one before you would have mastered the standing up bit by now.' Merky chuckled, and gave Erin a look to make sure she knew he was trying to lighten the mood, not poke fun. She smiled in return.

'When I was working with hedgehogs, I didn't have to use a Table. I just used to travel down there myself. There wasn't any need for a… contraption. Their lives are so slow and uncomplicated, you could just pop down for a week, visit everyone who needed your help. It all worked fine. The way things are done here is just so different.'

Merky nodded in agreement. 'When you get big, as in, you *are* the pantheon big, it's impossible to run the gig on your own, but you can't let on to the people down there. You just have to keep going. Obviously we're not really made for it, we're supposed to split the load. You take the hedgehogs, I take the oaths of agreement, Dermis takes the skin diseases. But more people means more problems, and more problems mean more prayers, and then it gets complicated, and people like *simple*. So they bundle it all up. Streamline it. One temple, one priest, one god. I know I'm glad I'm not that one god! Can you imagine having to manage all those prayers? It's no wonder Ava got help in. And, in a way, it makes all of our lives easier, even though it looks complicated.'

'But don't you miss being on the ground?' asked Erin.

'I never really did a lot of groundwork anyway. My lot was in the abstract mostly. Words, semantics, trust, that sort of thing. Very complicated business, lots of room for interpretation. Probably best that it's been rolled into the Fiat department.' Erin realised that Merky had been speaking like he'd learned it from rote. It had a tinge of falseness to it.

'I think I understand. I just hope the hedgehogs are doing okay,' Erin sighed.

'Oh, don't you worry about them. The Bestia team are top notch,' Merky reassured her. Erin tried her best to perk up.

'So, tell me how the Table works. I don't want the others to think I can't use it properly,' she said earnestly.

'Of course!' replied Merky, 'I don't know how much you already know, but there's no harm with starting with the basics.

So when the Progenitors sat down and made the world, they each made different parts of it. Then they all sat around a table, and took turns placing what they had made. An island here, a fjord there, the odd hill or mountain range. After a few aeons of placing they started to get bored and realised they still had a lot more to place before they were finished, which is why a lot of places on the edges have a lot of one thing, like endless forests and plains, and not a lot of the interesting things, like caves shaped like skulls.

The Table is a replica of the table used by the Progenitors to make the material world. It's such an infinitesimally accurate replica that, in way, it *is* the table used by the progenitors to make the world, and so therefore it is the world, with all that the world contains. Except of course it isn't, because it can't be the world because that would be absurd! But what it does allow us to do is monitor the world without having to go there via the usual astral pathways. Much more efficient, although we are limited to monitoring only. No interaction, that's for other departments.' Merky made a general motion around him as if to indicate that these departments were somewhere nearby, but their specific location was not something to worry about. 'Now you're wondering how it's possible to monitor anything on there when it looks like it's actually made out of a billion angry bees that don't want to be seen by our eyes. That's where the Specs come in.' At this juncture he produced the goggles that he had taken from Erin earlier out of his top pocket.

'These nifty little things have a few tricks up their sleeves. First of all they filter out all that particle noise. Smooths it out, converts it into something you can recognise and understand. Then this,' he tapped one of the adjustable runed rims, 'is used for zooming in. It's a little sensitive, which I'm guessing is what threw you off guard. The faster you turn it, the further it will zoom in. When you get near the level you need, slow down your movements and fine tune the zoom. You'll find there's more resistance when you move it slowly, so it gets easier. When you've had a practice you can start getting it accurate to within an inch of world-space.' He passed the specs to Erin, twiddling the rim back and forth in demonstration as he did so. 'Have a fiddle, but don't put them on yet, eh?' He raised his eyebrows.

'The good thing with this current iteration of Specs is that they have built in assistance. Just dial in roughly what you want to be monitoring using the other rim dial and it will guide your gaze to just about the right spot. It feels a little odd the first time you do it, like someone has grabbed your head and is moving it around. But as long as you don't fight it too much you'll be fine. You can always turn it off as well. Just remember not to turn it on when you're facing completely the wrong direction, or you might have to get used to looking down and seeing your own bum.' He grinned, but changed his expression as soon as he saw Erin's horrified look. 'Of course, I don't think that can actually happen, at the worst you'd get a bit of whiplash.'

Erin relaxed a little, but held the goggles a little further away from her face than before.

'And lastly we've got the hearing aids.' Merky pointed to the over-curved arms of the Specs. 'Make sure these wrap nice and tight around the back of your ears. They'll conduct the sound straight from what you're looking at into your head, as long as they've got a snug connection. Bear in mind that if you zoom in too close to, say, an active volcano, that you might blow a few gaskets, so to speak.'

Merky let Erin get used to the different parts of the goggles for a while. He always found that knowing exactly what you're putting on your face helps the whole process, and now that he knew that Erin was more of a traditional operator, he figured she should be given all the time she needed. Erin asked him to repeat a couple of his explanations and demonstrate exactly how the mechanisms worked, and Merky was happy to oblige. He didn't want to see her embarrassed again, if not just for her sake, but also for his own feelings of responsibility. At his primal core, he was a god of trust. If he could not be trusted to look after his team, he was nothing.

'I think I'm ready to go back now,' said Erin confidently, more to herself than to Merky. She had always been a surefooted god, and she knew that just because she had made one mistake it did not reflect who she was. To be a god of hedgehogs was to be resilient; the little buggers were half made of prickles, after all.

'Great,' replied Merky, 'just one tip before we go back. Hold the edge of the table with your hands if you can, it helps stop the temptation of reaching out and falling over.' He grinned, and so did Erin.

***

Rhev took one last look around the hovel. Most of the pots and pans were still on the floor where he had left them a few days ago. The empty locker was tucked back under his childhood bed. His mum's snuffbox sat on the mantelpiece. After a moment's thought, he took the snuffbox and placed it in the locker, locking it and pocketing the key. The key joined a piteously small collection of belongings that Rhev had decided to take with him. Naturally his new sword had been first on the list, followed by the clothes on his back, his ring, and some particularly well preserved rat jerky. He had realised that he had spent the remainder of his money on booze the night before, and was grateful for the fact that his new job would be paying for his board and food. If he hadn't been hired, he would have been finding out exactly how far that rat jerky could last.

He sighed, encompassing all the good memories he'd made in this home in a single exhalation. In truth, these were the only memories he had of any home. Twenty two years in this hole in the backstreets of the Underport. Rhev knew he could stand there and envisage his entire life thus far. It was a strange thought. Comforting, yet sad. Perhaps he was too familiar with this place. *Time for a change?*

'Right. Good,' he said aloud.

He stepped outside and pulled the door behind him. It remained in place, as doors are supposed to do, for approximately four seconds. Then it was on the floor.

The sun was rising, and if Rhev hadn't time to fix it in the last six months, he certainly didn't have time to fix it now. Unfortunately, his particular corner of Velheim was notorious for squatters, and he knew if he was ever to return, it would be to a hovel full of strangers. There was only one thing to do.

59

'Do you know what time it is?!' Josephine squawked.

'I know, I know, I don't want to be having this conversation either.'

'Then go away!'

'I am!'

Josephine paused, and drew her tattered shawl around herself.

'What do you mean?' she asked.

'I've got a job on a courier caravan. I'm leaving Velheim. Today.'

The haggard woman squinted at him suspiciously.

'Rhev Culluggan, I've known you your whole life, and you've never left Velheim in all that time. What has gotten into you?'

Rhev shrugged. 'Bored of the carnal pits, I guess.'

'Your mother wouldn't like it.'

'No, she wouldn't, but I need to make a living. It's something I need to do. Actually, it's something I *want* to do, I think.'

'You sound like your father.'

Rhev hadn't expected that. Josephine's usual stern visage had softened. She didn't say anything more. She just stared, and shook her head sadly. Rhev cleared his throat.

'My front door is broken. I haven't time to fix it, and I know you don't want squatters any more than I do. If you could board it up or something, I'd really appreciate it, Josephine.'

Then she did something he really hadn't expected. She hugged him.

'I know you've got a good soul somewhere under all that muck, Rhev Culluggan. I seens it when you was little. Follow it, and you'll find blessed Ava.'

He had no idea how to react. Thankfully, he didn't have to. Josephine released him, and said: 'Now leave me alone.'

Then she shut the door in his face.

'Bloody hell, I hope she didn't have plague…' he muttered as he went on his way.

The Underport was still dark at this time. Lanterns and lit braziers lead him to the docks where the lifts to the surface lived. Even now, there was a bustle of activity surrounding the ships making ready for an early departure. Curses and heave-hos abound. The creaking of jetties underfoot and the squeaks of pulleys created a song so familiar to Rhev that he had ceased to notice it, until now. He realised that he wouldn't hear this song for quite some time. In fact, it could even be the last. Overcome with melancholy, he sat down on a crate and drank greedily of the sights and sounds of Velheim. A new instrument joined the orchestra, a meow to his left. It was Steve the harbour cat, stinking of fish, and butting affectionately into Rhev's shoulder.

The sun peaked above the horizon. Its rays glittered over the waves and speared through the forest of ropes and chains that suspended the lifts.

It may be the pits, but it's not so bad in the right light, Rhev thought. *Why am I leaving it behind?*

His focus shifted to the colossal axes hanging over the seaward entrance of the underground cove. They were wielded by two statues standing at the foot of the cliffs, either side of the cavern's mouth. Each statue stood over three hundred feet tall. They were named Scrogi and Narl, mythical giants said to have carved out the Underport millenia ago. They worked so hard, the story went, that they developed severe arthritis, to the point where they could no longer move a single joint. Infirm and incredibly knackered, they resigned themselves to stand guard over their creation for evermore. The fact that Scrogi's left arm had fallen off fifty years ago and hadn't elicited as much as an 'owie' from him was something that the storytellers tended to leave out.

The interesting thing about Velheim's number one tourist attraction was that you could only see them from *outside* the city, either as you came into port, or left it. In his entire life, Rhev had never seen the statues in all their glory.

'Well Steve,' said Rhev to his feline companion, who was now affectionately yacking up a fishbone. 'I suppose there's only so much you can see from staying in one place. So long, fella.'

Rhev got up just as Steve threw up a little in the spot he had been sitting, and strode purposefully to the nearest lift. Up, up, into the dawn's light he went, then through the main square towards Mudditch Street. The long road was almost exclusively used for wagons, and the constant churning of their wheels was what gave it its name. Close to a hundred wagons, caravans, wains, and carts lined the road, and Rhev became nervous that by the time he found the one he was looking for he would most certainly be late.

He needn't have feared though. Steem Vennts' caravan was not difficult to spot. As advertised it was a magnificent bright red vehicle that stood out from the drab, unpainted wagons around it. Rhev saw Steem, easily recognisable by his top hat, busying himself on the roof of the caravan.

'Reporting for duty!' he said, out of habit.

Steem continued to secure various sundries to the roof. Rhev tried again. 'I hope I'm not late.'

Realising that someone had spoken in his direction not once, but twice, Steem raised his head. 'You look pretty alive to me, lad.'

'That's partly what you're paying me for,' Rhev chuckled, giving as good as he got. 'That, and being handy in a pinch, right?'

Steem looked baffled. 'I'm paying you?'

Rhev's hairy apple cheeks flushed. *Have I made a mistake? Are there two red caravans? That's possible. Are there two men in*

62

Velheim who wear top hats? That's impossible!

'You are paying him, Steem,' said a voice coming from the other side of the caravan. A second later Mercy walked around, brushing her hands together. 'This is Mister Rhev Culluggan. You hired him last night.'

'I did, did I?' Steem stroked his moustache thoughtfully. 'That must have been some powerful stuff in the old pipe, I can't for the life of me recall hiring a dwarf.'

'You said if I could transport my own arse from home to the tavern, I was qualified for the job.'

Steem considered this. 'That does sound something I would say. Rhev Culluggan, was it? Let me show you around your new workplace.'

Steem leapt from the caravan's roof and landed with a bend of the knees that was unexpected from a man of his age. Then he spread out his arms and gestured proudly to the faded gilt writing on the side of the caravan. It read '*Steem Vennts & Co - We'll Move It For You (We Don't Do Dragons)*'. Underneath this was scratched '*Maybe Little Ones*'. Steem grinned proudly.

'Why don't you do dragons?' asked Rhev. Steem's face fell.

'Ah, I'd rather not-'

'We ran out of horses.' It was Sterling, who came sauntering out from underneath the caravan. He appeared to be finding the whole thing quite funny.

'And they were excellent horses!' glared Steem. 'Who would still be with us today if someone had been able to cast the magickal padlock spell that he said he could do.'

Until that point Rhev had been watching Kevin's slender boots make their way around the caravan. They had now begun walking in the opposite direction.

'Let's move on,' Steem continued. He walked around to the wide rear step of the caravan, hoisted himself up, and opened the door. With a little difficulty Rhev hauled himself up as well, and was beckoned inside. He couldn't quite believe what he saw. Compared to his hovel in the Underport, the caravan was practically a royal suite. Plush bunk beds lined one wall, with the bottom most covered by a thick velvet curtain. A small area had been set aside for food preparation, and various utensils were strapped to the walls. Next to this was a series of heavy chests and crates, that could have been full of either food or gold, for all Rhev knew. The floor was covered by an ornate but fraying floral rug, which matched with a beautiful tapestry hung across the ceiling. Morning light streamed through the little window hatches, bouncing off the polished sconces and making everything glow.

'I've never seen finery like it,' marvelled Rhev.

'It's alright.' Sterling had crept in with them. He got another glare from Steem.

'I'm glad that we now have someone on the team who appreciates a good interior,' said Steem. 'Yours will be the top bunk I'm afraid, it's the only one left. I hope you have the, erm, requisite height to make it up there.'

'Oh don't worry about me, I've got a lot of practice getting up to hard to reach places.'

Steem looked at Rhev askance.

'Such as watchtowers, and so forth,' Rhev continued, cursing his loose lips.

'Indeed. Anyway, feel free to put your possessions in that chest there, but mind the box next to it. That's our cargo.'

Before Rhev had a chance to unburden himself of his rat jerky, Mercy called out.

'Time to get going if we want to avoid getting stuck behind a bunch of potato farmers, and you know they're a touched lot.'

'Right you are!' Steem called back. He kicked Sterling off the back step and turned to Rhev. 'You'll have to take the rear for now. The others have already picked out the other positions. It's not the most glamorous spot, admittedly, but you'll get a good view of the sunrise. Just mind you don't get a mouthful of mud when the wheels start turning.'

Steem swung himself up and over the caravan to take his seat at the reins. Rhev had the presence of mind to grab onto something just before the vehicle lurched forward. He sat down on the back step and watched Mudditch Street roll away underneath him. Rolling, rolling...

It was at this time that his body remembered that he should be experiencing a terrible hangover. The caravan turned a corner and the horizon wobbled dangerously. The hangover, furious that Rhev had as of yet managed to outpace it, decided this was an excellent time to remind the dwarf of the fundamental laws of inebriation: *what goes down, must come up.*

The caravan jolted as the large wood and iron wheels hit yet another muddy pothole. Velheim didn't have a highways agency, but if it did the people would probably get the wrong idea and use it as an excuse to say 'stand and deliver' to anyone who looked like they would be worth a bob or two. As Velheimnians would probably say if they were any good with aphorisms, 'better a hole in the road than a hole in the purse'. Unless you're a halfling of course, in which case it's probably best that you avoid any kind of hole in case you can't get out.

Rhev's legs, now a little spattered with the remains of his last meal, dangled awkwardly over the bumpy road that now seemed to be a metaphor for what might await him. His initial wonder at his plush new accommodation had quickly faded. He was now feeling horribly sick. He wasn't sure where he was going. He still didn't know what it was they were actually delivering. Then the thick stone archway marking the edge of the city passed overhead, and it reminded him that worst of all, he knew next to nothing about life *out there*. To Rhev, his perception of *out there* was constructed entirely from drunken stories told by the hundreds of travellers passing through Velheim every day. Out of habit, he played nervously with the ring on his finger.

Now you can tell your own story.

What a strange thought. It had come to him unbidden, from somewhere deep inside that had been locked away.

What's a life without daring deeds? Without adventure?

He recognised the thought now. It wasn't his own. It was his father's. *Had he really said that?* It did feel like something his dad would say.

Ah, but let's not get ahead of ourselves. Dwarves with questionable morals don't do deeds, they do jobs.

That was his own inner voice, booting the shade of his father right back into forgotten memory.

Do enough jobs and you get rich, then you can get drunk as often as you want and commission swords from people who can spell. If those jobs take you out of the city for a while, so be it. Ale tastes the same everywhere you go.

The first thought, that belonging to his father, had excited him and scared him in equal measure. This thought, however, calmed him. It was familiar. It rang like a bell through his head, loud and clear, and for now, Rhev ignored the fact that there was a crack forming in it.

Spears of pinkish light spilled across the plains and through the rows of crops, picking out the gold lettering on the side of the big red caravan. Steem sat at the front, his top hat bouncing comically on his head at every bump in the road. Next to him sat Sterling, a small lute making absentminded trills in his hands. Kevin was inside the caravan, pouring over some dog-eared tome. Mercy sat up top to act as look out, surveying the plains for any sign of thieves or aggressive potatoes. Indeed, the plains held very little danger for travellers other than the potatoes. Centuries before a wizard

66

had relieved himself in the irrigation system, giving rise to a breed of root vegetable that not only uttered profanities but, at times, would hurl themselves out of the ground at unwary farmers. Theories abound as to why they do this, but the most popular is that they were granted sentience by the magickal urine and word got around regarding all the mashing and frying that awaited them. They would have been culled years ago, if it wasn't for the fact that they made for a very tasty chip.

Beyond the potatoes, it was the Grippen Mountains that Steem and his party would be worrying about. The dappled plains ahead were interrupted by an almost sheer mass of grey stone, a vast wall of peaks that separated the barony of Velheim from the rest of Peninsula like a topographical tourniquet. The mountains were perilous to cross, uncomfortable to inhabit, and really, bloody, *mountainous*. There were a lot of your standard mountain features: stupendously narrow roads, sickening drops, unfortunately placed waterfalls, and goblins, because the goblins apparently thought *'we're ugly, unhygienic and fundamentally unlikeable chaps; let's improve our lot by moving to the mountains, where it's cold and wet and full of equally unlikeable things'*. Incidentally, goblins are not particularly bright.

The horses began to strain in their harnesses as the ascent into the mountains began. Rhev suddenly had the most beautiful view of the plains he had ever seen: the farmsteads picked out in the dawn light, the wheat swaying in the sea breeze, the high walls of Velheim and the keep behind that rising above the chimney tops, and far beyond the sun boiling out of the turbulent sea. The dwarf was seeing all this wonder for the first time in his life. For a moment, he forgot his worries, and began to look forward to the other wondrous things he might get to see. He felt vindication in his sudden career change. He cursed himself for not following this path sooner. The moment was rudely taken away from him, however, as the wagon turned a corner in the road, and the view was dominated by scree, moss, and a distastefully placed skull on a stick.

As they climbed, the air began to chill, and the hangover shivers reached a fever pitch. Rhev opened the back door of the caravan and hopped inside. Kevin was sitting reading on a small chest covered in shifting glyphs, similar to those that adorned the wizards shirt. He looked up from his reading to observe Rhev totter unsteadily through the wobbling caravan to bury himself in a pile of furs.

'I thought you dwarves were supposed to have iron stomachs,' he said, going back to his reading.

'Eh?'

'You look like you're nursing a fearsome hangover.'

'Never. I'm fine and dandy, me.' The wagon lurched again and Rhev felt the bottom of his stomach wobble. He diverted the conversation.

'What's that you're sitting on?' he asked.

'This,' said Kevin, looking between his legs, 'is our cargo.'

'I know that,' said Rhev unconvincingly, 'I meant, what's in it?'

Kevin shrugged. 'We don't know, that's what I'm trying to find out.' He went back to reading the tome.

'Have you tried opening it?'

The elf glowered at the dwarf from under his slender eyebrows. Rhev pushed on.

'Well, have you?'

'This box has no lock, no latch, no handle. The gap between the lid and the body is so small I doubt you'd be able to see it. It is, as you may or may not have realised from its appearance, inherently magickal. But to answer your question, yes, we have tried opening it.'

'I was just asking.' He didn't like how Kevin spoke to him.

68

Kevin was not the sort of person Rhev would usually socialise with. In fact, Kevin was the sort of person that Rhev might single out if a convenient tavern brawl erupted.

However, he decided not to chuck the books stacked beside him at the wizard's head. Instead, he picked one of them up and read the cover. 'How To Breathe Custard And Other Useless Spells by Ripley Gargunfungel'. He opened it to a random page. Across it was written a series of incomprehensible runes, accompanied by a picture of a duck with very long legs.

'You can do all these spells then, can you?' he asked Kevin, holding the book up.

'Well, yes, of course I can,' he said, surprisingly ruffled. 'Who told you I couldn't?'

'No-one. It's just all the wizards I've seen were either con men or barmy old buggers wearing very short trousers in very cold weather.'

'Those weren't barmy old buggers. Don't you know anything about wizards?'

'Look, all I know is that the last wizard I met down the pub said he could make everyone's beers disappear, and by the end of the night he was very drunk and very unpopular.'

'That one does sound like a con man, but the ones wearing the hotpants would have been certified masters of their craft. You see, contrary to popular belief, powerful wizards do not wear heavy, cumbersome robes with long dangly bits and billowing cloaks. All truly powerful wizards wear as little as possible.'

Rhev was almost certain Kevin was pulling his leg, but he bit anyway. It was true that he really didn't know much about wizards. 'Why?'

'Obvious, isn't it? If you saw someone walking down the street with a staff, pointy hat, and next to nothing on, you'd assume they were either mad, or someone you don't want to mess with.'

Rhev considered this for a moment. 'What if you just assumed they were mad?'

'Most wizards are by the time they get to that level, so you'd be right on either account. One thing's for sure though, only a person who is very sure of themselves would wear shorts all year round.'

You couldn't fault the logic, but it did leave Rhev with another question.

'Why are you so… *clothed*, then?'

Kevin's head shook rapidly as he made some incoherent mouth sounds, refusing to make eye contact with his interrogator.

'I didn't say *all* wizards, did I? Hmm? I could cut the sleeves off this shirt, as would be my prerogative as a wielder of magickal arts, but then I would ruin a very expensive shirt, so I'm not going to do that, am I?' Kevin continued to bluster.

'But you said all *truly powerful wiz-*'

'Give me that book!' Kevin interrupted. He leaned forward and snatched it before Rhev had a chance to acquiesce. There were a few ripping sounds as he flicked through the tome at speed. Finally, he pinned a page under a slender finger.

'Pass me a cup and a waterskin,' he said sharply. Rhev obeyed, more out of curiosity than subservience. The elf poured the water into the cup.

'Watch this,' he grinned. He took out a thin wooden rod that had been tucked in his belt and began muttering into the cup in a strange tongue. A flash illuminated his face. He drew back and nodded at the cup. What had been a cup of water now appeared to be a cup of fresh, frothy ale.

'Now that's the kind of magick I can get behind,' said Rhev with glee, taking the cup and putting it to his lips. *Hair of the dog would be good for me, right? Prove this smarmy elf wrong as well.* He glugged the liquid. The glugging soon turned to spluttering.

'This isn't ale!' protested Rhev. 'This is just scummy water!'

Rather than laughing at his expense as the dwarf had expected him to do, the elf looked genuinely perturbed.

'Are you sure?' he asked.

'Yes I'm bloody sure!' Rhev gagged.

'Oh.'

'I thought you could do magick.'

'I can!'

Rhev tried his best to calm down. His hangover had left him in a foul mood. As he cleared his head, he could see now that Kevin was almost upset. This was the last thing he had expected. Not quite knowing how to navigate this sort of situation this early in their relationship, he decided it was best to retreat. On his way out the back door, he turned.

'Just keep practicing, I guess.'

As he secured the door behind him and took his seat on the rear step, he realised that may have been the worst thing he could have said.

They made camp for the night at the side of the road. All were grateful for the fire that warmed their aching bones. Earlier that day the wagon and the horses with it had almost fallen prey to a subsidence at the edge of the track. It had taken all of them an agonising amount of time to push the whole lot back onto the stone road. For a second, Rhev had thought his career as caravan security was going to end abruptly at the bottom of a cliff. On the bright side, the exertion had sweated the hangover from his body.

'You've a strong arm, Rhev,' said Steem through a puff of pipe smoke. 'Almost as strong as Mercy here. You've already proven yourself as a good hire.'

Rhev shuffled about on his buttocks, not sure how to take the compliment. He glanced at Mercy. She returned his gaze with a wink that made him feel uncomfortable.

'Thanks Mister Vennts,' he replied.

'Just Steem, if you please, Rhev. I'm not the sort of man to stand on honorifics.'

'What do you usually use then? A box?'

Rhev froze. He had known his boss for barely a day, and this sort of tavern banter with a superior had got him in trouble before. Steem stared at the young dwarf, his moustache twitching ever so slightly.

'A box? A box!' he erupted. 'Brilliant!' He slapped Rhev on the back with all the avuncular charm he could muster. The dwarf relaxed.

'May I take a look at your sword?' Mercy asked. She had been sharpening her own formidable longsword with a whetstone. The question caught Rhev off guard. He was reluctant to show her his weapon, and although he wouldn't admit it to himself, he was intimidated.

'I suppose so,' he replied hesitantly. He drew the wide greatsword from its scabbard and held it in both hands in front him, catching the light from the fire. He walked over to Mercy and handed the pommel to her with difficulty. It was not the most agile weapon.

'You'd find it more balanced if you twist your left hand round the hilt a quarter turn more,' she said as she took the blade from him, almost absent mindedly. Rhev was shocked. He'd only been holding it in front of her for a few seconds, but he knew she was right.

'It's an urban-style grip,' he lied. Mercy didn't seem to be listening.

'It's well made, although I can't seem to place the alloy,' she muttered. 'What's this here... 'Onur'?'

Rhev's heart skipped a beat. He had entirely forgotten about the stupid engraving.

'A name,' he tried, 'the sword's name, that is. After a

72

famous… fighting…person.'

Mercy made no reply as she traced the word with her calloused finger. Then she spoke.

'I like that. A good sword should have a name. Mine is called Warum, after a brave soldier I once knew.'

Rhev breathed a sigh of relief. 'That's a good name too.'

She handed the large sword back to him with more grace than he had used. It was accompanied by a nod that appeared to communicate a certain respect, a respect that Rhev wasn't used to. The moment was interrupted by Steem hollering.

'Stop playing silly buggers and sit down!'

Sterling had somehow persuaded Kevin to stand against a dead tree to raise the stakes on his knife throwing practice. The wizard was surrounded by tiny knives. Sterling protested the summons, but Kevin was more than happy to acquiesce.

'Make yourself useful and play us a tune,' said the boss.

'Right you are, chief.' Sterling grabbed his lute from the wagon and began playing a rhythmic, chugging progression of chords. Steem began tapping his foot on the gravel. Then he launched into a sincere rendition of *Up The Ropes And Down The Hatch*. Rhev knew it well. It was a popular shanty down on the docks of the Underport, and he'd heard it often on his patrols down there.

At the beginning of the third verse Rhev's full baritone joined Steem's, and together they finished the song. By the end, even Kevin was smiling.

'By Ava above, that was beautiful!' said Sterling in awe. Enough of this delivery work; we should start a band.'

'I like a man who can sing for his supper,' Steem grinned. 'Excellent work, Rhev. A good arm and a good set of pipes, what more can I ask for. Soups up!'

Steem leant forward and began dishing out ladles of thin soup. As everyone's attention turned towards supper, Rhev allowed himself a smile. Later that night, as he settled into his cosy top bunk and stared at the beautiful tapestry above him, he looked forward to a new life of wealth and comfort. He realised there was a lot to be said for a straight forward job. Perhaps it was best that the deeds were left to people like his dad.

***

Two goblins sat in a bush. Their voices came through as a rasping whisper.

'Right, so you get the plan now, yeah?' said the first.

'No,' replied the second. The first sighed.

'Okay, this is the last time I tell you, Grunthry, and stop playing with that rock. So, we hold up these masks-'

'They look a bit splintery.'

'Doesn't matter. We hold up these masks in front of our faces so that any passersby will think we're human.' In his hands were two pieces of bark, a crude smiley face scratched into each of them. 'Then we ask them for help to lure them in. Actually, I'll ask them for help, you just keep shtum.'

The other goblin shrugged. 'Suits me, Gethin. But why the masks?'

Gethin smacked a mask against his brow in frustration. 'Because we don't look human, do we? If anyone sees us, they're going to think "oh no, it's those two infamous goblin robbers, the Nabbers Extraordinaire", and then they're never going to stop and we'll never have a chance to *nab*.'

'Oh, right, I get it, they're dis...disgo... disguises-'

'No, Grunthry, they're *ours*. Who's 'this guy' you're talking about? Never mind, shut up! I hear something...'

Around the bend came the long awaited caravan. Judging by how slowly it was moving, Gethin guessed that it was probably ripe with things for the nabbing.

'Put on your mask, Grunthry, it's nabbing time.'

Out of the bushes just ahead of the caravan stumbled two short, vaguely humanoid figures. A nasally voice spoke up:

74

'Hail, fellow humans. Oh woe, oh cursed fortune! Our wagon has fallen over yonder cliff, and we are without transportation. Can thay...thy...*you* help us?'

Gethin whispered to his side: 'I think that was pretty good, don't you? Very human.'

On the driver's bench of the caravan, Sterling nudged Steem: 'They speak a bit funny, don't they? Sound very la-dee-da.'

Steem grunted in agreement.

'Maybe we should help them, though. If they're as rich as they sound, there could be some money in it.'

'We don't really need the money. We're still heavy from the sack of ducats we got in Velheim for this job.'

'Fine, fine, do it for the reputation then. Pay it forward. Spread the name of Steem Vennts throughout the land. "Courier and all round fine gentleman".' He accompanied the phrase with a few choice chords from his lute, and beamed cherubically at his employer. 'Now surely that can't be bad for business?'

Steem grunted again, less enthusiastically. 'If it will shut you up...'

Steem slowed the wagon to a halt. The two figures approached cautiously.

'Hello there travellers. Sorry to hear about your wagon,' said Steem in a polite but forced tone. 'I'll gladly take you west out of the mountains, for the small fee of-'

He felt a small elbow jab him. 'Good will means good words!' hissed the halfling. Steem growled.

'-of nothing. No fee required. I'll take you out of the goodness of my heart. Me, Steem Vennts.'

'Oh, thank you, Steem Vennts. What an all round fine gentleman you are!'

'See,' whispered Sterling, 'told you!'

The second figure, who had not yet spoken, added to the

praise with a low bow. There was a *twang* of some sort of cord breaking, and his face fell off.

'Err...' mumbled Grunthry.

Gethin whispered sharply: 'Don't look up you idiot. You've blown us again.'

'Sorry, Gethin.'

'Just back up, real slow like.'

Both of the figures began shuffling backwards, one of them still doubled up with their face to the ground.

'Where are you going?' asked Steem.

'We just remembered that we don't need help. Nope, no help needed here. We're fine. We're going to live here now. Bye.'

Sterling and Steem looked at each other, suspicion etching its way into both their faces.

Grunthry was doing his best to shuffle backwards towards the bush he had come from whilst keeping his head bowed and face out of sight. Without a frame of reference, however, the goblin began slowly shuffling in a circle. By the time he had gone a full one hundred and eighty degrees, it was too late. The two wagoneers had a full, glorious view of the top of the goblin's pimply green buttocks as they peaked above the waistband of his trousers. Sterling pointed, almost gleefully.

'Goblin! Goblin!' he yelled.

Mercy jumped off the back of the caravan where she had been sitting and jogged to the front. Rhev and Kevin stuck their heads out of the windows on either side.

'Alright, alright,' said Steem as he forcefully lowered the halfling's arm. 'That's the last time I listen to you. "Good will means good words", my arse. "Stick to the job", that's a better motto. "Don't get involved": there you go, stick that in one of your poems. Mercy, sort those two out will you.'

'Leg it!' yelped Gethin, but it was too late. Mercy's long strides took her over to the two goblins in a matter of seconds.

76

She hoisted both of them up by their collars. They stared fearfully at the sword about her waist.

'Please don't stick us, we weren't going to nab anything, honest!' Gethin wailed.

'Stick you?' said Mercy with a smirk. 'This sword doesn't come out for little robbers like you. It's only for worthy adversaries.'

'We are not worthy!' squealed Grunthry, wriggling to keep his trousers up.

'No, I can't say you are. Now, when I put you down, what are you going to do?'

'Bugger off!' said the goblins in unison.

'Very good. I can see that you've done this before. Are you ready?'

The goblins nodded. Gethin's mask finally fell off with pitiful clatter onto the track.

'Go!'

Mercy dropped the Nabbers Extraordinaire on the ground and watched as they scarpered off into the hedges. One thing was for sure: they were very good at running away.

'Nicely done Mercy, as always,' said Steem, who had now taken the time to light his pipe. 'Although, I was rather hoping I'd get to see how far you'd punt the little fellas.'

'I thought you were going to chop their heads off or something,' said Rhev, still hanging out the side of the caravan. Mercy looked perplexed.

'Why would I do that?' she asked.

'They were goblins, right? Scum of the mountains, scourge of travellers, gnaw the meat from your bones with their little pointy teeth, sort of thing.'

'Did they really look capable of being the scourge of anyone taller than two foot?'

Rhev looked abashed. He had always believed the tavern tales of fearsome goblin raids on the shepherd communities in the mountains, and the strapping sellswords and mercenaries who brought vengeance upon them. He had to admit now that those tales seemed a little tall.

'You never know,' he said quietly.

'It's good to know *how* to use a sword, but it's just as important to know *when*.'

'Enough chat, everyone back in,' said Steem. 'We've got to make it to Wathgill by the end of the day.'

It was late afternoon by the time they hit another obstacle.

'Mercy should have kicked 'em,' Steem muttered as he slowed the horses to a stop.

In front of them was a gaggle of small creatures wearing masks. Their dress was more bombastic than the previous goblins, replete with eagle feathers and interesting twigs. They huddled around something that looked like a scarecrow made of shrubbery and bits of brambles. Without warning, they began dancing around the effigy in a stumbling, swaying motion. A chorus of reedy chants rose up to match the rhythm of the dance.

Steem called into the caravan. 'Rhev, time to see if you're any good at crowd control.'

Rhev popped his head through the hatch. 'What sort of crowd?'

'More goblins by the looks of it, wearing those silly masks again. They've plonked a totem of sorts in the middle of the road. Probably some sort of territory marker. Just get them off the road.'

'Just four, eh? Sure, I'll sort them out,' Rhev said with confidence. *A chance to show what I'm really good at.* He hopped out of the caravan and went to draw his sword, then thought better of it. If Mercy could sort out two of the rascals with her bare hands, doing four of them should go some way to showing his worth. He swaggered over to the group.

'Right you lot, take those silly masks off, you're not fooling anyone.'

One of the dancers stopped. It was covered in feathers to a comical extent. Rhev wasn't entirely sure that he wasn't talking to a large chicken. The creature walked over to him cautiously. Its mask was not as crude as he had expected. This one was actually recognisable as some sort of bird.

'Clear the road, we're coming through,' said Rhev, his confidence fading in the face of the implacable bird mask. The creature didn't answer at all. It was about half the size of Rhev, but it bared no sign of being intimidated.

'Enough of this,' he growled, and reached out for the mask, ripping it off in one smooth motion. Behind the wood was not the face he was expecting. Rather than black eyes and green skin, the tiny creature had a pale visage with rosy cheeks and piercing blue eyes. For a moment it looked quite innocent, and Rhev felt a pang of guilt in his chest. Then the creature opened its mouth. Two rows of sharp teeth, filed to points, flashed menacingly.

***

The caravan thundered down the mountain pass, torches leaving trails of light in the encroaching darkness. Mud flew from the wheels as Steem steered his pride and joy through the near horizontal rain. His throat was sore from shouting at the horses, and his arms were sore from holding the reins, but he wasn't going to stop, not now, not when he could still hear the cry: 'ECKI ECKI ECKI! P'TANG! P'TANG!'

Gnomes. Feral gnomes. The worst kind. They rode on tiny horses, spears in hand and murder in their hearts. Mothers would tell their children of the dreaded hoards of little people up in the mountains as a cautionary tale, a myth to keep them from straying too far from home. Some say they were driven mad through a curse, some say it was through their war with goblin tribes. The local drunk would always say it was 'short man syndrome', and get a good laugh out of it. It wasn't a joke

79

now though. It was real, and terrifying.

The sound of tiny hooves drew closer. Steem looked around for a second to see a fearsome face with fire blazing in its eyes. The gnome lifted its spear above its head to throw at Steem, but at the last second a hatch flew open on the caravan and the point of a sword hit the gnome in the armpit. The spear was dropped, and the gnome fell with it to the sodden ground. Steem rustled his moustache in thanks, and continued to steer the caravan through the night. It was far from over.

More of the tiny tribesmen began gaining on them. The roof hatch and rear door were thrown open, and the crew clambered out into the rain, balancing precariously as they lurched around a corner on the track. Rhev and Mercy stood together on the back step, both with their swords drawn. Warum scythed through the rain, reaping gnome after gnome. Rhev struggled to handle his greatsword as the platform beneath him bucked unpredictably.

'Grip!' yelled Mercy over the rain and battlecries.

He knew she was right. He twisted his hand and regained his balance. His first swing cleaved two riders in one.

'Nice kill,' said the warrior beside him. 'Keep it coming.'

A few gnomes flung themselves onto the side of the wagon, only to find knives quickly flying towards their heads. Sterling's blades were clearly not just for show, and they just kept on coming. Rhev was unsure where the halfling was even keeping all of them.

The onslaught of gnomes came as thickly as the rain. Blood was washed away by the downpour just as quickly as it was spilt. When it looked like it would never end, a new adversary emerged. Silhouetted against the light of the rising moon rode an imposing gnome in a chariot. The raindrops glinted off the polished surface of a large crystal in his hands. Ethereal green light flowed from the crystal into the rider. He laughed maniacally as his eyes began to glow with magickal fire.

Thunder deafened Steem's crew as the chariot rider raised his crystal. Rhev looked uncertainly at Mercy; stoney faced, she stared straight ahead at the wild mage, waiting. The closest gnomes parted as the grimacing wizard held the artefact aloft.

A crack of lightning ruptured the air and cut straight through the mage. A green explosion rippled from the crystal and the small wooden chariot burst, flinging debris in every direction. The gnomes fled, screams of 'ECKI ECKI' and 'AIEE, AIEE' retreating back into the mountains.

Sterling leant down into the roof hatch. 'Well done Kev, took you long enough.'

'Long enough?' replied the wizard trembling in the corner.

Sterling made a sound like an explosion and shook his hands about. 'Blow their leader up with a spell. Zap! Lightning, classic magick. It's been a good while since you've done one like that.'

'Right, yeah, classic…'

As the moon rose, so did the spirits of the party. The mountains shrank behind them as they rolled through the night. Ahead of them a twinkling settlement lay among fields, a salvation against the storm and those bloody gnomes.

Wathgill was, on the surface, a wholly unremarkable village lying between the foothills of the Grippen and Krovanian mountains, populated by folk who were both friendly and rather dim. It was surprising then, that the alderman of Wathgill was a chap going by the ominous name of 'Slicer Tom'. Tom 'Slicer' Pedallo was in fact the first person in the town to invent sliced bread, and this achievement alone had guaranteed lifelong loyalty from his constituents, who were previously burdened with having to cut their own bread. No-one had yet realised that the alderman's moniker alone had been inadvertently responsible for deterring several raids on the village over the last decade.

Steem carefully steered his caravan through the streets and

into the courtyard of a nearby tavern. He stopped, not because he had arrived, but because the back left wheel collapsed. His moustache twitched.

Kevin, who had been leaning against the back door of the caravan, rolled out into the mud. His sudden expulsion from the safety of the caravan triggered residual anxiety from their madcap dash from the domain of the feral gnomes.

'Get away! Get away!' he yelped as he surveyed the courtyard for gnomes. 'I wield the magick of Pingle, you know!'

A hand tugged at his trouser leg, roughly at gnome height. Kevin screeched and spun around.

'Calm down you daft elf,' said Sterling. 'There aren't any gnomes here, just the odd yokel-'

'Yokel? Yokel! The Cheesebearer? Where?!' Kevin looked around furtively, wand gripped tight in his hand.

'Simple folk, Kevin! Country people. Smell of manure, go "ee bah gum", you know.'

Kevin relaxed. 'Be more careful next time, I almost let off a fireball on instinct.'

Rhev couldn't help not chuckling. 'What's a Cheesebearer?' he asked as he hopped out of the caravan.

'You don't know?' Kevin replied with a derisive snort.

'Dairy-based fiend,' Sterling explained. 'Old wives tale, supposed to appear in cheese that has a particular configuration of holes.'

'What sort of configuration?'

'Well, like a face.'

Rhev nodded, satisfied. Mercy came out next, carrying the cargo. The glyphs on the box were moving noticeably faster. Rhev felt his curiosity pique again. He was desperate to know what was inside.

As they entered the inn they were bathed in a warm hearthlight and the intrigued gazes of the locals. A few nodded in acknowledgement. A few chewed on pieces of straw. One even said 'ee bah gum'.

Once everyone was settled into their accommodation and their cargo locked away in Steem's room, a team meeting was called.

'I'm afraid we might be here for a few days,' Steem announced. 'I've asked around for the blacksmith and carpenter to get a new wheel made for the old girl, but it's gonna take a while. Apparently their new blacksmith currently only knows how to make horseshoes, and the carpenter has to help his cousin in an emergency up on the top field. Something to do with angry parsnips... poultry... potatoes?'

'Probably potatoes', Rhev chimed in.

'Probably', agreed Steem, and the two shared the same grim stare as they pondered the maliciousness of the infamous strain of tubers.

'Drink?'

'I like the way you think.'

The rest of the night was spent in much needed relaxation and revelry. Ale gave way to mead, which gave way to a strong barley wine, which eventually gave way to something resembling lantern oil. Rhev was in his element. Here he was, enjoying an all too familiar pastime in an all too unfamiliar place. His thoughts drifted off to half remembered bedtime stories of adventurers and their exploits, the stories that always began and ended in a tavern like this one. His drunken synapses conflated the stories with his own recent experiences. *Am I an adventurer,* thought the drunk dwarf. *No, just a hired sword, nothing wrong with that, remember?* thought the sober dwarf. *But, then again,* retorted the drunkard, *can't they be one and the same?*

It depends on why you're doing it.

'Here you go lad, almost forgot in all the hullabaloo.'

Steem set three ducats spinning on the table in front of Rhev. The dwarf's eyes grew wide as the gold coins settled into a small pile in front of him. It was more money than he'd ever acquired in one go. Legally, that is.

'Don't worry too much about that gnome business, eh? Mercy said you proved your mettle back there. A broken wheel is a small price to pay to get the measure of a man.' A cheeky glint caught in his eye and he spread his hands from the floor to Rhev's head. 'About four foot two, I reckon. Hah!' He punctuated the joke with a firm slap on the dwarf's stocky shoulder.

One last round and the dwarf was off to bed. On his way he passed Sterling at the bar, perched on a stool far too tall for him. Rhev caught him beaming at a pretty girl further down the bar. The devilish smile was returned, and Sterling motioned with his head for her to come over. The woman blushed and began winding her way through the other patrons, but stopped short. Her eyes glanced over the halfling's legs, dangling in the air like a child on their father's shoulders. The blush covered the rest of her face as she bowed her head and diverted her course.

'Not worth it, mate,' slurred Rhev. 'Doesn't look like she'd get off her high horse for anyone.' He didn't stick around to catch Sterling's pained expression, but as he settled into his bunk, he realised for the second time that he'd said the worst thing possible.

Rhev awoke the next morning with a strange man in his bed. Suffice to say that he was not expecting this situation, and reacted in the only way he could.

'Bah!' he said.

'A reasonable reaction,' replied the man. 'My apologies, I got tired of standing up. It seems I timed my projection rather poorly, you were still asleep, you see.'

The man got up from the bed and began stretching. His

84

body made some noises that couldn't have been healthy. As Rhev's sleep encrusted vision cleared, he started to get a better idea of what this intruder looked like. The man appeared to be a walking beard. Purple follicles reached from just below his nose all the way down to his knees. For a horrible moment it looked like this was the only thing covering up the man's nether regions, but as he did another bone-popping lunge Rhev could see that he wore very short purple trousers. *Hot pants of mastery*, Rhev remembered. As if to verify his suspicions, the man bent over backwards to reveal a purple eye tattooed on the top of his bald pate.

'What do you want, wizard?' Rhev said calmly, while eyeing up his sword propped against the opposite wall. 'You're not here to rob or kill me, or you would have already done it.'

'Very astute, Mister Culluggan! As wily as the legends portray.'

'Legends?'

'Indeed, indeed. Ah, but I have yet to introduce myself. How rude. My name is Jengelwold Kaloop, master of the magick of Ohm, thirty-sixth mightiest of the gods... no, hang on, the rankings changed last month... thirty-fourth. Ah, it's all academic anyway. What is far more important is why I am here!'

There was an awkward pause between the near naked wizard now squatting in the middle of the room and the dwarf still tucked up in bed.

'Why are you here then?'

'I'm so glad you asked,' replied Jengelwold, clapping his hands together. 'I am writing a book about famous heroes and villains throughout history. Now, I've almost finished your chapter, but it was really missing a certain personal flair. I wouldn't usually do this mind you, it's *very* power intensive navigating the astral pathways as a mortal, especially when chronomancy is thrown into the mix. But, I really do need something special to make this one stand out. The adventure book market is very competitive, you know. First-hand accounts are always a selling point.'

'Heroes… and villains? Famous?' Rhev was having a hard time understanding what the man was saying, not least because he hadn't stopped doing stretches. This was all too much to take in before breakfast.

'Yes, exactly. Now, would you mind telling me how you actually *felt* after the affair with the giant moles?'

'Um.'

'No, no, sorry, completely understandable, bit of a sore spot. How about the time with the potato golem of Zinch? High points, low points?'

'I'm sorry, but what on earth are you on about?'

The wizard paused in the middle of balancing on one foot, arms set in a 'T' pose.

'You are Rhev Culluggan, yes?'

'I am. Rhev Culluggan from Velheim, that's me.'

'Good, good.' The wizard seemed placated, until he peered closer at Rhev's face. 'Where's your tattoo?'

'I haven't got any tattoos,' Rhev replied, shifting about under his sheet. 'Unless you're talking about the little one on my ars-'

'On your face. You haven't got the tattoo on your face...' The wizard lowered his leg and put a hand to his face. '...Yet. You haven't got it, *yet*. Oh my, not again. Too early, Kaloop, too early!'

Something clicked as Rhev became fully awake. 'Am I a… am I *going* to be a hero?'

Jengelwold Kaloop was now sitting cross-legged on the middle of the bedroom floor. He closed his eyes, and the tattoo on top of his head began to glow.

'Keep this to yourself, please. I could get into a lot of

trouble. Just forget you ever saw me, thanks!' His final words morphed into a shlooping sucking sound, and he was gone.

Rhev still hadn't managed to get out of bed. He sat up, leaning against the pillows, and tried to remember what he'd been drinking the night before. Whatever it was, he made a vow never to drink it again.

Famous heroes. He certainly wasn't either of those things, as far as he was aware. *And villains.* He considered that one more closely, but he concluded that petty theft could hardly be called villainy. *Yet.* So, maybe…

He slumped onto the wooden bench next to Steem.

'Here he is. Bacon is almost cold, but the hard-boiled eggs are good. Eat up lad.'

Rhev began clumsily peeling an egg. Kevin and Sterling sat leant up against each other, both worse for wear. Mercy looked surprisingly unaffected by the previous night's revelry, although Rhev was certain she had drunk him under the table.

'So our destination,' he began, affecting a casual air, 'would it happen to take us through a place called Zinch?'

'Never heard of it,' replied Steem through a mouthful of gristle.

'Oh, right. That's good.'

'What's in Zinch?' Mercy raised a dark red eyebrow.

'Potato gol… nothing, nothing's in Zinch. Just heard it had nice scenery, is all.'

'You didn't strike me as a "stop and smell the roses" sort of person,' Mercy said, her brow furrowing now.

'Just saying what I've heard, that's all.' Rhev ended the conversation by thrusting the egg into his mouth whole.

'Speaking of smelling the roses,' said Steem as he picked the gristle from his teeth, 'that's not what we're in the business of. Come on you lot, time to get a move on.'

He picked up his top hat, gave it a whack, and got up.

Mercy made him pause.

'I think you've forgotten that we've only got three wheels on our wagon, Steem.'

As his buttocks fell back down onto the hard wooden bench, the door of the inn swung open and the bloodied face of a manic young man came into view.

'The top field! He's dead! Reginald! By Ava, it's the plungdugglers! And this time they've got goats!' With that final confusing revelation, the young man collapsed.

'Reginald was the name of the carpenter, wasn't it?' said Rhev through a mouthful of egg.

The way Steem's moustache hairs bristled gave him his answer.

***

Reginald was not, in fact, dead. He did, however, think death might be preferable to his current state. A nasty bump was beginning to form on his brow where the goat had jumped up and butted him. He was trying to remember precisely why the goat had felt the need to do this. Normally they were perfectly content doing absolutely nothing besides eating things they shouldn't be eating. Reginald thought hard, resulting in an intense pain in his head: nothing too abnormal there then. Ah yes, something had been on the goat. Something with knobbly legs and arms wielding a stick above its grotesque bald head, its bat-like ears and nose a striking pink against the soiled brown of its face. And it had been grinning a big, wide, toothy grin. Reg cried out in dismay. A plungduggler! He turned to look in the direction of the village, down the long slopes of the fields. In the distance he saw them mounting some sort of amateur cavalry charge.

Plungdugglers are mysterious creatures. They always arrived quite literally out of nowhere. No-one had ever found a plungduggler village, or a nest, or a mound full of holes where they might have crawled from. They would simply

88

appear at the most inopportune of moments, wreak havoc, and then just like that, they would vanish again. However, the most perplexing thing about these creatures was that, despite their reputation as 'pillagers', they never actually took anything back with them. In reality, the plungdugglers were little more than pranksters, not predators.

At the bottom of the fields on the outskirts of the village stood Steem's team, and beside them the portly figure of 'Slicer' Tom.

'So what you're saying is that they'll eat all the food?' asked Steem.

'Aye, and they'll drink all the ale as well', replied Tom.

'*All* the ale?!' cried Rhev, then a mumbled 'impressive.'

'Aye, and they'll bugger everything up. Smash things, hide things. They don't usually hurt anyone, but there's always a fair share of accidents in the panic. Someone fell down the well last year. And the year before. We should really cover up the well…'

Mercy chimed in. 'What do you normally do when they turn up? Gather the militia?'

'What's a militia?'

Mercy's eyes nearly rolled into the back of her head. Slicer Tom had run on a single-issue platform during the alderman elections, and military policy was not it.

'No, normally we just all hide in hole somewhere. Got lots of holes round here. Quite a lot of people fall in them though when we're not being raided. We should probably cover up the holes…'

'It sounds like this raid, if you can call it that, is going to hinder us for a time longer than would be agreeable, if they stop us repairing the caravan. Kevin, Sterling, come with me to the blacksmiths. We've got to make sure that forge stays intact. Mercy, you protect the caravan. I don't want any more wheels falling off. Rhev, go to my room in the tavern and sit on that bloody box. Last thing we want is these pingledingles or whatever they're called running off with it. This better not carry on past lunch.' With that Steem set off towards the forge, Kevin and Sterling following at a casual pace. Mercy and Rhev headed off in the direction of the inn. Slicer Tom went off to find a hole.

'I've never been in a raid before,' said Rhev, doing his best to hide his nerves. He'd been in his fair share of fights in a tavern setting, but a full scale assault on a village defended by nothing more than a few strategically placed holes was something else. 'You been in many raids?'

'I've seen my fair share.' Mercy's reply was curt, as if she was reluctant to elaborate. 'But from what I've heard that alderman say, I'd have to agree with Steem. It doesn't sound like this will be much of a raid. More of a nuisance really.' She turned to look Rhev in the eye. 'No heroics necessary, Rhev. That's not the job. This isn't the Battle of the Gorge, or anything like that. Just keep an eye on that box and don't let anything happen to it. Nice and simple.'

'Hey, that's me, nice and simple.' He punctuated the words by lifting up his fists one after the other. 'Can't fail, eh?'

Mercy shrugged with her face, as if she was less than amused, but Rhev caught the flicker of a smirk at the corner of her mouth.

'Get to your post.'

She left Rhev at the door of the tavern, her long red plait bouncing on the back of her mail shirt.

He entered the tavern. It looked completely empty. He assumed that everyone had left for their respective hiding spots, so he hopped behind the bar and pulled himself a pint. After a moment of uncharacteristic consideration, he left a copper piece on the bar top for the innkeeper on his return. He trudged up the stairs, slurping as he went, and went into Steem's room. It smelt of smoke and moustache oil. Rhev noticed that there was an ornate silk sheet laid on the bed in place of the tavern's complimentary bed linen. It wasn't too surprising that Steem had replaced the linen: 'complimentary' was not a word Rhev would have used to describe the itchy sackcloth. What was surprising, however, was the pattern on Steem's sheet. It was covered in beautiful roses in a variety of colours, a significant contrast to the dowdy, monochromatic man himself.

The box sat on the opposite side of the room to the bed, its curious whorls moving more noticeably than usual. Rhev stared at it for a while, captivated by the patterns. He wasn't too sure how long he had been looking at it when he was torn from his trance by sounds from outside.

'Get in the hole!'

'That's my best cheese!'

'Ouch my big toe!'

Wood clattering, metal ringing, the occasional ping and paflooey sounds that could have been anything, all provided a backing to the whoops and giggles of the plungdugglers. The sound of the tavern door caving in was followed by gurgling as all the taps in the bar were opened, and the smacking of lips on meat as the kitchen was raided of all it had to offer. Then all went silent.

The sounds of revelry hadn't disturbed Rhev as much as the silence did. He decided to plant his feet firmly on the box in preparation for the inevitable robbery. They would have a hard time taking it away with a fully-grown dwarf on top of it, and besides, it gave him a much appreciated boost to his height. As a last thought, he drew his sword. *A little intimidation couldn't hurt, could it?*

In the distance he could still hear the little fiends faintly, probably giving Mercy and Steem's team some bother, but in the tavern it was quiet. Then came some chattering. Rhev couldn't pinpoint where it was coming from, but it was definitely close. The chattering faded away again, only to be replaced by a high pitched *eeeee* inside Rhev's head, as if the pressure around him had changed far too quickly. The air felt thick, bristling.

The door to the bedroom burst open. Filling the doorframe stood at least eight plungdugglers, all stood on top of each other, their eyes wide, their huge ears pricked forward. Before Rhev could stand up he was thrown backwards with a colossal force. The lid of the box that he had just moments before been standing on had flung open, catapulting him into the wall. Slumped on the floor, his sword lying out of reach, Rhev opened his eyes. At least, he tried to.

The light filling the room was blinding. Out of the box rose a myriad of dancing colours in a spectrum that defied the dwarf's senses. Ethereal shapes tumbled around the room, over themselves and through themselves, a twisted subversion of geometry that didn't have a right to exist. The plungdugglers were gathered around the room, chittering to each other, mesmerised. One of them leapt through the cacophony towards Rhev. He raised his arms up to protect himself, but there was no need. The little creature seemed to float momentarily in the air, surrounded by the chaos that had unfurled from the box. In fractions of seconds it lost all depth to its dimension, and then seemed to gain too much. At once it was magnified as if under a dome of glass, its face massive and ghastly, whilst in the recesses of its huge eyes reflected another image of itself, floating around its blackened iris. And then it folded in on itself, and it was gone. Others followed and disappeared in much the same manner. The last to go rode one of the village goats into the void, a large sack slung over its behind, and all together they left the world. The unimaginable storm, silent yet loud, continued to rage.

***

Rhev was sat at the bar guzzling hard liquor straight from

the bottle when everyone returned to the tavern.

'Rhev, what are you doing? You're supposed to be looking after the cargo' asked Mercy with reproach.

'Wash does it look like? Drunking,' Rhev replied as he wiped his lips.

'You better bloody pay for that,' said Steem as he entered the room behind Mercy. 'I don't want us getting a reputation for thieving.'

Rhev made an exaggerated gesture to the small pile of coins he had laid on the bartop. 'I'm a good boy now.'

'Seems like he has the right idea to me. Is it not tradition for the victorious to drink to vanquished?' Sterling jogged over to Rhev, climbed up a stool, and prised the bottle from his hands. There was a sharp *pop* as the neck of the bottle was loosed from Rhev's mouth, and then a prolonged *glug glug* as Sterling took a long draught.

Kevin came over and snatched the bottle away. Putting a foot on a nearby chair, he untucked a leg of his voluminous silk trousers from his boot and began pouring the liquor over a chaffed knee.

'What are *you* doing?!' Rhev and Sterling shouted in unison.

'Cleaning out this near-fatal wound, thank you very much. Who knows what kind of other-worldly diseases those plungdugglers carry?' said Kevin.

'Do you have to use the rum?' moaned Sterling.

'Considering it's already been bought and paid for, yes. Besides, another second and I could go catatonic from exotic flu. Trust me on this, I'm a wizard."

Sterling and Rhev both grumbled and mourned their rum. 'I'm pretty sure he got that scratch from when he fell over at the forge. He tripped over his shoe laces when he tried to run away,' Sterling confided. Kevin overheard.

'I wasn't *running*, I was maneuvering to a flanking

position, like Steem asked me to.'

'It looked like running to me,' interjected Steem as he took a seat next to Rhev. 'Two strikes now Kevin, lad. One more and I'm sending you back to Yedforth. Now what's with all this drinking, young Rhev? You know my rule, no spirits before noon.'

'You would be drunking too if you'd sheen what I'd sheen,' Rhev slurred.

'Oh, and what did you see? I did notice those prongledongle things could be a little... promiscuous.'

'Nope, washn't even that. I've sheen my share of arshes, any road. Nah, it wash that bloody boxsh! One minute it was closhed, the next-' Rhev clapped loudly and started waving his hands around erratically, punctuating his movements with spittle-flecked *whoosh* sounds.

'It exploded?' asked Mercy.

'If it exploded while in your care I'm going to have to take it out of your paycheck,' said Steem.

'It didn't exshplode! The *boxsh* didn't exshplode. It *opened*, and the shpace *around* the boxsh exshploded. And all the bitsh flew around and thoshe plongledongle blokesh jumped *in between* the bitsh! And then they dishappeared. POOF!' Rhev said that last part a little too loudly and a couple of people jumped, including Kevin and the recently arrived Slicer Tom.

'I saw one of them take a goat in here earlier. Did anyone see where it went? We don't want it falling into any of the holes,' huffed Slicer Tom. He had spent the raid running in circles around the well as all the nearby holes were already full of people, and those people had figured that if anyone was going to have to sacrifice themselves it should be their elected representative.

'It went into the boxsh,' replied Rhev. 'The plingplong fella rode it through the shiny shpace bitsh and POOF!' The abrupt noise made Kevin and Tom jump again.

'Oh, right... but the plungdugglers never take anything with them when they go back. I'm fairly certain they can't actually. A man in hotpants and a pointy hat told me they couldn't, and as someone who can't really pull off that look personally, I didn't think it right to argue," said Tom. 'Do you think the goat is... in the box?'

Rhev shrugged.

'Go on then, open it up,' said Steem from the back of the group in the doorway.

'Shorry Shteem, I don't know how to open it,' replied Rhev, 'and I don't wanna get shucked in.'

'Not being funny Rhev, but you're a little broad. I don't think you'd fit in that box anyway,' he replied. The intonation on the word 'broad' highlighted the beer belly Rhev had been cultivating over the last few years.

'An' I din't think that eight ploggadoggs, a goat, 'n shome cheeshe would fit in there either, but here we are.'

'Look, I'd be really grateful if someone could just get the goat out,' pleaded Slicer Tom. 'It was one of the communal ones you see, and everyone will be very upset if it goes missing.'

'Right, go on Kevin. I don't understand what's going on so I'm going to chalk it up to magick, and that's your area.' Steem shoved Kevin into the room. The scrawny elf stumbled and turned to look at the group.

'But I've already tried opening it. It can't be done,' said Kevin with a pout.

'No harm trying again lad. Get the man his goat back.'

Steem nodded slowly and made an encouraging motion for Kevin to approach the box. Kevin gulped and crept cautiously towards it. He took out his wand and held in front of him like someone about to pick up a poo with a stick. He muttered some words in the name of Pingle, traced some shapes in the air with his free hand, and prodded the box with

95

the wand. The shifting blue whorls on the surface of the box rippled away from where the point of the wand made contact, but after that, nothing.

Then the lid flew open, Kevin flew back, and a lot of madness flew up. The indescribable shapes and distortions that Rhev had seen earlier once again ripped the air around the box into tatters. Everyone gasped. In reply, a *shlooping* noise came from the direction of the box. Kevin's trouser leg, still untucked from earlier, has been caught in the inexorable gravity of the maelstrom in front them. Barely conscious, Kevin had still had the wherewithal to grab the leg of Steem's bed.

Sterling was the first to react, jumping to his friend's aid. He grabbed Kevin's free hand and began to tug.

'Harder!' screamed Kevin, 'don't let go!'

'I'm trying! You've been eating too much!' screamed back Sterling.

'How dare you!' screeched Kevin, 'You've just got tiny muscles!'

'How dare *you*!' screeched back Sterling, both their voices cracking.

The window crashed into the room under the weight of a steaming dwarf. He landed on his arse with an I and kicked out his right leg. Foot made contact with lid, and the box closed itself with a sharp snap.

Kevin pulled his trouser leg away. It had been perfectly severed where the lid had closed, the edge of the fabric slightly hard as if it had been cauterised. Rhev got to his feet.

'Itsh a good thing I'm dronk, int it? Don't think I would 'av done that otherwishe.'

'How did you get over there?' asked Steem.

'Put it thish way: there'sh more than one broken window.'

Steem grumbled under his breath, and then moved to go downstairs.

'So where did the goat go?' stammered Slicer Tom.

'I'm sorry alderman, but my problems are now a heck of a lot bigger than your missing goat,' Steem replied as he trudged down the steps. When he got to the bottom he found that Mercy was already there, tucked away in a corner with another bottle of pilfered rum. He noticed that the pile of cash on the bartop had grown larger. *Where was that innkeeper? At this rate the entire place was going to run on an honesty box.*

He sat down next to the hardened warrior, and she offered him some rum. He graciously accepted.

'I think I need to add to the "no dragons" sign on the caravan. "No dragons or boxes of undefined magickal hoo-ha".' Steem finished the sentence with a grunt that could have been interpreted as a laugh.

'We need to get rid of it,' she said bluntly.

'My my, Mercy Nazaar, veteran of the eastern front, Heptamil's finest, scared of a little box.'

'I'm serious, Steem. This one isn't worth it.'

Before Steem could reply, the rest of the group came fumbling down the stairs.

'Are we going to bury this thing and forget about it or what?' Sterling drummed out on the table. Kevin stood beside him, looking sadly at his damaged trouser cuff.

'It ate my favourite trousers,' the elf mumbled. He looked at Steem sternly. 'It has to go!'

Rhev punctuated the demand with a heinous burp.

'Look who's giving the orders!' said Steem. 'I didn't realise the enterprise was called "Kevin of Yedforth's Cowardly Couriers". Bah!'

Kevin shrank a little and went back to examining his wounded trousers.

"Be as that may, I am inclined to admit that this delivery may be beyond Steem Vennts & Co. I don't want to chance that thing going off in the caravan.'

'What are we going to do about the down payment we received?' said Mercy.

'The way I see it, the bloke who handed that thing over didn't mention it was a volatile item, the contract didn't mention it was a volatile item, but it is *most certainly* a volatile item. Under courier law that's a breach of contract, and the bloke's money is forfeit. I'd say we're going by the book here, if anything. I'll send word back to Velheim, let the authorities sort it out. In the meantime, we can't just leave it up in that room for any Dom, Nick, or Larry to stumble across. We need to dispose of it. Any ideas?'

A burp. "There'sh lotsh of holesh ready-made around here. Jusht pop it in-" Rhev managed before passing out on the floor.

***

Thonk. The box hit the bottom of the hole. Steem brushed his hands together, despite the fact it had been Mercy who had done the lifting. The hole was well placed on the outskirts of Wathgill. It had been dug by a lumberjack long ago, and was currently not in regular use as a plungduggler shelter. The lumberjack had left several years earlier after realising that living in a place under frequent attack from other-dimensional gremlins was not going to be good for property prices in the long term. If only he had stayed around for the advent of sliced bread: it had really put Wathgill on the map.

'Everyone get shovelling,' Steem ordered. There was a collective groan, mostly from Rhev, succeeded by the sound of shovels crunching into dirt. This sound continued, groans included, for another hour as the hole was filled in. When the rhythm of the shovels stopped, Steem took his hat off his face and got up from his dozing position.

'Good work. A problem buried is a problem... erm... that isn't ours anymore. Let's head down to Dankvyr and pick up a normal contract delivering artwork or geese or something.'

Everyone shrugged apathetically, and began the long walk back to Wathgill through the woods. As they reached the treeline they were met with a chocolate box view of the village, its rolling hills and jaunty windmills placed just-so around the quaint settlement. Only the odd hastily dug hole and incomprehensible plungduggler graffiti sullied the image. The group paused to take in the scene. *I suppose that was sort of an adventure,* thought Rhev, *although it was a lot shorter and more anti-climatic than the stories would suggest.*

After this moment of reflection, Rhev took a step forward. As he moved, he experienced the feelings of someone who is very sure that they have just dropped their keys down a drain, with all that entails: the sense of loss, the frustration, the disappointment, the anger, the fogging of the mind that causes rational thoughts go missing. All of this came to him in the time it took to take a single step. And then it came again, and again, like an endless tide with no time between waves and no time to react and no time to come to your senses. In half a second Rhev had felt the sense of losing his keys down a drain a million times, one after another, one on top of each other, intensifying exponentially, until eventually his foot hit the ground and his face was wet with tears.

He stumbled forward and then sank to the ground, drowning in loss, unable to move on. Through the fog of anti-emotion he became aware of the others, also weeping, moaning, and on the whole not having a good time. Their sorrow was inappropriately interrupted by a noise that, in all honesty, sounded like the wind farting.

'Woah, now this is a vibe that I do not like,' said a voice that sounded like it came from a punchable face. 'Can we all please just mellow out for a moment? I need to talk to y'all.' The vocal fry and the pronunciation of vowels in a way that they really didn't deserve was enough to stir the group from their malaise.

'Who's... this... bastard?!' screamed Steem hysterically.

'Look, I don't want to be here, ya know. There's some killer dune surf happening right now in the Sands of Time, and that stuff quite literally happens in no-one's lifetime.'

'Leave me alone!' shouted Kevin as he rolled into the foetal position.

'If you stop harshing for, like, a second, I can leave you alone sooner!'

'Buh,' Rhev wailed mournfully.

'Ugh, I shouldn't be doing this.' The owner of the voice, a tall man with long blonde hair and a seashell earring, began to pick up invisible bundles from the ground and throw them in the direction of the crew. 'Ew, this one won't stop squirming,' he said as he threw a fifth invisible bundle at Kevin. Whatever it was the man had done, it had worked. Rhev stopped crying uncontrollably, Kevin unfurled himself, and Steem stopped screaming into his hat.

'What the bloody hell is going on here? You better not have cursed us,' Steem said, trying to regain control of the situation. He smoothed his moustache, embarrassed at how brush-like it had become.

'You were breaking the contract, man,' drawled the unidentified person..

'The contract?' asked Steem.

'The... yeah, the contract. Come on dude, what did you think was happening?'

'I thought I had dropped my keys," Steem mumbled.

There were mumbles of agreement.

'Right. Exactly. That's what it feels like when you drop your *soul*.'

Rhev began examining the bottom of his boot. Mercy nudged him and shook her head.

'You're referring to the essence of what makes you, *you*?' she asked.

'I'm not going to get into the philosophy of it, babe.' Mercy's hand gripped the pommel of her sword. 'But yeah, you get it. So anyway, you guys were breaking the terms of your arcane contract, so you dropped your souls. Not cool, I get it. But it says here,' the man fished around in the long white shorts he was wearing without a care for how lecherous it looked, and retrieved a scroll, 'that you made an agreement to deliver, uh, "one normal box" to "the cottage at the end of the lane in Little Mosshill", brackets, "there's only one lane so it shouldn't be too hard", for a Mister Kowloon, "payment five hundred ducats in advance, one thousand on receipt". Wow, really guys? Just one normal box? You were going to sacrifice your souls for the sake of not delivering Mister Kowloon his normal box? What were you thinking?'

'It's not normal,' said Rhev, 'it's got something seriously wrong in there.'

'Woah, woah, *woah*,' interrupted the underdressed man. 'Don't tell me what's in there, for starters. Also, isn't it part of your job to, like, not look in people's private deliveries? And *also*, man, don't judge! We don't know what Mister Kowloon is into. Now, you guys signed this contract,' he pointed at their signatures, 'and Mister Kowloon signed this contract,' he pointed to a sigil-like signature that hadn't been on Steem's copy, 'which means that by the arcane power invested in it by,' he looked at the small print for a moment, 'this dude "Boswell", that you are bound to complete this delivery within thirty days. That's one month, people! Failure to do so, or *intent to fail*, which is very relevant right now obviously, will result in permanent souldrop. This here now? *This* is a freebie. Y'all should be thanking me for picking up your souls and reminding you to do your jobs.'

'Hey boss, I don't remember signing the part about dropping my soul,' said Sterling in an accusatory tone.

'Well you did, and that's on you!' grumbled Steem. 'I

didn't realise I had to read for my employees.'

'That is one of your few jobs, Steem. Check the contracts,' said Mercy, her voice dripping barbs.

'When a bloke walks up to you with a contract worth five hundred ducats up front to deliver a single box, you don't stop to read the fine print. Besides, we were all off our heads on goblin grass at the time. Except for Rhev…'

'I just really wanted a job,' he mumbled.

'This is bad, Steem. Arcane contracts are serious business. They're unbreakable, sealed by the powers of the gods themselves.' Kevin was shaking in his boots.

'Yup, true that,' the messenger interrupted. 'I'd love to stick around all day and watch y'all point fingers and flap your gums like a bunch of ghouls, but I should be catching sweet, sweet crystal on the infinite sands right now. So, you get it? You got it. I'm gonna peace out.' He shoved the scroll back into his shorts. 'Ahem. I have been Chardo, godly representative of the *Fiat* cohort of Ava, on behalf of Mercatrus, once-god of contracts. If you have any feedback, please pass it on through the usual astral pathways. See you on the other side, *boneheads*.'

There was a sound like wind farting in reverse, and Chardo was gone. In the silence that followed, gears turned. Only Rhev was able to find something positive in their situation. *This has officially moved up from 'job' to 'adventure'*, he thought. *But are you going to be a rich adventurer or a dead adventurer?* There was the cynic again, the dwarf whose eyes had sparkled when the coins had plinked onto the table last night. The little voice fought back. *Maybe there's a third sort of adventurer?*

'Stupid, stupid, stupid,' said Mercy as she ground her teeth violently.. Rhev tentatively put a hand on her shoulder.

'We all do mad things when we're off our heads. I once bet Hoskin that I could climb from the bottom to the top of the

102

Underport before he could get to the top using the lift. I chundered halfway up, and fell asleep on one of the ladders before I could even see the surface. He waited up there until morning, bless him.'

'And did this Hoskin demand you forfeit your soul?' asked Mercy through gritted teeth.

'Well, no. He's just a blacksmith.'

Mercy growled and quickened her pace.

'I hope you lot didn't pack the dirt too well. Back to the hole,' Steem said quietly. The group marched silently back to the resting place of the box. It took a couple of hours to exhume it.

'Chuck it up, Rhev,' said Sterling, hands outstretched over the top of the hole.

'There will be no chucking!' Steem barked. 'Mercy, get your rope out. We'll take it up gentle like. I don't want to think what will happen if we deliver damaged goods.'

Another few minutes of careful lashing and securing, and the box was solemnly lifted up out of the hole.

The sun was beginning to set on the picturesque fields of Wathgill, its rays slowly rotated by the canvas sails of the windmills. After the plungduggler attack the inhabitants of the village had spent the afternoon taking inventory and counting out the few pairs of underwear that didn't have holes cut in them. Now that evening was upon them they sat on their porches enjoying the sunset, and for some, the extra breeze.

Steem and Sterling went off to see if the carpenter and blacksmith had survived, and to tell them to get a move on. The other three members of the crew sat in the empty tavern.

'What happens now?' asked Rhev. The question hung in the air, unwelcome.

'Simple. Nice and simple. You're going to do your job. I will do my job. Kevin will do his job, whatever that is,' replied

Mercy, still smarting from their encounter with Chardo. She felt like she had allowed herself to be tricked into fighting a battle she couldn't win. What could dependable Warum do against such eldritch legalities?

'What was that supposed to mean, "whatever that is?"' retorted Kevin. 'I am one of the only wielders of the magick of Pingle *in the world*. I am the only one in this team who can cast any sort of magick, understand magick, and protect us from magick. As far as I can tell, guards are ten a penny.' He nodded in the direction of Rhev.

'Hang on!' Mercy and Rhev said in unison. Mercy continued: 'You did a fine job of identifying the decidedly *magickal* contract that we signed. In fact, I don't think I've ever seen a single spell that can be reliably attributed to you, Kevin.'

Rhev pushed back his stool and jumped off. He had quite enough of this haughty elf.

'I'd like to see you go up against *this* guard, matey!' He pulled up his sleeves and brandished his fists. 'I think I fancy my chances.'

'For Pingle's sake Mercy, there have been plenty of times my magick has saved us on the road, like back in... back in...' Kevin faltered, then pointed at Rhev. 'You're honestly saying that I'm worth less that this moronic, brutish drunkard?'

Rhev's face fell. He lowered his fists. It was true that he had been called similar before. He was reckless and impulsive, and often resorted to physical solutions by reflex, so it wasn't surprising that people would call him names like that. It wasn't even that he was surprised that the elf had been the one to say it. What was surprising to him was that he really cared this time. Usually he would just smack someone who insulted him, but now he just wished Kevin would take it back. He wanted to be part of the team. He had started to really warm to the idea. Up until that moment, he thought he had been doing alright.

Rhev stood there quietly, looking into the middle distance. Both Mercy and Kevin were shocked by how the jibe had perceptibly saddened the dwarf. They looked at each other, then back at Rhev, trying to work out how to move the situation away from this knife edge.

'Kevin didn't mean that, did you Kevin?' said Mercy, carefully.

'No. No, of course not! Just, you know, stressed from today's activities. Hah. No, no, definitely didn't mean it.' Kevin looked genuinely abashed, although whether it was out of regret or fear of Mercy, it wasn't clear. 'Sorry, Rhev,' he said under the warrior's withering gaze. She sighed.

'We've got no choice but to see this through together. We *all* have our parts to play.' Mercy made eye contact with Rhev.

'Why do you lot look like all the rum has gone?' asked Sterling as he entered the inn. Without waiting for an answer, he continued, 'Steem's struck a deal with the blacksmith's neighbour for a wheel off his cart. It was either that or wait here for a few days while the blacksmith and the carpenter worked out how to make one from scratch, and it looks like we don't have a few days.' He hauled a small coin purse, or a middling one by Sterling's standards, onto the bar top. 'Do any of you know where the innkeeper is?'

***

Duncan, the owner and proprietor of The Steaming Loaf in Wathgill, didn't know where he was either. To be more accurate, he knew he was in a large hessian sack, but as to the sack's relative location, he did not know. He took comfort in the fact that he at least knew why and how he had got in the sack.

It had become common for Duncan to react to the plungduggler raids by stepping into a large hessian sack that he had previously used for turnips. This wasn't in any attempt

105

to hide from them, far from it. When he had first moved to Wathgill after inheriting the tavern from his uncle, he had been unaware of the frequent attacks that plagued the town. When, a couple of weeks after moving in, he was caught off guard by a sizeable squad of small, hairy, bat-like people, he had done his best to put up a fight. Ultimately he was brought low by some strategic kidney tickling and playful kicks to the genitals, and put in a sack. The plungdugglers then used his writhing, sack-covered form as a sort of rugby ball in a village-wide game of underhanded sporting. The game proved so popular among the plungdugglers that at some point in every raid they all banded together to capture Duncan, put him in a sack, and resume their eternal and incomprehensible match.

After the fourth or fifth time Duncan was dragged from the attic or ousted from a hole, he decided that he could at least skip to the *being in a sack* part himself, therefore making the process slightly less painful and regaining a certain measure of agency in his own life. After all, the pummelling of little hands he received as he was carried around town was, in a way, quite therapeutic.

This time, however, he had been in the sack for quite a while. Usually he would naturally end his tenure in the sack after he was dropped to the floor when the plungdugglers popped out of existence. Now, though, he had started to worry. He was still in their tiny mitts, and by his reckoning, had been for at least a few hours.

Eventually he sensed he had come to a halt. Then, something that felt very much like the ground hit him in the face. He rolled over until he was resting on his back. There were a lot of squeaking noises all around him, suggesting that the plungdugglers were still there. Even so, he came to the conclusion that as he was on the ground, the game must surely be over, and it was time to come out. He moved his hands to where he could see light and prised the hole open. In the last several times he had done this, he had been met with a variety of interesting views: a rooftop, in a rowboat on a nearby river, and once even in someone else's bedroom. This view, however, really took the biscuit.

All around him was drab grey. Grey rocks, grey sky, grey moss even. Varying shades but consistently depressing, like a vast stone cave with no ceiling and no end. The scene was illuminated by a strange greyish light. The source of the light baffled Duncan. It seemed to be coming from far above, emanating in thin strips, like stars that had been stretched out into noodles. There did not appear to be any moons or suns, only the elongated stars punctuating the sky like tears in a tent canvas.

Duncan came to realise that about a hundred pairs of saucer-sized eyes were staring up at him. He was completely surrounded by plungdugglers, more than he had ever seen. They chittered quietly to each other. A couple moved to the front of the crowd and began prodding his knees. Duncan moved back reflexively, but they didn't seem to be prodding him with cruel intent. Their prods were curious, bordering on reverential.

He felt a leathery hand grasp his finger, and looked down to see that a plungduggler was trying to lead him somewhere. The crowd parted to create a path. Not really knowing what else to do, Duncan followed the plungduggler through the crowd, hunching slightly as the little creature pulled him forward by the hand. He noticed that there was something that set this one apart from the rest; he was wearing clothes. Not anything that would be available to purchase at a respectable tailor's shop, but they were technically clothes. They appeared to have been woven together from thick strands of the native monochromatic grass, creating a black and white striped shirt that covered the plungdugglers chest and what were presumably its private parts.

Duncan was led up quite a steep hill. As he climbed he became aware that the crowd was now following him in a solemn procession. A chill went down his spine as thoughts of ritual sacrifice flashed through his mind. *What's at the top of this hill? A big drop? Is there a nice cushioned surface at the bottom of the drop, or is it full of* bones?! Sweat began to bead on his forehead, but the sheer number of plungdugglers behind him made escape impossible.

He needn't have been afraid. Concerned, perhaps. Confused, maybe. At the top of the hill was a monument, an effigy of sorts. The plungduggler in the striped outfit stopped in front of it, and pointed. The thing in front of Duncan was made from a pile of rocks, covered in dried grass and other flora, and sitting atop this strange cairn was what looked like a coconut with eyes. If you squinted, you could be forgiven for thinking you were looking at a man in a sack.

Duncan's jaw dropped. He turned to see the hundred eyes behind him. He could have sworn some of them had tears in them. Turning back to the stripy one, he slowly pointed to himself, and then at the effigy. The stripy plungduggler nodded and smiled, and then made a motion to someone in the crowd. The sack was brought forward. The stripy one gestured for Duncan to get in it. He did so, pulling it up to his head in a reflection of the effigy. The chittering in the crowd increased. The stripy one then bowed to the crowd, and one of their number with unusually long hair moved forward to meet them. They carried some sort of tiny instrument. With great ceremony, the instrument was given to the bowing plungduggler. He received it, stood triumphantly, and raised it to his lips.

One short blast on the whistle, a cheer from the crowd, and the Great Game began anew.

***

The bean bag slid neatly into the central hole on the board. A cheer went up in the little tavern on the quayside.

'Blimey, Hammy, you just beat your high score, didn't you?' Hampton smiled at the eager young lad in front of him, a slice of beef jerky hanging from his mouth in awe.

'Truth be told, I don't keep track,' he admitted with a shrug. 'I just play for the fun of it.'

'You say this is just fun for you?!' a voice bellowed.

The man towered above Hampton, his white eyes glinting like the moon on a calm midnight sea. His dark skin was covered in a dusting of white powder. An ignorant sort would mistake him for a blind man man with an unfortunate skin condition. Hampton was not an ignorant sort though, and he knew this man to be one of the fisherfolk. His white eyes were not blind, far from it. On land his sight was like that of any normal man, but under the waves he could see as far as a shark could smell. From his skin, Hampton could tell that the man had just been at sea. The fisherfolk were unique in their regular consumption of seawater, their bodies able to filter out the salt through the pores of their skin. It was a neat trick that often came in handy when supplies of fresh water on ship were running low.

'Good, clean competition here, at The Blowhole, home of sack toss, amongst friends? Against the best chucker I've seen for a long time? Why yes, I call that fun sir!' Hampton beamed.

'The best... chucker?' asked the tall man, confused.

'Best I've seen. Good arm. Keen eyes. Heck, you'd think we were underwater.' Hampton winked. 'If you practised a bit more for the trivia rounds, you could have me easy, that's for sure.'

The tall man appeared to relax. 'I... am not used to the... trivia rounds.'

'It's traditional in Dankvyr. As I said, home of sack toss.

We play it how the elders played it, trivia rounds and all. Now, say you played a tournament in Velheim? I hear they've replaced their trivia rounds with mud wrestling. I reckon you'd be a shoo in there.'

'It is funny you say this,' the man replied. 'I am in Velheim not long ago. I win the sack toss. A lot.'

'My goodness, I bet you did! How about I get you a pint and you tell me all about it. I'm fascinated by the regional variants of sack toss.'

Hampton did his best to put an arm around the fisherfolk's shoulder and lead him to the bar. His height only allowed him to get an arm around his back and under the armpit, but the fisherfolk seemed to accept the gesture for what it was, and allowed himself to be lead to the bar

Many hours later Hampton and his new friend were sat at a quiet table in the corner of The Blowhole, surrounded by several empty tankards.

'So wait, say again, what brought you to Velheim in the first place, Manu?'

Manu hiccuped and shook his head, as if casting out his inebriation.

'We bring cargo across Bay of Larendor,' he said in a thick accent. 'Heptamil to Velheim, Velheim to Heptamil. It is a good trade. This day we are in Heptamil, the captain is bringing a small box on board. He hides it in the hold, like it is a secret. He says we set sail. This is strange. We always take big cargo. Wood, salt, marble stone. Our hold is very big, but now we sail with it empty. I do not question though. Our captain is a good man. He takes us on many voyages, always safe, good pay.'

The large man shook his head slowly and continued.

'It is a bad voyage, the worst I sail, and I spend my life at sea. First there are storms. Such storms that you would think the gods themselves set them upon us. Then the sea does strange things. Unnatural things. Whirlpools. One after another, everywhere we go we would run into one, two, three. "Whirlpool is a lone beast," I say, "he does not hunt in packs." The crew is scared, the captain is scared. He is a sensible man. He believes in his brass tools. It is not the old way, but I know it is a safe way. But this time we were not safe, and the captain knows this. He knew much that he was not telling.'

'What was he not telling you?' asked Hampton, his eyes wide as if he were a child listening to his grandfather's war stories, despite him being at least twenty years Manu's senior. Manu's deep white eyes bored into him.

'It is the tenth day, the crew gather outside the captain's cabin. We do not want to mutiny. He is a good captain, we know this. But we need to know why we are cursed. I stand at his door and knock. Ten times I knock. He does not come out. We ask Largish Basla to break down the door, but the man on watch cries out to us. "Land!" he shouts, "Land below!" I do not understand. None of us do, until we see it. It is a… gap. A chasm in the sea.'

Manu paused as he tried to find the words to describe it.

'The water parts, down to the bottom of the sea floor. In the seafloor is another gap. A gorge going down and down. An abyss. My people have tales of this place. It means in your tongue, "The Place Where Water Goes To Die". A bad place. Should never be seen.

It is now that the captain comes out. He orders hard to starboard. "I am sorry," he says. Our ship rides on the edge. Hull is in water, hull is in air. It is like this for a long time. At last we are reaching open sea. "I lead you astray," the captain says to us. "Our cargo is cursed." This is the first time the captain is admitting fault. We are silent but for one. Farrah is fresh to the crew. She does not hold faith in the captain. "Cast the cargo overboard" she says. The captain, he says he cannot. He says that if we cast out the cargo, his soul is cast out with

111

it. Farrah says the captain lies. I do not believe it. My eyes are sharp. I see when a man tells the truth. I say, "the captain does not lie to us. We have seen The Place Where Water Goes To Die. Even then, he still wishes to keep the cargo. There must be something worse waiting for him if we cast it out, and I will not kill my captain."

But Farrah and some others go to the hold and bring this cursed box up to the deck. Some of us stand between them and gunwale. They run at us with fire in their bellies. We fight. The box falls, and it opens.'

'What was inside? Jewels? A monster? Magickal orbs?" Hampton asked, totally and utterly hooked by the fisherfolk's tale.

'A place. A doorway to a place that is not here. I see people in this doorway, like... reflections in smashed glass. I swear I see my mother's face, and I know that this is a door to a lost place, because the sea takes her long ago.'

'This place... an afterlife?' Hampton murmured. The fisherfolk shook his head sadly.

'Not an afterlife, not like you are thinking, my friend. These faces I see, they are not souls. I know this in my heart. There are stories in Heptamil. Those who open gates to another place where there are trapped people... and worse. Terrible things that will not be spoken of, that should not exist. My people think this place and the Place Where Water Goes To Die, they are one and the same. The door should not be opened.'

The two sat in a much needed silence. Finally Hampton asked: 'So what happened? Did you throw it overboard?'

Manu shook his head.

'Largish Basla closes the box. He sits on it with all his weight. We are three days from Velheim. We say this is not far, we will take the cargo to Velheim to save our captain's soul. On the second day, I am too curious. I go to the hold and look at this cargo. I know now in my heart it is an evil thing. The door should not be opened. I know this. I worry that I was wrong to defend my captain. That he has turned to evil ways to make his coin. I vow that it is my last voyage with him.

As we are making port, the captain asks me to do one last thing for him. He asks me to go to a dangerous place in the Underport and pick something up for him. I do this for him, out of respect. As long as I stand on that deck, I am crew, and I obey my captain. It is our way.

I find this place. It is full of criminals and shadow people. I pick up this thing that has been left for my captain. It is a big scroll, very strange. I do not have the reading of your tongue, but I can see there are symbols that are not of your letters. A mage's scroll, perhaps? Another bad thing, I am thinking, but I give this scroll to my captain so as to be rid of it.

I do not take my pay. I cannot look my captain in his eye. I go to the taverns, I drink, I think. It is then I see my captain again. He has the box, wrapped in sailcloth. He has the scroll under his arm. He is talking to the barkeeper, barkeeper is pointing to a back room. Captain enters and comes out with a man. "Is this the man who seeks this evil thing?" I wonder. I must know. I follow them to a caravan, painted bright red. It is written on the side "Steem Vennts & Co"; a courier's caravan. "This box is not for this man", I am thinking. "Just another to bring this evil closer to its purpose." My captain shakes hands with this man. Then he has him sign this magick scroll. An evil agreement, surely. The courier locks the box in this wagon.'

'Did you do something? Did you take the box, destroy it?'

'You are thinking I should be, yes? I am sorry my friend. I do not do this thing. The captain sees me in the shadows. My belly is full of ale, my head is not straight. I am frightened of this doorway to The Place Where Water Goes To Die. I am running. I am distracting myself for days with drink and the sack toss. I am waiting for a ship to take me from Velheim. I am coming here.'

'I don't blame you for leaving, Manu. That sort of eldritch nonsense is far beyond people like us. Leave it to the wizards, I reckon.'

'But I am ashamed, my friend. I am allowing evil to exist.'

Hampton patted the thick arm of the fisherfolk.

'You saved your captain's life, and that's a good thing. You did a good thing, my friend.'

'I should do more.'

***

Rhev sat on the rear step of the rocking caravan, alone. Wathgill was becoming a distant memory to the south. Even though night was drawing in, Steem had decided it best they make their way to Little Mosshill as quickly as possible, and so had set out without delay. The new wheel wasn't quite the right size, and it had visibly pained Steem to allow it to be fitted, but it was just good enough to serve. Every once in a while Rhev had to grab something to keep him from falling off.

He sighed heavily.

Rhev felt the loud reverberation of heavy boots behind him. Mercy dropped down onto the rear step next to him, and took a seat. They sat in silence for a while, their eyes fixed on the twinkling lights of Wathgill. Mercy cleared her throat.

'Kevin is insecure,' she started bluntly. 'His magickal abilities haven't been up to scratch for some time now. But he does try, and for that I give him credit. I shouldn't have goaded him back at the inn.'

'Why are you telling me this?' asked Rhev, his eyes still fixed on the far distance.

'I'm telling you this because I could see what Kevin said affected you, and I wanted you to know that it was a lie. He

114

was lying. I attacked him, and he lashed out at you because it was easier than going for me. For that, *I* am sorry. I'm sorry, Rhev.'

Rhev turned to look at Mercy for the first time. Her body was tense. The sinews in her arms stood out ever so slightly and her expression was strange. She was not used to apologising. Not in the sense that she was cruel-hearted, but that she was careful to never do anything to apologise for. Rhev could see it was making her uncomfortable.

'Thanks, Mercy. I appreciate it.' He smiled in a way that caused his beard to bunch up around his chin. Mercy nodded, turned to look out across the rolling countryside for a moment, and then made to get up.

'I'm really glad I'm part of this group, you know,' he continued. Mercy sat back down with a thump.

'You *are* paid to be here,' she replied uncertainly.

'Don't worry, I know that. It used to be that I always did things for myself, looked out for number one, that sort of thing. But now I'm on this team, I'm getting to like having something to do *together*. Doing something against the odds. It's like being on a... quest.' The word slipped out before he could stop it. 'Not a *quest*, per say; obviously I'm not going to be fighting any dragons or potato golems or what have you. I meant to say... erm... *mission*.'

Mercy smirked out of the side of her mouth, the side facing away from Rhev. 'I understand why you would want to be in a squad, with an objective. I like that sort of structure too. That's why I signed up to go to the eastern front.'

'You went to the eastern front?' asked Rhev in a way that implied a million other questions were waiting in line behind it.

'I did. But I'd rather not go into it now. Things happened.'

'Oh.' Rhev was visibly disappointed. You could almost see his mind at work guessing what sort of things could have...

happened. 'I'd never stepped foot out of Velheim before this job.'

'I'm so sorry,' said Mercy, only a hint of sarcasm in her voice.

'Hah. I know, I know, it's an armpit, but I had no choice really. My dad left when I was a tiddler and never came back.' Realising how that sounded he quickly added, 'he was an adventurer, a *hero*, you see. He used to go looking for treasure and wars and that. When he wasn't doing that he was in the taverns listening for rumours about treasure and wars, and telling me stories.'

Rhev waggled his fingers in front of Mercy's face. 'This ring here is from one of them,' he grinned.

'It looks very valuable,' she replied.

'Aye, probably. I've never got it valued though. Never had any intention of selling it, you see.' He cleared his throat and took a breath. 'One day dad went off on another one of his adventures and never came back. Fact is, he's probably dead. To be honest, I *like* to think he's dead. That means he didn't have a choice about coming back for me and mum.' Rhev stopped for a moment. He couldn't see it, but Mercy had softened under her heavy chainmail.

'So it was just me and mum and I told her I would look after her, and I did in my own way. I stole, I swindled, I fought for money. Don't tell the others about that, by the way... When mum asked where the money was coming from I lied and said I had a job. I was hazy on the specifics, of course. She kept asking about it though, so I lied. I said I was with the Cliff Guard. It was respectable, and I wanted her to be proud, because I was all she had left.' Rhev made a sound like he was clearing his throat, but there was something wobbly about it. He breathed deeply.

'She started to tell everyone in the neighbourhood about it. "My Rhev is with the Guard. He's protecting the city. He's got

116

responsibility and respect." I couldn't take it.'

'So what did you do?' asked Mercy, sounding genuinely interested.

'Only thing I could do: I joined the Cliff Guard.'

Rhev laughed a big, rumbling belly laugh. Mercy couldn't help it: she let out a giggle. Rhev had never heard her laugh a real, uncontrollable laugh. He stopped laughing out of surprise for a moment, and listened. When she realised she was the only one laughing, she stopped. A pause charged with immense chortle potential hung like ancloud around their heads. It was no use. They both fell back into laughter, not sure now what they were even laughing at. Both gasping for air, they eventually stopped.

'Anyway,' Rhev continued, 'truth be told I didn't have many friends in the guard, for the obvious reasons. Most of them had run into me at one time or another, and not for a friendly catch up over a mug of fine ale, mind you. Being a… how can I put it? Being a cheeky bastard doesn't get you many friends in general, so being on this team, with all of you, that means something.'

Mercy just smiled.

'Could you, erm, help train me?' said Rhev suddenly. 'With the sword, that is. Not from scratch obviously, just, you know, *polishing*.'

'Now that *is* unexpected,' she replied, an evil smile crossing her lips. 'Your "urban style" not cutting it?'

Before Rhev could reply she continued. 'Of course, I'd be happy to. Like you said, we're on the same team.'

Rhev was about to thank her when he was interrupted by a shout from inside the caravan. It was Kevin.

'But where do you keep all of them? I don't understand!' he screeched.

'I don't know, around and about?' replied Sterling, not nearly as concerned about the issue as Kevin was.

'Around and about? What does that even mean? I can only see three on you!'

'Well it isn't polite to carry them about openly. It would give off the wrong vibe. I'm a lover, not a fighter. They just come to me when I need them- hey, hey! Stop touching me! What are you doing?!'

Rhev and Mercy stood up on the back step and peered through the window. Kevin was quite violently patting Sterling's clothes, and the halfling was not taking it well. Sterling caught their eyes and looked at them pleadingly. Kevin followed his gaze.

'I was looking for... he wouldn't tell me where he keeps all the daggers!' he exclaimed as he got off the poor halfling. 'I don't get it! You never see them until we're in some sort of dire straits, and then they just appear, as if by magick! And... and I want to know how to do it!'

Sterling winked and rolled away from Kevin.

'A wizard never tells his secrets,' he said with a cheeky grin, knowing full well what he was doing.

'Gah!' shouted Kevin. 'You, Sterling Panthelios, are a rapscallion of the highest order and I am ashamed to call you a friend! Thank Ava that I now have better company.' Kevin's eyes caught Rhev's and he smiled apologetically. It was a clumsy gesture, but Rhev appreciated it nonetheless.

The four of them spent the rest of the evening playing Stacks while Steem hummed an old travelling tune in his rich tenor. All the while, the box sat in the corner of the caravan covered in a thick layer of canvas, blankets, rugs, and enough detritus that for a while it could be forgotten about if you tried hard enough. Beneath all those layers, however, the glowing sigils on the box's surface pulsed and flickered like a deep sea creature sending signals into the abyss.

The following day it was Rhev's turn to sit up front. He took the opportunity to get the lowdown on their destination.

118

'Just past Relthorn, south of the Thicket. Never been there myself but I've met a couple of people from there when I was last in Relthorn. Nice enough lot, a little provincial for my taste. Quaint would be the word, I suppose.' Steem nodded to himself and adjusted his grip on the reins. The Krovanian Mountains were looming ever closer to the north.

'Do we have far to go?' asked Rhev.

'Hah! Aye, we have a ways to go before we get to Little Mosshill, lad. Over half the length of the Peninsula! But don't you worry, we won't be dawdling.' He raised an eyebrow at Rhev. Only an eyebrow as dark and thick as Steem's could convey the full weight behind that simple statement.

'We are going to make it in time right? Before the contract... terminates.'

Steem hesitated. 'We should be fine, lad. It took us a week to go through the Grippens. If the weather is decent we should be able to get through Krovania in another week, then it's straight through Falstyr and around the Lindentarn. All told, I reckon we'll even have a few days spare. You can take those as holiday time, if you like.'

The horses sweated and the caravan continued to trundle along the track. Clouds hung over the mountains ahead as if they had always been there, building in density and darkness over thousands of years. Rhev shivered as he felt the phantom of the cold damp to come.

***

Beckett awoke in his office. He had nested himself in a pile of unfinished paperwork and unsatisfactory reports. Last night must have gotten the better of him. He blinked in the single ray of light that had been slowly making its way over to his face for the last three hours or so. Hampton looked up from his desk, which had the handy feature of also being a stool.

'Ah, sir, you're awake. It seems you had a productive

evening getting your head stuck in the work, sir.'

'What time is it?' Beckett snapped.

'Almost noon, sir. I didn't want to wake you, seeing as you'd been doing overtime and all. You deserved the rest, sir.' Hampton smiled at Beckett as one would a recovering patient. Beckett replied with a harumph and moved to his desk.

The two sat in silence; one respectful, one morose. The only sound was that of Hampton's quill scratching away at papers on the rough wooden stool. It irked Beckett. His eyes flicked between his own desk and Hampton's. He was in a terrible mood, and he had nothing to occupy himself. No new reports to read. No new money to manage. No investment leads. Nothing. Nothing at all.

Nothing to lose.

He cleared his throat. It was rough from dehydration and tasted foul.

'Hampton,' he began, uncharacteristically politely.

'Yes, sir?' Hampton replied, immediately putting down his pen and fixing Beckett with a helpful look.

'You like your job, do you?' Beckett steepled his fingers together.

'Well, yes sir, very much,' Hampton said innocently. 'Keeps me out of the cold. Keeps my mind agile, what with all the numbers and that. I've got my own desk,' he gestured proudly with both hands to the stool in front of him. 'A man can't ask for much more really, can he?'

'No no, you're quite right. You are *very* lucky, Hampton. Now, what if I were to say that, hypothetically, you would lose these comforts and privileges if you didn't come up with a good idea to make money for this firm very quickly. What would you do?'

'Well, sir, I have no real business acumen, as you do, but I suppose I would rattle my brains as best I could and see what fell out.'

120

Beckett didn't reply immediately. Instead, he slowly folded his steepled fingers away, starting with his little ones, until only his index fingers remained pointing. Then he angled his hands down, until those index fingers were pointing straight at Hampton.

'Go on then.'

Hampton gawped like a fish. His eyes glanced back and forth to the comfort of his paperwork.

'Rattle. Your. Brains.' Beckett spoke each word slowly, accentuating each syllable. Hampton coughed.

'I, erm, I'm trying, sir. I really am.'

'Try harder, Hampton. Your job depends on it. Give me something. An investment opportunity. A lead. A whiff. A secret. The inside leg. I need something now!'

'I heard a story,' said Hampton abruptly. Beckett got up from his seat and leant over his desk. He loomed ever closer, prompting Hampton with a stare.

'From a fisherfolk. He'd been on a voyage from Heptamil to Velheim. They carried a cargo, a single box, that was cursed. It contained a doorway to another place.'

"What do you mean, 'another place'?" Beckett snapped.

'Inside the box, sir. When it opened, it showed a way to a place that isn't here. The fisherfolk called it The Place Where Water Goes To Die'

'Full of tall tales, those fisherfolk. They spend too much time underwater, and it puts pressure on their heads. Damages the brain, you. This all sounds like poppycock, Hampton. Is this it? Is this all you can offer to me? To this firm?'

'He said that when they docked at Velheim the captain asked him to pick up a big scroll, with lots of weird symbols on it. The fisherfolk couldn't read it, but he thought it might be magickal. Then the captain passed this box onto a courier, and made him sign this magick scroll. I don't know about you, but it sounds like some pretty serious business, right sir? An important new... thing, in the Peninsulan market, sir?'

Hampton looked imploringly at his boss. He was terrified that he had just lost his job out of the blue, after working for Beckett & Beckett for over thirty years.

'Sir?' Hampton tried. Beckett had been quiet for some time, and he was anxious to learn his fate.

'This story of yours, Hampton, may not entirely carry the stink of fisherfolk lies after all.'

'It doesn't?'

'It did, up until you mentioned a very specific detail. This may indeed corroborate with something that I myself heard when I was working on Fence Street yesterday.'

Beckett's mind slowly began to fill with new possibilities. If this so-called 'magick scroll' was what he thought it was, and it was real, then the cargo it secured could be real. If the cargo was real, then it could well be a portal to another realm. Besides, it stands to reason that if someone had gone to the lengths of commissioning what he *thought* had been commissioned, it would only be to secure the delivery of something incredibly valuable.

'Did the fisherfolk tell you who the courier was?'

'Esteemed Gents & Co, I think.'

'Esteemed Gents & Co?' Beckett trawled through the ledgers of his mind searching for a courier company by that name.

'It was a red caravan, I know that much, sir.'

'Red caravan, Esteemed Gents...' Beckett had an epiphany. 'Not Esteemed Gents, you bloody idiot, Hampton, it's *Steem Vennts & Co*. He uses a red caravan. I remember now, we used him around ten years ago when we were trading in dragons. Not particularly reliable if I recall correctly. Shoddy. Now, if they were in Velheim with a caravan they could only have been going west from there. Nowhere else to go but through the Grippen mountains into the centre of the Peninsula. From there they would most likely either go due south through the Tynewood towards us, or they would go north to Krovnia.'

'What are you thinking sir?'

'What I'm thinking is that I want that box,' Beckett replied, the edge of his lips curling to betray the scheme forming in his mind.

'But why, sir? The fisherfolk said it's cursed. Only evil could come of it!'

'Do try and *think,* Hampton. If we were in sole possession of a gateway to another world, we would control the only known route in and out. We would own the road, and what do road owners do? *They toll the road users.* And what do the road users take with them? *Goods.* And what do we do with goods? *We tax them!*'

'Sir, with all due respect, you're not a wizard. I think whatever powers are in this box may be a bit beyond your control.'

'Dear Hampton, but don't you know what the *greatest* power in this world is?'

'Sir?'

'Market forces,' he said with a manic grin. 'There is no stopping the power of trade once the dam is broken between one market and another. I will control trade between the Peninsula and this New World, Hampton. I will control a new economy, a new Fence Street. Beckett & Beckett will rise once again.' Beckett stood proudly now, looking up into the corner of the room, his bony chin pointed majestically.

Hampton was brimming with confused emotions. It looked like his job, *his life*, might be safe, but at what cost? Was he complicit in a fundamentally evil scheme, or was he helping to divert this evil box from its original evil purpose? The lesser of two evils? He had never had to think about so many moral quandaries in his life!

'Hampton, look up the address for Mister Boswell. I believe he may be able to help us determine which way our friend Steem Vennts is headed.'

'Boswell, sir? Yes, sir. Right away, sir.'

'And when you've done that, run down to whatever establishment you found this fisherfolk in and offer him a job with Beckett & Beckett. Tell him to pack his bags for travelling.'

'Travelling, sir?'

'We're going on a hunt, Hampton,' he replied menacingly. Hampton felt his left knee tremble uncontrollably. The small beam of light coming from the high window faded behind a passing cloud.

The foreboding atmosphere was broken by one of Beckett's sharp, barking laughs. 'Is this the sort of thing an *accountant* would do? Eh, Hampton? Eh?!'

***

'I swear that the sermons in Dankvyr just keep getting more and more ridiculous,' Aed said as he took the Specs off and moved back to his desk at the side of the room. He was tall and gaunt, and his head was shaved like an egg, in the sense that his head appeared to have never grown any hair at any point in his existence.

'That old bat at the Recently Orthodox Mega Temple spent a whole hour talking about how honey was Ava's gift to the people and that by using it as a moisturiser your hands would be "sanctified for her holy work", but then she asked everyone to queue up for their monthly divine embrace and they all got really sticky backs.'

Dermis and Cal snorted. A smile crept across Erin's lips.

'It's not funny!' Aed insisted. 'First of all, honey is not a moisturiser. Secondly, it is not Ava's gift to the people. It is a byproduct of bees, so if anything it comes under Bumblebas' domain.'

124

Cal interrupted him. 'Bumblebas works in Prayer Stratification now.'

'Yes, I know, but he started off the whole bee thing so you have to give him credit. And *thirdly*, the Recently Orthodox Mega Temple has just bought shares in Missus Milton's Marvelous Honey Limited, so no ulterior motive there,' he laughed smugly, amused by his own sarcasm. Aed was a nice enough god, but he did like the sound of his own voice.

'I had to monitor Chardo again yesterday,' said Erin. There was a wave of groans around the room.

'Go on then,' said Cal with an encouraging nod, 'what did he do this time?'

'He was complaining to these people that they were interrupting his sand surfing time. He called them *boneheads*,' she replied.

'Classic Chardo,' said Dermis. 'Really putting his own spin on "divine word".'

Erin giggled and continued, 'No, no, it was terrible! He was being so awful with these poor people. They had no idea what was going on and they had just dropped their souls.'

'Oof. I hate watching that. I don't like the way they start squirming, and how they can't stop crying. It's gross,' said Aed with a shiver.

Erin gave Aed a little sidewards glance that he didn't notice. His mortal skills had been notoriously lacking in his previous role, so it was no wonder they put him on the Table.

'He only helped them out because they were in such a terrible spot that he couldn't finish the script properly. He just wanted to get back to surfing. Do you think he does it on the clock?'

'Well that's the thing when you go to the Sands of Time,' said Dermis. 'You technically *can't* be on the clock because there are no clocks capable of measuring all the sand.' She finished her point by folding her arms and leaning back in her chair. Erin turned to Merky, who was deep in his reports.

'Merky, don't you think it's a bit silly that someone like Chardo is in charge of contracts?' she said.

Merky didn't look up from the paperwork, but replied: 'I don't think we should be second guessing top brass. They must have put him there for a reason.'

'Yeah, because he's one of the, like, million sons of Solari,' said Cal. 'I'm pretty sure he was only worshipped in some beach communities in Ellyndr. It wasn't a huge demographic.'

'And now he's in charge of arcane contracts. That's crazy! That used to be your thing Merky, and he's nowhere near as on it as you!' Erin said enthusiastically.

Merky put his pen down and turned around suddenly. 'It doesn't matter though, does it?' he snapped. 'He's on contracts now and I'm here, because contracts and agreements and *trust* aren't as important to a lot of people down there anymore, and some gods have better scriptures and prophets and are just more… *convenient*.' Merky's apple cheeks had flushed, and his already sparse strands of hair seemed to be moving away from each other in a haphazard fashion. No one could think of a reply..

'That's enough talking about Chardo. I don't want him ruining our work as well.' Merky turned back to his desk, and the other gods did the same.

Erin liked Merky. He was kind, helpful, and understanding. He was the de facto leader of the team, although technically the god in the crisp white suit was in charge. Merky seemed to enjoy the work on the whole, or at least he never showed signs of not enjoying the work. He was a person who structured his life around duties and agreements. It was rare, however, that he talked about his previous life as a god of Oaths. Although not entirely au fait with the world of humanoid gods, Erin understood that there was a time before the rise of Ava that Merky, or Mercatrus as

126

he was known to his worshippers, had been a rather popular and well-respected god. No doubt that Merky had been anything other than the most reliable and professional in his godly duties. It was a far cry from the likes of Chardo and the other *boneheads* in the Fiat department. It was enough to make you think that the current situation in the pantheon was something of a wrong step.

She sighed to herself as she filled out the monitoring report for Chardo's astral projection, and wondered to herself how those poor people were getting on with their quest.

***

'Push!' yelled Steem over the rain. 'Come on you lazy buggers! It's another three miles to the next village. If we don't hurry up this rain will drown us.'

Everyone apart from Steem had their hands planted on the back of the caravan and their feet planted in something that looked like black treacle. They were soaked to the bone. Sterling struggled to gain purchase on the caravan's relatively high rear step and slipped. *Thwap*. His face planted firmly in the treacly mud. A moment later he came up gasping for air, his eyes glued shut. A strong hand grabbed his suede jacket and hoisted him to his feet.

'Gotcha!' said Rhev as he lifted the little man. Sterling thanked him through a mouthful of mud.

'Go and see if you can help Steem with the horses,' Mercy said to Sterling. He nodded in her approximate direction and began to slip his way towards the front of the caravan like a blind man on rollerskates.

'We've been through this part of the world before, and it's never been as bad as this!' Kevin complained. 'What's the point of a caravan if you have to push it the whole way there? We really are having some rotten luck.' He paused, a look of worry spreading across his face. 'You don't think it's because of the *Box?*'

127

They had taken to referring to their burden with a capital 'B', as one is want to do with a thing they fear. Mercy dignified Kevin's dangerous superstition with a stern look, and nothing else.

'Just keep pushing, Kev,' grunted Rhev, 'you heard Steem. Not far now.'

After another half an hour of trudging through the molasses of the mountain pass, the caravan gave a lurch as the gradient began to change in their favour. Everyone hopped aboard, and the horses began their thunderous descent into the valley below.

On the lower slopes of a valley stood the village, the slate-covered roofs overly tall and pitched, as if they were mirroring the surrounding mountains. Civilisation was a welcoming site, but the green tinge to the lights in the windows did not promise comforts and warmth. The incessant rain ran like a waterfall down the roofs of the buildings, and the slick tiles reflected a dark and brooding sky. The whole village dripped forlornly. Steem's caravan bumped a road sign on the edge of the settlement that read 'Haven' in tall, seriffed letters.

He slowed the horses when they were among the houses. The small, bottle-thick glass windows gave nothing away. Most of the houses were dark and could well have been empty if it wasn't for the odd pile of freshly cut firewood or chamber pot effluence that suggested life. Some glowed faintly from within with the eerie green light they had seen from the pass. It was a constant, smooth light, like the sun, not the flickering of candle flame or hearth fire usually found in a home. Steem shivered. He was wet, cold, had a bad case of the heebie jeebies, and worst of all he was late, although he wouldn't admit it to his crew. Then he rounded a tight corner into a wide cobbled square, and was met by a reassuringly normal orange glow.

128

A large tavern at the end of the square bore the name 'The Rosy Brewer'. At the pitch of the roof stood a carved figurehead of a chubby man holding a brimming tankard, wearing trousers that seemed impractically short for this sort of climate. Steem deftly steered the caravan through the coach entrance into the yard at the rear of the building. He banged on the wood behind him.

'Right you lot, we're here. Get the horses stabled and secure the Box. I'm going in to find the innkeeper.' He hopped down from his perch and made his way to the front of the inn. Before he entered he took off his top hat and emptied the water that had gathered in the brim.

Inside the tavern was blessedly warm and dry. Steem revelled in a pleasant shudder as he began to feel his bones again. The hearth was large and welcoming, and he made straight for it with his hands stretched out in front of him. There were already some damp travellers sitting nearby tucking into a hearty stew. Steem nodded cordially, and they nodded in return.

'Yes yes yes! Come in! Warm those bones of yours and dry off that wonderful moustache.'

Steem span on a sixpence and found he was alarmingly close to a ruddy faced man carrying four dripping tankards.

Steem mumbled his thanks, not quite sure how to react to such an unprompted compliment.

'No no no! Thank *you* for your custom. We always treasure a fresh face here in The Rosy Brewer,' said the innkeeper. He turned to the people seated for supper. 'Here are your ales, ladies and gentlemen,' he crooned as he placed the tankards carefully on the table. There was a call from somewhere behind the bar. 'Rudy!'

'That's my cue,' said the innkeeper to no-one in particular, and hurried off before Steem could catch him.

'Seems like a nice bloke,' he said to the people seated

129

nearby.

'It wears,' replied one of the travellers. 'I have to come this way for work once a month. The only reason I stay here is because it's the only place that doesn't glow green, but every time I stay here he seems to get chirpier and chirpier. I swear, one day I'm going to be passing through and he's going to be there in the middle of the square surrounded by the bodies of all the townsfolk with that insufferable grin on his face.'

The rest of them nodded sagely and slurped their stew.

'Lovely,' replied Steem. There wasn't much more he could say, so he left the group to their food and went to find Rudy.

He wasn't hard to find. He had set himself up at a table next to the bar with a huge red sausage on a plate in front of him. The sausage was already half gone, and much of its viscera lay on Rudy's large black and white checkered bib. Steem walked up to him and cleared his throat. Rudy swallowed his most recent morsel and smacked his lips.

'Do excuse me! I always say an inn is like the innkeepers stomach: it's only good if it's full!' Rudy's bulging stomach seemed to have been full daily for most of his life. 'But though rude by name, I am not rude by nature! Hah! So please, how can I help?'

'Board for five and four horses. Also I must ask, do you have secure rooms? Good, strong locks and that?' Steem replied.

'Of course! Locks made from the strongest iron mined right here in the Krovanian mountains. And plenty of room for you, your company, and your steeds. That will be six ducats for the night, if you please.'

It was steep, but it sounded like he didn't have much choice. Steem counted out the coins from his soggy purse and placed them in Rudy's hand. Rudy turned his head towards the kitchen and yelled: 'Gerty! Four, five, seven, nine, and thirteen please!'

Five sets of keys seemed to fly out of the kitchen one by one, and Rudy managed to catch them all, although only just. He grinned at Steem and handed him the keys. 'Can I interest you in a slice of blood sausage? Gerty does the best. Uses only the finest blood!'

Steem grimaced and shook his head.

'Suit yourself. Do call if you need anything!'

Steem left the sounds of blood sausage being attacked behind him and went to find his crew. He found them at the front of the tavern wringing out their clothes. Rhev was holding a box sized bundle of canvas and blankets.

'Where do you want me to put it?' he asked.

'Not in my bloody room, that's for sure,' Steem replied. 'Stick it in Sterling's room.'

'Hang on, why me?' the halfling asked incredulously.

'Because you drew the short straw a long time ago,' Steem snorted. Rhev chuckled, but judging by Mercy and Kevin's resolutely neutral expressions this wasn't the first time that line had been used.

After everyone had settled into their rooms, they reconvened for dinner. The inn was surprisingly full with patrons who all gave the distinct impression that they were just passing through. Despite his avuncular personality, Rudy was obviously a shrewd businessman. He had positioned his inn in just the right spot as to make it the only logical option for travellers passing through Krovania. Not only that, but his exclusive offer of bottomless ale while you ate your dinner had made it a no-brainer for all concerned. It was just the thing Rhev needed after the gruelling journey into the mountains.

Struggling to find space for all of them at the same table, the party decided to split up and find seats where they could. Rhev found himself opposite a grizzled gentleman wearing an eyepatch. The man eyed him, singularly of course, and then

131

went back to his haunch. Rhev paid him no mind for quite some time, instead choosing to focus his attention on drinking as much ale as possible while eating as slowly as he could.

However, he couldn't fail to notice that his table companion was wearing a macabre collection of crude talismans about his neck. Most had been tucked under his stained shirt but a few had popped out over the course of the meal. They were made of bone and were carved to bear the resemblance of a menagerie of strange creatures. Rhev was utterly fascinated. His experience with beasts didn't extend much beyond the farmyard or vermin variety. Here in front of him were the faces of monsters that he had only heard of in tales. He had to know more.

'You've got some nice jewellery there,' he said to the one-eyed man. He realised immediately he had said the wrong thing. The man stopped mid bite, the juice from the meat dribbling down his stubbly chin. He stared at Rhev for a good while. Eventually he finished his bite, chewed laboriously, and swallowed loudly.

'Not jewellery. Trophies,' he replied slowly in a low gravelly tone.

'Right, right,' said Rhev. 'What did you win?'

'Win? Win!' the man scoffed and choked out a smoky laugh. He fingered one of the trinkets. 'Every time I gained one of these, I won my life, laddy. Won it back from the jaws of certain death.'

'Sounds like a difficult competition.'

'You don't get it, do you? It wasn't a competition, it was a job. Nay, a calling. Each one of these is carved from the bones of a monster that I killed. I am a Slayer.' He said those last words with a healthy serving of relish.

'You get paid to kill monsters? How did you get that job?' Rhev asked. He hadn't touched his food at all. Even though the man's manner was coarse, he was undeniably captivating.

'I was destined for it. As a babe I killed a snake with my bare hands. Ripped its head off and wore its blood. When I could walk I set out into the woods searching for bigger prey. I stalked a five-tusked boar for three days. On the third day I skinned it with the hunting knife I had been given the week before for my first birthday. At aged ten I saved my village from the northern wolves using a single fireband, and the chief bowed low to me. When I came of age I left my people and their mundane threats behind. I knew I could handle more, you see. I needed to handle more. Bigger, faster, stronger. More claws, more teeth, more venom sacs. My first truly great kill was a Many-Eyed Spinal Crab.' He sat back and smiled to himself. Rhev sat with his mouth agape.

'I don't even know what that is,' he said in awe.

'You don't even know what that is? Well, I'll tell you what that is. Or should I say *was*, because I killed all of them forty years ago. The Many-eyed Spinal Crab is a fearsome creature, both at sea and on land. It has eyes pointing in all cardinal directions, so it can never be surprised. It can walk sideways just as easily as backwards and forwards. Truly, an abomination.' He paused again, as if trying to find more words to describe the horror.

'And... a pointy spine?' Rhev ventured.

'No!' the Slayer replied. '*No spine*. It's called that because it *eats* spines. Sucks them up in its maw and pulverises them to grit. But as you can see my back is still intact. It wasn't going to eat my spine, no laddy, *because I needed my spine*. So I made a plan. Its strength was its biggest weakness: it could look in all the cardinal directions, but *up* wasn't one of them. And they can't walk upwards, only sideways and forwards and backwards. So what did I do? I climbed the tallest palm tree I could find, and waited. After hours and hours of patiently waiting in those leaves, breathing perhaps only three, four times at most, one of the bastards came out of the sea and into

133

my kill zone. I leapt with my sword pointed straight below me and plunged it up to the hilt. A quick, clean death. You have to respect your quarry you see. No fannying about.'

'Blimey,' said Rhev under his breath. 'And you did that same thing to every other living one?'

'I did,' said the Slayer with a smirk.

'Didn't that take quite a while?'

'It did,' he replied, 'but you don't get to be a Slayer if you're afraid of commitment. Now this,' he fished out one of his trophies from the depths of his shirt, 'this is truly my greatest kill, and also my greatest loss.' The Slayer indicated his eyepatch. 'I had been hired by the city of Dankvyr to rid its sewers of a great evil. The top dog had come to me and said "Slayer, my people are in desperate need of a hero, and only someone with your skills, sword, and succour can help. A beast from the sewers has been roaming the streets at night and dragging innocent young women back to its filthy lair. It is said it has the head of a man, the body of a crocodile, and the limbs of a man.' The people were calling it Scaly Dan, though only in hushed murmurs at the backs of taverns, mind you. I had seen something similar in my travels; a man with the head of a crocodile and the limbs of a crocodile. The locals had called it *Corpse Ripper*, by dint of how it liked to consume its prey. I had dealt with it swiftly enough, so I know a Scaly Dan would be no match at all. Oh how wrong I was, and *I'm never wrong*.

At midnight I slid into those Dankvyrian sewers, covered myself with filth so as to be invisible to the monster, and stalked those stinking tunnels for three hours. Then, a scream! I followed it around a corner and found myself looking at a sordid scene. Scaly Dan himself, macking on a young lady dressed in finery. It was abhorrent. He must have used his hallucinatory bile to bewitch the lass, because she made no attempt to fight back. I had to fight for her honour! I drew my sword and span it five or six times, moving ever closer to the wretched thing. He was clearly in awe of my manoeuvres, because he made no attempt to flee. The young lass screamed out "No, don't!" as I came closer. Her fear for my safety was ill-placed though. She threw herself away as I reached the monster, and my sword slashed clean across its chest. Its thick green torso did not splinter though. As soon as I made contact with the knobbly hide my blade broke and flew into the muck below us.'

'I bet you didn't see that coming,' said Rhev, slowly beginning to spoon stew into his gaping mouth.

'Far from it,' replied the Slayer icily. 'It was entirely deliberate. I knew the creature would have an impenetrable hide, and so I had brought a dud sword made of brittle iron. By striking him so confidently on his chest and breaking my sword, I lulled him into thinking that I had made a grave mistake; that I was outmatched and had no further recourse. But remember, dear dwarf, I am a Slayer, and I killed a rat with my bare hands before I had even fully emerged from the womb.'

Rhev choked on a potato, but the Slayer continued.

'I had no need for a weapon. My hands were steel enough. I stepped away from the creature to lure it towards me, anticipating its over-confident advance. As I expected, it lunged at me, filthy arms outstretched. A simple half-turn and I was at its side. I grabbed those foul appendages and twisted. Hard. A simple technique, the Shantese Burn, but quite powerful in the right hands. Within moments the creature's arms went limp and useless. It tried to kick at me to no avail. It slipped on the wet stones and fell, cracking its head open like an egg. The woman screamed and became petrified in horror. It was indeed a gruesome sight, but I had seen worse. I took her by the arm and led her to the surface. She forgot to thank me, but I put it down to the bile. I let her go into the cold night, certain she would sing of my deeds for all the city to hear.'

The Slayer sat back and crossed his arms smugly, pleased with a tale well told. Rhev swallowed the last of his meal and sat back in turn.

'So when did you lose your eye?' he said after some consideration.

'Severe conjunctivitis. There was a lot of crap in the water.'

Rhev bobbed his head, a little disappointed.

'Why are you here in Haven, then? Here to slay another monster?' he asked. The Slayer smiled a thin, sickle smile.

'The Slayer code forbids me from discussing contracts until the contract is complete. But suffice to say, I'm here in regards to some unfinished business.'

The bone necklaces jangled together as the man got up from his chair. He took a long stretch, and the sinew beneath his tight black tunic bulged.

'I hope my story inspired you, master dwarf. What is your name?'

'Rhev Culluggan,' the dwarf replied.

'A good name, Culluggan. I feel I have heard it somewhere before. You can call me Rygert, if you ever see me again,' and with that the Slayer kicked his chair back under the table and took his leave.

There goes a real adventurer, Rhev thought. *Maybe I should start wearing necklaces.*

Steem, Mercy, Kevin, and Rhev reconvened after their meal by the large hearth at the front of the tavern. Sterling was nowhere to be found. Kevin pointed out that it was easy to lose someone so small.

'Never mind him,' he continued. 'I just had a long chat with that Rudy fellow.'

'Couldn't you get away?' said Mercy. She had been on the receiving end of a particularly long and reluctant conversation

136

about her unusual hair with the proprietor.

'Why would I want to get away? He's a very nice man. Very complimentary. He said it was an honour to have such an accomplished wizard in his inn.'

Mercy snorted. Kevin glared daggers.

'I learnt a great deal from him actually,' he continued. 'For instance, did you know that the locals have more than seven, *yes, seven,* words for rain? And that the lightning here is green? *And,* that there's an excellent example of a traditional Krovanian castle not far from here, but he wouldn't recommend visiting because-'

'And I heard,' Mercy interrupted as she leant forward in her seat, 'that the green glow in the villager's houses has turned them all mad, and no one knows why.'

'Now there's got to be a story behind that,' said Steem.

Kevin furrowed his brows. 'Are you just trying to one-up me? Architectural history not good enough for you?'

Mercy put her hands up in mock surrender. 'All I'm saying is that I've seen enough castles, forts, and bastions to last me a lifetime.'

'I met a man who had single-handedly wiped out an entire species,' said Rhev.

'Oh come on!' Kevin wailed.

'Guys, we have a problem.'

Sterling had appeared at the foot of the table, breathless and shirtless. 'I messed up,' he continued, 'big time.'

'You wagered the shirt off your back in poker again?' asked Steem, lighting his pipe as he did so. 'I'm afraid all I can offer you is a sack.'

'It's not that. I've got my shirt. It's in my room. What I don't have is the Box.'

Steem spluttered as he rapidly exhaled his first drag from the pipe.

'What?! How on earth did you lose it? Dropped in down

137

the lavvy, did you?!' he choked out, rising from his seat in preparation to wring Sterling's neck. The halfling was petrified.

'Oh gods, I can feel my soul slipping away already,' said Kevin, picking at his clothes and patting himself down like a tweaking junky.

'Calm down Kevin," said Mercy. 'I can't feel anything at all. Sterling, answer the question.'

Sterling looked sheepishly at the group. 'I was sitting next to this girl at dinner. Absolutely beautiful, she was. Pale skin, dark red cherry lips. Long black hair. Zero split ends. Incredible. Anyway, we got to talking obviously. I threw out some of my best lines. Made her laugh. Lovely laugh by the way, like crystal glasses vibrating-'

'Get to the point!' Steem flexed his best wringing hand.

'Right, yes, well,' replied Sterling, a little put out. 'She said that she lived around here and that the most interesting thing that had happened in the last year was the three days in a row that it *hadn't* rained. I said "Oh boy, have I got a treat for you." Well actually I said something a lot more poetic than that, obviously, I just can't remember right now, I'm very stressed at the moment.'

Steem's hand was very close to his neck now.

'So I took her back to my room and showed her the Box!' he blurted out.

'By Ava, we're not a bloody travelling museum!' shouted Steem.

'I know, I know! But she was just so lovely, and she said I looked like a swashbuckler, and you know that's the look I've been going for. And did I mention her hair? Like fresh spun midnight. Hmm, *that* was a good line. I'm saving that for later.'

'Later? Later?!' Steem had resorted to balling his hands into tight fists to resist the urge to wring.

'*Anyway*, she loved it. It lit up like a firework when I took the canvas off. All the little blue whirls and that were pulsing. I let her touch it. Just for a moment, mind you. She was just so into it, I couldn't *not* let her touch it. Then I started to take my shirt off because, *well you know*, and in the time it took to get the bloody thing over my head she had disappeared and the Box was gone! Some thief! First my heart, then my burden,' he finished dramatically.

'You romantic fool,' chastised Mercy. 'She may as well have stolen your bloody soul!'

'Where does she live?' asked Rhev, trying to help the situation.

'I'm not sure. She did seem like a local though. Knew a lot about Haven,' Sterling replied, glad that at least someone wasn't insulting him.

'Perhaps my good friend Rudy will know,' said Kevin. 'He seems to know a great deal about this village and its inhabitants.'

The group hurried over to the bar to find the ever-welcoming innkeeper. They found him standing there in his signature pose, a brimming mug of beer in one hand, his cheeks positively bursting with rosy goodness. A customer looked at him with dead eyes.

'Just give me the drink Rudy. You've stood there long enough,' said the patron.

Rudy's cheeks deflated and he passed over the tankard. 'Just trying to make you smile,' he said, crestfallen.

The man took his drink and left in a hurry. Kevin approached the bar with the group in tow behind him.

'Rudy, I was wondering if you could be of assistance,' said the elf.

'Ah, my dear friend Colin of Yeti! Of course, I live to serve,' Rudy replied, his frown turning upside down in an instant.

'Many thanks, Rudy. And it's Kevin, by the way. Kevin of Yedforth. But that's beside the point. My short-witted friend here,' Kevin placed his hand on Sterling's head, as if to drive the vertical metaphor home, 'has been robbed by one of your patrons.'

'Oh no! A robbery? In my establishment? It cannot be! It's enough to change the red in my cheeks from a jovial blush to a rash of anger! It will not stand! But, of course, I am not liable…'

'It's okay, Rudy, we're not blaming you. Sterling is too quick to trust whenever a lady gives him the slightest bit of attention.' Sterling's cheeks flushed even more than Rudy's. 'Our precious cargo was taken by a woman who dined here this evening. Go on Sterling, describe this woman to Rudy.'

'Well,' Sterling began, 'she-'

'The quick version,' growled Steem. Sterling cleared his throat.

'Pale skin, black hair, red lips. Can't have seen more than twenty five winters.'

Rudy caressed an imaginary beard on his chin and hummed ponderously.

'Does she have a tinkling laugh?' he asked.

'Yes! Yes!' replied Sterling, nodding furiously.

'Sort of like this?' Rudy tilted his head back and delivered an uncanny impression of the young woman giggling. It was really quite unnerving.

'Yes, that's right,' Sterling admitted, not quite able to meet Rudy's eye. The rosy cheeked innkeeper became quite grave.

'This is not good I am afraid. The woman who you suspect of stealing from you is not someone you would want to have dealings with. Her name is Mina. She is the daughter of Lady Varylla.' Rudy finished his sentence, trusting the weight of this name to do the rest of the talking for him. He was met with five blank expressions.

140

'*She is the daughter of Lady Varylla,*' he repeated, sotto voce. 'Don't you know what that means?'

Five blank faces shook side to side in unison. 'She's the daughter of the most monstrous woman I've ever met! The spawn of an abomination!'

'Where does this abomination live?' asked Steem impatiently.

'I wouldn't go there, sir. I could tell you the worst stories-'

Steem hadn't the time.

'Sorry Rudy, but if we don't get our property back we're going to be the main characters in our own worst story. Now where does she live?' He punctuated his question by jabbing a finger onto the bar top.

'In the castle. It's on the northern edge of town, across the deep chasm,' said Rudy reluctantly.

'Of course it is,' muttered Mercy. 'Is there a bridge across this deep chasm?'

'There is,' said Rudy.

'Narrow, wooden, suspended by fraying ropes?' she continued.

'Yes, that's right. Surely you must have been before?'

'No, just figured as much,' she sighed. 'This Lady Varylla, is she a vampire by any chance? A bloodsucking demonspawn? A dark succubus?'

Rudy blinked, taken aback. 'What? No! I don't think so. She's just a bit mean. Very judgy. She doesn't like the way I do business. The last time I saw her she said I try too hard and that my manner is "suffocating and sickly". I'm just trying to be welcoming to my patrons!' Rudy's lower lip began to tremble slightly.

'I can assure you, Rudy, that your manner is anything but suffocating,' Kevin assured him. Rudy straightened up and puffed up his chest.

'Thank you, Kellern. That means a lot coming from an

141

esteemed man of magick like yourself. But please, if you insist on going to that castle, be sure to go with a thick skin, that's all I can say.''

'Right, yes, thanks Rudy,' said Kevin, trying his best to ignore the flagrant mispronunciation of his fairly common name.

'Looks like we're going to have to pay a visit to this Lady Varylla and her daughter if we don't want our souls to fall out of our, well, soles,' said Steem with an air of purpose. 'Sterling, put your clothes on.'

The chasm on the northern edge of Haven was very, very deep. The bridge that spanned it looked barely sufficient to withstand the rain, let alone the weight of a body. The group stopped before daring to take a step on the rickety wooden planks.

'You think there's another way across? Something with fewer holes and more bridge?' asked Kevin, water dripping off the tips of his pointed ears.

'Do we have much of a choice? I don't want to chance our souls dropping out if we deliberately move away from the castle for any reason,' said Steem dourly.

Here's my time to shine, thought Rhev.

'Don't you lot worry, there's hundreds of bridges like this in the Underport. The trick is to get across them quick, before the bridge realises you're on it. I think it's called physics.'

'Rhev, I'm not sure that makes sense,' said Mercy, but it was too late. The dwarf pulled up his belt, made a *hup* sound, and started running.

'You've got to hand it to the lad, he's no yellow belly,' said Steem with a slight smile.

Rhev's heavy boots slipped and slid across the planks slick with rainwater and slimy rot. It was going alright, until one of the planks became detached at one end, causing it to flip up as Rhev put his weight on it. The dwarf was catapulted towards

142

the edge of the bridge. There was no barrier, only the odd frayed rope acting as a support for the wood. Rhev fell. Everyone held their breath.

At the last moment his calloused mitt caught hold of one of the ropes and he swung around it like a chirpy chimney sweep on a lamppost. He landed back on the bridge, and everyone breathed again. Rhev looked back and saw their faces awash with various levels of concern. He threw them a reassuring grin and kept going, slower now that he had lost his momentum. He could feel the physics catching up with him. Creak. Crack. Sway. A gulp of vertigo. Shuffle, shuffle, hop. After another five excruciating minutes Rhev made it across, throwing himself onto the muddy ground. He turned again and waved.

'I was wrong, you'd be bloody mad to try that!' he shouted across the ravine. 'Don't do it!'

It was too late. Sterling was already halfway through his run up. If he had stopped he would have more than likely slipped and fallen into the ravine. He had no choice but to barrel across the rickety bridge as quickly as he dared. At least he had the advantage of being significantly lighter on his feet than the dwarf. Even so, at one point the wind got up so high that it almost flipped the bridge right over. As the halfling neared the end there was a horrible whip crack. The bridge was caught at one end by a thermal from the ravine, causing a wave of motion to travel down its length. The kinetic energy had nowhere to go. The wave reached the main supports of the bridge and ripped them from their moorings. Mercy, Steem, and Kevin looked on in horror as the bridge fell away from them. Sterling still had a couple more yards to go. He hung for a moment in the place where the bridge used to be, and then he fell.

'Making a habit of this, aren't we?' said Rhev as he hauled Sterling up onto the ledge by his jacket. The two of them sat now in the rain on the precipice of the ravine, staring back at their friends.

'Why did you do that, mate?' asked Rhev.

'It didn't seem fair that you go on your own. I was the one that got us into this mess.'

'It's very noble of you to come over and help, but when I said '"don't do it", what I was trying to say was "please don't come over because the bridge will probably break and then I'd be stuck". I probably should have elaborated, but it's hard work shouting into the wind.'

Rhev got up and cupped his hands to his mouth.

'Stay there, we'll go get the Box!'

'How are you going to get back?' Mercy shouted back over the howling wind.

'We'll cross that bridge when we come to it!' He could make out Steem slapping a palm to his forehead.

'Come on then mate,' he said to Sterling. 'Let's go pay your new lass a visit.'

The two of them marched through the downpour and the mud towards a rocky outcrop. There was no sign of a castle.

'Rhev, are you sure we're going the right way?' asked Sterling.

'The bridge can't exactly lead to nowhere, can it? Besides, Rudy said the castle was around here, and he seemed honest to a fault.'

There was a flash in the sky. The dwarf and the halfling were lit up green, looking like two ghouls stalking the rocky mire of the Krovanian lowlands, hunting for flesh. Ahead of them, a structure appeared on the outcrop for just a moment, as if the lightning had brought it into existence. Rhev was certain it hadn't been there before. He nudged Sterling and pointed towards the building, now appearing more solid as green lightning continued to rage.

After a trudge up the steep western face of the

144

outcropping they reached level ground. About a hundred yards ahead was a dark castle, classically foreboding. It was the sort of castle you don't accept dinner invitations to.

'So what I say is that we storm it. I've always wanted to storm a castle. I feel it's the sort of thing that adventurers do, right?' Rhev was clearly quite excited. He pummelled his hands together slowly, readying them for action.

'We can't storm a castle! By Ava, Rhev, are you sloshed or what?'

Rhev stifled a hiccup in reply. It would be a lie to say the bottomless ale hadn't gotten him at least a little tipsy, *but what was the harm in that?* He certainly couldn't recall a time, at this particular moment at least, when booze had led to anything bad. The fire in his belly was as comforting as ever.

Sterling continued, 'There's only two of us, and it looks like the sort of castle that has a lot of halberds lying around everywhere. Besides, I much prefer using my words. It's more my style. I think the best plan is for us to knock calmly, request to talk to Lady Varylla, and tell her what her daughter has done. I'm sure she'll make her give the Box back. It's not like the nobility are in the habit of stealing.'

'The baron of Velheim quite literally stole his title from the last baron. So he basically stole a whole city. And probably lots of boxes too.'

'Alright, alright, but that's *Velheim*. That sort of thing is expected there.' Rhev looked at Sterling with a wary eye. 'From the nobility! It's expected from the nobility... in Velheim,' Sterling added hastily.

'Alright, alright. Your problem, your solution. Lead the way.'

They hurried to the entrance of the castle. In front of them was an impractically tall door made from blackened wood and blacker iron. A large and ornate knocker hung there, asking to be used.

'Come on then,' said the knocker with a sneer. 'Give us a go. Or are you too afraid? Is the idea of willingly inviting doom into your lives too much for your little hearts? And I do say little of course, because look at you! If you were stacked on top of each other you'd barely fill out an overcoat!'

Sterling and Rhev looked at each other in consternation. Then Rhev pointed at something to the side of the door. It was a chain that hung down the wall, its upper end disappearing into a hole in the brickwork. Sterling shrugged and went over to the chain. He pulled hard. Inside, a bell could be heard ringing sweetly.

'No! No, no, no, don't use the bell! Use me you cowards. You're probably just too weak to lift my immense weight. No-one is strong enough or brave enough to ring the knocker! You are one of a long line of pathetic bell ringers, and you will be consigned to history as such.' The knocker went on and on like this while Rhev slowly raised his middle finger at what he guessed was its face.

The door opened, so very, very slowly. A face peered through the crack. Bright blue eyes framed by half moon spectacles pierced the gloom, flicking between the dwarf and the halfling. Suddenly, the door was swung the rest of the way open. In the frame stood a short man with wild white hair and a welcoming grin on his face.

'Visitors, oh my! Please come in out of the wet, you poor things.'

Bemused, Rhev and Sterling did as they were bid.

'Please let me take you cloaks. By the gods you could wring these out and fill a pond!'

Rhev and Sterling shrugged their cloaks off and looked at each other, both trying to discern what the other was thinking.

'I do hope the knocker didn't give you any trouble. It's been terribly rude lately, even more so now that we've

146

installed the bell pull. He pines for the days when all thuds were booming and accompanied by lightning, I'm afraid. Now, I'm assuming you two gentleman are here for the taxes.'

'No,' said Sterling quickly.

'Yes,' said Rhev, even quicker.

'Sorry, is that a yes or a no? I'm aware that we owe quite a bit for the turret tax and I wouldn't like to get in trouble with the duke.'

'How very... noble of you, sir,' Rhev replied, giving Sterling a quick wink as he did so. 'We are indeed here to collect the tax you owe the duke. My name is... Blev, and this is my associate...Berling.'

'Pleased to meet you,' Sterling said, and he bowed hesitantly.

'No no, it is *my* pleasure. My name is Victor, but of course you will already know that from your records!'

'Yes, indeed. Nonetheless, it is *my* pleasure to meet *you*, Victor. Now sir, may I ask that you take my associate to your coffers for the tallying forthwith?' asked Blev the tax collector. 'In the meantime, may I be permitted to use your privy?'

'Certainly Mister Blev! Up the stairs, first on your right. Come this way Mister Berling. The coffers are in the basement.'

The group divided. Rhev hurried up the stairs, while Sterling went with their hospitable host down to the lower floors. Rhev couldn't believe his luck. If all went to plan, he might be able to find the Box while Sterling filled his pockets with gold in reparations without ever having to run into the infamous Lady Varylla or her daughter, Mina. Now surely *that* was the sort of story worthy of a book.

'Rylla!' The voice of their host echoed off the dark stone walls of the castle. 'We have visitors!'

A heavily accented voice called out from somewhere in the upper levels.

'Oh joy! Thank you for letting me know Victor!' It was dripping with sarcasm.

This must surely be the horrible woman who Rudy so despised. To so publicly air her contempt for guests while they were in earshot signalled to Rhev that they were dealing with a person who lived wholly outside the rules of the social contract. A true monster. He would have to keep his wits about him.

The upper levels were decorated in much the same manner as the entrance hall. Abundant dark red carpet and wall hangings, polished wood, and portraits of very white people. It was opulent, but the presence of the cold, black stone that lay behind all the soft furnishings and tapestries was oppressive. You simply couldn't escape it.

Rhev began to open all the doors that he passed, as quietly as he could for fear of alerting that foul lady of his presence. The upper rooms were mostly full of what Rhev would regard as junk: beds that were very wide and very short, pillows so heavily embroidered that they looked to be more thread than stuffing, and a few polished wooden chairs that seemed to suit the sort of person with a very tall spine and little to no arse. Any boxes in the room were always found at the foot of the beds, and were of the oak and iron variety. No sign of telltale blue whorls.

After more than ten rooms, Rhev stopped and took stock. Perhaps his plan wasn't a particularly good one after all. He had left Sterling in the lurch and in the hands of a gentleman that could at any moment realise that Sterling was not a tax collector, and then he may not be very gentle at all. Rhev was now aimlessly searching through empty rooms while a mysterious and no doubt dangerous woman hounded his footsteps. *Think, you stupid dwarf. It was the lady's daughter who took the box. Where would a young woman living with her parents hide stolen goods?* He racked his brains for the answer, and it was not long before it came to him. *Under their own bed!*

The dwarf made a beeline for the next set of stairs leading upwards, having exhausted all the rooms on the first floor. *People at the top, live at the top*, he reasoned. Surely the daughter of a Lady would sleep in the tallest tower, away from potential suitors and, most of all, her parents. Rhev grabbed the central pillar of the spiral staircase and swung himself up there at quite a speed.

***

'By the way, please don't call me Victor. My wife only uses that name because she knows it irks me. Vic is perfectly adequate, or Doc, if you prefer that sort of thing.'

The kindly man had been making pleasant chit chat with Sterling, or Berling as he was now known, as they picked their way through the dimly lit basement of the castle. All Sterling had been thinking was: *when it comes to castles, what exactly is the difference between a basement and a dungeon*. He definitely wasn't on board with whatever crazy plan Rhev had pushed him into. He had caught on to the idea that he would soon, presumably, have his pockets brimming with gold coins from Victor's coffers, but he was still turning over the morality of it in his head. It's not like Sterling was particularly fond of the idea that landed gentry hoarded their wealth and kept it from the hands of the hard working man in the field. He prided himself on his egalitarian sensibilities, that's for certain. You had to be a populist if you wanted to maintain an air of easy charisma as Sterling did. On the other hand, Victor seemed like such a nice guy, and *he* wasn't the one that had done the stealing. Besides, he was certain that Mina's theft had been some sort of mistake. *It had to be,* he thought. *She was too lovely.*

'Here we are, Mister Berling,' said Victor with a keen smile. 'I had actually done the estimates myself earlier this year and put aside the amount we owed. I know, I'm a boring old fart!'

He gestured to a very, very large sack with the sort of knobbly bulge that only a sack bursting with over a thousand coins can have. Sterling gulped.

'But of course, you'll be wanting to count it all out before you take it back to the treasury. Once you're done we can compare numbers, eh? Make sure everything is in order. I wouldn't want you to have to trudge all the way up here again.'

Sterling nodded absently, unable to take his eyes from the wealth in front of him.

'Oh goodness, I almost forgot!' Victor crouched so that he could look into Sterling's eyes. Sterling's heart jumped. He could feel those blue irises boring into his skull. The older man whispered conspiratorially. 'You know what you deserve, Mister Berling?'

***

'What do you think you're doing up here?'

The voice belonged to a woman who had obviously never experienced self-doubt, anxiety, fear, or any emotion that would have given her cause to think that she was anything but infallible. The effect was amplified by the fact that she had exceptional skin and hair, so exceptional that Rhev felt it was rather condescending. She stood now at the top of the stairs he had been so carelessly barrelling up. The dwarf had been sure her voice had not come from this part of the castle earlier, but it seemed his ears had betrayed him.

'I was looking for the privy,' he replied lamely.

'Then you weren't looking very hard, were you? The privy is back the way you must have come, at the top of the first flight of stairs. I imagine you must be quite desperate by now, Mister...?'

'Rhev- err, Blev. Mister Blev. I am here for the... the taxes,' he stumbled.

150

'Oh thank goodness you're here for the taxes,' the lady replied, sarcasm yet again dripping from her words like a wet rag hung out to dry. It made Rhev's skin crawl. 'I thought the duke would never get around to leeching from me.'

Rhev made no reply. He thought it best to not get into a conversation regarding the duke's unfair economic policies. He wasn't even sure who the duke was.

'Here, follow me Mister Blev.'

The imposing woman forced Rhev into a crevice as she walked past him. Rhev took a searching look up the stairs onto the next floor, and then thought better of disobeying Lady Varylla. She waited impatiently at the bottom of the stairs.

'Come on. We wouldn't want you to soil yourself, would we?'

Rhev began to laugh politely, but the unamused glance Varylla shot him made him think that it wasn't a joke.

'You're rather heavily armed for a tax collector. I didn't realise it was such a dangerous occupation.'

A cold sweat washed over Rhev. *The sword.* He had forgotten about his sword. It was impossible to miss really. Come to think of it, he was surprised the old man hadn't mentioned it.

'Then again, I don't suppose you exactly make many friends in your line of work. Quite sensible to make a show of being able to defend yourself, even if you don't know how to use that thing. Here is the privy.'

She gestured to a noticeably smaller door than the rest. It was indeed at the top of the stairs. Rhev bowed awkwardly and went inside. It was a modest affair, but then again castles aren't exactly known for their plumbing. He sat on the bench, trousers still on, and waited. The more he waited the more he got the horrible impression that Lady Varylla hadn't moved an inch. *What kind of person stands outside the privy door while their guest does their business? Was she listening to make sure he didn't steal the toilet seat? Did she need to do her business too? Weren't there other toilets she could use. Go away!* Rhev had never felt more uncomfortable. He began to think it might be better if he just de-trousered and tried to force something out. Eventually, he resorted to the only power of communication left to someone bound to the seat of a toilet that is not their own; he coughed.

'Are you quite done, Mister Blev?' came the reply.

He couldn't believe it. Not only had she implicitly admitted that she was standing right outside the door, but she was now implying that Rhev's evacuations were not timely enough. *She really is a monster!*

'Aye, quite done... thank you. Just a minute.' Rhev made a point of loudly adjusting his belt and splashing some water in the sink.

When he came out Lady Varylla stared at him like she was judging him for a non-existent stink. For a moment Rhev was worried that he *had* left a stink. Perhaps she could just smell the fear.

'My husband referred to visitors, plural. I assume your companion is another tax collector?'

'Yes, Mister Berling,' he replied warily.

'*Mister Berling.*' Her lip curled as she said it. 'And he will no doubt be down with the coffers. Since you have already proven yourself inept at navigating this castle without entering places you don't belong, I will escort you there.'

She set off briskly, and Rhev saw no alternative but to follow her. It wasn't long before they crossed paths with Victor.

'Oh hello darling,' he said with a start, his eyes still adjusting from the darkness of the basement. 'I see you've found our other guest, Mister Blev. Did you find the privy all right, Mister Blev?'

152

Rhev looked at Varylla briefly before answering, 'Yes, I did sir, thanks to the lady here.' He gave a deferential bow to her.

'Excellent, excellent. Your colleague Mister Berling has already begun the tallying I believe. I was just popping off to get him some hot cocoa. It looked so terribly cold out there in the rain. Would *you* like a hot cocoa, Mister Blev?'

Varylla answered before Rhev could say anything.

'Who said you could offer them hot cocoa, Victor? Whose money buys the cocoa, Victor? Do you even realise how expensive cocoa is? Come, Mister Blev, you've work to do.'

The atmosphere became so highly charged that Victor's wild hair seemed to stick out even further. Without allowing Victor time to answer any of her questions, Varylla continued down the steps into the basement, Rhev in tow. They found Sterling sitting on the floor methodically counting out coins into little stacks. Their sudden arrival out of the gloom of the corridor made him knock over some of the stacks. His eyes grew wide in despair. This was not the first time this had happened.

'Mister Berling, I presume? I am Lady Varylla, but I'm sure you already know that from your records. Please, don't let me keep you and Mister Blevington from your hard work.' She took a seat on a chest nearby. Then, quite deliberately, she crossed her legs. placed her hands together on her knee, and watched.

Rhev sat next to Sterling, making a point to avert his eyes from the stern woman sitting across from them.

'So, Mister Berling, is everything in order? Are we ready to take this back to the duke?' he asked, slowly.

'Yes, Mister Rhev- Mister Blev, I've almost finished counting out the tax. Did you... conduct your business upstairs satisfactorily?' Sterling asked in reply, his eyebrows raised high in implication. Varylla leant forward, putting her chin in her hands, and smiled. Rhev caught her gaze momentarily and looked away.

'The business was not as satisfactory as I had hoped, Mr Berling. Must have been that suspicious mutton we had for lunch.'

'Oh dear,' replied Sterling, not sure where to go from here. 'That's... not good.'

There was a rapid clip-clopping of house slippers on flagstones.

'Gentlemen!' said Victor, cutting through the rapidly thickening atmosphere. 'I've just realised that it's time for our evening meal, and I must insist that you join us.'

He beamed at them. Varylla's perfect skin cracked as she scowled at her husband. Victor caught her eye and, for a second, his smile turned into a smirk.

'We still have some counting to do,' said Rhev, thinking quickly, 'and we wouldn't want to impose.'

'Quite right, it wouldn't be proper for these men to join us at the dinner table. They're on duty, after all,' said Varylla.

'Nonsense! These are representatives of the duke of Krovania, and we shall serve them as such. Come, my friends.'

Neither of the would-be fraudsters moved until Victor forcefully lifted them from the floor and ushered them from the castle's vault. Varylla seethed behind them.

Rhev and Sterling allowed themselves to drop back from Victor so as to whisper out of his earshot. 'What's the plan now, Rhev? Even if we get out of here with a fat sack of coins, *we still need the Box*. I think all this skullduggery has gotten a bit out of hand, too much for even my charm to fix.'

'I know, I know!' Rhev replied, his voice dangerously close to being audible to Varylla, who was now only a few steps behind. 'Keep calm. I've got myself out of stickier spots than this. I'll come up with something over dinner.'

Sterling grimaced. With a face like his, he was always going to be the marketing guy; he left the logistics up to Steem or Mercy. Although he did like him, he wasn't so sure that the dwarf could match their planning capabilities. Maybe it had been a mistake to follow his lead.

The dining room was decorated with the same unique brand of oppressive chic as the rest of the castle. Dark polished wood, dark red velvet drapes and table runners, and paintings so imposing that the subjects seemed to be dining with them as well. The chairs were set up awkwardly. Two high-backed elaborate affairs sat at either end of the long table. Three more chairs were set up at the centre of the long table, two on one side and one on the other. The Lady and the Doctor clearly didn't get many dinner guests.

Rhev and Sterling hiked themselves up onto the high seated chairs at the centre of the table, both their legs dangling ungainly. Varylla took a seat at one end of the table, slowly and with grace, and Victor took the seat at the other end. A suffocating silence ensued.

'Will Mina be joining us?' Varylla asked, nodding towards the single empty chair.

The two interlopers froze simultaneously, then slowly turned to look at each other with panic in their eyes. Sterling mouthed the name 'MINA'.

'I'm not sure Rylla, I'm sure she'll be down at some point. You know what she's like, she'll probably only want desert or something.' Realising that his guests presumably did not know who Mina was, Victor continued: 'Mina is our daughter, by the way. She's an adult but she still lives at home with mum and dad, you see. Lovely girl, takes after her mother in the looks department, but a little rebellious, I'm sure she wouldn't mind me saying. I really do hope you meet her.'

'If she's anything like her mother,' Rhev replied carefully, 'I cannot wait to meet her.'

155

Varylla let out a quick exhale that could have been interpreted as either amusement or annoyance. Then she picked up a little silver bell from the table and rang it.

Without much of a pause, someone new entered the dining room carrying a platter. Then another, and another, and another. Whoever were carrying the platters were small, smaller than Sterling. Rhev couldn't see underneath the platters to get a good view of any of them. *Are they gnomes?* The thought crossed his mind but it would be very unlikely; gnomes were feral and certainly couldn't be trusted with cutlery. *Then what are they?*

His question was soon answered. The last of the mysterious figures came into the dining room carrying a small step ladder. It placed it carefully at one end of the table. And then, one by one in an orderly fashion, the creatures climbed the steps with their platters in hand and mounted the table. They were, to be frank, quite horrible. Twisted little green things with bulging eyes and hands that you wouldn't want touching you. In a way they resembled goblins, about half the size and about half the charm, which was saying a lot. Each one had some sort of large growth on part of their body. The growths resembled vestigial body parts; extra toes or fingers, sometimes whole feet. What made these growths even more unsettling was their size; they were at least twice the size of what they should have been, and some of the poor wretches were quite unbalanced by them. Rhev and Sterling gawped as they proceeded to walk down the table and unload their platters in the appropriate places. Rhev couldn't help himself.

'What are they?' he asked, still staring at the monstrous parade.

'Wonderful, aren't they?' Victor replied. 'These little beauties are my latest project. I call them goblobs. Easy to produce, easy to train, surprisingly obedient.'

Rhev saw that the nearest goblob looked quite vacant

156

behind its bulging eyes.

'I'm hoping they will be my magnum opus. In five, maybe ten years, I'll be able to roll them out across the Peninsula. Everyone will have a goblob in their home!'

'I'm sure they can't wait,' said Sterling, who looked a little sick.

'Of course, they're not perfected,' continued Victor. Rhev and Sterling let out an audible sigh of relief.

'Of course,' Rhev encouraged.

'Yes, yes, I still need to work out how to make them a more pinkish skin tone. I don't think green will go down well in a lot of households. Stereotyping is such a terrible thing.'

One of the goblobs let out a noise that sounded like a baby drooling bubbles as it placed a plate of roasted potatoes in front of Sterling. He closed his eyes and threw up in his mouth a little, and didn't open them again until he was sure all the goblobs had got off the table and left the room. 'Victor,' said Varylla in an icy tone, 'nobody wants to hear about your disgusting little pets. Now please shut up so we can eat.'

Everyone began eating at a different pace. Victor ate enthusiastically, spearing parsnips and cuts of beef left, right, and centre. Once the morsels were on his plate, he prepared them for his mouth with the precision of a surgeon, filleting and dicing and so forth. Varylla ate much more slowly but no less deliberately. Each piece of meat that met her lips was savoured for all it was worth, and it was only meat that she savoured. Rhev and Sterling ate like two people who weren't supposed to be eating at all: only guilt-free leafy greens for them. Between mouthfuls the two of them communicated quietly.

'We're eating dinner now. What's your plan?' asked Sterling urgently.

'We're going back to the original plan,' Rhev replied.

'Wait, you don't mean–'

'Yeah. We storm the castle. The great thing is that we're inside, so we've done the hard part already. Now we've just got to clear it-'

'You don't mean *kill them*? We can't kill them. Victor's really nice.'

'Everything alright gents?' Victor managed through mouthfuls. 'You're not vegetarian are you? Ha!'

As the sounds of his scoffing resumed, so did the whispered conversation.

'Okay, maybe we just bop them on the head, tie them up, that sort of thing. *Hold them hostage,*' said Rhev with an arch of his eyebrow, as if this was an inspired solution.

'What about Varylla?' replied Sterling nervously.

'What *about* Varylla?'

'She doesn't seem the sort to just lay down when you ask her to.'

'Look, she may be a monster of a person, but she's just that, a person. I'll flash the steel, and she'll do what she's told. Besides, she deserves what's coming to her. She listened to me do a fake poo.' Sterling didn't know how to react to that.

'Alright, alright,' Sterling conceded. 'I'll wait for your mark.'

Rhev looked first at Victor, then at Varylla. To his surprise, she was staring right at him as she placed another cube of rare sirloin in her mouth. He faltered for a second, and then resolved.

'Right!' he shouted as he climbed up onto his chair. 'I'm sorry to announce we are not tax collectors.'

Both Victor and Varylla stopped eating.

'So you're not here to take our money?' said Victor.

'Erm- well, no. I mean, maybe. It's not top of our list though.'

'That's a shame.' Rhev honestly couldn't tell if he wanted the money gone or not.

'Then what have you come for?' asked Varylla impatiently.

'Your daughter has stolen a very important box from us, and we've come to get it back.'

'Why didn't you just say that when you arrived?'

'Well, we, erm…'

'Is it because my cretinous husband took you for tax collectors and you thought you could get away with the levy yourselves? Like a couple of opportunistic rogues?'

'It was his idea,' Sterling mumbled. He remained seated, looking at his potatoes.

'How shameful, gentlemen,' said Victor scornfully. 'I'm very disappointed, especially in you Mister Berling. I judged you for a man with more sense and backbone than to go along with a shoddy plan such as this."

'It's Sterling, actually.'

Victor dropped his cutlery on his plate and threw his hands up in the air in despair.

'Hang on, *we're* not in the wrong here. It was *your* daughter who stole from us in the first place,' Rhev said, exasperated. This wasn't how storming a castle was supposed to go, he knew that much. At the very least Victor could have gotten out a couple of halberds.

'I don't doubt it,' Varylla replied coolly. 'Mina is a free spirit, she does what she wants. *And* she is an adult. Victor and I are not responsible for whatever crimes she's allegedly committed. Now Mister Blev, or whatever your name is, please sit back down. You're both far too short to storm a castle, or whatever you think all *this* is."

Rhev remained standing on his chair. 'You are just the worst person.'

'Am I, Mister Blev?'

'Yes! And it's Rhev!' With that fierce proclamation, Rhev unsheathed his sword from the scabbard slung on his back. It

159

sang as it came free, and the word engraved on its blade caught the candlelight.

'Mister Rhev, you really should put that thing away,' said Victor in a worried tone.

'That's what you would want me to do, but why should I? Now both of you, get up and take us to Mina.'

He held his sword out with both hands, swinging it back and forth between Varylla and Victor at either end of the table.

'Oh dear,' said Varylla in mock fear, 'the dwarf has unsheathed his weapon. Whatever are we to do?'

Out of nowhere, her tone changed to one deep and dark and terrible. 'If you're showing me yours, I'll show you mine.'

She stood up impossibly fast. One moment she was seated, the next she was standing. There was no inbetween. Then she opened her mouth. Wider, and wider, and wider. Her jaw unhinged like a cobra's and from her upper jaw two stiletto incisors grew to almost a foot in length. Next, her fingernails extended, growing cruel and pointed. They danced together and clashed menacingly. Rhev froze, his sword outstretched in front of him in a defensive position. Sterling stood up from his seat purely out of fear.

'Rylla, please, there's no need for that' said Victor hysterically. 'Not in the house! This was supposed to be a nice, civilised dinner. I don't even care that they're thieves, or brigands, or whatever they are. Mister Rhev, please put your weapon down, and we can sort this out by talking, like *gentlemen*.'

Varylla sneered at her husband. It was a grotesque movement.

Rhev knew he was no match for whatever this thing was. He was fairly tasty with a blade, but only when the person he was fighting had conventional weaponry. As far as he could count, Lady Varylla had five daggers on each hand and two

160

coming out of her face. Velheim was a dunghole, but at least you never met someone in an alley who could hold more than two weapons at a time.

Sterling patted him on the leg. 'Come on, Rhev, put it down. Let's talk. Please.'

Against every instinct and bad habit in his body, Rhev decided to put the sword down. He tried to put the sword down. He really did.

'I'm trying to put it down,' he said aloud.

'Great, then do it,' said Sterling, encouragingly. 'We just want to talk, don't we? No need to get into a fight.'

'Yup,' replied Rhev. 'No fighting, just talking. Civil. Let me just put this down.'

He really couldn't put it down. Then the blade began vibrating very, very quickly. Flash.

'UNHOLY SPAWN. TAINTED BLOODFIEND. SHADOWDWELLER AND SHIRKER OF AVA'S GRACE.'

The rich soprano filled the room. It lifted the cobwebs and stoked the fire. It had come from the sword, and the sword continued.

'I SHALL SPILL BLOOD AND THE BLOOD WILL BE THAT OF THE UNCLEAN.'

'Rhev, are you saying that?' asked Sterling in a loud whisper.

'No, I'm not. I think it's the sword.'

'IT IS TIME TO STRIKE DOWN THIS ABOMINATION.'

Varylla and Victor looked on in disbelief.

'It's not me,' said Rhev nervously. 'It's the sword. This hasn't happened before. It's not supposed to talk.'

'I CANNOT SLEEP WHILE TRUE EVIL WAKES.'

The sword flashed again and leapt about in Rhev's grip. His whole body was pulled along by the hilt.

'Stop it!' Rhev wailed.

Varylla made an inhuman noise that grew in intensity as

161

Rhev edged closer and closer along the floor towards her, dragged by the sword. The blade started moving in short, stilted bursts, performing thrusts and parries in the air.

'Rhev just drop it!' shouted Sterling as he raced after his compatriot.

'I can't!'

It was true. Try as he might he found he couldn't release the sword from his grasp. It moved inexorably towards its target, and all Rhev could do was follow it like a bound prisoner. He was moments away from making fatal contact with Varylla's lethal claws.

'NOT. IN. THE HOUSE.'

Victor's voice echoed louder than Rhev had thought imaginable. Truly, there is nothing more fearful than the anger of a gentle man. All eyes turned to the demure man with his half moon spectacles. They were fogging up from the heat of his face.

'I'm sorry gentlemen, but you've really forced my hand.' He sighed. 'Be comforted in the knowledge that you will be a great help to my work.'

He strode over to a painting with an ornate gilded frame. The carving around its edge was replete with classical *fleurs* and bunches of bobbles that were probably grapes. He surveyed the scene once more, carefully, and then reached out and pressed two of the bobbles. The flagstones immediately beneath Rhev and Sterling disappeared, and gravity played its part.

***

'Oh thank Ava, dry land!'

Hampton tottered along the gangplank onto the docks of Falstyr Point. The eponymous point, a white cliffed crag topped by a gleaming castle, was like a ship in a sea of muck. The stench of fish and refuse lapping at its feet ever threatened to stain the homes of the isolated nobility high

162

above.

'Hampton!' screech Beckett. 'Just because we are no longer in Dankvyr does not mean that you are released from your duties as my assistant! Come back here and carry my luggage!'

As he said this a rogue wave buffeted the vessel that they had called home for the last week. The sight of the deck rising and falling was enough to strike terror back into Hampton's heart. He turned bright green.

'I'll get your bags, Mister Beckett,' said Manu, the broad fisherfolk now in the financier's employ. He gave a slight nod at the stricken Hampton, which was returned in kind.

Once all their possessions were safely evacuated from the ship, the motley group of three began their journey through the bustling streets of Falstyr Point. If it weren't for the gently guiding hand of the towering Manu, Hampton would have quickly become lost in the forest of thick set elves.

'I will charter us passage up the river tomorrow morning,' announced Beckett to his two employees. 'For now, we shall find accommodation. Manu, we have established that you are a well travelled man. Perhaps you can point us in the direction of an inn that doesn't stink to high heaven of halibut.'

'This, I can be doing,' the fisherfolk replied, 'but if you are wanting to be avoiding the smell of fish, we are walking a long way. Even then, you cannot be avoiding the halibut. Please, be following.'

He was right. The halibut reigned supreme in the Point. Statues and banners of leaping halibut, a notoriously flat and un-acrobatic fish, lined the rotten streets. It seemed that most people had had enough of their city's patron fish. Many of the statues had been defaced with sticks of chalk and charcoal. To the left, a halibut wearing a monocle. To the right, a halibut with an ostentatiously twiddly moustache. Somebody had placed a dunce hat on top of a particularly hard to reach statue, an act that must have been achieved by someone either incredibly acrobatic, or incredibly fed up with all the halibut.

'Where are these people's civic pride?' questioned Beckett, never one to like seeing a monument defaced. 'Surely the halibut is their lifeblood. Why do they hate it so much?'

'They are having good reason,' replied Manu over his shoulder.

'The goggly eyes, is it?' mused Hampton.

'It is more… political. These people can only be catching the halibut. It is illegal to be catching any other fish. The market is saturating, too much halibut. Now the people work, work, work, for less and less coin.'

'Why on earth is it illegal to catch anything other than halibut?' scoffed Beckett. 'That can't be right.'

'It is pride,' said Manu. He pointed to the glittering crag above them. 'The rulers of this city see the halibut as their own creature, their symbol. They are wanting to be the only city that catches the halibut, and now they are making it so.'

Manu shook his head. 'People with power to control are controlling for its own sake, even if it is not making sense. It is hurting these people.'

As his boss was distracted by yet enough graffitied halibut, this one bearing the words 'Hali-*butt*' and little stink lines, Hampton spotted something rather curious. A fishing line and hook descended with deft precision between himself and Manu, and then flicked over onto Beckett's money purse, which had been strung over the fisherfolk's shoulder.

'Um, Manu…?' said Hampton, his brow furrowed.

The fisherfolk stopped and turned around. 'Yes my friend?'

As he turned around the money purse detached from his broad shoulder and ascended, accompanied by a tinny *whrrr* sound.

'Oh, dear.' Hampton froze. 'Sir? Sir! Mister Beckett! The

money is getting away!'

'Nonsense, Hampton, money doesn't have a mind of it's-by Ava! Get back here!'

The coin purse continued to float jerkily up towards the rooftops. Beckett, Hampton, and Manu followed its trajectory until they saw the culprit: a lanky elf bearing a woven tapestry of scars. In his hand he held a fishing rod, and in a few more seconds he would also be holding a weighty purse.

The sight of the last of his liquid assets in the hands of a ruffian from Falstyr Point was too much for Beckett to bear.

'Both of you, retrieve my money now! And bring me that man. I'll see him in the stocks, mark my words!'

Both Manu and Hampton were hesitant. Hampton, because he really wasn't very good at chasing, and Manu, because he didn't really care for Beckett one iota.

'Nowww!' continued Beckett. 'Or none of us are leaving this putrid city!'

That did it. Hampton and Manu set off, the fisherfolk taking the easy lead. Their quarry wasn't difficult to spot; his rod stood straight up like a standard, bobbing along the rooftops to their right.

'I think we need to get higher,' suggested Hampton in between mouthfuls of air.

'There!' shouted Manu.

He pointed to a cargo net that was in the process of being repaired. It was hung down the side of a building from the top floor. Without a word of warning Manu picked Hampton up like a bag of groceries and began leaping up the net with practiced grace. Then he flung the little assistant above him onto the pitch of the roof and pulled himself up after.

They could see the thief a few rooftops over. It became obvious by the way he moved over the tiles that he knew every inch of this domain, and would be almost impossible to catch in a straight chase.

165

'Sack him Hampton!' said Manu.

'I don't have the authority!' Hampton replied.

'No, my friend. Montefort variant!'

'Oh, I see!'

The Montefort variant was, of course, a rare variation of the classic sack toss game that replaced the hole at the end of the ramp with your opponent's body. Much like the Velheimnian variant, it was regarded as less civilised than the standard game, but that hadn't stopped Hampton reading a lot of books about it.

Hampton fished out his prized sack, weighted especially for his compact musculature, and proceeded to take aim.

'Quickly, my friend, he is getting away!'

'Now, now, Manu, what did I say? Most of the game is when you *don't* toss the sack.'

When it seemed like the thief was most definitely out of range, Hampton launched the sack with surprising sluggishness. It skimmed across the tiles, *accumulating* speed as if by magick, before reaching its intended target. A faint *hurk* echoed over the slates.

'You are truly the master of sack toss, my friend.'

'I hope not, the games would be too one sided!'

They watched as the thief, now stunned, keeled over and slid down the rooftop and off the edge.

'Oh dear...' said Hampton.

After a few minutes of carefully picking their way over loose tiles and down the side of a ramshackle building, they found the thief. Miraculously, he had landed on a pile of surplus halibut. Hampton bent down to retrieve the purse lying next to him.

'Are you alright? I didn't mean to knock you off the roof,' he said apologetically.

'Wassat?' said the thief, a little woozy.

'Can you stand? I'm afraid we have to walk you back to

our employer to face, erm, justice.'

'Up you are getting,' said Manu as he hooked his thick mitts under the thief's armpits and hauled him to his feet, transferring his grip to the man's wrists as soon as he was standing. Now vertical, the felon came to his senses.

'Please sir, I'm sorry about what I has done. I got no other choice, you muss understand! I don't think I can handle any more justice.'

The elf's face really was the most awful criss-cross of scar tissue. Tears began to run in zig zags down his cheeks, following the scars like wonky guttering.

'I has got a family, sir.'

Hampton didn't like seeing people cry. It made him cry too.

'Now, now, none of that, we can talk. What is your name?'

The thief hesitated.

'Montague Wollingsworth.'

Hampton tutted reproachfully.

'If we're going to have an honest conversation about this, we need to be honest with each other. My name is Hampton, and the gentleman behind you is Manu. And your name is…'

Montague Wollingsworth looked at the ground and muttered: 'Rodney.'

'Right, Rodney, what's all this about not having a choice? One can always choose not to thieve.'

'Not true, sir, not true.'

Manu tightened his grip, making Rodney flinch pathetically.

'Not a good time to be calling Mister Hampton a liar. Speak your truth.'

'I am, sir, honest!' whimpered Rodney. 'I have to thieve now. I didn't use to though sir, oh no. I used to be a good, honest fisherman.'

'Now, I can believe that. You handled that rod very

167

preciesly. You must be a master of your craft, Rodney,' said Hampton with an encouraging smile.

'Yes sir, I was... I am! But the markets, they're so chock full of halibut, I was making barely enough to keep my baby fed. So I started fishing for salmon. Lots of money to be made on the black market with salmon. A much more attractive fish, but illegal, you understand. I got ratted out by some of the other fishermen, got locked up by the city guard. They wanted me to rat on the black market, but I wouldn't do it sir. Ten months, stuck in that cell. Each time I refused to rat on the other salmon fishermen, I got a new mark on my skin.'

'I'm sorry you had to go through that, Rodney. It sounds very unfair,' said Hampton. 'But you're not telling us why you absolutely *had* to steal from our employer.'

'Sorry sir, yes, you're right. I just wanted you to know the full story, is all. When I got out of the tanty, I couldn't get any work fishing. I was banned from all the markets, overground and underground, and if I even set foot in as much as a dinghy, I'm fish bait. I needed money real desperate like, so I took a loan off this fella. Long story short, it was a right rotten deal. Now I'm stuck working for him as a pickpocket, and if I don't, it's fish bait for me *and* my family.'

'So you're saying that you're stealing under duress?'

Rodney nodded enthusiastically.

'I am smelling a stink, and it is not the halibut,' said Manu gravely. 'What if this man is telling tales? Thievery is a bad thing. Bad people are doing it. They are deserving punishment.'

'My dear friend Manu, sometimes things are not so black and white. I know you know this as well. Bad things can be done for good reasons.'

Hampton smiled sadly at Manu, and then took a good, hard look at Rodney's pocked, tear stricken face.

'And I think here we have a man who did a bad thing for a

168

good reason.'

He took three coins out of the purse, and offered them to the thief.

'Let him go, Manu.'

'What about Beckett?' the fisherfolk replied.

'I'll handle it.'

Manu let Rodney's hands slip from his own. The reluctant thief took the coins carefully from Hampton. He slipped them one by one into a pocket, all the while looking the little assistant dead in the eye, in case it was some sort of ruse.

'Off you go, Rodney. No more stealing for today, eh?' said Hampton.

Lost for words, Rodney nodded hastily and ran down the alleyway and out of sight.

'I am not sure that was the right thing to do,' said Manu.

'You heard his story, didn't you?'

'As I am saying Hampton, he could be telling lies...' There was a lack of conviction in his voice.

'He could, yes. But he may also have been telling the truth. If I'm faced with a choice between believing the best in people rather than the worst, I'd rather take the best. It makes life much more bearable.'

'But even if he is doing this for a good reason, it is still a bad thing. Bad things should be-'

'Punished, yes, I know. But sometimes knowing that you've done the bad thing is punishment enough, and doing the bad thing teaches us how to do the good thing.' Hampton sighed. 'Manu, I apologise if I'm going too far, but I think I know what this is really about. You're still feeling guilty about sticking up for your captain when he got himself involved in something unsavoury. You chose to believe in the best of him, rather than the worst. You didn't know why he did what he did. It might have been for a very good reason. Just like with our Rodney. Which means you did a good thing in protecting him.'

Manu walked alongside Hampton in silence. The little man put a hand on his arm.

'Pity takes strength, if not more than judgement does.'

The fisherfolk's shoulders relaxed. He turned to look Hampton in the eye.

'Thank you, my friend.'

'You quite took your time!' Beckett screeched as he came striding towards them. 'Where's the culprit? The filthy cur who deigned to steal from an innocent man such as myself?'

'He was a slippery customer, I'm afraid, sir,' replied Hampton. 'Must be something in the water, what with all the fish…' Hampton tailed off with a nervous chuckle.

'Useless, the both of you.' Beckett snatched the purse from his assistant, weighing it in his hands quite deliberately. 'If there is as much as a copper piece missing from this purse, it will be coming out of both your salaries.'

'Surely just my salary, sir?' said Hampton. 'The luggage is ultimately my responsibility, yes?'

Beckett looked surprised. 'My my, Hampton, taking responsibility for a change. I thought I would never see the day. Very well, on your head be it.'

Beckett threw the purse over to his assistant and motioned for Manu to pick up the luggage he had left behind before chasing after Rodney.

'Hurry up Manu and get us to a suitable inn,' Beckett demanded. 'Try not to hand over the rest of my belongings to any other thieves while you're at it.'

Manu simply nodded and began marching up the steady incline towards an area of the city some distance from the estuary. Hampton joined him at the head of their procession, while Beckett busied himself turning his nose up at so many sights and smells that it threatened to fall off his face.

'You do not have to be sharing the blame, my friend,' said

Manu quietly. 'I am not minding losing some pay when he is finding out there is money missing from the purse.'

'Don't you worry about that Manu,' replied Hampton, his voice low and conspiratorial. 'He has no idea how much money is supposed to be in that purse. I'm the one that keeps the books, remember?'

Manu chuckled to himself. 'You are a clever little fellow, my friend. I am not understanding why you work for a man like Beckett.'

Hampton shrugged. 'Beckett & Beckett was ...*is* a very respectable firm, and I'm proud to work there. It's been my whole life. I've never known any different.'

'What if different can be better?'

'We're really throwing around the aphorisms today, aren't we?' Hampton chuckled, and then sighed. 'Sometimes the satisfaction of doing a job well is all a man wants from life. Can't blame someone for... for wanting to hold onto that.'

The Hackneyed Halibut was a pleasant enough inn, situated roughly equidistant from the putrid fishing district and the ivory towers of the ruling elite. The proprietor had been canny enough to invest in incense, succeeding in masking the scent of fish with patchouli at the expense of nearly choking all his guests.

'Do elves not have a sense of smell? How can anyone live like this?' said Beckett through a handkerchief.

'In fact, I believe elves do have a less acute sense of smell than men. An elf I knew once told me that it's Ava's way of balancing out their superior hearing, height, musculature... actually, seems like a pretty good deal to me. Then again, did they invent sack toss? I think not!' joked Hampton.

'You are forgetting to mention the glossy hair,' said Manu, chuckling along.

'Enough!' coughed Beckett. 'Enough about the elves. A dim lot, all of them. You know what elves also didn't invent?

Money. Money doesn't care how glossy your bloody hair is- yes, hello, I would like the smoked halibut with braised turnips please.'

Just when Beckett's diatribe was beginning to veer into some questionable territory, the elven innkeeper arrived at their table to take orders. When he left, an awkward silence fell on the table, and didn't break until after they had all finished their meals.

'Mister Beckett,' began Manu in a very serious tone, 'I am wondering this past week, how are you going to be destroying this box when you are getting it?'

Hampton's breaded halibut almost swam right up out of his stomach there and then.

'Hmmm?' said Beckett, still dabbing fish oils from his lips. 'Destroy?'

This was the conversation that Hampton had desperately hoped Manu would leave alone. He had already been lucky that the fisherfolk hadn't broached the subject on their week long voyage, but now his luck had run out.

When Hampton had gone back to The Blowhole to recruit Manu on Beckett's orders, he had been deliberately vague on the details of his employment. He had explained that Beckett wanted the fisherfolk to come along to confirm that they had secured the right box when the time came, as well as acting as extra muscle. As far as Manu was concerned, this presented a welcome chance to redeem himself in the eyes of his ancestors, to set right the wrong he believed he had been complicit in on the ship by destroying the box. Desperate to keep his job, Hampton had neglected to mention his boss' intention to capture and exploit the box for his own gain, albeit technically diverting it from its original and undoubtedly far more evil purpose.

Manu was about to find out that Hampton had omitted a rather large and important chunk of truth, and Hampton was

172

about to lose a friend and, potentially, his job. Hampton panicked.

'Look out sir!'

He picked up what remained of his boiled halibut and slapped Beckett across the face. His boss was stunned.

'Hampton, you... what possessed you to... insolent little-'

'Gremlin, sir! On your head. Creeping and crawling, would have gone right up your nose, sir.'

'A gremlin? Oh, by Ava...' Beckett began to wretch. 'On me? On my skin? Full of disease and disgusting whimsy.'

He stood up quickly and began brushing and patting his body violently.

'Are there any more? Quick Hampton, are there any more?!'

Hampton made a show of frisking his employer for any remaining imaginary gremlins, pictsies, or galumphs.

'All clear, sir, I think.'

'I was not seeing any gremlins,' said Manu.

'No, no, definitely a gremlin. Covered in its own snot, it was,' said Hampton, nodding his head furiously.

'Damn this city!' cried Beckett. 'Damn these blasted elves! Hampton, please convey my fury to the proprietor. I will be retiring to my quarters to wash this filth from me.'

Beckett stormed upstairs. Manu's attention turned to Hampton, who shifted nervously in his seat.

'Fancy a game of sack toss?'

***

Erin flicked through the records in front of her. She just couldn't believe it. This man, a Mister Umway, had prayed sixty two times in the last year for his failing mushroom farm to yield a sustainable crop, and nothing had been done about it. He'd prayed to Almighty Ava fifty seven times, and to Foonghi, God of Mushrooms, five times. By the look of his profile, Mister Umway was a good man who had rarely asked for anything, be it from his neighbour or from the gods, but his prayers to Ava had gone unanswered. All he had to show for his diligent work was a tiny pile of shiitakes. Erin picked up a smaller, dingier volume, its leaves loose between the covers. Her fingers carefully rifled through the thin pages. *There*! In faded ink it was written that almost fifty years earlier Mister Umway had prayed *once* to Foonghi, and within a week he had been blessed with a threefold growth in his cave farm.

This can't be right. Why was the divine system failing this man? Of course, Mister Umway didn't know that Foonghi was probably working somewhere in the Flora department now, but with Ava's prayer stratification system, surely the mighty god herself should have answered him by now?

'What are you doing?'

The question made her jump. The Table chamber had been empty except for her. She looked up and saw the Flaw Manager, dressed as ever in impeccable white, leaning over her shoulder. The god gave her severe anxiety. His job, after all, was to ensure that their departments were run without the slightest hint of divine imperfection. As far as the Flaw Manger was concerned, gods shouldn't have personality or be fallible in any way, which Erin thought was a little unreasonable. *How long has he been standing there?*

'I was just, erm, cross-checking the prayer asked and prayer answered reports,' she said quietly. She was certain he would spot the deception in her voice.

'Is that so?' he said dully, his low tones burrowing into the base of her neck. 'Then why do you have a pre-conglomeration ledger?'

Naively, Erin quickly slid the volume underneath the other binder, as if that would make the evidence no longer exist. She racked her brains furiously. When she finally answered, she knew her pause had been suspiciously long.

'I must have accidentally grabbed it when I picked the binder up from the library. I think it had slipped between the pages.' Her heart was racing. She had no idea if that had been a good lie or not; she was so unused to telling them.

'I don't believe you.'

Not a good lie then.

'In fact, I don't *like* you.'

Oh dear.

'You have not integrated well, Erin, *Once-God* of Hedgehogs. I have heard reports that you have been questioning the conduct of our divine agents, and the efficiency of the new pantheon. May I remind you that you willingly joined this pantheon? And that you are here to monitor, not to judge? When you question these things, you are questioning Ava herself. That is *Ava*, also, in case you have forgotten, named the All-Mother by her loyal worshippers. The *Almighty.* Remember that, *Erin.*'

With a clean precision, he swiped the old ledger from underneath the binder and tucked it neatly under his arm.

'And you still need to sort out your clothing. You look like you live in a bush.'

***

As Rhev slid ever downwards in what appeared to be a near vertical shaft, he lost all sense of speed, distance, and time. The darkness was beyond pitch. The dwarf had no frame of reference apart from the ever moving smooth stone beneath his buttocks, an uncomfortable feeling in his belly, and the smell of damp. At least his sword had stopped shouting.

This situation continued unchanged for an indeterminate length of time until something new began to tickle at the edge of Rhev's perception. A scream, slowly rising in pitch and volume. Faster and faster it came. Then with a sudden lurch he found himself in a giant basin, a sort of massive funnel with steep edges that was dimly lit from whatever was at the

175

bottom. Almost at the same time as the dwarf started slipping down the funnel, the source of the scream became apparent. Sterling plopped out of another shaft adjacent to Rhev's.

'Arghhh,' he said, very, very loudly.

'Arghhh,' Rhev replied.

Together they slid inexorably towards the light at the bottom of the funnel, gripping each other tightly and continuing their screamed conversation.

Gethin and Grunthry had stopped plinking small pebbles at each other a while ago now. They had resorted to plinking pebbles at their own faces. It required less effort. The goblins had lost track of time some, well, time ago, and had stopped making attempts to escape the iron barred cell. They were beyond elated to see a halfling and a dwarf enter through the ceiling and land on the conveniently placed sacks of flour, or possibly bonemeal. Finally, they had new targets to plink pebbles at.

Rhev let out a long exhalation as his velocity hit zero for the first time in what seemed like forever. He was so pleased it hadn't been terminal. He could feel a new appreciation for being stationary wash over him. Then a pebble hit him in the head.

He turned to see none other than the goblins they had ran into on the Grippen mountain trail. A glimmer of recognition crinkled across the goblins' faces and they began to shuffle backwards.

'Sorry sorry sorry!" Grunthry grovelled.

'He usually misses! He was trying to miss. He didn't mean it!' cried Gethin.

A pebble hit Grunthry on his crooked nose.

'Take your pebble back, stay there, and shut up for a moment,' Rhev said, pointing his chunky finger at the goblins. He turned to Sterling. 'What now?'

'Gods, Rhev, I don't know. We came in here, we tried to

steal from them, then kidnap them, then *your sword insulted them*, and we were put in a dungeon with some goblins. I say we got what we deserved.' He kicked a sack angrily.

'I don't like the way he said "goblins",' whispered Grunthry to his companion.

'The sword part wasn't my idea!' retorted Rhev. 'It's obviously faulty.' He gave it a tap with his knuckle. He was relieved to find it didn't react verbally.

'I am sorry about the other things, though. I got distracted, and greedy, and I just thought that storming the castle was the thing you were supposed to do in this type of situation. It's just like Kevin said, I'm a brutish moron.'

He sagged as he sat down against the damp stone wall at the back of the cell, and buried his thickly bearded face in his hands. Sterling said nothing, and continued to kick the sacks.

A small green hand rested itself on Rhev's shoulder. 'I don't think you're a moron. Grunthry's a proper moron and you don't look as stupid as him.' Grunthy had gone back to quietly plinking pebbles at his own face.

Rhev looked up into Gethin's ugly little green face. His pointed teeth smiled what Rhev assumed was supposed to be a sympathetic smile, but could have been easily mistaken for the last thing a goblin's dinner sees. The dwarf gently removed the goblin's hand.

'Thanks…'

'Gethin.'

'Rhev,' and he pointed at the halfling, 'Sterling.'

'Grunthry,' Gethin replied, pointing at his own compatriot.

'How did you two end up in here then?'

'We got tipped off by another nabber on the road that there was loads of gold here for the nabbing. So we crawled up the privy chute, sneaky-beaky like, except there was this bloke on the lavvy. He asked if we were there to fix the

177

plumbing, so I said "sure, that's us". Clever, right? He took us to the water tank room thing, 'cept we went past the room with all the gold in 'n Grunthry had never actually seen gold before so he went a bit mad 'n started sticking it in his pockets 'n licking it. The bloke musta realised we weren't plumbers 'cos he said "how disappointing, we've been without hot water for weeks, but at least you can comfort yourselves in knowing that you'll be helping a great deal with my work here". Then *woosh*, floor gone, ended up here.' The goblin shrugged. 'Pretty much par for the course for the Nabbers Extraordinaire.'

'Sorry, are you referring to yourselves?' asked Sterling.

'Yep, that's us. We nab, grab, dab...ble in thievery. You know how it is.'

'What about you two?' said Grunthry, after missing his face and losing his pebble.

Rhev and Sterling looked at each other.

'A worryingly similar story to yours,' said Sterling. Rhev grimaced. 'But we weren't supposed to be here to nab anything, not technically anyway. We were stolen *from*, and the thief lives here.'

'They steal gold?' asked Grunthry excitedly.

'No, just a box,' replied Sterling.

The goblins were clearly disappointed. For a while there was just the sound of Grunthry looking for his pebble. Then a troubled thought crossed Rhev's mind.

'You said that Victor told you you'd be helping him with his "work", yeah? Well, he said something very similar to us. Now, I see why you two might be useful to him, but what he'd want with us, I... don't... know...'

He looked at the two perplexed goblins, and the equally confused Sterling standing next to them. The halfling wasn't much taller than the goblins, a little broader and more filled out, more well-rounded. More pink.

Rhev's gaze began to move back and forth between the goblins and the halfling. Sterling was becoming visibly concerned.

'What is it?' he said.

'Oh dear.'

'What?!'

'Goblobs,' said Rhev darkly.

Sterling looked at the goblins aghast, and then back to Rhev. He could see the dwarf's eyes wide and staring right at him. Sterling glanced down at his own body.

'Oh dear,' Rhev repeated.

'We've gotta get out of here Rhev! Now! I don't want to be chopped up. I've never liked the idea of it! I look much better as a whole. Everybody always says it!'

Gethin interjected. 'We usually pronounce it "goblins" actually.'

Rhev turned to him. 'We're not talking about goblins, we're talking about gob-LOBS. Old mister nice bloke Victor is making them. Little green buggers, thick as planks, good at menial tasks and dribbling. I think he grows them out of goblin... parts.'

'But now he's going to make them out of me!' wailed Sterling, rattling the bars of their cell.

'Or maybe worse, mix you and the goblins here together into something even more ungodly.' Rhev shivered.

'So if me and Grunthry stay here we're going to be choppy choppy-ed up for parts and have goblins grown out of our toes?' asked Gethin. Grunthry began inspecting his own rather gnarled toe, which no doubt already had intelligent life growing out of it.

'Looks like it, unless we can all get out of here,' said Rhev. 'Have you two even tried escaping?'

'Locked, innit,' replied Grunthry, 'and we ain't got the keys.'

Gethin shrugged to confirm that they did not, in fact, have the keys. Rhev turned to Sterling. 'I can try picking the lock. Give me one of your knives.'

Sterlings stopped rattling the bars for a moment and patted himself. The patting yielded nothing. 'Bugger. Bugger bugger bugger.'

'Come on, mate!' said Rhev, starting to feel the walls close in on the situation.

'I think I left them back at the inn. I took them off when I got undressed, and then I must have forgotten to put the bandolier back on in the confusion.'

Rhev gave his beard a sharp tug in frustration. A couple of hairs came off. The stress was getting to him.

**

Mina was absolutely transfixed by the patterns on the box. It was, in her opinion, the prettiest thing she had ever stolen. It outshone everything around it, even the gilded silk pennant of that Falstyrian knight and the exquisitely carved ear trumpet she had nicked off that gullible dowager.

She had tried opening the box to no avail. Now she sat cross-legged on her bed, just watching, much in the same way the people in the village below stared vacantly at her father's lights. *Why did I steal it?* she thought. She had always stolen out of boredom. Haven was so *boring*. It rained all the time and all the villagers were dull as muck. The only excitement she had was causing trouble in The Rosy Brewer, and even that was wearing thin.

Then the funny halfling had come along with a silly bow in his hair and he had made her laugh. It was notoriously difficult to make her laugh. She realised, in a flush of anxiety, that this was the first time that she had regretted doing something. She had stolen from someone that she actually liked. *Really* liked. She wasn't the sort of person that *liked* people. She didn't even like her parents. In fact, she hated

180

them: they were literal monsters.

Now she had ruined it all by stealing from the first person that she had liked, out of sheer habit. No, worse, out of wanting attention. Wanting *his* attention. For the first time in her life, she considered returning what she had stolen and apologising. *What has he done to me?*

She looked out of the open bay window into the rainy night. The rooftops of the castle were covered in her father's abandoned apparatus, and they glimmered and dripped under the rain water. A crack echoed through the drowned air as a bolt of green hot lightning struck one of the brass pylons on the roof. Its elemental power arced from pylon to pylon towards the bay window. At the last moment Mina threw herself behind the bed as the bolt flew from the last pylon to the ornate ear trumpet on her dresser. Inside the cone the energy coalesced and fired directly into the box beside it.

With a crack louder than the thunder that preceded it, the box opened. In a flash its inside became out and Mina found herself sliding, though she knew not where and in what direction.

She stopped sliding in a grey wasteland. Tall cliffs of blocky stone stood to either side of her. Their walls were sheer, as if cut deliberately. As her gaze tracked further up their face, she realised that the sky was gone. At least, *her* sky had gone. What was above her was a firmament that felt oppressively solid, although she could not say for sure where its solidity started or ended from so far away. She shivered, and realised that she was very cold. The finely embroidered lounge trousers and blouse she was wearing were not designed for outdoor wear. Her long hair at least gave her a measure of warmth around the base of her neck.

She shivered again. This time, it wasn't from the cold. A primal instinct wriggled its way up her spine, and she turned quickly. A horde of creatures grew steadily larger in her field

181

of vision. They were a monochrome mass of heaving bodies. Before Mina could make out their forms fully, she began to hear their terrible cries. Wails and moans and screeches and chitters emanated from the advancing army. She stood fixed in terror as slippery white forms and black edges peeled towards her down the gorge. It was only until she could make out their cruel, shiny eyes that her legs got the message and began moving away from the horrors.

It is true that Mina had seen horrors before. She had grown up with them. Mina remembered well the times her mother had grown tired of her father's ramblings and let loose her inner demon, all teeth and fury. She had seen the failed creations of her father career out of the depths of his laboratory to feast, desecrate, and more often that not, self-combust. But the things chasing her now were *unthings*. It was less their appearance that frightened Mina, and more the sickening energy they gave off. They simply had no right to *be*.

The unthings were gaining ground quicky, driving up a cloud of ashen dust. Mina's breath came in quick short gasps as she willed her legs to move faster. Then she began to notice more movement around her. Things were moving down the sheer sides of the gorge. Colourful things. Streamers of vibrant colour flowed behind their forms as they descended. Mina didn't stop to see if these newcomers were friend or foe. She kept moving, tripping over scree and rubbing dust from her eyes.

The sound of stampeding creatures behind her was replaced with battlecries and wails. She risked a look over her shoulder, and saw that the unthings were surrounded by the colourful ambushers. Swords and clubs and spears joined the unthings' sharp limbs and barbs. The ring of attackers slowly closed in and trampled the fallen creatures underfoot, until there was nothing left but a pile of grey flesh.

The warriors turned as one to look at Mina. She realised that she had stopped moving some time ago to watch the carnage unfold. Feeling their eyes on her, she instinctively began to turn away and make ready for another desperate flight, but one of their number cried out.

'You're safe now! You can stop running!'

Mina stopped, but she didn't move towards the group

'Who are you?' she called back.

'We're Lost, just like you.'

'I'm not lost!' replied Mina indignantly. 'Just point me in the direction of Haven.'

The person she was talking to began walking towards her, and their group followed slowly. Mina flinched, but stood.

'And where might that be?'

'Oh, for goodness sake. Haven, you know, the Krovanian mountains? Surely you can point me there?'

As he came closer the figure resolved itself. He was short and stocky, and wore a long beard almost down to his waist. It flapped in the wind that blew down the gorge, kept in check only by the cinches of coloured fabric tied down its length.

'Ah, Krovania, I know those mountains,' he nodded to himself. He spoke with a thick accent common to the eastern Peninsula. 'Majestic and muddy, aye.'

'Excellent. Then you can *tell me where they are*,' replied Mina, impatience bleeding into her tone.

'Of course!' the dwarf replied, only ten yards away now. He made a broad sweeping gesture with both hands and swung them upwards towards the sky. He grinned at Mina. She followed his hands and looked up.

'Are you joking?' she asked.

'Oh dear, I am sorry,' came the exaggerated apology. 'Perhaps I am a bit off.' He swung his arms again and pointed at an entirely different section of the sky. 'That seems more like it.'

Mina stared at him angrily. The dwarf slowly lowered his arms and his expression became dour.

'I need you to realise, missy, that you *are* Lost. We're all Lost here.'

The group of individuals behind him all nodded their heads sadly. They were a motley bunch. Humans, dwarves, halflings, elves, fisherfolk, and other races she did not recognise. There was one thing they all shared though: vibrance. In this wasteland of grey they were the one source of colour. From head to toe they were covered in bright fabrics. The cloth was wrapped around their arms, their legs, worn as bandanas and tied to the hafts of weapons. They formed a brigade of chromatic brilliance, in defiance of the oppressive anti-colour around them.

Mina tried to process what she had just been told. The dwarf in front of her could see her indignance slowly fade to confusion and panic as she surveyed the new world around her.

'What's your name, lass?'

'Mina,' she replied faintly.

'Nice to meet you, Mina of Haven. Remember that, remember where you're from, or you'll go mad here. For my part, I am Bratzva Culluggan of Velheim.'

***

'Don't sit on that.'

'Ooh, sorry Merky the Almighty,' replied Cal. He hopped off the edge of the Table where he had been sitting while talking to Aed. 'Isn't it like an unbreakable artifact or something?'

'It was made by gods, so presumably it can be unmade by gods,' Merky replied sternly. Cal shrugged and took a seat next to Aed to continue their conversation. The Table did look quite old though, even by eternity's standards. Like a poker table, the world replica was sunken in the middle, with about

184

six inches of wood acting as a raised frame on each side. Because of this, you couldn't actually see what the cross section of the world looked like, although the Specs did allow a monitor to penetrate a certain amount rock and water to report on any subterranean or underwater incidents. The fact was, there wasn't an awful lot to bother looking at on the edge of the Table; the world was entirely surrounded by a deep ocean where nothing much happened.

'You alright Erin? You've been a little quiet,' said Merky, offering her some ambrosia. She politely declined.

'It's nothing. I just had a bit of a run in with the Flaw Manager.'

Merky nodded in understanding and leaned in conspiratorially.

'Don't pay any attention to him. Before all this, he was a just small time tribal god. Just happened to jump on the Ava band-wagon early on, back when it wasn't such a sure thing. He took a gamble, and it paid off. He's where he is now because of luck, and that's it.'

Erin smiled a little. She appreciated Merky's words, but ultimately it didn't really change her situation.

'I suppose I'm just not really used to being under scrutiny. I've always been my own boss, until I got here.'

'We all have to deal with change at some point in our existence. It's for the greater good, and all that.'

'Is it though?' Erin couldn't believe what she was saying. Neither could Merky. The cherubic god took a hasty look at the others in the room to see if they were listening. He replied, his voice low.

'Be careful, Erin. What are you saying?'

Erin bit her lower lip and considered what she was doing. She suddenly realised that she wasn't entirely sure that she could trust Merky. After all, he was the most senior member of the team, and hadn't exactly agreed with the rest of them

185

when they were talking about Chardo. On the other hand, Merky was kind and level-headed. She decided to take a chance. It was no use working alongside him if she couldn't have faith in his empathy.

'I'm saying that the pantheon hasn't been doing a very good job. Almost all earthly appearances are for bureaucratic reasons, wizards have been struggling to draw from their gods' magickal energies, and so many prayers are going unanswered it's unreal! But down there people are still worshipping Ava, despite the fact that things have objectively gotten worse. It's less of a church, more of a weird... cult.'

Merky winced. 'Don't use that word, please.'

'I'm sorry, Merky, but it's true. Prayers to Ava have gone up, which is great; more power to the pantheon. But they've gone up *because they're not getting answered*. It's all built around desperation, and that can't be right? Can it?'

Merky didn't answer for quite some while. Erin thought at any moment he would burst into anger and condemn her seditious thoughts. Then he leaned in closer.

'These are wild accusations, Erin,' he whispered. 'I would urge you to keep them quiet.'

Erin's heart fell. *He's trying to protect me, but he doesn't believe me.*

'Meet me back here when the others have gone,' he continued. Without waiting for acknowledgement, he went back to his work.

Erin's mind fired off ricocheting bullets of anxiety as she walked down the corridor later that day.

It's a trap, it's got to be a trap, right? Everyone else gone, no witnesses. It's probably not even going to be Merky there. Probably the Flaw Manager. Or even Ava herself? No, that's ridiculous. Unless...

Erin reached the entrance to the Table chamber. Merky was sat at his desk with his legs up, eating more ambrosia.

'Mmm, you're here,' he said through a mouthful of the nectar. 'I was worried you wouldn't come. While I was sitting here I realised how all this subterfuge might have been construed as a trap, but I knew I was just being paranoid.' He wiped a speck of ambrosia off his cheek with a handkerchief. 'Come in, come in.'

As Erin entered, Merky got up and closed the door after having a brief inspection outside.

'First of all, I wanted to assure you, *yes*, I've come to the same conclusions as you. Why, I wandered into prayer stratification earlier and it was an absolute shambles. The prioritisation system is all over the place. Some of the prayers on their board have almost faded with age! But hey-ho, doesn't matter as long as they keep coming in, right? More power for the pantheon.' Merky's sarcasm was punctuated by wild gestures, quite uncharacteristic. Erin had never seen him this animated. She was quite stunned. He grabbed her by the shoulders suddenly.

'There's more. I need to show you something.'

He let go and walked over to the edge of the Table where Cal had been sitting earlier that day.

'A long time ago when it was just me on the Table, I discovered something. Something big. I was fiddling around with the Specs one day, and I dropped them. They skidded right under here.' He disappeared. Erin knelt down and saw him lying underneath the Table. 'I went to pick them up, and when I looked back, I saw these.'

He pointed to the corners of the Table, where the legs met the main body.

'I can't see anything,' Erin said cautiously. 'It's just wood.'

Merky beckoned her to come closer. She got down on her hands and knees and crawled over. He pointed again.

'See? The wood within the wood.'

She squinted hard, and then she saw it. Wooden buttons,

flush against the joinery, almost invisible.

'Weird, right? Let's get back up.'

They both hauled themselves to their feet.

'You take that end and I'll take this end. If you feel the grain really carefully, you'll be able to find the button.'

Erin ran her hand along the perfectly smooth wood until she found a little inconsistency in the shape of a square.

'Got it? Now when I say go, push it and grab the side of the Table.'

Erin nodded, and Merky counted down from three. On 'go', she pressed the button. It only went in a nanometer, but it was enough. She felt the side of the Table loosen. Together, they removed it.

Erin didn't know what she was expecting to see, but it wasn't this. The full cross-section of the world below was revealed. Along its entire edge a curtain of water veiled a whole other realm *beneath* the one that she knew.

'What… how… what is it?' she asked breathlessly.

'The first gods' dirty little secret,' replied Merky, a look of grim satisfaction on his face. 'Here.'

He passed her a pair of Specs. Tentatively, she put them on, and flicked one of the dials with a now practised motion. Her vision flew through the curtain water, and as it did so, she realised that it was in fact flowing upwards, not down. Beyond the waterrise, a grey desert was all she could see. Its topography lay discarded randomly, as a child would with its toys. The mass of the world that she knew seemed to be balanced on the tops of this wasteland's tallest mountains. As she looked closer, it became apparent that the world above seemed to be warped slightly around these fulcrums.

'I know,' replied Merky when she mentioned it. 'It looks like they did a shoddy job. I believe that in order to make sure nobody up here or down there found out, they made the second world incredibly thick, which of course made it incredibly heavy. If you look very, *very* closely on top, you'll see it's actually cracked in some places from the strain. But that's not the worst of it. Zero in on that point there.'

He gestured to a speck on the grey plains beneath the world. She twisted another dial on the Specs and zoomed her vision in towards a patch of pale, undulating movement. She gasped in horror.

***

'What you said to Kevin the other day, in the caravan, was that true? That you don't even know where the knives come from?' Rhev asked Sterling.

'I mean, no. Well, I'm not sure. I know where most of them come from,' he replied.

'But when we got in a spot of bother back in the Grippen mountains, you threw at least twenty knives. There's no way you were carrying that many. You'd cut yourself.'

'I confess, *you're not wrong*,' agreed Sterling, 'I just… can't explain it. Whenever we get in a tussle I just seem to have no problem finding them. I thought it best not to question it, or it might stop happening. I always just thought it was some sort of curse from a wizard with a dodgy sense of humour.'

'Or a blessing,' Rhev mused, stroking his beard. He paused for a moment as if an idea had struck him, and then walked over to the goblins. A word or two passed between them, and Grunthry ran over to Sterling and slapped him.

'Oi!' he shouted. 'What was that for?'

Instead of an answer he got a swift kick to his most prized possessions, followed by a bite to the calf. Gethin called over.

'He hasn't eaten in almost a week. We're starving for some meat!'

The other goblin turned to Rhev and leapt at his face, his sharp little teeth gnashing at his hairy chin. Rhev cried out in surprise.

The scuffle lasted for less than a minute. There was a clang as Sterling finally managed to throw Grunthry against the bars of their cell, the goblin letting out a pathetic yelp.

Rhev was struggling. 'My sword is stuck in the scabbard!' he yelled over to Sterling when he was momentarily able to push Gethin away from his face. 'Help!'

The was a *woosh* and Gethin grunted in pain. He fell back and Rhev stood up, smiling broadly.

'Perfect!' He went over to Gethin and helped him up. 'Ah, not too bad, worth it in the long run, eh? You alright, Grunthry?' Grunthry raised his hand in a weak thumbs up.

Sterling looked at the goblins and then back to Rhev in confusion. 'What's going on? Why are you helping him?'

In answer, Rhev bent over Gethin and yanked at something. The goblin squealed. Rhev stood up and walked over to Sterling.

'See. I knew this would work!' In the dwarf's hand lay a small, bloodied, stiletto dagger. 'Now where did you get this from?' he asked Sterling.

'It was just in my hand,' Sterling replied in amazement. 'Owww,' he continued, as he realised the bite on his leg was beginning to bleed.

'Sorry about that, your mate told me to sell it,' Grunthry apologised as he dusted himself off. 'I likes to bite,' he shrugged.

'You told them to attack us?!' Sterling's fists clenched.

'I just wanted to test my theory! And it worked out, didn't it? With minimal collateral damage I might add. Now, time for me to do *my* magic trick.'

Holding his tongue but grimacing nonetheless, Sterling watched as the dwarf slid his arms through the bars around their cell door. His short, thick fingers were deceptively nimble and he handled the stiletto in them like a venerable grandmother with a knitting needle.

'What are you trying to do?' asked Sterling.

'Suffice to say I know my way around a cell door,' Rhev grunted in reply, concentrating on his handiwork intently. He felt the halfling's judgemental gaze burn into his back.

'As a watchman, of course,' he added.

A series of scrapes and clicks came from the lock, accompanied by the occasional grunt of profanity.

Rhev stood up, turned to his audience, and bowed. As he did so, his buttocks pushed against the cell door. It swung open with ease.

'After you.'

The corridor outside the cell was dimly lit by glowing green orbs connected by some sort of rubbery rope. The passage smelt of mould. As they cautiously made their way further down, that smell gradually gave way to a strange metallic taint that stung the nostrils. After a few more twists and turns and ups and downs the motley group arrived in a large vaulted hall. Its walls and ceiling were stained with soot in odd places, illuminated by more glowing orbs and a much larger orb hanging in the centre of the room. This larger orb fizzed and cracked with imprisoned lightning, casting odd reflections on the polished brass instruments that littered the room. A series of large hoses connected the orb to various points in the room, with the largest leading somewhere through a hole in the wall. Rhev didn't really understand what he was seeing, but he knew well enough not to like it.

'Keep moving, we've got to find a way out,' he said, taking the first step into the room.The group began winding between the strange contraptions. It was slow going. The obstacles in their way had been left in a haphazard manner, and there was no clear path between them.

Suddenly there was a loud clatter. Rhev span around to see Gethin and Grunthry desperately trying to hold an armful of shiny brass spheres. As Gethin added one to the top of Grunthry's pile another would slip out and fall to the floor, bouncing and rolling with a horrible tinny sound.

'What are you doing?!' Rhev yelled at them.

'Nabbin'' Gethin replied, matter-of-factly.

'Uninhibited nabbing was what got us all here in the first place!'

'Rhev, hush. Look!' whispered Sterling, pointing at something on the other side of the room.

Two of the hideous green creatures had entered the room by the door the gang had been making their way towards. They were communicating to each other in a disgusting, garbled tongue. One of them giggled. They hadn't noticed the escaped prisoners it seemed, but Rhev hit the deck instinctively and watched through some table legs.

The goblob closest to him picked up some sort of fork-like instrument with brass balls on each of its two tines. It chuckled, and pointed it in the direction of its deformed colleague. The target put its hands up, one of which was much larger and entirely out of proportion with his body. There was a charged pause. Then both goblobs opened their well-toothed mouths and laughed.

Zap. The goblob had touched the other with its mysterious instrument and sent an arc of lightning coursing over its victim's tiny deformed body. A sizzling sound and a stream of black smoke signalled the end of the goblobs sorry existence. Its murderer continued to giggle. Rhev could see that the creature was quite mad, insane in a way that almost made him feel sorry for it. Almost.

A ting-ting-ting noise echoed through the chamber. The goblob stopped giggling and looked in his direction. Rhev turned around wide-eyed as Grunthry continued to fumble every last one of the brass balls he had been carrying. He looked at Rhev apologetically.

The goblob began advancing on their position. Its disproportionate left foot slapped on the stone floor as it walked.

'Bugger this,' said Rhev. He stood up, cracked his neck, and ran at the creature. In what seemed like less than a second he had punted the goblob with his heavy boots over to the other side of the room, where it landed with a satisfyingly wet sound.

'Creepy little bastard,' he grumbled, and knelt down to pick up the brass zapper it had dropped. 'This could come in handy,' he mused, careful to only touch its wooden handle.

'Good kick,' said Sterling. 'You should play bladderpunt.'

Rhev was surprised by the compliment. He had been certain that Sterling now hated his guts.

'Thanks,' he replied, 'I used to play street bladder back in Velheim.'

'Which position?'

'Left under the bridge.'

'Nice.'

They kept on through the labyrinthine passages. As they progressed, another smell met their nostrils: earthy, mixed with some sort of chemical. Moisture crept into the air around them, and there was a new warmth to the stone floors.

They rounded the next corner and were met with a curious sight. Rows upon rows of what Rhev assumed were raised flower beds lined the walls of the chamber. The ever present green glow highlighted sprays of water droplets coming out of pipes in the ceiling. Rhev noticed some sacks stacked near the entrance of the chamber, and could see they were filled with a white powder, the source of the irritating chemical smell.

Some sort of underground farm then, Rhev thought to himself. *Perhaps this is where the castle gets all of its food from.* He wandered over to one of the mounds of dirt. What he found made him jump back with a start and trip over the flagstones beneath him. Sterling lifted him onto his feet.

'What is it Rhev?'

'Something growing, in the dirt. It was… wriggling.'

Sterling looked over at the mass of earth, and in the green gloom he could indeed see something wriggling. Grunthry fearlessly, or perhaps stupidly, walked over to the bed.

'Ey, look at this, Geth. Someone's got themselves buried alive. Stupid or what?' He reached into the dirt, grabbed at the wriggling thing, and pulled.

What came out of the earth was, simply put, an abomination. Grunthry had grasped a tiny, malformed hand that was attached to an even more amorphous green body. The body seemed to be growing like a tumour out of the ankle of a goblin-sized foot. Sterling gagged a little.

'That's how he's making the goblobs? He literally grows them?'

'It looks like it,' said Rhev, turning a paler shade of green. 'Chops them up, propagates them like a plant.'

'I swears I recognise that foot,' said Gethin, seemingly unperturbed. 'Spitting image of cousin Gerry.'

'Gerry was a bastard,' said Grunthry.

'Gerry was a bastard,' agreed Gethin. Grunthry threw the creature unceremoniously back onto the pile of dirt.

'You're taking this very,' Sterling gulped down another urge to vomit, 'well.'

Gethin shrugged. 'Horrible stuff gets done to goblins all the time, innit. It's just the goblin way of life. Can't get all boo hoo about it or we'd never get any nabbin' done.'

Rhev squinted at the goblin. Behind the bravado, he sensed a deep sadness.

One of the mounds began to move, then another. Shapes arose under the sickening green light.

'Time to go,' said the dwarf abruptly, and began jogging for the exit.

The dimly lit corridors ahead were just as winding, but

years of living in the Underport had given Rhev an innate sense of direction underground, and it told him they were on the right track to freedom. There were a few wrong turns here and there though, leading them to storage areas, seething vats, and one incredibly dark and rotten smelling pit.

'I have definitely changed my mind about Victor,' admitted Sterling as they made a swift retreat away from whatever lay at the bottom of the pit.

'Agreed. As much as I often have the urge to give a goblin a good whack around the chops, no offence lads,' the goblins didn't seem to care, 'what this bloke is doing is definitely in the realms of evil. And as far as I'm concerned, his wife is just as bad,' said Rhev.

'Because of the whole 'inner demon' thing?'

'That, and because she's unnecessarily passive aggressive and listened to me poo,' replied Rhev with genuine sincerity.

'Truly monstrous.'

They had reached a gate. On the other side of the gate was a shaft that was shrouded in darkness both up and down. In the darkness, they could make out a thick rope dangling down the shaft. Beside the gate was a lever.

'This is the only potential way out we haven't tried,' Sterling said, 'but I wouldn't climb that rope even if Ava herself told me to do it.'

'You clearly haven't spent enough time in Velheim. My money is on this being a lift,' replied Rhev. He grabbed the lever, and yanked. The rope started to move upwards, followed by a platform. It stopped level with their corridor, and the gate unlocked itself with a *clank*.

'After you, sirs.' Rhev ushered the halfling and the two goblins into the lift, then followed them and closed the gate. As the gate locked itself with another *clank*, the lift started moving upwards again.

'This is handy, innit,' said Gethin. 'Why aren't there more

of these?'

'Do they make them going forwards and backwards, instead of up and down? I spend lots more time going forwards and backwards,' mused Grunthry.

'They don't, but that's a pretty good idea,' admitted Rhev.

'Is it?' said Sterling. Rhev considered for a moment.

'I'm not sure.'

The lift reached its final destination. Rather than a wrought iron gate, they were faced with a heavy wooden door. On the other side was a study. It was covered in loose sheets of paper emblazoned with alchemical symbols and nonsensical diagrams. A chalkboard leant against a bookcase showed a drawing of a dissected goblob in shocking detail, and next to it the words *'improve base stock: halfling / gnome / pictsie'*. Rhev felt sick to his stomach, and turned away.

Sterling was studying a map on the other wall. It depicted Haven and the surrounding countryside, including the castle itself. Curious lines connected the castle to the village, each one ending at a different house. The only building that didn't seem to be connected to the castle was The Rosy Brewer.

Next to the map lay an open book. Sterling could see that the chapter heading read 'Studys In The Applycashun Of Light In Relayshun To The Mind'. He didn't understand a word of it.

Shouting could be heard from somewhere in the castle. It appeared that Victor and Varylla were arguing.

'Twice, Victor, twice now. You naive fool.' Varylla's tone was measured, but dripping with venom.

'Tell me, what is naive about wanting company? Civilised conversations?' Victor was near hysterical.

'You know that I despise company.'

'Maybe that's why I invited them!'

There was a notable pause in the conversation.

'You petty little man!' replied Varylla, her composure

broken. 'Remember who it is who funds your work, your experiments, your *life*. Remember that no-one else, and I mean *no-one*, is remotely interested.'

'That's not true.' Victor was quieter now.

'You should know, Victor, that you're quite mad. A man who yearns to converse with stupid peasants, to impress these dullards with his so-called achievements, yet at the same time showing no remorse for cutting those same people up into little peices in the name of progress. What's even more insulting, is the fact that the "progress" that these people die for doesn't exist! It never will! At least when I kill people, I eat them. There is a purpose to that. An honest purpose.'

The voices were quite close now. Rhev spied through the keyhole of the study's door. Immediately outside was the entrance hall, where Varylla and Victor were stood arguing.

'We're boxed in,' he said. 'I hate to say it, but...'

'Storm the castle again?' said Sterling with a smirk.

'Really? I was going to say surrender, but if you mean it...'

'It was definitely an overreaction before, don't get me wrong. You jumped the gun. It's all very well and good if we were on some sort of whacky adventure, but this is serious business. On the other hand, now we know for sure how evil these bastards are, it feels a bit more proportionate.'

Rhev nodded sagely. 'Only use your sword on a deserving enemy.'

'Exactly. Plus, it makes for a good song.'

Rhev considered for a moment. 'As much as I don't like to be a pessimist, if this goes south, we've buggered it for the others. We need insurance. You two, you're good at nabbing, right?'

'We ain't called Nabbers Extraordinaire for nothing, mate,' replied Gethin.

'Yeah, it's 'cos that's what we called ourselv-,' added Grunthry, before receiving a sharp elbow to the gut.

'We need to find a box, about this big, with magical whirly bits on it,' Rhev continued. 'I'm pretty certain it will be up in one of the towers. I reckon you'll be able to pass off as goblobs, should make it easier for you if you run into anyone else in the castle.'

'Look out for someone with lovely hair,' said Sterling. 'Don't hurt her...'

'Like he said, just avoid anyone if you can, and get the box out of the castle. If we don't make it, get it to Steem Vennts. He's at The Rosy Brewer in Haven. What do you say?'

'Yeah, alright,' said Grunthry, recovering from the jab.

'Wait, Grunths!' interjected Gethin. 'We could just sneak out while these two pink lads do all the smashing. Mister Rhev, what will you give us if we do this nab for you? ' He had a sly look on his squashed green face, as if he was making the deal of the century.

'Something you can't nab.'

Gethin rolled his eyes. 'What's that then?'

'Friendship.' Rhev stuck out his hand for a shake. Gethin looked at it, confused. He laughed nervously. Then he glanced back at Grunthry. His companion was nodding enthusiastically.

Hesitantly, the goblin reached out his small green hand to Rhev's stout pink one, and they shook shortly and firmly.

'Everyone ready?' said Rhev. Everyone nodded.

'Wait, aren't you going to get your sword out?' Sterling asked.

'We'd lose the element of surprise if it starts banging on again. Don't worry though, I've got something better.' He brandished the brass instrument he had looted earlier and winked. The wink disguised a maelstrom of nerves, excitement, and adrenaline. He thought of the Slayer, how fantastic his monster hunting stories had been, how he longed to live a life like that. Here was his chance.

He slammed his broad boot into the door. The goblins were off in a flash, incredibly fast for their size, no doubt experienced from years of running away from things. Taking advantage of the distraction, Sterling flung his stiletto straight and true at Victor's heart while Rhev jabbed the lightning weapon into the small of Varylla's back. For a moment, it looked like they had done it. Quick and easy.

It was only the briefest moment though. Out of nowhere, a loyal, or more likely brainwashed, goblob threw itself into the path of the flying dagger. The momentum threw it back into Victor, who discarded it with a yelp. Rhev's luck was no better. His weapon did nothing. There was no discharge of lightning. Varylla didn't fly over to the other side of the hall as he had anticipated. Frantically, he slapped the instrument in his hands in a vain attempt to make it work. He jabbed again, this time into Varylla's tightly bodiced gut as she turned to face him. Nothing. *That's what you get for playing at being a wizard, you lead-headed dwarf*, he thought. Slowly he lifted his gaze to meet Varylla's. Her eyes turned from blue to black. Rhev tentatively reached for the hilt of his sword.

'Restrain them!' ordered Victor, and suddenly Rhev and Sterling were surrounded by a throng of goblobs. Tiny hands prevented the dwarf from unsheathing his sword, and he was lifted bodily from the ground. It was over.

'See, Victor, this is what happens when you don't eat the peasants,' Varylla chided, a sickly satisfaction in her words.

'I'm sorry, Rhev,' Sterling whimpered as he was lifted up by goblobs as well.

'It's my fault, Sterling. Stupid, drunk dwarf playing at being adventurer...' he replied, staring straight up at the ceiling with an air of miserable resignation. He recalled with vivid clarity the events that led him to leave Velheim in the first place, and realised that it was a series of similar poor decisions that had got him into a bind again. *When will I learn?*

he thought. *By the looks of things, I won't have time to!*

'I lost the Box in the first place,' Sterling consoled. 'You're a good dwarf for trying to help, really.'

Rhev strained against the grip of countless goblobs to look at Sterling.

'Really?' he asked desperately.

'Really' his compatriot smiled.

There was a thunderous knock on the castle's great door.

'More visitors, Victor? I swear to the gods I will eat this one on the spot!' screamed Varylla. 'Get the door, you cretin.'

Victor stomped over to the huge iron door pull and opened the door in a sulk.

'Yes?' he asked.

'I'm here on business,' came a gruff reply. Victor was pushed away from the threshold so roughly that he almost fell over, and from out of the night a figure emerged. The squeak of leather on leather and the *click clack* of bone hitting bone preceded him. Rhev managed to incline his head and take a look.

'Oh thank Ava, we're saved,' he said to Sterling with a relieved grin.

The Slayer walked slowly into the middle of the hall. He shook the rain from his long locks and pulled at the sodden black tunic that had pasted itself to his body. He seemed to ignore Rhev, Sterling, and the crowd of goblobs. Instead, his steely gaze was fixed singularly on Varylla.

'Don't fear Sterling, he's a Slayer! He'll kill all these bastards and make jewelry out of their bones!' he said *sotto voce*, as if waiting for the show to start. The Slayer spoke.

'Varylla. I've waited a long time for this moment. It's been very... painful. You know how much it hurts me to have unfinished business.'

'Oh, I know, Rygert the Slayer,' Varylla replied with a wicked smile. 'I knew this moment would come. How I've so longed for a return to the... *baser* pleasures of life.'

'I am glad you remembered,' said Rygert, his eyes locked so fiercely on hers that Rhev could swear he could see a visible connection between them. The Slayer and the monster both cocked their heads, and with terrible speed ran at each other. Rhev's heart leapt. He couldn't wait to see the Slayer in action.

Varylla and Rygert met under the warm glow of the candle-lit chandelier, and embraced tightly. Their kiss was long and passionate. Their hands slid feverishly over their entwined bodies. Rhev frowned in confusion.

'Rylla, what are you doing?!' screamed Victor, chemical-stained hands clenched into fists. Varylla came up for air just long enough to reply.

'Being loved by a man who knows how to really appreciate a monster! I had a life before you, Victor!'

'Rylla, please!' wailed Victor. 'No, no, no!'

A wild look had taken him, and he glanced around in desperation. His eyes fell on the horde of goblobs surrounding Rhev and Sterling, and he made a series of gestures, finishing by dragging his thumb across his neck. The goblobs surged towards Rygert and Varylla, more and more filling in from surrounding rooms.

Distracted by their passions, the two reunited lovers didn't notice their attackers until it was too late.They were mobbed by hundreds of grasping hands, dragged away from each other, their embrace finally broken. The Slayer desperately tried to draw the swords on his back. Varylla tried to transform into her demonic alter-ego, but she only had so many teeth and claws to go around. Their screams were eventually muffled by the weight of green flesh on top of them, and Rhev could tell they were dead.

The only sounds in the hall now were the faint chittering of goblobs and the sizzle of rain outside. A cold, wet wind blew in through the open door. Victor's wild hair fluttered as he knelt beside the corpse of his wife, surrounded by his foul creations.

'Look what you made me do, Rylla! Look what you made me do!' he wailed as he pounded his fists on her body. Rhev and Sterling were no longer restrained, and slowly they crept towards the door.

'What happened here then?' a voice said beside Rhev. It was Gethin. 'Who's this new fella?'

Victor didn't acknowledge the goblins. Grief and madness had taken him. All thoughts of killing the pathetic man had left Rhev's mind for now.

He saw that Gethin was wearing a sort of colourful silk flag as a cape, and Grunthry had an intricately carved trumpet gripped in his mouth. Between them, they held their prize. The sigils on the box glowed and snaked across its surface more than ever.

'Well done lads,' said Rhev quietly. 'I don't think that's supposed to go in your mouth though, Grunthry.'

Grunthry clearly didn't care. He exhaled sharply and a resounding toot echoed about the hall. Victor was roused from his revery.

'Treachery!' he shouted at the escapees.

'Time to leave,' said Rhev, and the group made a beeline for the open door.

'Treachery all around me. No more, I say! Quite mad, eh? I'll show them madness!' His declaration reverberated around the hall and out into the night air.

The dwarf, the halfling, and two goblins slipped and slid their way down the track leading from the castle. In the gloom, they could see three torches swaying ahead of them. They ran towards the lights.

'Rhev? Sterling? What's going on?' asked Steem, his voice raised over the sound of the storm.

'We'd rather explain later!' shouted Sterling as he ran past his companions.

'At least explain the goblins,' Mercy demanded.

'New friends!' answered Rhev, as he too continued running away from the castle.

'Gross,' said Kevin.

Steem's cohort turned to follow.

'We found another bridge a couple of miles west of the broken one. Make for there!' ordered Mercy.

As the seven strong group crossed the significantly more robust bridge, a flash of green light lit up the horizon. The flash was followed by many more, a series so rapid and arrhythmical that it was nauseating to look at. After a minute or so the flashing stopped, the afterglow burned on everyone's retinas.

'What was all that nonsense' asked Steem. Rhev and Sterling's minds flashed back to what they had seen in Victor's study, but neither could come up with a reasonable explanation.

'It's definitely not good, I can tell you that much. We should get our things and go as soon as we get to Haven,' said Rhev.

When they neared the settlement they could see right away that the streets were far more busy than they had been on their arrival, despite the lateness of the hour. Groups of dour looking villagers milled around the outskirts. As the gang drew near a choler rose in their eyes and shouts went up among them.

'Why are they pointing at us like that?' Kevin asked nervously.

'Take the side streets to the inn. I don't like the look of that mob,' said Mercy.

As they detoured and entered a dim alleyway, Rhev could hear the sound of many footsteps behind them. The first street off the alley was blocked at one end by another mob of villagers, as were the next two. Through some canny navigation by Mercy however, the group managed to make their way to the central square without running into any of the strange folk that seemed so interested in them. Nevertheless, they could hear many of their number closing in.

A warm, comforting glow still spilled from the windows of The Rosy Brewer, and Rhev let out a sigh of relief. They clattered through the doors of the inn and drummed the floor with their wet boots.

'Please, please, a little quieter,' begged Rudy from behind the bar, his hands clasped together. 'I have guests upstairs, you understand.'

'Sorry Rudy,' said Kevin, 'but there is something seriously odd going on. The whole village is out for a midnight stroll, and they don't seem very welcoming.'

Rudy wiped his hands on a dirty dish cloth and came round to the other side of the bar.

'The inhabitants of Haven being unwelcoming? Sounds pretty normal to me. Hah! Let me have a look anyway.'

He peeked his ruddy face through a window looking out onto the square.

'I confess, that is a little odd. No one told *me* about this nighttime jamboree!' His chuckle turned to a shriek, and he pulled his head from the window. A woodcutter's axe fell in the place his head had been just moments before.

'So the time has come!' Rudy shrilled. 'Haven has finally turned on their friendly neighbourhood innkeeper! It's been a long time coming.'

'I don't think this is about you Ru-' began Rhev.

'No, no, it is. It must be. Always going against the grain, that's me. "We don't want outsiders in Haven", they said. "Stop encouraging them." "Why won't you adopt the same oddly foreboding yet highly efficient lighting system as the

204

rest of the village?" Because it's green! Nobody wants to stay at an inn with green lights!' Rudy was out of breath by the time he had finished his tirade.

The sound of the crowd outside was growing louder by the second. Mercy grabbed the heavy wooden plank next to the door and barred it shut.

'I really bloody hope this isn't happening because of what you two jokers got up to in the castle,' said Steem. 'There will be words. Now everyone, pack your kit and meet by the door to the courtyard quick smart.'

There was a frantic scramble up the stairs.

'Please, do not disturb-' Rudy began. The *boom* of someone ramming the door interrupted him. 'Oh, bugger it.' He went back behind the bar and unhooked a large, cruel cudgel from underneath the countertop.

A minute or so later the group was assembled by the backdoor. Gethin and Grunthry sat on the Box with their small legs swinging idly.

'What should we be doing?' asked Gethin enthusiastically.

'Get your green arses off that damn box and bugger off to wherever you came from,' replied Steem, the stress making a vein in his forehead bulge. The goblin's eager expression turned to dismay. Steem shoved them away from the Box and picked it up. Gethin and Grunthy frowned at Rhev.

'Wait, Steem,' he said, his palm open in a calming gesture. 'The goblins come with us. They did us a favour back in the castle. We're comrades now.'

'A favour? How the bloody hell did you get indebted to a couple of goblins?' Steem asked, the vein fit to bursting. Rhev hesitated, not wanting to detail the farce that he had gotten Sterling and himself into.

'It's a long story, Steem,' interjected the halfling, 'one that requires a lute and a decent campfire. The goblins are with us. I vouch for them.' He looked at Rhev and gave him a supportive look. Rhev nodded back in thanks.

'It better be one of your better ones Sterling, and with a happy bloody ending! For now, they better keep up and not get under my feet.'

The goblins looked at each other excitedly and stood beside Rhev, ready to go. Rudy appeared at the door, brandishing his club.

'Allow me to provide a checking out service,' he said as he opened the door to the courtyard.

'Bloody hell,' breathed Rhev. The courtyard was thronging with armed villagers. They were systematically vandalising everything they could see. Wagons lay toppled on the cobblestones among broken crates. A welcome sign had been ripped from its hangings and snapped in two.

The sound of the Box hitting the floor with a thud reverberated around the space.

'No!' wailed Steem, as he saw his own pride and joy mercilessly torn apart by axes and billhooks. 'Wait, wait! Stop, please!' he yelled as he ran outside. He was knocked to the ground by a blow to the head, and looked on helplessly as the majestic red caravan bearing his name began to topple over. Accompanied by raucous uproar, it finally succumbed to the efforts of the villagers and came crashing down on its side. The sound of someone carefully ripping the floral ceiling tapestry to shreds, the tapestry he'd spent so many years staring up at during those long nights, cut right through his heart.

Mercy ran to Steem's side, kicking his assailant in the stomach. When she lifted him to his feet, she saw that he was weeping.

'She's gone. She's gone,' he sobbed, clutching at her shoulders.

'Pull yourself together, boss. This isn't the time! We can... we can get you a new one.' Mercy's awkward attempt at comforting her boss only yielded more tears. Steem's legs buckled beneath him.

The rest of the group fought their way through the ever thickening crowd towards them, accompanied by Rudy swinging his club with mad enthusiasm.

'Mercy, we've got to get to the horses. They're still in the stables, look.' Rhev pointed to the four nags in their stalls across the courtyard. Their eyes were wild as they surveyed the violence around them. Froth bubbled from their mouths.

'Take the Box. I'll have to take Steem, he's lost his faculties. Damn these villagers, what is going on?' Mercy was becoming enraged. Rhev could see it in her eyes. 'Go!'

Kevin was the quickest, his innate desire to avoid danger giving him a near supernatural ability to dodge his attackers. He reached the stable and began sorting out the bridles. Sterling soon reached him, and Kevin gave him a leg up onto one of the shorter nags.

'I can't ride,' he admitted to his friend. 'My legs are too short.'

'Yes, yes they are.' Kevin said, relishing the moment. He mounted Sterling's horse, seated behind the halfling. 'Oof, bareback riding. How inelegant.'

The rest of the group arrived, battered and bruised. Rudy was still with them, his cudgel marred here and there by spots of blood.

'Come on Rhev, I'll get you and the Box up onto this one,' said Mercy, cupping her hands by the horse to act as a step. After some awkward effort, Rhev managed to mount the beast with the Box cradled precariously between his arms.

Finished with helping the dwarf, Mercy turned to the goblins. 'I suppose you want a leg up too?'

'What's the point? We can't ride a horse! Look at us!' replied Gethin. Grunthry demonstrated by lifting up one of his tiny legs, almost falling over in the process.

'They can ride with me,' said Rhev. 'Stick 'em on the back.'

'Your call,' Mercy shrugged, and she placed the two skinny goblins onto the back of Rhev's nag. 'I'll take Steem on mine. I don't think he's in any condition to ride.'

By the time everyone was mounted up, the mob had grown to the point where they were entirely blocking the exit. Steem's nags were no warhorses, and they cowered at the sight of so many angry men and women.

'Leave my guests alone!' shouted Rudy, addressing the mob. 'I know you all look down on the travel and tourism industry, but if you hurt these people word will get out that Haven is the armpit of Krovania and then we're all in for it! Now move!'

The crowd was not swayed. In fact, they barely registered what he was saying. Grunts and growls were the only thing they seemed to be vocalising, and their eyes remained fixed on the riders. If they wouldn't part, the horses were going nowhere.

As the mob began advancing as one, screams began coming from the village square. From atop the horse, Rhev could just see over the crowd and into the square beyond. A massive fist swang into view. Another followed it, and villagers went flying at its impact. Through the newly cut swathe came a goliath, almost as wide as it was tall. Its blonde plaited hair flew about its head as it systematically removed people from the vicinity. The nightgown it wore followed its exaggerated movements gracefully, like a teepee flying in the wind.

'My dear, I didn't want to wake you. Please, go back to bed, I can handle this,' Rudy said, addressing the goliath.

'You're having a laugh if you think I can sleep with all this racket going on' replied the goliath. Rudy turned to the riders and smiled sheepishly.

'Gertrude, my wife.'

Gertrude the goliath, the mysterious creature whose lair was the kitchen of The Rosy Brewer, had now cleared a path out of the inn's courtyard.

'You better leave while you can, there's more of those barmy locals around the corner,' she said as she threw a straggler out into the square like a sack of rubbish.

Mercy kicked her horse into action. Reluctantly, the nag began to canter away, and the other horses followed it.

'Please tell your friends about The Rosy Brewer! We do roasts on Sundays!' Rudy yelled after them.

Rhev was terrified. He very quickly realised that he had no idea how to ride a horse. He'd grown up on the streets of Velheim for goodness sake. It seemed like his nag was following the others by instinct, but he was struggling to stay seated without a saddle. He was also trying to balance the Box and two goblins at the same time.

He swayed side to side on the horse's back, using the reins to steady himself. He realised pretty quickly that wasn't what they were for. As he pulled on the bit the horse swerved erratically towards a new group of angry villagers on the roadside.

'Hang on!' he shouted to the goblins as they careened towards the men.

It was no use. He heard a shriek behind him. He turned to see one of the goblins get pulled from the horse by one of the villagers.

'Grunthry!' shouted Gethin. Seeing his partner in crime struggling in the grips of a wild-eyed washerwoman, he valiantly leapt from the horse himself. Rhev didn't know what to do.

'Gething, wait!' The nag continued galloping out of the crowd and back en route towards Kevin's horse.

'No, you stupid animal!' Rhev yelled into the beast's ear. Desperately he tried to wheel the horse around, but the more

209

he tried the more the Box began to slip from his precarious grasp.

'What are you doing? Don't lose the Box!' Kevin shouted as he disappeared around a corner.

Try as he might, Rhev knew he had no choice but to let his horse carry him to safety, and away from his new friends. The guilt burned in his chest.

***

The conversation regarding Chardo's *bonehead* incident had been ringing in Merky's ears for days. Unprofessionalism, in his name no less, was too much to bear. Emboldened from finding another conspirator in Erin, he had decided to pay a friendly visit to the Fiat department 'just to see how things were going'. Besides, he was an alumni, of sorts.

While the lazy and, in Merky's opinion, completely underqualified gods had been busy talking about their latest sand surfing trip, he had taken the opportunity to sift through Chardo's files. Apart from the fact that the god could barely write his own name, the gross negligence apparent in his work was astounding. He had allowed an arcane contract to be written up in regards to a particular item without full disclosure of what that item *was*. 'Normal box', it said. Such a contract should have disintegrated as soon as the scribe had finished it, but Chardo had allowed it to survive out of sheer apathy. Merky knew all too well of the evil that could be hidden in a contract written with such vaguery. He wanted to do nothing more than get to the bottom of the matter and track down the two signing parties and the item that was bound to them.

Paranoia, he thought to himself, *that's all it is, it can't be that bad.* He sat down in his chair by the Table, Specs in hand, and breathed. His left eye had started doing that thing again.

He managed to go an entire seventeen minutes before the compulsion overtook him. Five minutes after that, and he was glad it had. In the entire world he couldn't find anyone by the name of Mister Kowloon. No records, no trace. Evidently, he was on to something. He tracked the subject of the contract to a castle in a village called Haven. It was there, to his horror, that he had witnessed this 'Box' *suck a girl into it*. His Specs had told him that the girl no longer existed in the world, either in the Box or outside it. Following the sickening feeling in his stomach, he had waited until he was alone to check the world *beneath* the world. His suspicions had been correct.

'We might be the only gods in existence who have any idea how bad this could be. We have to do something about it!' Erin flapped her arms about like a distressed bird.

'Like what? We can't just go down there and *poof* it out of existence. There's limits to our powers, both of us,' replied Merky, defeated. Erin got out of her seat.

'Then we get Ava to intervene.'

'Are you kidding? She's a progenitor. She would have to admit that this other world existed, and even worse, that she had a part in creating it. She'd never help. She'd just brush it, *and us*, under the carpet.'

'She's one of the wisest gods in existence. She wouldn't just "brush us under the carpet".'

'She literally brushed an entire world under the carpet, Erin. I don't think Ava is as wise or level-headed as we would like to think. Besides, she's surrounded by so many small-time, small-brained gods like our own Flaw Manager that we'd be shut down before we'd have a chance to flag it.'

He was right. It was bad enough that they couldn't speak out against the flaws in the new pantheon system. Now they had a potentially world-altering disaster on their hands that would be denied by anyone who could actually stop it.

Merky chuckled.

'Why are you laughing? *Why are you laughing?*' Erin's freckles disappeared into her flushing cheeks, as they often

211

did when her emotions were high.

'Well, it's ironic isn't it,' he replied, trying to stifle his amusement. '*We* can't do anything, so we've just got to hope that the people *down there* can do something about it.' Merky threw his hands up for the punchline. 'The gods have to believe in the mortals!' He brushed a tear of laughter from his apple cheek. 'Oh dear, what a terrible situation this is.'

***

'Do come in,' said the old man. 'Make yourself at home.'

'Cor blimey sir, that's mighty kind of you. This storm came out of nowhere, it did.' The merchant stepped into the house and allowed himself to be ushered into a very modest drawing room. The old man left him drying by the fire, and came back some time later holding two clay mugs of dark liquid.

'Thank you sir, much obliged.' The merchant took the steaming drink and peered into its black depths.

'Cocoa, is it , sir?'

'Rose tea, actually. Brewed with my own roses. A special variety,' replied the old man, who took a sip from his own mug.

'Oh, right, lovely.' The merchant took a sip as well. 'Not half bad!'

'Thank you. Now tell me, what is it you sell exactly?'

'It doesn't seem right to reel out my patter to such a gracious host, *but* if you insist!'

The merchant stood up and began to unroll his pack across the floor. It seemed to go on forever, but just when it looked like it was going to go out of the door, he stopped.

'Right, sir, here we are. A wardrobe fit for a baron. A marquess, even. A man, dare I say sir, such as yourself!'

The merchant gestured to the pile of clothes before him as if he were announcing a debutante. Then he crouched and lifted up an exquisite silk shirt from the pile between his thumbs and forefingers.

'The foundation of any respectable man's ensemble, the shirt. Sir, we live in a world of starch, of rough wool, of hessian, even. To put it bluntly sir, we live in a world of chaffed nipples. But, sir, there is hope! This silk shirt will not only protect your nipples from unwanted wear, but it can also be bought in two dazzling colours - green, and sage.'

'Fascinating,' replied the old man. 'What exactly is the difference between green and sage?'

'An astute question, sir! You possess a curiosity only found in the most discerning of customers. I can see that you are quite the connoisseur. Now, if I may draw your attention to these boots, sir.'

The merchant carefully laid the shirt down and retrieved a pair of knee-length boots.

'The trouble with boots these days, sir, is that when the buckles go, they're in the rubbish. What a waste! What I can offer you today sir are boots that you will never have to throw away. Observe. Not one, not two, but ten buckles sir! If one of the buckles breaks, you simply tighten the other nine. Ten buckles, ten times the durability.'

The merchant shook the boots in front of the old man's face, starting a cascade of tinny jingles as the clasps wobbled together.

'For you sir, I can again do two colours: red, and vermilion.'

'And if all the buckles break at the same time?'

'A forward thinker, sir. A man of infinite foresight. If only men like you were in the ruling class, oh what a jolly nice place this Peninsula of ours would be. Well, you know what they say, "dress for the job you want, rather than the one you have". In that vein, may I present to you this magnificent regal cap.'

The merchant set down the jangling boots and fished out

something resembling a giant fingerless glove.

'Now I know what you're thinking. You're thinking "by Ava, he's gone mad, that's clearly a giant fingerless glove," but you would be wrong! Attend, if you will, to my bonny nonce.'

The merchant grasped the cuff of the item and stretched it over his head. Once firmly on, the 'fingers' stuck up like the points of a crown.

'Majestic, is it not, sir? Note how the points have flexibility in them, for when one must pass through low doorways. Practical and pontifical. What's more, I can offer this beauty in either purple, or mauve.'

'I'll take everything.'

The merchant was visibly shocked. 'Everything, sir?'

'I like the colours. I enjoy them very much. Please, would you be so kind as to take these garments upstairs?'

'Of course. Of course! Right, away, sir.' The merchant was beaming now. He rolled his pack back up and gathered it under his arm. The old man carefully rested his mug on a small table beside him and rose slowly from his chair.

'Follow me, please.'

The two of them climbed the stairs onto a dark landing. The old man stopped and pointed at a door hidden in darkness at the end of the corridor.

'In there.'

'Certainly, sir.'

Reluctantly, the merchant went to the door, all the while ignoring the doubts in the back of his mind in favour of envisaging the great sack of ducats that would soon be his. The door creaked open.

The room beyond was filled with colour. Clothes, paintings, furniture, candles, wax fruit, all of it was as vibrant as a summer sunset over Dankvyr.

'My goodness, sir, this is quite the collection you have

here. I don't think I've ever seen so much beauty in one room. A true sight to behold.'

'Is it? I'm afraid I wouldn't know.' The merchant realised that the old man hadn't moved from his spot at the top of the stairs. He was staring wistfully in the direction of the room.

'Sir?' prompted the merchant. It had just occurred to him that nowhere in the house had he seen anything else of colour, except for the fire in the drawing room, and even that had seemed... odd.

'If I look for too long, the colours run.'

'You don't have to worry about that with my wares, sir. These colours will maintain their integrity even after one hundred washes.'

'I'm afraid you don't understand. The colours are... afraid of me.'

'Oh.'

'But I desire them. Greatly.'

***

The party's desperate flight from Haven led them north through the Krovanian mountains and into the lowlands of Falstyr. Cold grey rock gave way to lush pasture, babbling brooks, and tree lined thoroughfares. While they had still been in the oppressive shadow of the mountains very little had been said between the companions. Their bodies were sore from riding bareback, made worse by the chafing caused by riding two to a horse. It was not long before they resorted to taking turns between walking and riding. They all missed the comfort of the caravan, and the knowledge that they were at least a day behind schedule added to their sense of impending doom.

Rhev, however, had other thoughts that preoccupied him. His mistakes weighed heavy on his conscience. There was a time, when it had looked like they were going to die at the hands of a hundred goblobs, that Rhev had been happy to accept Sterling's acquittal. After the devastation that followed, and knowing that he had to live with it, the guilt and doubt returned.

Steem's caravan smashed to pieces. Friendship promised to those who sorely needed it, left in the dirt surrounded by enemies. A silly scheme for gold that endangered his companions in the process. 'Reparations' he had thought at the time. 'Justice'. Now he was sure it was just base greed, a lust for coin still lingering within him, a disgusting trait born from years of desperate survival in the city. Here he was, thinking he had left that Rhev behind, traded it for a new model shaped in his dad's noble image. What a stupid thought that had been. The question that had been burning in his heart since the wizard's visit was answered then: he must be a villain, not a hero.

On their first night out of the mountains, as they camped under a tree beside a busy stream, the dreaded conversation began.

'I've been turning it over and over in my head,' said Mercy, 'and I still can't figure out what the hell happened back in Haven.'

Rhev could feel his heartbeat rising. He felt like everyone was looking at him, their talons out. The fact it was Mercy leading the hunt made him sweat even more. He respected her, more than any of the others in fact, and now he was going to be hung upon the gibbet by her hands. He swallowed, knowing there was no way out. He knew his mistakes would be revealed, if not by him then by Sterling. He was surprised the halfling hadn't already accused him of treachery.

Rhev cleared his throat, and readied his confession.

'I messed up,' announced Sterling. Rhev met the halfling's eyes and knitted his eyebrows. Sterling gave him a look that said 'keep quiet'.

'We tried to sneak into the castle to steal the Box back but

216

we were caught by a madman called Victor. He threw us into a dungeon, but Rhev got us out. He made friends with those goblins and they helped us get the Box back. Victor spotted us on the way out. I think he used some sort of magic to control the villagers and command them to stop us.'

Mercy considered the explanation for a moment. 'Sounds like you were lucky that Rhev was there to get you out of your mess, Sterling.'

'I was,' he replied, nodding at the dwarf. Rhev nodded back in unspoken thanks.

'Shame he wasn't there to stop you losing the bloody Box in the first place.' It was the first time Steem had spoken in two days. 'If it wasn't for your weakness for any woman who gave you more than five seconds of her time, none of this would have happened.' Steem started to choke up. 'And now she's... she's gone!'

He got up from the log he was sitting on and walked away, running his hands through his sparse black hair.

Kevin broke the silence. 'I don't get it, who is he talking about?'

Mercy looked around to make sure Steem had gone, and sighed.

'His wife.'

Kevin looked at Sterling and Rhev to make sure he wasn't the only one who didn't understand. After a moment's pause, Mercy continued.

'Before we all started working for Steem, it was just him and his wife. I don't know much about it, just what he told me one night he had a few too many in Dankvyr. He said they'd married young and put their money together to buy the caravan. She was the one that painted it red. Apparently, it was her favourite colour. They started doing delivery work, just simple jobs around the south of the Peninsula. From what I gathered, they were very happy. One day they were taking the road through the Tynewood and she saw a grove of rose bushes through the trees. She told Steem to keep going while she jumped off to pick a few for him. He waited for her, but she didn't come back. He panicked and went looking for her in the grove, in the surrounding forest, back down the road, everywhere. He didn't know where she had gone. Eventually another caravan passed him. When he told them what had happened, they said there had been talk of fey creatures returning to the forest causing all sorts of trouble. He kept searching for another month. Nothing. She was gone. After that he started taking more risky jobs, so he hired me.'

Mercy blinked. She had been staring straight into the campfire.

'That caravan was their home. Now it's gone.'

No one felt like talking after that. Rhev lay down in a spot a little way from the fire to be alone with his thoughts. Up until that moment, Steem had just been a curmudgeonly man in a battered top hat. Now when Rhev pictured his face he saw a sadness hiding behind the big moustache. He realised then the significance of the floral silk sheet he'd found in Steem's room in Wathgill. He hoped that it was not lost too.

Just as Rhev was starting to drift away, he spotted Sterling walking nearby, searching for a soft spot to sleep.

'Sterling,' he whispered.

'Rhev?' the halfling replied.

'Why did you take the blame for what happened at the castle? Why didn't you tell them about my stupid plan?'

The halfling shrugged.

'We're friends, right? We cover each other's arses. You made a mistake, I made a mistake, but we're all still alive. Guilt doesn't have a use unless you learn from it, so learn from it and stop beating yourself up. What happened doesn't have to stop us being good people, and I reckon you're good people, Rhev. Mad people, but good people.'

218

Rhev wasn't sure what to say. He went with: 'Thanks mate.'

'Don't mention it. But maybe lay off the booze a little, yeah? Doesn't always make for the wisest decisions.'

The halfling winked, flopped down on a patch of moss, and fell asleep within seconds, tired from the day's hard journey.

'Don't I know it...' Rhev said quietly to himself, before dropping off as well.

He was awoken early in the morning by an inconvenient patch of sunlight hitting his face. The nearby stream continued to gurgle, and the willows swayed in the breeze. This land was far more welcoming than Krovania had been, Rhev decided, if only the sun wasn't so bright.

A noise disturbed his tranquil bower. The undergrowth cracked around him, as if the trees were coming alive. One of their nags woke up and snorted. It was answered by another horse. Not one of theirs.

Into the riverside clearing rode ten knights, their armor gleaming in the dappled reflections from the stream. Rhev thought about waking the others but there was no need. One of the riders lifted a long brass trumpet to her lips and blew hard. The blast woke everyone up and sent a score of birds bursting from the treetops.

'On the orders of Duke Kerroulach of Ponstrad, we are searching for the thief known as Steem Vennts, and his associates. Present yourselves now.' The knight spoke in a haughty manner that cut through the campers' morning brain fog. Rhev looked over at Steem, waiting to see what he would do.

'And who might you be?' he asked, standing to his full height in front of the speaker. The knight's horse twitched and shimmied under its barding, but Steem stood firm.

'I am Istla, daughter of Istrar, a knight of Falstyr,' replied the woman. She took off her helm to reveal a bob of jet black hair tucked behind tall pointed ears. 'The same question to you.'

'I'm a grumpy traveller who has just been awoken at this early hour by an inconsiderate bastard with a kazoo.'

The elf knight shifted uneasily, as did the herald behind her. She cleared her throat and straightened herself in the saddle. 'Justice never sleeps,' she replied smugly.

Somewhere behind Steem, Kevin snorted. 'They're novitiates, you can tell by their tabards,' he whispered to Rhev beside him. The fabric draped over their plate armour was light blue with a silver egg emblazoned on the chest. 'The egg hasn't hatched yet.' Before Steem could speak again, Kevin stepped forward.

'Indeed, justice may never sleep in Falstyr, but did it bring a warrant?' he asked slyly. The knight gulped and turned to her compatriots. Urgent whispers and gestures passed between them. One of the knights smacked another on the back of the head and tutted loudly. Istla turned back to Kevin.

'We, erm... don't need a warrant. We are on direct orders from the Duke himself. As knights of the realm we-'

'*Novitiates* of the realm,' Kevin corrected. 'I don't see the golden mallard on your breast.'

Istla was bristling now. She was clearly not prepared for this situation. Her fellow novitiates watched her with baited breath.

'What is your name?' she asked Kevin through snatches of exasperated breath.

'I don't think I have to tell you that, do I?' he seemed to be enjoying his verbal spar with the young knight. 'May I also point out how stupid it is to announce your purpose *before* asserting whether or not this Steem Vennts is in the company you're addressing. What reason do I now have to tell you my name? Presumably you were not given a description of Steem

220

Vennts, for then you would not have to ask the question. For all you know, *I* am Steem Vennts.'

Istla's eyes flashed in the reflection of her drawn sword. 'You heard him, he said he's Steem Vennts! Surround them!'

Before anyone had time to react Istla's fellow warriors raised their own swords and spears and made a circle of sharp metal points around the group. Mercy vainly tried to reach for her sword but the cold tip of spear in her neck stopped her.

'Easy now,' said Steem, waving his hands in a downward motion in an effort to calm everyone. 'Now what did this Steem Vennts character allegedly steal?'

Istla opened her mouth to say something, stopped herself, and then said: 'You think me so stupid that I would reveal what the stolen item is, just like that? So you can deny that it is in your possession? I think not! Haldo, search their belongings.'

The herald dismounted and began kicking through the sparse gear the group had managed to save from Haven. Rhev's eyes darted to the gnarled willow roots where they had stashed the box the night before. The herald was hovering dangerously close to its hiding spot.

'The magic box does not appear to be here Istla,' announced the herald in his nasally tenor.

'By Ava, Haldo, I just said we weren't going to tell them what we were looking for!' Istla replied through gritted teeth. 'Are you sure it isn't here? Check by the horses.'

Istla's eye twitched as she surveyed the group in front of her. Rhev could swear he could actually see the cogs in her head turning.

'Haldo, what's that behind the nag?' she said, without even glancing that way.

'You mean this brown pile of- OOF.'

The nag panicked as Haldo walked around to its rear. A loud clang resounded around the clearing, and Haldo lay sprawled in the muck with a hoof shaped dent in his helm.

'Assaulting agents of the peace!' Istla declared, a smug look of satisfaction on her face. 'Grounds for arrest, I think even this ingrate would agree.' She prodded Kevin's chest lightly with the tip of her sword. 'Get these criminals moving,' she ordered.

The circle of weapons corralled the 'criminals' into a file and they were marched away from their encampment. Rhev brought up the rear, the point of a spear hovering dangerously close to his nape. It was no use trying to fight his way to freedom. Green as they may be, the ten warriors around him were mounted and heavily armoured. Tension buzzed between him and his compatriots, as no doubt they were thinking the same thing. Amid his frustrated and panicked thoughts, something of deadly importance rose to the forefront of Rhev's mind.

'Wait!' he shouted, but it was too late. At the front of the line, Steem made a *hurk* noise and stumbled to the ground. The retinue stopped.

'What's wrong with him?' asked Istla. A fellow knight prodded the pale writhing body with the butt of his spear, but Steem didn't seem to notice. 'Ah I see, trying to pull another fast one on me, eh? Pretending to be sick? Pathetic!'

'We have the magic box!' Rhev shouted from the back of the line. 'Take us back and we'll show you where it is!'

'Hah, I knew it,' said Istla, her face lighting up at confirmation of her suspicions. She had completely forgotten about Steem. 'It was only a matter of time before you craven thieves crumbled under the weight of your own guilt. Knights, about turn!'

As the cadre reorganised itself Mercy lifted Steem up and away from the spot where he had fallen. Steem felt something slide back into his body, but the effects of a second souldrop had already taken its toll on the wearied man.

222

'I'm losing it, Mercy,' he croaked. 'Forgot about the contract, didn't I? So much going on...'

'Don't worry about it boss. These are confusing times. Just stay on your feet, eh? We'll find a way through it.'

They returned to the hastily abandoned camp and retrieved the Box, which still glowed faintly. While Istla was distracted by its strange sigils, Steem tried to surreptitiously retrieve something from his pack.

'Stop that!' ordered Haldo. 'Istla, he's trying to retrieve a weapon or something.'

'Step away from the pack, scum,' she said. 'No more tricks from you.'

Reluctantly, Steem dropped the crumpled lump of delicate silk. His jaw was set tight as he rejoined the others.

It took three days' journey west to reach Ponstrad. Falstyr was a pleasant country at least, with its vast rolling hills, ponds, and abundant duck population. The countryside was filled with the sound of peasants scything wheat, quacks, and profanity from the odd freshly uprooted potato. Squat stone towers dotted the landscape, the follies of every minor baron with delusions of grandeur and enough grain money going spare.

Any attempts to ask their noble captors more about their situation were quickly shut down, most likely because Istla feared any further embarrassment. The entire incident at the camp had left her prickly, and all she wanted now was to see these interlopers in the dungeons of Castle Ponstrad.

In the evenings the gang talked over their predicament. There was confusion as to why they had been accused of theft, considering it was their job to be in possession of the Box. Sterling suggested that perhaps Victor had accused them, but Rhev thought it unlikely a message could have been sent so quickly. Perhaps it was their employer who had alerted the duke, impatient to receive their delivery, but again this seemed unreasonable. The arcane contract they were bound to was watertight, and besides, a terrible fate awaited them if they didn't deliver by the specified date, which now seemed perilously close. Conjecture was thrown about wildly by everyone apart from Kevin. The closer they came to their destination, the more quiet the elf became. Gone was his bravado at the encampment, now replaced by a fidgety anxiousness.

Passing over the crest of a particularly large escarpment, the city of Ponstrad finally came into view. Its suburbs sprawled over wetlands surrounding a central stone causeway that lead to the inner city. Many of the houses in this exterior of the settlement were raised above the water on wooden stilts, and their residents stalked the lands on similar contraptions strapped to their feet. It was a comical sight watching the peasants awkwardly go about their business alongside the more stable herons and storks.

The inner city was a different matter. The causeway allowed access to a sizable tract of land buttressed by stone foundations. It was encircled by a tall wall made from the dark stone of the Krovanian mountains nearby, and upon those battlements was mounted a colossal statue of a duck. As they were pushed through the gates, Rhev saw that the impressive townhouses that lined the streets were similarly adorned in waterfowl statuary. Immaculate front lawns were dominated by carved sandpipers, waders, and snipe. Doors were guarded by frescos of enlarged herons. They had really gone *all out*.

Other knights, similarly garbed as their captors but bearing intricately embroidered mallard ducks on their tunics, rode by on their steeds. More of them came into view as the prisoners were led towards an imposing central keep. Warriors trained in sandy yards with sword and spear, regimented and disciplined. Gardeners refined topiary of geese watching over the path to the keep's tall entrance.

The party was led into an entrance hall festooned with faded tapestries. Rhev had to stifle a chuckle as he studied them. Many depicted a monstrously huge duck battling with various predators, such as lions and gryphons. In every instance, the duck appeared to be victorious, bathing in the blood of its kill. In none of the tapestries did the duck's expression show anything other than a cool, merciless placidity. It was, to be perfectly honest, quite chilling.

Istla had gone to talk to a guard standing by an inner door. She returned now, a smile on her lips.

'Time for you to stand before the duke and answer for your crimes, you... criminals,' she said, grimacing a little at that last part. Rhev exhaled and braced himself for what was to come. Kevin, however, groaned in annoyance.

The doors to the throne room were triumphantly pushed open by Istla to reveal an amusing, if not entirely unexpected, sight. A tall, muscular elf with a greying goatee looked up at the intruders, a loaf of bread in his hands. He was knelt down in front of a large, artificial pond. Its waters rippled in the wake of a variety of ducks as they hunted down floating crumbs. They began quacking in annoyance when the elf stopped feeding them.

'You would interrupt the daily giving of bread?!' he bellowed, standing to his full height and dropping the entire half loaf into the water. Mandarins and mallards circled it, unsure of what to do with such a large crumb. 'You better have a worthy excuse!'

Istla knelt imperceptibly fast at her lord's chastisement, and kept her head bowed low.

'My lord Duke Kerroulach, my sincerest apologies.'

'I should think so! Look at poor Willard, he doesn't know what to do now that you've interrupted his routine,' said the duke ruefully. He pointed at a particularly large mallard who span aimlessly in the water with its feathered arse in the air.

'My apologies to Willard too, my lord,' continued Istla, 'but I have I captured the thief Steem Vennts and his accomplices, as well as the item they stole.'

'You've captured who?' replied the duke, genuinely confused.

'Steem Vennts, my lord. Two weeks ago you ordered my cadre to hunt down and capture him.'

'Ah yes, to keep you out of trouble. Really thought it would take longer than this...'

'My lord?' said Istla, raising her head.

'Nothing, nothing. Well done Istla, you've done your family proud.' The duke turned and shouted in the direction of a side room. 'Istrar, she did it! She actually found him!'

A voice echoed out of the adjoining space. 'Who?'

'Steem Vennts!'

'Oh, really?' it replied. 'That's a shame, I thought she would be gone longer than that.'

There was an awkward silence as the duke met Istla's gaze.

'She's right here, Istrar. In the throne room. Now. With me...'

A clatter and a string of muffled profanities preceded the arrival of a flustered elf wearing ornate green-blue robes, his pointed ears balancing a tall yellow hat.

'Hello darling! It's so nice to see you. I hear the criminal hunting went well?'

'Yes, father,' replied Istla through gritted teeth. 'We have apprehended Vennts.'

'Excellent, excellent. Beckett will be so pleased. So where is he then?'

Istla issued an order to her fellow novitiates to bring the captives forward..

'Great. Very good. Which one is he?' asked the duke.

'We, erm, we're not sure. One of them is. They won't tell us their names though,' Istla replied, her high cheeks turning a pinkish hue. 'But they do have the stolen box, so it must be them!'

'I see. We'll just have to get Beckett out here to confirm. You there, Haldo, go and get the money man. He's in one of the guest rooms.'

Haldo nodded eagerly and ran off to fulfill his quest.

'Who's that skulking at the back? Come forward.'

Reluctantly, Kevin stepped to the front of the group, doing his best to hide his head. Without warning, Duke Kerroulach burst into laughter. He slapped his knees hard.

'Oh my, oh my! This is priceless! The heir to the throne returns! And with a group of vagabonds no less. Ha! So much for glory and riches eh, Kethlan?'

'What's he talking about, Kevin?' Steem whispered. Kevin made no reply. He was shaking softly with rage.

'Istrar, look, it's my son, the wanna-be-wizard! Come back for some pocket money no doubt.'

'By Ava, it is!' exclaimed Istrar, lifting a hand to his face in surprise. 'Little Kethlan, still skin and bones I see. Didn't ever quite fill out like your father here, that's for sure.'

The duke and his seneschal laughed heartily.

'Kevin, is that your dad?' asked Rhev. Kevin turned. His lips were drawn tight.

'He's a brutish, duck-obsessed idiot, that's what he *is*. But yes, he also happens to be my father.'

'Well, that's great, isn't it? You can just tell him we're not thieves and we can be on our way,' said Sterling excitedly.

Kevin tried to reply but a nasal screech cut across him.

'Severin Beckett of Dankvyr, you lordship!' cried Haldo at the top of his lungs.

Duke Kerroulach and Istrar halted their fits of laughter to clasp their hands to their ears.

'Yes, yes, thank you Haldo. Please do try and work on that tone,' said Istrar.

The newcomer stood next to Rhev, although a little ways apart, as if the dwarf gave off a bad stench. Behind him stood a short fellow with a worried look on his face, and a large, well-weathered fisherfolk.

'Mister Beckett, we have apprehended the man you have accused of stealing your property, and the property itself,' announced the duke.

Istla nodded for her men to place the box down in front of Beckett. He turned briefly to the fisherfolk behind him. He nodded silently, and Beckett turned to address the duke.

'My sincerest thanks, Duke Kerroulach. Justice has clearly been served.' Istla nodded to herself at that remark. 'You can be sure to receive the loan for your new waterfowl gardens on my return to Dankvyr.'

The duke's eyes lit up, and he couldn't help but rub his hands together.

'This is nonsense!' bellowed Steem. 'The box doesn't belong to this Beckett bloke at all! We're on contract to deliver it to a Mister Kowloon of Little Mosshill. He's a bloody liar!' He shoved a fat, calloused finger in Beckett's direction.

'Please put your finger down, Mister Vennts. Mister Beckett here is an upstanding member of the Dankvyrian financial sector. You, on the other hand, appear to be the leader of a gang of scruffy brigands. I know which one I'm more inclined to believe.'

'Are you having a laugh?!' Steem screamed hysterically. 'Kevin is your son for Ava's sake!'

'I am well aware that *Kethlan* is my son, Mister Vennts,' said the Duke coldly. 'If anything that makes me *more* inclined to believe Mister Beckett's accusations.'

'We're under an arcane contract,' protested Mercy. 'If we don't deliver to Mister Kowloon, we will suffer a fate worse

228

than death.'

The duke and his seneschal laughed.

'What an absurd story! An arcane contract?' said Istrar. 'Forbidden, as I'm sure you well know. I'm certain nobody even knows how to make them any more. Can you even produce this contract?'

'It was left back at our encampment,' said Steem.

'*Convenient*. My lord, your son really has picked the dullest group of ingrates to associate himself with."

'Quite so,' the duke agreed.

Rhev turned to Istla. 'You saw what happened to Steem when we left the box behind. His soul was dropping!'

Istla didn't even make eye contact with Rhev, addressing Duke Kerroulach instead. 'Petty tricks my lord. Feigning illness in captivity. I didn't fall for it.'

Rhev threw his hands up in despair. Istrar gave his daughter an enthusiastic thumbs up.

'This is pointless,' Kevin said quietly. 'He's been trying to get the money together for that duck garden for as long as I've been alive. Having an excuse to punish me is an extra bonus.'

'You see now why this is a very simple matter,' said the duke in a tone of finality. 'I have already discussed the sentencing with Mister Beckett, and he has agreed to-'

'Wait!' shouted Kevin, suddenly gaining an air of confidence. 'As heir apparent to the duchy of Ponstrad, I... *Kethlan*, hereby invoke the right of trial by combat. If I win, all charges will be dropped against me and my cohort. If I lose, we will accept the punishment that you have deemed fit, *father*.'

The duke, agape, turned to Istrar. In a low voice he asked: 'Can he do that? I thought we abolished trial by combat?'

Istrar cleared his throat and replied quietly: 'We did, my lord, except in the case of your lineage.'

'Why did we do that?'

Istrar paused, and said: 'Because you said, and these are your words I may add, that it "sounded pretty fun".'

'I did say that, didn't I?'

'You did.'

Duke Kerroulach shrugged and addressed his son. 'Very well. I cannot deny you the rights of your title. I will however add a caveat to this trial. If you do indeed lose, which you will, you will forfeit your inheritance and right to the duchy of Ponstrad.'

'Fine with me,' replied Kevin through gritted teeth.

'Excellent! Mister Beckett, please choose your champion.'

Disarmed by this unexpected turn of events, Beckett blustered.

'This is most unorthodox, Duke Kerroulach. A champion you say? Um, err…'

He looked at the fisherfolk behind him imploringly. He was met by a dour expression and a stern shake of the head. He turned then to the short, bookish man beside him, and then apparently thought better of it.

'I will be Mister Beckett's champion,' declared Istla, saluting the duke. 'It will be an honour to do my lord's justice.' She looked sideways at the accused, her lip curling into a sardonic smile.

'Good thinking, Kevin,' said Mercy, putting a hand on his shoulder. 'Just pick me and I'll make short work of this upstart.

'No, Mercy,' replied Kevin, turning to the group. 'I'll be the champion.'

'You can't be serious?' Mercy raised an eyebrow. 'You've got many… talents, Kevin, but you're not much of a fighter.'

'He's knows that, Mercy,' said Sterling. 'It's personal, isn't it Kev?'

Kevin nodded grimly. Steem grumbled.

'Kethlan. I assume you'll be choosing the muscular woman

behind you as your champion?' asked his father.

'Wrong, dad. I'll be my own champion.'

The duke chuckled. "My dear boy, you're no warrior. I saw you slapping those training dummies around with a wooden sword when you were a sprog. As I seem to remember, it was you who came off worse.'

'At least we agree on something, dad. It's true that I am no warrior,' Kevin admitted, his hands balling into tight fists. 'But I *am* a wizard.'

***

'I was all up for you standing up to your dad, Kev, but are you sure you're up to this?' Sterling asked as he massaged his friend's shoulders. 'Your magick hasn't exactly been very reliable for quite a while now.'

'Let's not put any doubts into the lad's head,' said Steem, wringing the brim of his hat nervously. 'He's got enough to worry about.'

In the opposite corner of the training yard, Istla was stretching her lithe limbs. The sound of Haldo sharpening her sword dominated the scene like the drums of war.

'Sterling's right though. Kevin hasn't cast a proper offensive spell since that time in Montefort, and that was years ago,' said Mercy. 'Why couldn't you have picked me? I could take down that little girl one on one, no problem.'

'I saw you bring down a lightning bolt from the sky back in the Grippen mountains though, right? Proper fried those gnomes you did, and this lass is wearing metal armour. Easy peasy,' said Rhev, in a desperate attempt to lift their spirits. Mercy gave him a pointed look and a very slight shake of the head.

'Look everyone, I know you're worried about me. But if can't do this now, what was the point in me running off all those years ago to show my stupid father that elves *could* learn magic? That my worth wasn't based on my ability to swing a

231

sword? By Ava, I *am* the wielder of the magick of Pingle, forty-seventh mightiest of the gods, and I'm going to prove it to these jug-headed elves.'

Kevin stood up and removed his billowing silk shirt. Without the bulk of the garment covering him, it was painfully obvious how skinny he was. But he was tall, and he cut a proud shape as he held his ash wand by his side, like a duellist readying his rapier.

'Come on then, let's get this over with!'

Istla looked to the duke, who sat on a portable throne by the side of the training grounds. A large duck sat on his lap. The duke nodded, and Istla took her sword from Haldo and brandished it two-handed. The two combatants, their glossy black hair catching the sunlight, circled each other.

Kevin muttered under his breath. In his free hand he made intricate shapes in quick succession, pinching the air, then cutting it in two, then pointing with his index and little finger. He had yet to raise his wand. Istla came at him suddenly, sword raised up, tip forward, blade parallel to the ground. Just as she reached Kevin she swung it around in a horizontal circle above her head. It could have decapitated Kevin, but it was a flamboyant move and clearly telegraphed. Kevin ducked and dodged out of the way, causing Istla to stumble from the momentum as the expected resistance left her range. She cursed.

'You know, once you're out of the equation, my father will be next in line for the dukedom,' she hissed.

'You clearly don't know my father,' Kevin retorted as he retreated to the other side of the yard. 'He's more likely to give the duchy to his favourite duck.'

The wizard finished gesturing and a faint purple light illuminated his free hand. He lifted it to the wand, grasping it much like Istla had her sword, and swung it around his head. He aimed at her. There was a faint pop, and an impressively large bubble grew out of the end of the wooden rod.

The crowd that had gathered around the arena burst into laughter. 'There's the boy I know,' cackled the duke. 'Forever blowing bubbles like a baby. I thought you said you were a wizard now? I thought *real* wizards were supposed to wear little shorts?'

'Not shorts, you oaf! Hot pants!' Kevin grunted in frustration and smacked the wand repeatedly against his thigh, as if trying to dislodge something. Istla came in for another attack, passing her sword from hand to hand in an attempt to confuse her opponent.

'Look out, Kev!' shouted Sterling, as the blade whistled towards his friend's head. Kevin's almost preternatural ability to avoid danger kicked in quickly, but not quite quickly enough. He cried out in pain as the tip of his pointed left ear flew onto the dirt.

'Half an ear, half an elf!' mocked Istla. 'It suits you. You shame your father and our kind by dabbling in cowardly magick, Kethlan. And even in that, you fail!'

Kevin took his blood soaked left hand away from the stump of his ear and began frantically gesticulating once more. He raised his voice to utter the verbal components of whatever fresh spell he was attempting. It was total gobbledegook as far as Rhev was concerned, but he dearly hoped it would work.

Twice more Kevin dodged out of the way of Istla's blows. Her form was good and she was clearly well trained, but the elven swordsman seemed intent on dealing a final crushing death blow on every strike, giving Kevin time to gauge her angle of attack. No doubt if she had treated this fight with any modicum of respect, Kevin would have been dead in an instant.

Finally the spell seemed to be ready. With another flourish he set the energy he had conjured into the wand and fired a rule-straight beam of light in Istla's direction. Whether through chance or skill, her sword deflected the beam away, causing it to hit a nearby training dummy. There was a collective intake of breath as it appeared that Kevin had finally unleashed the full potential of Pingle. Then, with acute comedic timing, the training dummy raised its stick arms in the air and began to jiggle and dance on the spot. More laughter rained down on the struggling wizard, his mouth agape at yet another failed spell.

'It's a shame you left court,' sniggered Istrar, as his tall yellow hat began to slip from the shaking of his laughter. 'You would have made a fine jester for your father!'

'Quite so, Istrar, quite so!' the duke agreed, slapping his seneschal on the back. 'Come now Kethlan, admit defeat and we can stop all this before you lose any more dignity or body parts!'

'Come on you silly sod, summon that ball of fire, like you did in Montefort!' yelled Steem. His hands vice gripped the fence surrounding the yard as images of a life in a dungeon flashed before his eyes. Kevin faced his comrades for a moment.

'I... I can't. I've lost it, I... there's so little magick to gather. It's like Pingle isn't even there! Oh Ava, what have I done!'

The blade swooshed past him yet again, the force of the swing burying it into the wood of the fence between Steem's hands. Kevin continued backing away, abandoning any attempt to prepare a third spell. With a start, he stumbled backwards and fell on his arse. He had tripped over something at knee height, something soft and feathery. Looking up, he saw a large mallard duck pecking curiously at the severed tip of his ear. His breathing grew heavy as a wild idea crossed his mind.

After many tugs and grunts of frustration, Istla finally drew her sword from the wood it was embedded in, and grinned triumphantly as she saw her quarry sprawled in the dirt. She raised her sword high above her head. Her pace quickened. A bloodcurdling scream issued from her lips. In her blind fury she barely noticed Kevin grab the duck and raise it in front of him as a shield. Committed to the strike, she heaved her weapon.

'Stop! By Ava, stop!' The duke wailed and stood up shakily from his portable throne. 'Let him go! Let Willard go!'

The two combatants froze and looked at the duke. A confused quack echoed across the now silent yard.

'You always did prefer your precious ducks to your only son,' Kevin sneered. He pushed himself up off the ground, one hand around the duck's neck. 'Ducks do what you expect them to, right? No disappointments with ducks. A duck is always a duck. Ava forbid they would want to be something else.'

'The metaphor is a little mixed, but I think I get it,' Rhev whispered to Sterling, sotto voce.

'Kethlan, please! I just wanted you to live a respectable, noble life, like me! None of this deviant wizarding nonsense. It's beneath you.' The duke's voice quivered as Kevin tightened his grip around the duck's neck. 'Now, just put Willard down, and we can talk about how you can improve.'

'I don't think so, dad. I'd prefer to be a deviant wizard who can't even do proper magick than a narrow-minded brute. It's elves like *you* that give us a bad name. Now let us go with our possessions and the Box, and I'll let Willard live.'

'Listen here you duck-molesting-' began Istrar, but Duke Kerroulach held up a hand to silence him when Willard let out another confused quack.

'Very well, your possessions will be returned to you and you will be free to leave, but *not* as the heir of Ponstrad. It will be exile for you. I will also say this: do not speak of me being a brute, when you are the one threatening the life of a noble duck.' Kevin rolled his eyes.

Istla backed away at a nod from her father and reluctantly ordered her fellow novitiates to return the accused's poessessions. As they went to take the Box from a dumbfounded Beckett, he finally spoke up.

'This is insanity! What about the bloody duck garden?' he said hysterically.

Duke Kerroulach turned on him with tears in his eyes. 'What is a duck garden... without Willard?'

Beckett blustered. 'Manu, take the box, we're going.'

Hesitantly, the bulky fisherfolk bent to pick up the box. The duke waved a hand, and before Manu could reach it several spear points jutted into his frame of vision. He stood up straight with his hands up in surrender, and shrugged at Beckett. The spear carriers picked up the Box and dumped it at Steem's feet. Other novitiates left the few weapons and token belongings that had been pilfered from the group's encampment on the ground in front of them as well. Cautiously, Rhev, Mercy, and Sterling re-armed themselves, and Steem picked up the Box. Kevin backed slowly out of the gate of the training yard and rejoined his compatriots, duck still in hand.

'We're taking that wagon,' he said, pointing at a modest two-horse cart. 'Don't follow us. I'll leave Willard somewhere near the border. I'm sure he'll find his way back. He must be a *very* smart bird, yes?'

Duke Kerroulach nodded slowly, and motioned for the noviaties and fully fledged knights milling in the castle grounds to make way for the band of ornithological terrorists. They parted like water, and with a crack of a whip Steem drove the wagon through the cobblestone avenues of Ponstrad proper and out into the wetlands.

The seneschal spoke cautiously to his lord. 'Does this mean that I am next in line for the duchy?'

Duke Kerroulach glared at him. 'No, you bloody fool. That honour goes to Willard, the son I never had. It's the least he deserves after this.'

***

'Your dad is quacking mad,' said Rhev, shaking his head at the terrible joke. They had stopped the wagon a mile outside the boundaries of Ponstrad. Kevin stood at the banks of a tributary with Willard held tightly in his hands. By all accounts, it seemed like the duck had quite enjoyed the events of the day. Rhev had a suspicion that it had never left the city of its birth until now. *So now I'm empathising with a duck.*

Unceremoniously, Kevin plopped the oversized mallard into the river. After a second of manic flapping, the creature settled and bobbed serenely in the current. Then, with a quack that sung of determination, the duck began paddling upstream, away from Ponstrad.

Kevin sighed forlornly, and then realised that all eyes were on him. He smiled sadly.

'Dad's always been like that, ever since I was born,' he said. 'My mother died giving birth to me, and I got the blame. When it became obvious that I wasn't going to be a fantastically muscular and meat-headed warrior like him, he stopped giving me the time of day entirely. He became obsessed with his pets instead. Maybe it was a coping mechanism, I don't know. I don't care, actually. All I know is that there was no room for me in that castle, so I left when I was fourteen. Went to Yedforth, changed my name, used the last of the coin I'd pilfered from the treasury to get old Sedrach to teach me magick. Pingle wasn't exactly my first choice for a magickal conduit, but there weren't many mages in Yedforth willing to take on an apprentice, so here we are. Now I'm a disinherited wizard who can't even do proper magick. Maybe I should have just stayed at court, been a jester.'

'You did a glorious thing, Kevin,' said Mercy, placing a hand on his shoulder. 'You chose to live outside the shadow of your parents. Walk your own path. Not measure yourself against their achievements. That's a difficult thing to do, and you should be proud. For what it's worth, I don't care if you can do magick or not. As long as you do your best to help, that's all that matters.'

'But if you ever *do* feel like doing some magick, don't *not* do it, you know? It would be nice-' Steem stopped talking under Mercy's withering gaze.

Sterling broke the silence. 'So, where are we going now?'

'To the Lindentarn ferry. It's the fastest way to Relthorn, straight across the lake,' declared Steem, intent on taking charge of the situation once more. 'Originally we weren't going to take it, seeing as the old girl exceeded the ferry's weight limit,' his voice wobbled a bit, 'but now that we've got this lean, mean, stolen vehicle, it's back on the cards. Silver linings and all that. It's a good thing too, actually, because we've got time to make up after that Ponstrad debacle.'

'How much time exactly, Steem?' asked Mercy.

'I won't lie to you,' he replied. 'It's going to be close.'

***

The old, grey man sweated feverishly in his attic. His hands had stiffened into claws, and he was struggling to hold the chalk. He had grown lazy. He had left it too long. It was this world. It spread procrastination and ingratitude like a disease, and it had gotten to him. If only its people could appreciate what they had here.

Two more symbols, that's all he needed to draw. Two more symbols would complete the circle. Two more symbols is what it would take to harness Ava's magick.

A line and a loop. One symbol left now. The old man could feel the forces pull on him. Not yet. Not now. This would be the last time he would have to do this, if all went

238

well.

A cross. A dot. The chalk marks glowed in the dark. He could feel his fingers loosening now. The invisible forces pushing and pulling his body abated. He sighed, and chuckled to himself.

How clever he was. How superior. He was defying the gods, and they had no idea. Nothing would stop him.

***

'I've been thinking,' said Erin. 'Mortals are quite stupid, aren't they?'

'Undoubtedly so,' replied Merky, 'but you can't help rooting for them.'

'The other day, I saw an elf try to cross a shallow river. He started wading across, and then slipped. He started shouting "don't you run away from me", and punching the water.'

'This was an elf you say?' Erin nodded. 'Doesn't really surprise me.'

'There was a bridge less than a quarter of a mile away.'

'Alright, that *is* bad, even for an elf.'.

'My point is, they're not very good at... directing themselves. I know we can't get anyone else to intervene, but we've got to do *something*, right?'

'What were you thinking? An omen?'

Erin raised her eyebrows. 'Like omens have never been misinterpreted. We're talking about people who have been arguing whether the pointy rock on Mount Riszla looks like a rabbit or a duck for the last two thousand years.'

'Something more direct then?'

'I've been giving it some thought. I can only astrally project to hedgehogs, so I'm going to have a hard time communicating anything meaningful without some context. That's where you come in.'

Merky looked confused. 'I haven't even thought about astrally projecting for years now. Besides, I can only appear to

239

mortals when oaths or agreements are concerned.'

'And contracts, of course.'

'Well, of course. When contracts are conceived, broken, that sort of thing.'

'Conceived, broken, *and completed*.' Erin bobbed her head forward, trying to get Merky to understand. It took him a moment.

'Oh, I see. But won't that be a little bit late?'

'Better late than never, right?'

Merky conceded. 'There is one issue though. Astral projection in the new pantheon is heavily restricted. The Bestia and Fiat departments are going to have the astral pathways locked down, we're not going to be able to use them.'

'Don't worry about me, I've got a friend in the Bestia department. Nisca, looks after the woodlice, you know her?' Merky shook his head. 'Well, we've become quite good friends, and she knows how much I miss the hedgehogs. I'm certain she would let me use the pathways for a while.'

'Okay, great. But what about the Fiat department. We're hardly best chums with Chardo and his pals. No way I'm going to be able to do something as obvious as astrally project around them.'

'I've thought about that too,' replied Erin, tapping her nose. She seemed to actually be enjoying all this subterfuge now. Without warning she cleared her throat, relaxed her shoulders and lifted her chin. 'I've been, like, reading up on astral surfing man. Haven't you heard, the Sands of Time are bogus, man. It's all about the Winds of Change now, man.'

Merky had to stifle a laugh. 'Okay, okay, please stop. Maybe drop a couple of the 'mans' and steer clear of 'bogus', but I get where you're going. You'll keep those *boneheads* distracted all day if you can keep up that act.'

Erin beamed. 'Looks like we've got ourselves a plan!'

240

For three days the group trundled at a good pace through the green kingdom of Falstyr. On the evening of the third day the wagon pulled up to the docks of the small lakeside town of Wetbank. Huge nets lay strewn across the shingle beaches, and the scraping sound of dinghies being dragged ashore filled the air. Though Wetbank was small, it was also industrious. Almost all the inhabitants participated in some way towards the fishing trade. Netcasters, boatwrights, filleters, smokers: everyone had a role to play. The Lindentarn was very wide and very deep, so large in fact that it was a wonder that it hadn't severed the Peninsula from the mainland long ago.

Apart from the thriving population of trout, pike, and carp, the lake was also home to a very unique species. The Ull'bek, or the lindenfish as it is known colloquially, is neither flora nor fauna, but both. Its appearance is that of a broken branch, its leaves and twigs flowing behind as it gracefully maneuvers through the water with motions not unlike an eel. They vary greatly in size, number of twigs, and leaf density, and appear to possess no eyes, nose, or mouth. They are, however, able to navigate the waters as a fish would, and thrive near the surface where they can still catch the sun's rays. The people of Wetbank and their counterpart across the lake, Relthorn, learnt long ago that the lindenfish can be caught and dried like any other fish. Its leaves can be ground into a healing paste, while its branches can be burned to produce a heady, relaxing smoke, inducing visions in some who are open to them.

Stories tell of the origins of the lindenfish. They appear to originate from the waters that flow through the great and mysterious forest of Ull'Thranos to the north, from which the Lindentarn is fed. Grandparents delight in telling their grandchildren of the solitary and enigmatic woodland

241

dwarves who make their home there, and their habit of casting twigs and branches into the mystical waters of the river as a form of amusement, to see whose twig will reach the lake first. In ancient times, when people were fewer and there was more magick to go around, these dwarves would enchant their sticks in an effort to win the race, giving the wood the ability to propel itself through the water. Although it does seem like a mighty tall tale, one has to wonder whether a people who named their lakeside village 'Wetbank' would even have had the imagination to conceive of such a thing. Perhaps, then, there is some truth to it. Whether the dwarves still create all the lindenfish to this day, or that the Ull'bek evolved by some other means, it is not known.

Steem left the wagon and picked his way through the stacks of drying fish towards the largest jetty in Wetbank. The lanterns hanging on the wooden piles of the structure illuminated a small but motley crowd, all burdened with large packs of goods to trade in the settlements on the northwestern bank. Steem found who he was looking for, a gentleman sitting at a crude desk where the jetty met the dock.

'Looking for passage, sir?' the man said, looking up from the tattered volume he had been scribbling in.

'Aye. When's the next ferry?'

'The last ferry of the day will leave in about half an hour, assuming it gets here on time.' The man looked over his shoulder, out over the lake. 'It is currently running a little late.'

'Room for a wagon and horses?'

'Usually no, but it looks like we're light on passengers tonight. I hear some bastard has been telling folk tales again in the tavern. People do get so easily spooked. All nonsense of course, nothing in that lake to be worried about. Unless, of course, you're afraid of water!' He chuckled to himself.

Steem was not afraid of water, but he took some stock in

242

folk tales. He knew from experience that there could be truth to them. Unfortunately, time was not on his side, and the marshlands skirting the lake to the south and west would be slow going for a wagon. If they didn't get this ferry, it could be souldrop for all of them.

'Passage for five then, plus wagon and two horses.'

The ferry turned up not long after that. It was more of a huge floating pontoon than a boat. Wide and flat, and it moved under donkey power. The poor weary mules were harnessed into huge treadmill wheels that turned in the water, churning up a modest wake. The ferry nestled into the jetty with a series of bumps. A few passengers, similarly burdened as those waiting to get on, alighted and scurried off to find accommodation for the night. The ferry master, a surly looking fisherfolk with bright eyes began ordering his men to lay down the planks that would allow Steem's wagon to board the boat.

With some effort, the wagon and the horses were corralled on board. Once done, Steem and the others breathed a sigh of relief, grabbed their precious cargo, and went to find seats under one of the canvas tents on the deck. Only Rhev stayed outside. He made his way to the blunt prow of the ferry and sat looking out over the dark, starlit waters ahead of him. Despite growing up in a port city, this was the first time he had ever been aboard a vessel. He couldn't help smiling just a little at the new experience, one of many he'd had recently.

Just as the ferry master shouted the order to draw the gangplanks back in, a call went out to wait. Rhev heard the sound of hooves clop on wood. Then the work resumed, and the ferry was pushed away from the jetty and out onto the calm water of the lake.

Rhev was enjoying the relative quiet of the voyage. He focussed on the water in front of him. It looked like hot tar, sloshing and shining in the light of the moon and stars. It was mesmerising and relaxing to look at, but in the back of his mind Rhev couldn't help think that he wouldn't feel the same if he was *in* it, rather than *on* it. For one thing, he wasn't entirely certain that he could swim.

The rhythmic sound of lapping water and the filtered murmurs of the passengers in their tents was marred by the sibilance of nearby whispers.

'My friend,' said the first voice in a thick eastern accent, heavy with sorrow, 'I know you are lying to me.'

'What… what are you talking about, Manu?' answered the second voice, small and tremulous.

'Mister Beckett is not wanting to destroy this box, is he? He is wanting it for his own purposes. All he is talking of is money, money, money. He is just as bad as this Mister Kowloon the couriers are speaking of.'

There was a pause in the conversation. The sound of the lapping water somehow became more insistent.

'I did… lie to you Manu. I'm sorry. I'm so, so sorry.' The voice wobbled. 'I just wanted to keep my job. It's been my life, Manu, don't you see? If this plan fails, Beckett & Beckett will go under, and I'll go under with it.'

'You are thinking that your life is tied to Beckett, my friend. I do not think this is the truth.'

'But he's been my employer for so long. He's the reason I have a roof over my head and food to eat. I'm grateful to him. I am loyal to him… just like you were loyal to your captain!'

'This is not the same. My captain is making a bad choice, yes. This is not making him a bad person, I see now. He is always treating me with respect. This is why I am loyal. But Mister Beckett, he is not treating you with respect, Hampton! I am seeing how he treats you. You are his slave. Every day he is throwing something at you! You cannot be having loyalty to people who throw things at you!'

'His brother respected me…'

244

'I am thinking he is not his brother.'

'You... you are right, Manu. He is not Haverly, more's the pity. Oh, by Ava, I have been so stupid! I can't even listen to my own wisdom. Can you forgive me?'

'Sometimes, people are doing bad things for good reasons. It is you who are telling me this. Sometimes the bad thing teaches us the good thing. Yes, Hampton, I forgive you. Do not be keeping the burden of your guilt. It is bad for the soul, I can tell you.'

'Thank you, Manu.'

'You are welcome, my friend. But now we must be doing something, and it is bigger than you or me.'

'And you're huge!'

There was a shared chuckle.

'Indeed. Will you help me be rid of this evil box?'

'I think I would be rather a hypocrite if I said no, don't you think? Yes, I shall, Manu. But how?'

'I am thinking you are causing a distraction. Untie the horses, it will cause much fuss. When the couriers leave their tent to secure them, I will take the box and cast it into the lake. The Lindentarn is very deep. Even my people cannot see its bottom. The box will belong to the water then, forever.'

Rhev peered around a tent to get a proper look at the two plotters. One was a broad fisherfolk, the other a diminutive, balding man. He realised at once that they were Beckett's associates from Ponstrad. *I thought we were done with this lot!* He dearly wanted to jump the two of them right there and then. He knew he could knock the little one out cold with a good left hook, and he was pretty sure he could give the big fellow a run for his money too. If it came to it he could just run him through with his blade... No. No, he couldn't. That was the old Rhev talking. *Learn from your mistakes, stupid dwarf. Think of the consequences.* If he jumped these two now, he'd seem like the bad guy to everyone on the ferry. They would

245

have the watchmen on him as soon as he got to Relthorn, and that would cost all of them time they didn't have. He took another peek. The smaller man had vanished. *Time is running out. If you're going to do something heroic, better do it now.* So he did.

'Hello,' said Rhev jovially as he approached the fisherfolk. Manu's deep blue eyes widened.

'It is you. One of Steem Vennts' friends.' The fisherfolk began shifting his stance, his muscles stretching and tightening.

'Employee, actually, but I like to think we have a certain camaraderie. Name's Rhev Culluggan. What's yours?'

'Manu,' he replied, uncertainly. 'We do not have to fight, Rhev Culluggan. I only ask that you are handing over the box. It is an evil thing, it must be destroyed.'

'Yep, I'm not too fond of it either. Gives me the heeby jeebies, and has gotten us into a lot more trouble that even *I'm* used to. If I could be rid of it, I would be, quick as a potato.'

It was taking every ounce of Rhev's will to keep his muscles relaxed. The fisherfolk was clearly prepared for action, and if Rhev had misjudged his character, he was certain he would have him overboard in a matter of seconds.

'Why do you continue to bring it towards its purpose then?'

Rhev shrugged. 'We've got no choice. All of us.'

'I am hearing this a lot these days. No choice. No choice in doing the bad thing. Why are you having no choice?'

'You were there in Ponstrad, you heard what I said. We're under an arcane contract, one that we signed not knowing the full extent of what we would be taking part in. We were tricked, and now, if we don't deliver that box, we suffer a fate worse than death. Our souls will drop from our bodies, forever. I had it happen to me for about two minutes and I'll tell you this much: wasn't much fun. I wouldn't wish it on my worst enemy.'

'This is sounding like a very tall tale, Rhev Culluggan. How can I be sure that you are telling me your truth?'

Rhev looked long and hard into Manu's eyes. They shimmered in the reflection of the moon infused waters.

'You can't,' he replied.

It was a slight movement, but Manu was beginning to relax.

'What are you wanting of me?' said the fisherfolk.

'Let us deliver the package. Let us live. Let us live so that we can do our part to fix the wrong that we've got caught up in.'

'I am making this mistake before. It is eating me alive, Rhev Culluggan. You are asking much of me.'

'I know.'

Rhev couldn't bear the silence that followed. At this point he usually would have walloped someone or ran away. Unfortunately, you couldn't do either of those things when you're asking someone to trust you.

A bump. Another bump, reverberating along the hull of the ferry. More bumps, and some scraping too. It sounded very much like they were going over a large patch of driftwood. A very, very, large patch of driftwood.

The blunt prow of the ferry lifted several feet out of the water and slammed back down in a wash of foam. Rhev was lifted bodily off his feet and fell onto the canvas of a nearby tent. Muffled cries of alarm came from the bodies moving beneath him. He apologised and crawled his way off the writhing canvas. Manu had been thrown onto his back as well. Without hesitation, Rhev grasped his hand and lifted him to his feet. They stood once again, eyes locked.

The sound of falling timber diverted their gaze. Rhev looked up in horror at the impossibility before him. A tree as tall and broad as an oak was crashing down onto the ferry. He

247

dived out of the way as it made impact with the comparatively fragile deck, sending huge splinters in all directions. With the sharp sound of snapping branches, the huge tree began to slide back into the water. Rhev could see in the gloom that where the tree's roots should have been was a massive, amorphous bulk instead. He could no longer see Manu, so he turned and ran.

Rhev's companions released themselves from their collapsed tent just as he arrived.

'We've got to go,' the dwarf said.

'We're on a boat Rhev, there is nowhere to go,' replied Mercy. 'What's happening? Are we being attacked?'

'Never heard of pirates on an inland lake,' said Steem, popping out his top hat.

'We hit a tree, or an island, or something!' Rhev tried to explain.

'This ferry has taken the same route, day in day out, for as long as I can remember,' Steem said with a scoff. 'There's no way we've just hit an island.' He paused. 'There is *no* way we hit an island, so what the bloody hell is going on?' he continued with more urgency, then panicking: 'Where's the box?'

Sterling and Kevin were dragging it out of the wreckage of the tent. 'Thank Ava,' he sighed, seeing it was safe. 'Now where's the ferry master...'

The sound of falling timber echoed across the water again, except this time it sounded like an entire forest. One of the peddlers standing near them muttered to herself. 'By Ava, the bard was right. He was right...' Another voice cut through her mutterings, loud and terrified. 'Lindenkraken!'

There was no time to draw weapons. Trunks and boughs fell on the ferry from every angle. Bark and splinters flew around like arrows, piercing some unfortunate souls. Horses whinnied manically, some of them falling in the water. One of

248

the water wheels was crushed, its donkey *heehaw*-ing as it miraculously escaped the wreckage.

There was no plan. Nobody shouting orders. Most of the lanterns broke and were either extinguished in the water or set fire to tents. In the firelit gloom Rhev could see Beckett cowering in a barrel, eyes flitting nervously from one scene of carnage to another, and Hampton, his assistant, hemmed in by panicked horses. Rhev scanned the deck for the fisherfolk. The smoke was starting to make his eyes water.

Out of nowhere another massive trunk fell on the group. It crashed between them and tore a ragged hole through the ferry. All were cast aside by the impact and lay barely breathing on the deck, all apart from Rhev. By some miracle, all of the boughs and branches had missed him. His initial euphoria at his salvation quickly turned to dismay as he saw the box sliding inexorably towards a newly formed hole in the deck. He leapt at it, landing hard on his belly, and stretched out his stubby arms. It was too late. Just as his fingers touched the edges of the box it slipped into the bubbling waters below. Rhev watched in horror as the faint blue glow of its glyphs receded into the dark waters, the light growing ever smaller with each passing second.

He looked up to see the fisherfolk standing over him. Rhev tried to speak, to plead, but that dreaded feeling overcame him. All he could see was despair, and Manu could see it inside him. A fey look fell over the face of the fisherfolk. Then Rhev blinked, and he was gone.

Manu plunged into the cold depths of the lake. His blazing blue eyes adjusted in the water, compensating for its differing refractive properties. Now fully submerged, he could see even better than he could on land, and what he saw terrified him. A great leviathan stretched down into the depths from the ferry, its huge, heaving body made of dark, saturated wood. He had heard tales of the lindenfish from other fisherfolk, and whispered rumours of an ancient ancestor of their kind, birthed in a time long ago. He dodged a bark covered limb as it cast through the water with surprising speed and grace. He heard it land on the deck above him with a crack. He swallowed his fear. Water was the domain of the fisherfolk. He would not succumb to the despair of the dark depths that so often takes the heart of lesser men.

His broad, powerful form was but a speck against the monstrosity beside him. His legs moved in a single fluid motion, thrusting him down into the gloom below in search of the ill-fated box. The lindenkraken did not pay him any heed, but occasional limbs swung through his path, and more than a few he was unable to avoid. Still, he continued downward.

Rhev lost count of how long his soul had eluded him for. Indescribable misery filled his very being. Just when he thought it would never end, it did. Something etheric poured back into him. He gasped, and rolled onto his side to see a slick, dark-skinned man emerge from the hole in the deck beside. With great difficulty the man heaved a box onto the boards, and then himself. Rhev realised that the shine on the man's skin was not from water, but blood. The fisherfolk spoke quietly, barely audible through the sound of splintering wood around them.

'I am choosing to believe in your story, Rhev Culluggan.' He coughed, and blood welled around his lips. 'I am choosing to believe you are not a bad person... only bad- *cough,* choices. You are not deserving to suffer. I can not allow it. Take the box, be free of your burden. But please, do not let evil be coming to pass.' No longer possessing the strength to hold himself up, Manu collapsed onto his back. 'There is always another chance... to do... the good thing.'

Hampton came running over and fell to his knees. Weeping, he took Manu's head in his lap and shook his shoulders gently.

'Manu, what happened?' he whispered.

What breath was left in Manu's lungs escaped in the form of a single word.

'Pity.'

Hampton's smiled through his tears, and cradled his friend.

'Hampton. Hampton!' Beckett was shouting at his assistant from the shelter of his barrel. 'What are you doing? Leave the bloody fisherfolk! Get the box while they're still down!'

Hampton choked back his tears and replied: 'No, sir. I quit.'

Beckett was about to reply when he was suddenly launched, barrel and all, into the air and far across the lake. The sundered ferry had finally given up under the force of a final blow from the lindenkraken. It broke explosively into pieces.

Some time later, the sun now peaking over the horizon, Rhev and his companions drifted ashore. Flotsam surrounded them. A horse paddled awkwardly to the beach and set off at a canter as soon as it made landfall. Rhev loosened his grip on the Box that he had been holding so tightly, and coughed up some residual water. He saw the still unmoving body of the fisherfolk and his friend a few hundred feet down the beach.

Not too far away stood the town of Relthorn, the steeply pitched thatch roofs easily recognisable on the horizon. A few curious workers had stopped at the edge of the docks to watch the remains of the ferry float towards their town.

A hand on Rhev's shoulder made him start. 'You looked after the Box,' said Steem, his voice tired and raspy. 'Good lad. Come on, no time to lose. We've got until noon to get to Little Mosshill.' Rhev took one last look at the odd couple further down the beach, then nodded silently and joined his bedraggled crew, who had gathered together on a nearby dune.

The trudge along the sand was wearisome and frustrating. By the time they reached Relthorn the group were so desperate to get going that they simply ignored the frantic questions of the dock workers and their offers of help. Instead, they continued resolutely down the modest streets, dripping water onto the cobblestones. It wasn't long before they reached the edge of the town. There stood a sign that read 'Falstyr Point, Wetbank, Kippering, Hickscoombe', each line etched into planks of wood that pointed in different directions.

'Where's Little Mosshill then?!' blustered Steem, throwing his hands in the air. 'I know it's near here. I know! I remember seeing the sign when I came here last with Leila.' His body slumped as he choked out the last words. Everyone looked at each other and shared a sad grimace. Mercy put an arm around Steem. He was shaking ever so slightly.

'It must be nearby if you say so,' said Sterling.

'Maybe the sign fell off,' added Kevin, kicking around in the tufts of grass surrounding the signpost. He didn't find anything.

'I'll ask around for directions.' Rhev put the box down, and eyed a woman sowing seeds in a field nearby. He wandered over and leant against the fence.

'Hello there! I was wondering if you could tell me how to get to Little Mosshill?'

The woman stopped what she was doing and let a handful of seeds pour back into her basket. She gave Rhev a hard stare. 'Why would you be going to Little Mosshill?'

'I've got a delivery to make there.'

The woman snorted. 'Sounds like someone is having you on, lad. Ain't nothing in Mosshill 'cept empty homes and weeds. Nobody lives there, nobody goes there.'

'All the same, I-' Rhev was interrupted by the woman, who now had the look of someone who really enjoyed telling people more than they needed to know.

'It's a ghost town. People 'round here say it's cursed, you know. Ten years back, word stopped coming out of Mosshill. A merchant arrived in Relthorn one day, saying he'd passed through there. He said he hadn't seen nor heard a peep from anyone. But that wasn't the strangest thing, no. He'd gone through there at the height of spring, but there weren't a single flower or blossom in sight. Nothing at all, just an eerie drabness to the whole place. Some folk reckon whatever happened, happened 'cause they lived too close to the Thicket. A cautionary tale, that one, mark my words.'

Rhev was stunned. If indeed the mysterious Mister Kowloon did live there, why did he live in such a mysterious and abandoned place? Manu's words rang in his ears; he was almost certain now that evil awaited them.

'But if you *really* want to go there, you take the north road for twenty miles and take a left at the black stump. If you do come back, not that I think you will, but if you do, come tell me what you find. I love a good gossip.' The farmer cackled softly to herself and went back to sowing her seeds. Rhev returned to the group, who had taken the opportunity to rest and despair in equal measures.

'Good news, Little Mosshill is nearby.' Rhev clapped his hands. 'Ish.'

'How far is "ish"?' Mercy asked.

'Twenty or so miles.'

'Twenty?!' cried Kevin. 'How are we going to travel twenty miles by noon? That's it then! An eternity of soulless misery for us.'

Steem stood up and carefully adjusted his top hat. His eyes were dry now, but red. 'Pull yourself together, Kevin. We can make twenty miles on horseback.'

'On what horses?' he asked. 'In case you didn't notice, we lost ours somewhere in the middle of the Lindentarn, along with most of the money.'

'Stolen horses it is then,' replied Steem firmly. 'Let's go to the market.'

Relthorn's market was just starting to get into full swing. It was a popular trading hub for the north of the Peninsula, and people came far and wide from Falstyr, Wetbank, and even the deep forests of Ull'thranos. Fish was a major commodity here, as well as woodcraft from the northern forests and crops from the kingdoms to the south. Horses, a rarity in the north, were brought here as well. A corral had been built in one corner of the main square to facilitate their trade. As Steem led his crew through the throng of traders, they caught sight of at least ten worthy steeds jostling and bucking in their enclosure.

'How are we going to steal them?' Sterling asked, already shifting nervously as if he was a wanted man. 'I hope you don't think I'm going to do any razzle dazzle. I'm a rogue, sure, but I'm not a robber.'

Steem made no reply and tugged at his whiskers as he thought. A couple of watchmen wandered past wearing sturdy chainmail tunics and carrying spears. Kevin almost jumped out of his skin when one of them accidentally bumped into him. The watchman apologised and continued on his patrol.

Mercy looked hard at Rhev. 'What?' he said.

'You've got some experience in this sort of thing, haven't you, Rhev?' she insisted.

'What is she talking about?' asked Steem.

'That's not... now isn't the...' Rhev stumbled over his words.

'We don't have the time. Out with it lad.'

'She's, erm, talking about my past experience with being a

254

watchman, right, Mercy?' said Rhev through gritted teeth. '*Catching* thieves and that. You're right I suppose, I do have *a little* knowledge of how they operate.'

At the edge of the square a bell rang out. They turned to see an ornate four-horse carriage working its way through the slowly parting crowd. It stopped near the corral and a handsome couple got out. The gentleman took his lady by the hand and led her to the enclosure. She tittered as he whispered something in her ear, and pointed eagerly at one of the horses.

'Alright,' said Rhev. 'Forget those horses. I have a plan.'

Just as Rhev had suspected, the horse traders flocked to the finely dressed couple as soon as their bulging purse was revealed. Distracted by the desperate need to take advantage of the wealthiest punter at the market, none of them were paying attention to the gate of the corral. With a practiced walk that screamed "I belong here", Rhev approached the latch and awaited the signal.

The carriage's coachman leaned back in his seat and closed his eyes. He knew it would be a while until his master was done spoiling his new beau, and he always took the opportunity for a catnap if he could manage it. He was certain it was the key to youth. That's what his father, who had gone through approximately sixty jobs in his lifetime, had always said.

Just as he was settling in, there was a thump from the back of the carriage. It sounded like something had been loaded onto the luggage rack. Surely his master wasn't done yet? He sat up and looked around. No sign of him, but he better check just in case. He wound the reins around the arm of his driving seat and hopped down to the ground. A cough came from inside the carriage. He mounted the step and peered into the darkness of the carriage's interior.

'Sir? Finished already are we?'

255

He leaned in closer, not able to make out any forms in the velvety interior. Without warning, someone hoisted him off his feet. Another pair of hands pulled him headlong into the carriage.

Rhev lifted the latch on the gate and whistled sharply. Seeing an escape from their enclosure, the feisty stallions whinnied and bucked their way towards the opening. With their handlers distracted, there was nothing to stop them galloping into the busy square. Havoc ensued. Carts tipped, vegetables were trampled into mush underfoot, and traders ran in a panic towards the nearest watchmen. Amidst the mayhem a four-horse carriage driven by a man in a top hat cantered out of the square, with a dwarf clinging onto the back of it.

The carriage careened towards the edge of town. Steem drove the horses like a man possessed. It wasn't long before they reached the signpost, where the carriage screeched on its axles as it was flung in a sharp turn up the north road. The coachman landed comfortably in a nearby hedgerow. Behind them, Rhev caught the gaze of the farmer he had spoken to earlier. She was leaning on the fence, chewing on a stalk of wheat, slowly shaking her head.

The road northwards was not well kept. Weeds had started to grow in the grooves left by regular wagon traffic that had long since ceased. It wasn't long before they had left behind the tilled fields surrounding Relthorn, and entered a land of overgrown wild grasses and crooked trees. As the sun was close to reaching its zenith, they reached a fork in the road. In between its tines crouched a hideous tree stump. From a certain angle, its hollows and knots eerily resembled a screaming face. Steem slowed the horses down.

'A bad omen,' muttered Sterling as he leant out of the carriage window. He was yanked back in by Mercy's strong grip.

'This whole job has been a bad omen. Keep your head on and let's get this finished,' she hissed.

Steem urged the horses back to a trot, but they seemed reluctant to take the track towards Little Mosshill. Slowly, the carriage rolled onwards.

Half a mile down the track the thick greenery began to change. Where before the green-brown trunks of oak and beech had lined the road, they were now hemmed in by curious yews. Their trunks were faded and grey in colour, mottled with patches of white. Their leaves were equally colourless, various hues of grey, and in some places, black. The track itself devolved from a dusty brown to a blackish mire. Then they started to spot houses. Quaint stone cottages stood neglected, their thatch rotten and their gardens untended. From the back of the carriage, Rhev watched as they left behind the light of the noon sun. In the distance he could see that it still shone brightly, but here in Little Mosshill its light was diffused and weak, as if it were being filtered by a gauze. Greatly perturbed, Rhev clambered up over the top of the carriage to join Steem on the coachman's bench.

'How do we know which house is Kowloon's?' he asked. His tone was hushed. He had become aware of the silence draped over the village, and thought it best to avoid breaking its fragile web.

'Contract said end of the row,' replied Steem, equally quietly. 'Something tells me it's this one up ahead.'

The house in front of them was the only two story building in the whole village, and by that fact alone it seemed grand. As they drove closer they could see that it was built upon the edge of an escarpment which sloped away behind the house. At the edge of the wooded land beyond they could see the dark foreboding mass of the Thicket. Steem stopped the carriage, and everyone disembarked.

'Chins up, you lot,' Steem said as he stood by the gate to

257

the house, holding the Box before him. 'All we have to do is hand over the Box to this Mister Kowloon, and we're free from this bastard contract. No more living in fear of having our souls drop out of our arses.' He looked up at the weak sun above them. 'Just in time as well.'

'Wait,' said Rhev. He was the only one that didn't move. 'What do you think he's going to do with it? It can't be good, surely? That fisherfolk on the ferry said that it would be used for evil. I'm fairly certain he said that with his *dying breath*.'

There was a pregnant silence as the rest of the group weighed the potential morality of what they were about to do.

'Who are we to judge what's right and wrong, eh?' said Steem. 'I don't even understand what this bloody thing is. So it sucks people into it? Maybe this Kowloon bloke is going to put all the evil bastards of this world inside it. Maybe it will be used to *rid* us of evil! Had you thought of that?'

'But this all just *feels* wrong,' Rhev replied, unmoved. 'You must be able to feel it, right? In your bones, you know this is the wrong thing to do. Just look around us, this very place is forsaken! There must be another way.' He looked imploringly at Mercy, whose stern eyes betrayed a momentary flicker of agreement. Yet, she said nothing, and broke eye contact with the dwarf.

'Bugger all this right and wrong nonsense,' said Kevin. 'Makes no difference to me. I don't want to die. I don't want whatever happens if we don't hand over the Box. I'm going to live, damn it! In fact, I've *decided* to live, and none of you have the right to make that decision for me! I'll... I'll fight you if you try!'

'Calm down, Kevin,' said Steem. 'We're all going to live, because I'm going to hand over the blasted Box and fix the mistake I made when I got us all into this mess.' He turned to Rhev. 'No more talk of imagined evil, eh lad? Let me fix this.

Let me get us all off the hook and then we'll all be free to do whatever it is we feel like we should do. Please. Besides, if we don't hand it over now, we're going to suffer for no reason at all, because this Kowloon fella is just going to take it from our soulless hands anyway.'

'He's right, Rhev,' said Mercy finally. 'It's just a job, remember? No need to die over it...' The conviction just wasn't there.

'Just a job... right,' said Rhev, glowering. Sterling cautiously patted him on the back.

'That's settled then!' Steem smiled weakly. 'It's almost noon. Enough debate. We're getting this done.'

He nudged open the front gate with his foot, and led them up the garden path towards the house. Like the other cottages, it was grey and foreboding, but had been well maintained. The path was lined with white tulips in neat flower beds, and around the whitewashed door climbed a rosebush, its blossoms jet black. Steem hesitated for a moment, then knocked sharply three times.

'Delivery!'

A voice answered from somewhere behind the house. 'I'm out the back. Come around!' The voice was quavering and reedy, but friendly enough.

Cautiously, the group walked around the perimeter of the house and into a much larger back garden enclosed by tall, neat hedges. A glossy black rectangle, so still that it took Rhev a moment to realise it was a pond, was set in the middle of the lawn. In the opposite corner of the garden knelt a small, wizened figure in the shadow of the hedgerows. A modest collection of gardening tools were laid neatly on the grass around him.

They all stopped awkwardly by the pond, waiting for the figure to rise and face them. Steem coughed. There was a sharp snipping noise and the person stood up slowly. He was

259

the very definition of a grey, old man. So colourless was his hair and skin that if he had been seen in any place other than this monochrome garden he would have been presumed dead. Here, however, he looked very much at home.

He smiled, his skin bunching around well-worn wrinkles. 'So glad you came when you did,' he said. 'I think I've finally done it.'

As he walked over towards them he raised both hands outwards. Carefully gripped between them was a small iris flower, it's soft purple-blue petals and yellow centre starkly bright against the paleness surrounding it. But as he came closer the delicate white lines surrounding the yellow began to bleed outwards, until the entire thing was as pale and colourless as the person holding it. His face fell.

'Oh bother. I thought I had finally cracked it after all this time. Ah, well, I suppose it doesn't really matter now.'

'You are Mister Kowloon?' asked Steem, his business-like tone hiding the kernel of fear within him.

'The one and only, I suspect,' replied the man. His eyes feel on the object in Steem's hands. 'And that is my delivery, I hope?'

'It is.'

'I do hope it wasn't too much trouble bringing it here. I know it can be a bother delivering to people who live out in the sticks!'

'It was, erm, no bother, Mister Kowloon.'

'Good. Very good. Now, if you could please bring it to me...' The old man dropped the flower to the floor and thrust his frail hands towards the box. Mercy gently barred an arm in front of Rhev as he began to move.

'Shall I just put it down here?' Steem asked. 'It's quite heavy.'

'Pish posh, I'm stronger than I look,' the man replied. There was no way he had anywhere near enough muscle in his wiry frame to lift much more than the flower had just been holding. Steem shrugged and offered up the box. The man's claw-like hands gripped its sides and tugged gently. Steem hesitated, then let go. The old man smiled. It was a different smile to the one they had seen earlier. This one was much, much happier.

There was a pop that sounded like a fart in reverse, followed by a splash.

'Ugh, seriously? Gross.' Chardo was standing knee deep in the pond, the hems of his shorts dipping into the water. Slowly, he floated up into the air and began wringing them out.

'On behalf of the Fiat cohort of Ava and the once-god of contracts, Mercatrus, I, Chardo, hereby blah blah blah *has this stained?*' The minor deity began licking his thumb and rubbing it into the dark spot on his shorts. Seeing that it wasn't doing anything, he finally looked up at the dumbfounded group in front of him and narrowed his eyes. 'Seriously? You boneheads again? I can't believe you actually completed the contract.'

'We're free?' Kevin asked in an embarrassingly high pitched voice of disbelief.

Chardo rolled his eyes. 'Duh. So anyways if you could leave a review-' He didn't have time to finish his sentence. Instead, he was sucked into an invisible hole hanging in the air. As his body compressed into the infinitesimally small space, another form began to squeeze out. With a sound of a particularly *drawn out* fart in reverse, a new figure replaced Chardo.

'I haven't much time,' he wheezed. He seemed quite out of breath. 'My name is Mercatrus, I'm a god of... well, technically not any more... what am I saying, this isn't important! This man, he's not a man, he's an... um, a demon, of sorts. Actually, an Unfinished, really. You see, before the world was made,

261

well, *made for the second time*... time, time, there's no time! This box, it's a demongate. You've just given a demongate to a demon. Demons can go in, *demons can come out*! He'll take it to the world below and- no, wait, wait! Stop-'

Just as abruptly as Chardo had disappeared, Mercatrus was sucked out of existence.

'Oh-ho-ho, what fun.' The old man's chuckle was deep and languid. It didn't at all fit his body. His voice began changing as he spoke, lowering in octaves with each syllable. 'A little divine intervention. That was certainly unexpected. It has been so very long since the gods have bothered to go to such lengths.' He stared down at the Box in his hands. His eyes turned a deep, soulless black. 'Alas, as always, too late.'

The creature's manic grin widened beyond the confines of his face. Teeth multiplied to fill the ever expanding maw, sharp and dripping. The frail body grew thricefold in size and gained innumerable muscles and prominent ligaments. It laughed again, a sound like a boulder tumbling down the side of an abyss. The blue sigils covering the Box turned black and began pulsating.

Rhev drew his greatsword. It was released from its scabbard with a flash, and then it began to shout.

'AFFRONT TO THE SANCTITY OF THE SECOND WORLD! FORGOTTEN MISTAKE OF THE UNTERWELT! END THYSELF OR SUFFER!'

In a sickeningly deep bass, the creature said softly: 'How rude.'

It opened the box and released the refractive maelstrom inside. There was a crunching noise as the creature's bulk was compressed and sucked into the eye of the storm, and then it was gone, and this time, the Box with it.

There was perfect silence. Even Rhev's sword had stopped shouting.

'What have we done?' the dwarf whispered.

'According to that Mercatrus guy, we've just helped a demon to do a very bad thing' Sterling replied nervously. 'I'm really starting to distrust kindly old men...'

Everyone stood there in the grey garden, not talking, just processing what it was exactly they had just done. Mercy was the first to speak, after a loud, measured exhale.

'I've seen one of those demons, whatever Kowloon is, before,' she said as she sat heavily on the grass.

'What?' Steem started. 'Where? On the front lines?'

Mercy shook her head. 'At home, in Heptamil. I was a child. Many years ago there was a surge in... *alternative* worship. My people were tired of the old gods, how useless and impotent they had become. They began looking elsewhere. My parents were scholars at the Great Library, intellectuals. They had an intellectual curiosity in what was happening, that's all. Just an intellectual curiosity. At least, that's what I tell myself.'

Mercy paused and closed her eyes. She was finding this difficult.

'They had been working on something in secret. They were consumed by it. They started to forget that I even existed. I tried to talk to them, begged them to play with me, to sing me to sleep like they used to, but they were always too busy. One night I woke up and heard them talking downstairs, in our cellar. I wanted to know what it was that was so much more important than me.'

Her voice caught for a moment.

'So I crept downstairs and watched them from behind a crate. They were standing in a circle of runes they had daubed on the flagstones. They were chanting, or something, I couldn't understand the words, and there was this explosion of light. This... *thing* appeared between them. It devoured them. Completely. So many mouths... I was too frightened to even scream. It ran past me and out of the house. When I

263

could finally bring myself to leave my hiding spot, I found...
just, slaughter. The sand in the street was dark red, there were
bodies of my neighbours lying everywhere. I heard that it
took almost twenty soldiers to take that thing down in the
end. The officials reported it as a chimera attack. I guess the
truth was too confusing and horrible.'

'And Kowloon is one of these things?' Steem asked.

'He... *it* looked just the same.'

'Well, that clears it up then,' said Sterling. 'These demons,
or Unfinished or whatever that god called them, are *very bad*.
But hey, look on the plus side, it's gone! No demons here
anymore. When you look at it that way, we've done very
well.'

'Are you kidding me?' burst out Rhev. 'Where did it go *to*?
It can't just be in the Box. That would mean the Box is now in
the Box. Gods dammit, my head hurts!'

'Your sword,' Kevin replied. 'Your sword called Kowloon
'forgotten mistake of the Unterwelt.'

'Yes, yes, are we not going to address the fact that Rhev's
sword talked?' said Steem.

'Swords talk sometimes, don't worry,' Kevin continued
academically. 'It's the 'Unterwelt' bit that's got me thinking.
I've heard of it before, just once. My old teacher was
discussing it one night with a friend of his. I think it's some
sort of forgotten realm. No records of it, just a vague oral
history. The fisherfolk call it the Place Where Water Goes To
Die. I gather for them it's a sort of purgatory, they think that
anyone who gets lost ends up there.'

'Lost, you say? What do you mean?' Steem pressed.

'I'm not sure, my master wouldn't tell me anything when I
asked him directly. I think the fisherfolk believe that when
their people dive too deep and don't come back, they've gone
to the Place Where Water Goes To Die. Other folk have their
own stories, about those who go missing and are never found.

I figured the 'Unterwelt' was a myth, a way of making sense of losing someone.'

Rhev started pacing around the pond. 'Look, we're free, that's great. Excellent. But you heard that god bloke. Now we need to go to this Place Where Water Goes To Die, or the Unterwelt, or Demonshole or whatever you want to call it, and stop that *thing* from doing whatever it's going to do!'

'Did he actually say that *we* should stop it?' mumbled Kevin as he fidgeted with his wand out of habit. 'What can we even do?'

'By Ava, Kevin, did you not listen? Demon goes in, demon *can come out*. What if it comes back? What if there's more like it? We have to try… we have to try something. We're the only ones that *know* that *something* has to be done. How do we get to this place, huh?'

'I don't actually know *that*. And like I said, it's probably a myth anyway…' Kevin replied

'Rhev, just stop, please,' said Mercy quietly. She was staring at the ground. 'It's not worth it. The job is done. We should move on while we can. Let's just be thankful we're still alive.'

'I know you don't mean what you're saying, Mercy,' Rhev implored. 'You know if we stand by we're no better than accomplices to this bastard Kowloon. I will *not* be the villain here.'

'Come now,' Sterling mollified. 'If anything we're the victims here, not the villains. We were *unwillingly* coerced into aiding a demon from the Unterwelt in obtaining a means to teleport itself, and *perhaps* others, to *maybe* anywhere in the world. Not our fault… right? Right?'

Rhev growled and threw his sword down in frustration. The tip buried itself into the pristine lawn.

There was an indignant squeak. Rhev looked to where the sword now stood, and saw a prickly ball vibrating next to it.

As he went over to inspect it, the ball slowly unfurled itself.

It was a hedgehog. It raised its small snout in the air, and looked the dwarf dead in the eyes. With great difficulty it raised its front paws in the air. Hesitantly, Rhev waved back.

'I think this hedgehog is trying to tell me something.'

'I know this is a very stressful situation Rhev,' Mercy said gently, 'but let's just try to stay sane and-'

'Ever since we got here we haven't seen or heard a single living animal. Everything that could leave Little Mosshill, did. But now here's a hedgehog, who has come straight for us, out of nowhere, and I swear to Ava, it just waved at me.'

'What the!' Sterling jumped. Another hedgehog was insistently bumping into the halfling's ankle.

The group looked around in awe as at least ten more hedgehogs bumbled out of the undergrowth towards them. The first hedgehog tentatively put a paw on Rhev's heavy boot. When he didn't immediately kick it away, the little creature began to climb his trousers and his tunic.

Rhev daren't move. The hedgehog disappeared. A few seconds later its small face poked out of Rhev's beard. It squeaked contentedly.

Meanwhile, the other hedgehogs had formed up in a rough line in front of the group. The hedgehog in the beard squeaked again, and its compatriots rearranged themselves to form the unmistakable shape of an arrow.

'I don't really understand any of this,' grumbled Steem, 'but even I have to admit that these hedgehogs really want us to go somewhere.'

'What if it's a trap?' countered Kevin. Steem looked at him incredulously.

'They are hedgehogs, Kevin,' Sterling chided. 'I don't think hedgehogs are capable of malicious intent.'

'I'm pretty sure this one is smiling at me.' Rhev was staring cross-eyed down his nose, trying to get a good look at his hitchhiker. 'Let's be honest here, what have we got to lose? None of us has a plan of action, but it looks like someone, somewhere, is on our side. This is how adventures work, I know it. It just makes sense to me. Let's follow the hedgehogs.'

No one answered.

'Please. For Ava's sake, I'm looking for something, *anything* to do that seems *right*, and this is all I've got. I'm going, with or without you lot.'

Mercy finally looked up from the ground and made eye contact with the dwarf. 'There's no stopping you is there?'

Rhev shook his head, his brow furrowed in determination. Mercy smiled and bowed her head in acceptance.

'Let's follow the hedgehogs then,' agreed Mercy.

'It sounds barmy, but this little creature by my foot is being very pushy. Let's follow the hedgehogs,' said Steem.

Kevin raised his eyebrows at Sterling, who grinned in response.

'Fine,' he said, 'let's follow the hedgehogs.'

The hedgehogs formed a conga line of wiggling bottoms and led them through a small gap in the hedge. On the other side was a steep path into the wooded land below the escarpment. The creatures were surprisingly fast despite their tiny legs, and the group had a hard time keeping up with them as the undergrowth grew gradually thicker. The hedgehog in Rhev's beard appeared to tell its friends to slow down whenever they lagged too far behind.

After an hour or so of walking the flora began to change. Where the woodland below Little Mosshill had been relatively common for this part of the Peninsula, the trees that now surrounded them were densely packed and blackened, their boughs gnarled and dragging low on the ground. They had reached the Thicket, an inhospitable tract of forest that grew across the north western borders of the Peninsula, from the mountains in the north down to the sea. Those who entered the Thicket rarely returned, presumed dead or lost in the bewildering maze of spiky shrubs and trees. Any suggestion to fell the Thicket was always ignored, as it did have one vital importance to the inhabitants of the Peninsula: to protect them from the ever encroaching wastes beyond.

'I can't believe I'm willingly entering the Thicket with only a bunch of hedgehogs to stop me getting lost,' Kevin complained as he jumped at yet another shadow. The hedgehog in Rhev's beard squeaked.

'I think they're doing quite a good job,' he said.

'Are they? Where are we supposed to be going? How can you tell that we aren't lost already?' Kevin whined.

'Something tells me that getting lost is part of the plan,' Steem said quietly.

The canopy grew denser. The shadows thickened. The group started to lose sight of their intrepid guides and had to rely on following the sound of the odd squeak or soft grunt. Finally, the hedgehogs stopped. As Rhev's eyes adjusted to the darkness he could see that they had formed up in two columns, an honour guard of sorts, and in between them lay the entrance to a narrow ravine. His face tickled as the hedgehog climbed out of his beard and back down to the ground. It nudged the back of his foot.

'I think they want us to go down there.'

'I know I said that hedgehogs aren't capable of malicious intent,' said Steem, 'but I have been known to be wrong before.'

'Did anyone bring a torch?' whispered Sterling.

'Nothing good ever happened at the bottom of a dark ravine...' said Kevin.

The head hedgehog squeaked defiantly and nudged Rhev's foot again. He turned to address the group.

'You lot are probably thinking the same as me. "What am I

doing here?" I reckon I know. It's because deep down, even if you won't admit it, you want to do the right thing. If you didn't, you'd still be up there in Little Mosshill looking for the gold we're owed. I know you people don't put a lot of stock in tales of adventure and all that guff, but my dad told me enough of them for me to know that it's times like these, where you've a choice between walking away from the problem or trying to help, that make heroes. There's no gold in it, no fame, no nothing. That's why I know it's the right thing to do. Now, if you don't mind, I'm going to walk into this abyss at the arse end of the world, and bugger you if you don't think that's a proper adventure.'

With that, Rhev strode solemnly past the hedgehogs and entered the impenetrable darkness of the ravine.

'The lad's mad, isn't he?' said Steem. 'He really thinks he's in some sort of madcap story.'

'You know what? He *is* mad,' Mercy replied sternly. 'Let's be honest here, his sword is called 'Honour', for the gods' sake. *But* he *is* trying to help, and that takes courage. Maybe his reasons for helping are a little idealistic, but what's wrong with that? Are we just going to stand around here being cynical? Sounds like cowardness to me, and I'm no coward. Maybe... maybe I *have* been for quite a while now, without realising it. But I remember a time when I did the right thing just because it was right. It's been a long time, but by the gods, did it feel good. I won't leave Rhev to face whatever's down there alone. Time to put Warum to some real use again... and get some bloody revenge while I'm at it.'

Warum was pulled from its scabbard, and she, too, entered the darkness. The remaining three stared at each other.

'I've got my own reasons,' said Steem. 'Better come up with yours, or you're out of the running for employee of the month.'

He followed Mercy.

'Does the dwarf seriously expect me to be a hero?' said Kevin. 'Me? You know, statistically heroes are much more likely to die than normal people.'

'You don't have to be a hero, Kev,' said Sterling. 'You just have to not be a coward.'

'What if I *am* a coward?'

'Would you say that to your old dad, the duke of ducks?'

'Never!'

'Good! Down you go then.'

'Please, the common folk go first.'

Sterling punched the elf playfully on the knee, and they grinned at each other. Together, the darkness enveloped them.

The hedgehogs, satisfied with the completion of their task, hastened away to the south east. After they had left, a haggard figure stumbled out of the shadows of the trees, and made its way tentatively down into the gorge.

***

Erin and Merky rushed back to the Table chamber, casting furtive glances about for any sign of the Flaw Manager.

'I'm sorry, Merky, I should have known sand surfing was out and soul skating was in.'

'Not your fault,' Merky replied. 'Neither of us knew. It's just our bad luck that Chardo actually did his job for once. Your play with the hedgehogs seemed to work though, yes? We got the mortals to where they needed to go.'

'But Chardo knows we're up to something now! When he finds his way back from purgatory, that's it.'

'Don't worry, I'll come up with something, some excuse. Who's going to believe Chardo anyway? He's drunk on godsmead more often than not.'

They rounded the corner and entered the chamber. Several pairs of eyes stared straight at them: their coworkers, the Flaw Manager, and...

'Nisca? What's going on?' The demure god from the Bestia

department looked at her feet sheepishly.

'I'm sorry Erin,' she said in a small voice. 'I was scared.'

'You did the right thing, Nisca,' said the Flaw Manager, his voice reverberating around the room. 'You've protected the pantheon from sedition, from revolt, *from imperfection*. Ava herself will hear of your noble act, let me assure you.' He turned his attention to the two newcomers. 'And she will hear about *your* deeds as well.'

He walked towards them, his tall frame looming. Instinctively Erin and Merky backed away, only to find two other gods, similarly dressed in crisp white suits, standing behind them. 'Let's not behave like petty mortals. No struggling, if you please.'

The two accused were herded from the room and maneuvered down the corridor by the grip of strong hands on their shoulders. After a long and disorienting march they came to an area that neither of them had ever seen before. The beautiful rays of light that pervaded the rest of their realm were dim here. The firmament that they walked on seemed to creak. There was something ancient and terrible about this place. In her despair, Erin found the courage to speak.

'You're not taking us to Ava, are you?'

The Flaw Manager sniffed out a small laugh and rolled his eyes at his silent lackeys. 'Ava is far too busy being the Almighty Mother of millions. We're not going to bother her with upstart godlings like you. She trusts in gods like us, *true* divine beings, to manage her affairs for her. That means making sure her divine will is done. There will always be jealous renegades trying to undermine that will. You're not special. I hope you know that.'

'*True divine beings*? You're cogs in a broken machine! When was the last time you even looked down there? Churches are corrupt. Prayers are going answered. Magick is failing. You're so obsessed with keeping the new status quo that you've forgotten what divinity is supposed to be about.'

'Erin, please, you're going to make it worse.' Merky was close to tears.

The Flaw Manager seemed amused. 'Oh no, please, do go on. It doesn't get any worse than this.'

They had stopped in front of a hole of pitch blackness. In the tone of an executioner, the Flaw Manager continued.

'I hope you have a pleasant eternity.'

***

Rhev plodded through the darkness doggedly, but even with the enhanced darksight that his dwarvish eyes allowed him, it was not long before he was moving blindly. On the one hand, he was glad that the walls of the gorge were narrow. With both arms stretched out he could just about touch either wall and keep his balance on the loose scree. On the other hand, the feeling of being at the bottom of something so deep yet so narrow quickened his breath. The only thing stopping him from despairing entirely was his faith in whatever hand had guided him to this place. After all, it's only an adventure if you keep going.

The gradient increased. Each slip on a pebble represented a potentially unstoppable slide. Rhev's hands were becoming raw as they scrambled at the walls for balance. Another slip. The wall was now unexpectedly smooth and sheer. The inexorable slide began. He cried out. There was no echo, as if the rock around him was absorbing the sound.

His feet finally slipped out from under him. He landed hard, but not on the sharp scree he had been expecting. The ground had become as smooth as the walls, and grew exponentially steeper. He was reminded of the chute in Victor and Varylla's castle. He was beginning to lose perception of time, space, and his own speed as he hurtled down the slide. It was almost vertical now. Punching through the instinctive thoughts of fear running through Rhev's mind were chilling

272

doubts. He thought of how sensible Kevin was to suggest that this was all a trap. He started to hope that the others hadn't followed him down here. He knew that wouldn't be able to take the guilt of another one of his stupid ideas getting his friends into trouble. Then again, would he even be able to feel guilt once he's dead?

The air around him began to change. It gained a stifled, dusty quality. The ground below him began to bottom out. His eyes started to detect an ever so slight change in the pervading blackness. Without warning, his trousers filled with pebbles right up to his bottom, and the sickening falling sensation ceased.

As far as he could tell, he was in a narrow cave. There must have been an exit somewhere, as there was just enough light for his eyes to make out the shapes of stalactites and piles of collapsed rock. He stood up and shaked the stones out of his clothes. They were covered in a fine layer of dust. He coughed as some of it floated into his mouth.

It took him ten minutes and two scraped knees to find his way out of the cave. The entrance stood at the top of a crag, and what it looked out over took Rhev's breath away. A grey wasteland, gloomy and barren, punctuated only by oddly shaped mountains and bluffs cast like unused clay on a potter's wheel across the plains. Looking upwards, Rhev could see from his lofty position that the sky seemed to have an actual solidity. Faint, second-hand light seeped from cracks in the endless ceiling.

'Unterwelt seems like a good enough name for this place as any.'

Rhev turned to see Mercy, slightly bruised, standing next to him.

'You came?'

She shrugged. 'Stupid or brave. I wanted to see which you turned out to be.' Rhev frowned, but he was met with a wry

273.

grin.

'At best, both,' said Steem, accompanied by the sound of him gently dusting his top hat. 'Alas, I can't just let my employees walk off unsupervised.'

Just then, Kevin and Sterling tentatively made their way onto the crag.

'Bugger this,' they said in unison as they surveyed the barren landscape in front of them.

'I don't think buggering it is an option,' said Rhev. 'That sure felt like a one way trip.'

'We should try to find a settlement of some kind. Some sign of civilisation. Then we can reassess.' She spoke as a soldier would. There was a discipline there that Rhev was glad of.

The progress down from the crag was slow going. The rocks were sharp and sheer, and there was no well-worn path to follow. They had only made it about two hundred yards or so when they were stopped in their tracks.

'Wait! Please!'

They could just make out a person waving at them from the top of the crag.

'Who's that?' asked Rhev. No one could make them out. 'Have they followed us here?'

'Through the Thicket?' said Steem doubtfully.

'I don't like it.' Kevin twiddled his wand in his hands nervously. 'It could be one of those demons. We've seen them change shape, look like harmless old men.'

'Could be someone trying to warn us,' countered Mercy. 'I say we go. The worst that could happen is that it's a demon and I can practice killing it.'

'There is one way to tell for sure,' Rhev said, stopping Mercy in her tracks. 'I think.'

'Your sword?' Sterling asked. Rhev nodded.

'Twice now when I've drawn this here sword in front of

something really bloody evil, an abomination if you will, it's cried bloody murder. Shouts curses and battle cries and what have you.'

'Does your magick sword happen to do anything else?' asked Steem hopefully.

'I wouldn't exactly say it's magick. It doesn't glow, or shoot lightning, or whatever magic swords are supposed to do. It just yells at things. And sort of... pulls me towards that thing. It's hard to control. Hard to put away once it gets going. If anything, it's a bit of a bother.'

'But you're saying that we could use it as a sort of detector,' asked Mercy, her interest piqued.

'Sure, if you're happy losing the element of surprise. I don't know how to turn it off or make it quieter.'

'Whatever is up there has already seen us, and has the high ground, so we're going in at a disadvantage anyway. I say the more we know about what we're up against, the better. Lead the way.'

Rhev scrambled up the rocky slope at the head of the group, his sword unsheathed and resting on one shoulder so he could keep a hand free for balance. They lost sight of the figure on the crag as their approach became steeper. When they reached a boulder that they were sure was the only thing separating them from the potential demon, Rhev stopped and looked at the group. Mercy gave the affirmative, and as one they hauled themselves over the boulder, weapons and wands drawn. Rhev landed hard but steady, his greatsword brandished two-handed in front of him. It was silent.

'Beckett?' Rhev spat the question out in astonishment.

'Oh thank Ava, you came back,' came the muffled reply. Beckett had curled into the foetal position as soon as they had charged him.

'You're the bastard who accused us of stealing!' yelled Steem. 'Ruined my reputation! You stupid, selfish, cowardly

275

idiot. I'll-' Steem raised his calloused hand, ready to strike the quivering financier. Mercy caught his arm before the blow landed.

'Why did you follow us?' she asked.

'I wanted to help,' he mewled.

'Bollocks.' Steem shook off Mercy's grip and crouched down, face to face with Beckett.

'I'm pretty certain now that anyone trying to get their hands on something as dangerous as that damned demongate hasn't got anything good in mind. We know you're not one of them demons, but that's not to say you're not a monster. Now spill, or we leave you out here to die on this blasted rock.'

Beckett paused as he tried to gather his thoughts carefully. 'I was desperate. I run an investment firm. A failing one. I got a lead on the box you were carrying. I was told it would allow access to another realm. I thought if I had it I could use it to my advantage. Imports, exports, tolls, that sort of thing. Just capitalism, you see, nothing *evil* about it. A friend of mine, the man who wrote your contract, told me where you were going. I got Kerroulach to intercept you in Falstyr. When that didn't work, I fled, and followed you. I was going to... to steal the box, I don't know. I don't know! After the ferry incident, I went straight to Little Mosshill. I was watching, when you handed it over to that *thing*.' He drew in a sharp intake of breath, and exhaled slowly. He was trembling. 'I listened to that god, I heard what you said could happen. I knew I had made a mistake. I'd let avarice take hold of me. I am but a man, made of corruptible flesh. I need to repent! To help you!'

Steem stared into Beckett's wet eyes, his moustache twitching as he considered the man's story.

'If you knew the details of our contract, you knew that by taking that Box from us, you'd be consigning us to a fate worse than death. How am I supposed to believe a man like that just wants to-'

'You're right, that's not all. I haven't told you the whole truth' Beckett said quickly. When your wizard said that this Unterwelt is a place where people who are lost end up, I thought that perhaps... my brother, he disappeared some years ago. He was inspecting a mining operation in Krovania. There was no trace, no-one could find him. I thought... I don't know, I thought he might be here. I know, I know, it's stupid.'

Steem stared long and hard into Beckett's eyes, searching for something. Finally he stood up and wandered to the edge of the crag. He cleared his throat.

'He comes with us. No arguing, this is an order. At the very least we can use him as demon bait.' Steem had never spoken with such authority. Although everyone disagreed, they dared not go against him.

They wandered for what was presumably many miles. It was difficult to tell in the Unterwelt. Everything was so grey and drab that the lack of contrast made judging distance difficult. Beckett lagged at the rear of the group, complaining now and again about the state of his feet.

After a considerable time, during which the muggy twilight barely changed, the party resigned themselves to rest. In their haste to enter into this strange land they had brought no provisions, and they had yet to pass a source of water. Rhev coughed loudly. The dust was slowly beginning to choke him.

Just as they started stretching to prepare for the next leg of their journey to nowhere, they heard a noise. A chittering, whooping sound. It seemed to come from many mouths. They looked towards a nearby hill and saw a cloud of dust slowly billow from its surface. Weapons were drawn.

A wave of plungdugglers crested the hill, hundreds of saucer eyes catching the faded light.

'Not these little buggers again!' said Rhev, as he raised his sword.

Suddenly there was a piercing whistle, and the plungdugglers stopped in their tracks at the top of the hill. A taller figure joined them, a man wearing a sackcloth robe, looking for all the world like a shepherd among his flock.

'Ho there!' His voice rang out across the plain. 'I am Duncan of Wathgill, do not be afraid!... Hang on, don't I know you?'

The man made a couple of low whooping sounds directed at the creatures around him, and then began to make his way down the slope. The plungdugglers stayed put.

'Is that the innkeeper from Wathgill? The one that went missing?' Sterling asked incredulously.

'Surely not,' replied Kevin. As the man approached them, it became clear that it was.

'By Ava, it is you!' beamed the man. 'Steve Bents, right? And, erm, sorry, I don't remember the rest of your names. You lot were the last faces I saw in my inn before I ended up in this gods forsaken place. What a small world, eh?' The innkeeper paused. 'Actually, turns out it's a heck of a lot bigger than I thought it was, but there you go.'

'Steem, actually, Steem Vennts.' He shook Duncan's hand. 'We're just glad to see another person here.' He introduced the rest of the crew formally, but let Beckett introduce himself.

'Are they with you?' asked Rhev, pointing to the crowd of plungdugglers shifting about on crest of the hill.

'They're with me, I'm with them. It's an interesting relationship.' Duncan told them about his experiences since arriving in the Unterwelt, about how the plungdugglers had treated him like a god as long as he was willing to be thrown around in a sack from time to time. Their language was, unsurprisingly, quite rudimentary, and he had developed a crude form of communication with them.

Conversation turned to the matter of other humanoid inhabitants in the Unterwelt. To their relief, the party found

278

out that Duncan was not the only one.

'They call themselves the Lost. A gathering of people who have, one way or another, wound up here. Most of them live about a day's walk away, near one of the great lakes. They eke out a living, if you can call it that. Precious little grows here. A lot of the Lost spend their time tracking and hunting the Unfinished. Hideous things they are. Pure violence. I lost some of the plungdugglers to a pack of them last week.'

Duncan agreed to guide them to the encampment. He wasn't surprised to find that the group had found their way here through the Thicket; apparently many of the Lost had fallen foul of its confusing paths and dark chasms. When they told him about the Box they had been carrying and its power, he was, for a moment, quite happy.

'So that's how I ended up here!' he exclaimed. 'I've been racking my brains trying to work out how the plungdugglers managed to take me back with them.'

Duncan frowned. 'Oh, but that's not good. You say an Unfinished has this box? We definitely need to talk to the Lost then; there are scholars among them. They'll have a better understanding of this than I do.'

They quickened their pace across the dusty fields towards a glimmering pillar on the horizon, as tall as the sky. As they drew closer Rhev realised that it wasn't a pillar at all. From high above, somewhere in the roof of the Unterwelt, an endless stream of water poured down into a vast lake below. The torrent was so cyclopean that it dwarfed the surrounding mountains. Rhev now realised that the low rumble that had been teasing his eardrums for the last couple of miles was in fact emanating from those churning waters.

'There are others like it,' Duncan explained to the slack jawed dwarf. 'This is one of the smaller ones. The Lost seem to think the water comes from the deeps of the oceans up top. As you can see, the Unterwelt doesn't seem to be flooded, so the

279

water must go somewhere. We haven't run out of water up there, right, so maybe it finds its way back? Who knows? There's so much about this place that I don't understand.' He made a popping noise with his mouth. 'But then again, I'm just an innkeeper.'

'And a god, apparently,' remarked Sterling. Duncan gave him a wry look.

'How many gods do you know who get thrown around in a sack as part of a holy ritual?'

They continued down a long, shallow slope towards a settlement on the lakeside. Duncan explained that many of the Lost settled here because it was one of the few places they could find fish; not cod or herring, but strange, alien breeds, ghostly pale with huge mouths full of razor sharp fangs.

They could see the encampment more clearly now. Rhev was struck by how bright it was against the grey landscape. Coloured bunting hung about the perimeter, and tents were patched with patterned cloth. If he didn't know better, he would think they were entering a faire. At the edge of the camp Duncan signalled his plungdugglers to stay where they were, and then waved to a couple of hard-looking dwarves sitting on rocks nearby. Handaxes, worn but well looked after, lay in their laps. They nodded at Duncan and went back to talking to each other.

The inhabitants of the camp all looked like they had tripped and become tangled in the bunting that hung around their tents. They were covered in scraps of coloured fabric, on their arms and legs, braided through their hair, and even in their beards.

The innumerable lines of bunting seem to lead towards a central yurt, much larger than the rest of the tents. Duncan led the party towards it. Apart from the two dwarves at the edge of the camp, no one seemed to have any intention of stopping the newcomers. It seemed, Rhev thought, in a place like this, as long as you weren't Unfinished, you were a friend. They entered the yurt.

Sat at a crudely fashioned desk covered with scraps of books and dog eared papers was a very ancient, dark skinned woman. A bob of tightly curled grey hair framed her tired eyes, which were dimmed by cataracts. Under a woven shawl she wore an emerald green cropped top revealing her near skeletal liver spotted midriff. Her shorts matched the top. Rhev realised that this woman must be the most accomplished wizard he had ever seen.

Duncan spoke. 'Mara, these people have just arrived in the Unterwelt. They have some important news.'

With difficulty the old woman rose from her stool. "Hail to you, newcomers. My name is Mara of Heptamil. I am pleased that you were able to find your way to one of our camps. Many are not so lucky.'

The rest of the group made their introductions, taking care to include where they were from, as seemed the custom here.

'It is not often we see another from Heptamil in these parts of the Unterwelt,' said Mara, addressing Mercy. 'There was a time when my hair was as red as yours. Better days.' She smiled sadly as Mercy tugged at her braid self-consciously. 'But let us look to the present. What news do you bring?'

Steem nudged Rhev to speak. It seemed the honour was to be his. The dwarf proceeded to explain, honestly and in detail, what had befallen them since leaving Velheim many months ago. Mara listened intently, scribbling notes in shorthand periodically. When Rhev finished his tale, she smiled.

'You have done well to make it this far. In my experience, misfortune tends to surround demongates wherever they go. Please know, also, that I do not blame you for handing it over. There is a reason why arcane contracts were forbidden. To experience the pain of dropping one's soul for an eternity is, as far as we know, the worst possible way to go out. At least now you'll get into the habit of reading the fine print.' Mara wheezed out a chuckle, but her face grew serious once again. 'The fact that an Unfinished, or 'demon' as you call it, is now in possession of such an artifact is troubling. That it was able to somehow escape the Unterwelt in the first place suggests that it was very powerful indeed. As far as we know the only way out, apart from demongates, is to travel through rifts.' She gestured outside towards the towering waterfall in the distance. 'That is such a rift, as is the ravine you entered in the Thicket. The Thicket, we believe, is host to a high concentration of rifts. As you have just arrived, I'm sure you're wondering why we don't just travel *back* through the rifts. Unfortunately, as our predecessors discovered, there are greater forces acting on the rifts than gravity or water pressure. Forces that I suspect are divine in nature, there to prevent the Unfinished, and by extension us, from ever reaching the world above.'

Rhev's mind was working overtime trying to parse what Mara was telling them.

'Hang about. How do the plungdugglers get into our world then? Do they use these rifts?' The old woman looked to Duncan.

'Right, yes,' he began hesitantly. 'From what I've seen, the plungdugglers seem to be able to sniff out temporary, um, what did you call them Mara? Port-alls, that's it. These port-alls just pop into existence at random times, random places. They give you passage back up top.'

'So have you gone through one of these port-alls?' asked Mercy. 'Can't you escape through them?'

'You think I would still be here if I could?' Duncan laughed humourlessly. 'The port-alls allow you to get back up top, but only for a while. It's like, how did you put it Mara? Like silk. If there was a piece of silk hanging between you and an apple, the silk is flexible enough for you to grab the apple

282

through it. You're holding it, you can move it a bit, but the silk is still between you and the apple. Now imagine that the silk gets pulled taut suddenly. You drop the apple, and you're back where you're started. For me, the silk seems to get pulled taught almost straight away. The plungdugglers seem to get longer, like whoever's pulling the silk takes longer to notice them. Perhaps because they're small.' He shrugged. 'Who knows, I'm just an innkeeper.'

Mara spoke up again. 'Thank you, Duncan. I'm glad that you finally seem to grasp the allegory.' She returned to addressing the group. 'Our friend here is right. The plungdugglers' case is an anomaly. They are a... unique species. How that Unfinished entered our world, I cannot be sure of. I can only surmise that it found a way through a rift in the Thicket and somehow overcame the divine forces keeping it down. Perhaps the reason it was settled so close to the Thicket was due to residual forces still acting upon it. The fact that it required assistance in requisitioning a demongate, rather than getting one itself, seems to support my theory.'

The wizard pulled her shawl around her bare shoulders as a dusty breeze began to blow into the yurt.

'But never mind this. What's important is the demongate. A new factor has been introduced. The study of demongates have always been more the realm of occult fanatics than wizards, but from what I understand, they are a type of artificially constructed portal. They're designed to allow passage both to and from the Unterwelt without the restrictions of the 'silk effect', or the divine forces I mentioned earlier. It explains how Duncan was able to be brought here without being pinged back.'

'So that means the demons, the Unfinished, can escape from the Unterwelt permanently?'

'You catch on quickly, master dwarf.'

'It's been at least a day since it got its hands on the box, though,' said Mercy, 'so by now it could have released every one of those monsters into our world!'

Mara put up a single, wrinkly digit. 'Possible, but unlikely. Demongates are notoriously hard to control. They go against the laws the very gods themselves created aeons ago. As a result, they are volatile. If my studies, limited though they are, tell me anything, it is that if this particular Unfinished wanted to take the box to a specific place in the Unterwelt, likely the one demon stronghold we know of, it would have to use it many times before it arrived near its destination. That is, unless, it was very lucky.'

'So we have time,' Mercy continued, 'maybe. But what are we going to do with that time? How do we intercept the Box?'

'Finally storm that bloody castle, that's how.' The newcomer sounded parched. He stomped right past the group towards a waterskin on Mara's desk without giving them a second look. He was dwarven, heavily adorned with coloured scraps of cloth woven into his long matted hair and beard.

'Name's Bratzva.' He took a long draw from the skin and turned. 'Bratzva of-'

'Velheim.' Rhev stared, tears budding in his eyes, at the grizzled face of his father.

***

'Upsy daisy, on your feet.'

The voice was kind, but very, very old. Erin felt a hand take her arm and lift her gently to her feet. She opened her eyes wearily. The figure in front her did indeed look ancient, but not in a gaunt, skeletal way. Instead, he had the look of a man who was sustained from the love of so many grandchildren that he had lost count somewhere around the two hundred mark. Erin couldn't help but smile at him, despite the killer hangover she was experiencing. The old man smiled back.

'You must be Erin, god of hedgehogs. A noble breed, I

must say.' That kind voice again. Erin couldn't help but feel that he was very proud of her for some reason. 'I am very pleased to meet you. We have already found your friend. He's safe and sound, don't you worry. Ah, I've forgotten something, haven't I?' His chin shook slightly as he tried to remember. 'Of course, my name! My name is Anteus, god of memories.'

Anteus lead Erin through a stygian cavern, its walls slick with slime, its ceiling covered in menacing stalactites. Sorrow seeped from every crevice. She asked the kindly old god where they were.

'A prison,' he replied. 'A very, very old one. Almost as old as me, in fact.'

'And how old is that?' she asked.

Anteus stopped walking for a moment, drew in his lips, and finally, shrugged.

They crossed a perilously thin bridge of black rock. The chasm it traversed was infinitely deep, and Erin couldn't shake the impression that if she were to fall, her immortality would prove to be her greatest curse.

The colossal cave system was dimly lit by greenish fog that poured like water from the roof high above. Soon though, Erin began to make out a warmer light up ahead. As they walked closer she saw that the light came from a huge stone basin filled with orange flame, almost thirty feet across. Around this basin, rough seating had been carved into the rock, giving it the appearance of an amphitheatre. Erin could make out shapes on the seats, some supine, some sitting up and showing signs of movement.

Out of nowhere, someone gripped her tightly in an embrace. 'Erin! I'm so glad they found you. I couldn't see you when I woke, and I thought the worst had happened.'

'It's okay Merky, I'm alright,' she replied, pushing him back gently and smiling. She took a moment to take in her surroundings again. 'Then again, *are* we alright?'

'We're in Nirgond, Erin, *Nirgond*. I didn't even know this place was real. *A prison for gods.*' He bit his lip. 'Nowhere, forever.'

Anteus politely interrupted them. 'Please, come join the others. They'll be wanting to meet you. It's been a while since we've had visitors. Ah, sorry, wrong word. Erm, you're not visitors, you're… *damned*. Yes, that sounds right.'

Slowly, he led them to the centre of the amphitheatre.

'Everyone, I'd like you to meet Erin. She is the god of hedgehogs. Please be nice to her, she's only just found out that she's stuck here for eternity.' Anteus turned to Erin. 'Did I mention that before? The eternity thing? My apologies if I didn't, but it is, erm, true.' He grimaced.

There was no reaction from the crowd. Some of the gods appeared to be sleeping. Others stared blankly at Erin. Apathy flowed like custard down the tiers of seats. Anteus tried again.

'*I said*, Erin here is new. Please make her feel welcome. I don't believe she's been cast down before.' He turned again. 'You haven't been cast down before, have you? I only assumed, as you appear to have all your teeth.' Erin shook her head numbly.

This time there was a response from somewhere at the back of the amphitheatre. 'Does she know how to play Gin Rummy?' Erin made no response.

Anteus shouted back. 'I don't think so.'

'I've been playing Foonghi here for the last five years, and I'm not even sure if *he* knows how to play. The least she could do is be able to play Gin Rummy.'

'Pingle, I think you're being a little unreasonable to expect everyone to know how to play, and dare I say, *want to play*, Gin Rummy.'

'Whatever.'

'Sorry about that Erin, Pingle's been complaining about the lack of Gin Rummy challengers for quite some time. The fact is, no one has really been in the mood. One rarely is for Gin Rummy. I'm more of a poker fan myself, although I was a lot better at it when I could still count the cards properly.'

Anteus smiled, but Erin detected something missing in his eyes, a glimmer that she instinctively knew should have been there.

'Merky, have you told them what's happening in the pantheon?' Merky shook his head.

'I haven't, no, I was more worried about you.'

'In that case, I'll tell them. They need to know.'

She turned to the crowd and breathed deeply.

'I'm sorry to disturb you, and... I'm sorry that I don't know how to play Gin Rummy, but Merky and I have some very important, very bad news to tell you all.' There was no reaction, but she powered through and lifted her voice as much as possible. 'Ava's pantheon is corrupt. The prayer system is failing. Faith is getting stronger, but conditions down there are getting worse. Religion is broken.'

'We know.' One of the gods who had been slumbering near the front opened their three eyes. Erin thought she recognised them. *Were they called Ack? Or maybe Ooh?* 'Why do you think we're here?' they continued. 'We all saw the new system for what it was; inferior. We all tried to do something, and Ava's cronies chucked us in here to rot. No faith, no ambrosia, cut off from the astral paths, just Pingle up there complaining about winning Gin Rummy for the ten thousandth time. *Who complains about winning?*'

'Shut up Urgh! You have no idea how frustrating it is to not have a proper challenger.'

'It's 'Ohm', you second-rate godling!'

'I do try,' said the god presumed to be Foonghi.

More bickering started among the incarcerated gods. Erin

287

couldn't believe it. What had happened to this band of renegades?

'Please, please! Can you all just be quiet for a moment. You're behaving like mortals!' That shut them up for a moment. 'There's something else. Merky found another world below the one we know. It's filled with horrible beings, unnatural creatures, and we have reason to believe that those things have found a way to break through to the world above. Without magick, without divine intervention, I don't know what will happen, but it will be terrible.'

There was a decidedly disinterested grumble from the crowd.

'Oh dear,' said Anteus. 'So it's finally happening then?'

'It is!' said Erin, a little too loudly considering how close she was standing to the ancient god. She lowered her voice. 'Hang on, did you say "finally"? Did you know this was going to happen?'

'I was hoping it wouldn't, but I had my suspicions that the Unterwelt would come back to bite us on the arse some day.'

Merky piped up. 'You've a name for it? The Unterwelt?'

'Yes, that's it. I think I was actually the one who came up with that name in one of our board meetings. I believe the fisherfolk down below came up with a slightly more poetic one. Mine sounds a little uninspired now.'

'Are you saying that you're one of the progenitors? You made the first world?'

Anteus looked embarrassed. 'Yes, I was… involved. But I did say it wasn't a very good idea at the time, let me just make that clear. All those headstrong gods, going off and coming up with bits of the world on their own, tinkering away with no system of peer review or scheduled feedback rounds. No cohesion at all. When we got back to the Table and plonked it all on there, it looked very naff, let me tell you. It was a good thing that we started again. Well, it *was* a good thing. In

288

hindsight, it sounds like it might have been a bit of a silly thing to do.'

'You think?'

Merky was not impressed. Anteus looked so sheepish, Erin couldn't help feel sorry for him.

'Anteus, you want to help, right? Fix the mistake? Stop those monsters from ruining the second world?'

'If I could, I would, believe me, but we're a little limited in what we can do down here.'

'Then we escape. There must be a way out of here.'

'You think we haven't tried?' scoffed Ohm, who had gone back to lying down, but couldn't help overhearing. 'It's a prison specifically designed to hold gods. The nearer you think you're getting to the edge, the closer you get to the middle. It's an unsolvable maze.'

'Now now, Ohm, you know that's not strictly true,' said Anteus. Ohm let out a mirthless laugh.

'So there is a way out, Anteus?' Erin probed. Ohm answered for him.

'He says there is, *but he can't remember.* God of memories, was it?'

'Leave him be, Ohm. None of us are in our prime. Your third eye doesn't even work any more.' The defender was a small but stout god with a streak of white in her hair. Erin recognised her as the god of badgers, but she couldn't remember the name.

'Ohm is right though, I'm afraid,' said Anteus. 'I have waned somewhat since being in this dreadful place. Too long separated from the faith of mortals. I was here when Nigrond was created. I *know* there is an exit. Alas, it was so many millennia ago, I cannot remember exactly how to reach it. One too many lefts, or maybe rights, for my mind to hold together. Or perhaps you have to walk backwards…' The effort of remembering was tiring him, and he was forced to take a seat.

289

'So that's it then,' said Merky to the floor. 'The world will be trampled under the feet of jealous demons and the gods above won't even notice.'

***

'It's good to see you lad,' said the older dwarf as he slumped down on the cot in his private tent, 'but I wish you weren't here. The Unterwelt is no place for a kid.'

Rhev sat down gingerly on a rickety stool on the other side of the tent. Since reuniting, he had been unable to take his eyes away from his dad's face. It had changed a lot. The burly, ruddy man he had known as a child was now weatherbeaten, and lean for a dwarf. The muscles were still there though, sinewy, under his clothes.

'I'm not a kid any more, dad,' Rhev said gently. Bratzva looked up. Until then he had avoided making eye contact. He smiled sadly.

'You're right. You're a fully grown dwarf now. Bushy beard and all. Perhaps a little on the tall side, but you get that from your mother.'

Bratza reached down under his cot and grabbed a leathery bladder full of some sort of liquid. Uncorking it unleashed a powerful smell.

'Grog?' he asked, offering the bladder to Rhev. His son paused.

'I... better not,' he replied stoically. 'I need to cut down. Got to be sharp at a time like this.'

Bratza laughed. 'My, my, wise beyond his years as well. Your mother was always trying to get me to cut down, but she never quite succeeded.'

He paused, and pulled his eyes away once more. 'How is she?'

'Mum?' Rhev cleared his throat. 'I looked after her, dad. Made sure she never wanted for anything.' He cleared his throat again. 'Right up to the end.'

290

His father said nothing for a good while. Rhev couldn't tell if he was sad, or angry; angry at himself, or his son.

'I'm proud of you, Rhev. You're a good lad. You did what I couldn't.'

'What do you mean? It's not your fault that you ended up here. You couldn't do anything about it.' Rhev was starting to get breathless, insistent. 'You were a good dad!'

'I was not!' Rhev's heart skipped a beat. 'I'm sorry, Rhev, seeing you here, now… the guilt is too much. Gods, it hurts.' His father was breathing hard now. Short, staccato breaths. 'I was *not* a good dad. I was absent. I wasn't there for you, or your mother.'

'That's not true! The stories… you were out adventuring, doing deeds, bringing riches back home. You were a hero, you were a-' Rhev was silenced by a terrible look in his father's eyes.

'I was a criminal, Rhev. A mercenary, a grave robber, whatever paid and gave me that jolt in the heart that told me I was still living. I wasn't a father, that's for sure. I didn't know how to be one, so I ran away from it whenever I could.' Bratzva sniffed. 'I'm sorry, son. I'm not the dwarf you thought I was.'

Rhev didn't know how to respond. For all these years he had imagined his dad as a valiant hero, off fighting dragons and evil wizards, liberating oppressed villagers, recovering sacred artefacts. All those bedtime stories… were lies. Everything he had wanted to be… was that a lie too? How ridiculous it all sounded now.

Bratzva could feel the silence filling the tent like a choking gas. The weight of judgement lay heavy on his shoulders, squeezing out more confessions.

'The day that I came to the Unterwelt, it was not entirely… unexpected. I had been offered a lot of gold to join a wizard's expedition to "an unknown land". They had specified that the length of the expedition was indefinite.'

He sighed heavily.

'I went along anyway. Found myself in this godsforsaken place with no way back. I took it as a punishment. Punishment for not being there for you and your mum. Punishment for all the bad things I had done to earn a living.'

Bratzva got up from his cot and paced in tight circles around the tent.

'I found the Lost. At that time they were being raided often by the Unfinished. They lost more and more every week. I helped organise a proper defence. I trained the people. We defeated that band and went out hunting others. I helped turn the tide, just a little bit. I tried to do a good thing.'

'To save your own hide.' It came out as barely a mumble. Neither Rhev nor Bratzva was entirely sure that the young dwarf had said it. But he had, and Rhev realised he meant it. He got up, knocking the stool to the floor.

'Rhev, please!' said Bratzva, going to his son. 'I'm better now. I'm *trying* to be better. I'm trying to be a good dwarf to these people.'

'Maybe you should have tried twenty years ago.' The tent flap kicked up a small storm of dust as it fell in place behind Rhev.

He barely registered the fishermen hauling in a catch of supremely ugly fish as he sat at the banks of the vast lake. His mind was elsewhere, set adrift in his own lake of lies. He had spent so long believing his father was a hero, used that thought to give himself hope that perhaps he could be better. Now it was clear that his father had been a bandit: a hero in his own story, and a villain in others'. Rhev couldn't help think that perhaps he was just like his dad, that thievery and deceit simply ran in his blood.

He absently twisted his ring around and around his finger until it hurt. That ring, which had been a holy artifact in his eyes, a symbol of aspiration, turned out to be stolen property. He slipped it from his finger and eyed the pure silver band with its glistening verdigris engraving. No wonder his dad had stolen it. Anyone with greed in their heart and no moral compass couldn't have resisted it.

Rhev grasped the ring tight in his fist and prepared to hurl it far into the lake, tensing his muscles and focussing all his anger and shame into the throw. As he moved to release, he found he was unable to do so. A hand gripped his wrist like an iron shackle.

'Now why would you be doing that?' asked Mercy.

'It's got no worth to me now,' Rhev replied sternly, shaking his hand free from Mercy's grip.

'I thought it was priceless? From one of your dad's stories, you said.'

'Lies, more like.'

'Oh, I'm… sorry Rhev. I know they meant a lot to you.'

'He wasn't a hero after all. Just a brigand. A plunderer. A fraud.' Rhev's face started to glow red from the effort of holding back his tears. 'Looks like the apple doesn't fall far from the tree, eh?'

'What? Who says you're a brigand?'

'Half of bloody Velheim!'

'Well, who cares what they think! *You* know the truth of what you are, no one else.'

Unexpectedly, Mercy drew her longsword, drove it into the ground in front of Rhev, and took a seat beside him. The dwarf was stunned.

'Let me you a story, Rhev, and this one isn't a lie. You remember who this sword is named after?'

'Yeah. Warum, right?'

'Yes, Warum. When I was a corporal in the eastern army, Warum served under me. He had been pressed into service. He was a convict, Rhev. He had been part of a gang that ransacked burial sites under the false guise of the Cult of the Absent God, which was a popular movement in Heptamil at the time. Warum was sixteen. To the rest of the squad, he was a no good rat. Nobody trusted him.'

'And now you're going to tell me that Warum changed his ways and became a model soldier?'

'No, not at all. He continued stealing things. He couldn't help it. Hair combs and whetstones, brooches and buckles. The quartermasters cursed his name. Warum didn't even realise that what he was doing was so bad. He didn't even see his conscription as a punishment. As far as he could tell, he was just in a more well equipped gang with its own uniform. So, tired of having to deal with his mischief, I took it on myself to drill some discipline into him. To understand right from wrong. It took over a year, but eventually he stopped stealing. He was turning out to be a canny young man. Then something awful happened.

The Cult of the Absent God, the real one, set fire to the temple quarter in Heptamil. Our battalion was the only one on leave from the front at the time, so we were called in to evacuate everyone. It was a nightmare, Rhev. I was tasked with getting everyone out of the Temple of Ohm. It was a bloody labyrinth in there. I managed to find two people, but I could hear more. The fire was spreading so quickly that I knew I would be dead if I spent any more time searching, so I had to make a tough decision. I came out into the air and there was Warum, covered in soot, looking for me. When he saw the two priests in my arms he asked if that was everyone.'

Mercy paused, and touched the blade of her sword lightly, catching her own reflection in the polished steel.

'I didn't think. I said no. So he went in. He went in and he came out with two more priests, and before I could stop him he went in again. Two more priests, then again he went in. And then... and then he didn't come out. The roof caved in

294

and the blaze erupted and I was... I was too afraid to go back in.'

'He died, then?'

'He died a hero, Rhev. And he started as a criminal. Nothing is set in stone. People can change. It's up to them. It's got nothing to do with their past, or their family, or the world. I've been talking to some of the people here, in this camp. You see all the colours they wear on their clothes? It's their mark of defiance. They won't let this grey world get them down, no matter how bleak their future looks. So yes, maybe you've got into your head the frankly stupid notion that you're the villain here, because you think it's in your blood, or because you think heroes don't exist, and *you don't like that thought*. Then defy it! Wear the colours you want people to see.'

'I only brought one set of clothes though.'

Mercy shot Rhev a stern glance, and saw that his eyes were wet, but his grin was broad. She punched him in the shoulder.

'I hope you know this is a one time thing,' she said. 'I don't usually do emotions, they tend to take me to funny places. I spent years running away from the thought that I had taught someone to do the right thing, to make the selfless choice, and it had led to their death. I convinced myself that going above and beyond would only get blood on my hands, and I've been trying to scrub that blood off for so long, Rhev. That's why I was so reluctant for you to go after Kowloon. I saw it all happening again. Warum, you, both the same, jumping into the fire. But now I know what my mistake was. My mistake wasn't teaching that little street rat from Heptamil how to be a hero. My mistake was not following him down that path, standing by his side until the end. I'll follow you to the end, Rhev. I've got you to thank for helping me see my life as something more than just a job once again.'

'And thank you for following me down here on this half

baked, well, *quest*,' Rhev replied. 'To Warum.'

'To Warum,' she replied.

Sterling observed quietly. Kevin and Mara were deep in conversation. Although he still doubted his own magickal abilities, Kevin was determined to learn as much as he could from this master of their craft. It transpired that Mara had come to the Unterwelt many years before amidst the confusion of a sorcerous bombardment on the frontlines of the eastern wars. Since finding her way to the Lost, she had dedicated her time to the study of the Unterwelt and its denizens, for what little good it would do for those who found themselves in that unfortunate place.

As the discussion turned to Kevin's own experiences, he let slip that his control of magick had been declining for some time now. To his surprise, Mara confessed that she too had felt the power of her god, Ghazi, waning in recent years. She had chalked up her inability to harness the residual arcane energies of her god to general infirmity and old age, but with Kevin's confession she began to rethink this. She theorised, wildly, she admitted, that something was awry in the realm of the gods.

Steem popped his head into the tent. A crude meat cleaver swung awkwardly from his belt, a new addition to his previously non-existent arsenal. 'Everyone's kitted out. It's time.'

Sterling and Kevin got to their feet. Mara remained seated.

'Aren't you coming?' asked Kevin nervously. Mara smiled and shook her head.

'Does it look like these knees are fit to march twenty miles in a single day?' She shook her head and chuckled softly. 'I will stay here with the rest of those not able to fight. Don't worry, Kevin of Yedforth, as long as all goes well, you'll have the demongate back here by tomorrow and we'll all have a chance of getting out of this wretched place.' Kevin smiled unconvincingly and backed out of the tent.

It was a motley band of warriors that had gathered at the edge of the camp. Indeed, some of them were not even warriors, unless wielding a sharpened bit of metal made you one. Apart from Steem's crew, which at his own insistence included Beckett, the group consisted of Bratzva, a squad of hardy dwarves wielding pickaxes, various scarred humans, a few burly elves in rusted plate, and a curiously petite creature.

'Mina!' exhaled Sterling in surprise. The girl, her long black hair now plaited with ribbons in various shades of red, immediately tried to sidestep behind one of the large elves. Unfortunately, the elf knelt down to tie his greaves, and Mina made direct eye contact with the halfling. He walked over to her.

'You, erm, you walked out before-'

'I'm sorry!' said Mina, overly loud. 'I shouldn't have stolen from you. I, um, I didn't want to, I couldn't help it, you see I have this… problem-'

'I met your parents.'

'My parents? But you're still alive.'

The halfling shrugged and grinned. 'I guess they must have liked me.'

Mina looked at him sternly. 'They're evil people, Sterling.'

He dropped the grin and stammered: 'Actually, they tried pretty hard to kill me.'

The girl tried desperately not to smile, but in the end she couldn't help it. 'I'm glad you're still alive.'

'Me too.'

Straps were tightened, blades were sharpened, prayers were made. Finally, the scratch company was ready to set off. Bratzva was to lead them to the stronghold. Rhev and his friends brought up the rear.

297

They had made it no further than three feet when Duncan came jogging over, shouting for them to wait. He was carrying a large brown bundle with great difficulty.

'What is it Duncan?' asked Bratzva.

The innkeeper panted. 'I've talked it over with them. They've agreed to take you. It'll be much faster.'

'Who's they?' the dwarf asked, a thick eyebrow arched in suspicion.

Duncan pointed with a thumb behind him. A host of plungdugglers careened towards them, stopping just short in a haze of dust. Duncan threw the bundle he was carrying on the ground.

'One condition though. You'll have to get in these.' The wrapped bundle unfurled to reveal about twenty large hessian sacks. 'They said it's alright if you want to poke your head out.'

For the umpteenth time, Rhev tried to adjust his position. Whichever way he tossed and turned, he couldn't escape the unfortunate probing of tiny hands. At least, he thought, there was a layer of sackcloth between him and the plungdugglers dirty mitts. He caught glimpses of his companions bouncing along the top of the stampede. Only Duncan seemed at ease, or as much as one can be when being transported with the same care as an armful of dirty laundry.

Despite the discomfort, they were travelling almost as fast as they would be on horseback. As Rhev understood, there were no horses to be found in the Unterwelt, so this was probably as fast as it got. Just when he had started to get used to the constant pummelling, the journey came to its end. Duncan chittered authoritatively, and the plungdugglers set them all down, panting like sled dogs.

As the dust settled, they finally saw their objective clearly; and what an objective it was. From a distance it had looked like a terribly tall mountain, sharpened to a point like a pencil.

Now that they were closer, Rhev could see that it was constructed after a fashion, but not by any hands that he knew of. It appeared to have been built in many dripping layers of compacted dust, fused together by some unknown solvent. Gargantuan spires rose from its bulk, tapering to savage points high above.

Holes dotted its surface. Windows or entrances, Rhev couldn't be sure, but the more he looked the more he realised that there were features that he did recognise: twisted parodies of crenellations atop winding walls, carved shapes that appeared to be statues of grotesque proportions, and a gatehouse that looked more like a toothed maw than an entrance.

'It's terrible,' Mercy said quietly, 'like a huge termite mound.'

'Aye, it is. Full of creepy crawlies too,' Bratzva replied.

One of the men, white scars criss-crossing his dark skin, spoke up. 'If it's anything like a termite mound inside, we're going to have a hell of a time finding our way around. That's if we can even make it in.'

'I think I can help with that too,' said Duncan. 'The plungdugglers have an uncanny knack for sniffing out port-alls and the like. If that demongate is here, they'll probably be able to find it. You can use them like bloodhounds.' He squeaked at the plungduggler nearest to him, who turned to the crowd of his kin and called out, gesturing to the monstrous keep behind him. It was met by an almost tangible air of reluctance. But, when it seemed like none would come forward, there was a movement in the crowd. An unusually small plungduggler, their eyes almost too big for their face, walked forward. A quiet noise accompanied a determined nod.

'Looks like we have our bloodhound,' Duncan said. There was an indignant squeak. 'Sorry, "sniffer supreme", I think.

299

She'll go with you, just follow her nose once you're in.'

'You're not coming?' Rhev asked.

'I'm not much of a fighter. Better that I stay here to wrangle the plungdugglers, if you need a quick getaway.' He caught Bratzva's eye. '*When* you need a quick getaway.' Bratzva nodded.

'We'll make our way around to the right. Last time I scouted this place I spotted something that looked like a culvert, if a place like this has a need for such a thing. No one was guarding it, and we can approach it from an angle that keeps us out of view of most of those battlements.' He patted the hilts of the two shortswords he carried on his back. 'Buck up people. We've got a demon invasion to stop.'

Bratzva caught the eyes of his son, and smiled grimly. He didn't wait for a response. They all jogged after him, taking care to keep the low ridgeline on their left to cover them from the watchful eyes of any Unfinished. When they reached a small gap in the ridge they hooked a left and entered into a dark gully that ran around the foot of this section of the stronghold. An ungodly howl rose from one of the holes above them. Everyone froze and looked around nervously, imagining a wave of black teeth and white barbs descending upon them any moment now. The howl died away, and the silence returned. Bratzva signalled for them to move up. The culvert, as he had described it, came into view. It was indeed a hole, smaller than those on the rest of the keep, but large enough for regular folk like them to enter. It leaked a thin greyish ooze into the gulley.

'This is our entry point,' said Bratzva. 'We'll follow the, erm, the "sniffer" once we're in. Draw your weapons now. If we make contact with any of the demon scum, we'll try to take them out as quickly as possible before they get a chance to call on any others.'

Beckett put his hand up.

'Yes? Bucket, was it?'

'Beckett. I have a question. If we do make contact with any of these things, not that we will hopefully, but *if we did*-'

'I think it's fairly certain that we'll run into at least one Unfinished in their own stronghold, but go on.'

'Fine, fine, *when we do*,' Beckett gulped, 'how exactly do we kill them?'

'They bleed like anything else, but they're tough as old boots. You'll have a hard time even breaking the skin with that knitting needle,' he pointed at Beckett's dagger. 'That is until they change. The Unfinished will shift their bodies to meet threats more effectively: moving their mouths to different parts of their body, growing extra talons, becoming smaller and faster, you name it. They're weaker when they're changing, more fluid, easier to stick your needle into. That's the best way to get them.'

Beckett expressed his thanks but didn't seem convinced. He'd never wielded anything more lethal than a pen in his whole life.

Bratzva made the signal and everyone piled into the tight tunnel. The dwarves among them seemed quite at ease in the space, but the mighty elves in their plate armour had more difficulty. With audible disgust they were forced to get on their hands and knees in the sludge. Their route wound tightly left, then right, then right again, repeated randomly until they were thoroughly disorientated. All they knew is that they were going ever so slightly upwards, but they couldn't be sure where to.

Finally, the tunnel opened up into a pit. There was a dim light here, illuminating the area just enough to reveal the gruesome form of an Unfinished. Without a moment's hesitation, Bratzva rushed forward and cleaved what head-shaped lump, swinging both his blades in a scissoring motion. Nobody else had moved, not even the Unfinished. Bratzva grunted.

'Looks like this one was already dead.' He looked around and spotted another form. He walked over and gave it a kick. 'This one too. A grave of some sort, or a cesspit.'

The rest of the group crept out of the tunnel and over to where Bratzva was inspecting the second Unfinished.

'It appears to be decomposing,' suggested Kevin. 'That must be where the sludge was coming from.' A chorus of gags rose up from the elves behind him.

'I can't see any wounds on this one,' Bratzva continued as he rolled the body over with his heavy boot. 'I've never known them to die from anything other than grievous bodily harm.'

'Maybe they got sick, or died from old age.'

'I've never seen the like, but then again, there's a lot we don't know about these bastards. If they're kicking the bucket by natural means, I'm all for it.'

'This poor sod definitely didn't die of natural causes.'

Rhev was kneeling by a skeleton. It was human, intact except for a caved skull.

Mercy knelt beside Rhev and inspected the corpse herself. 'This injury doesn't look like a hammer blow, or a fall. I've seen both. It almost looks like the head's been... squeezed? How did they get here?'

'There's been no attempt to assault this place before, as far as I know.' Bratzva was met with mumbles of agreement from the other warriors of the Lost.

'Maybe they were brought here by the demons,' said Rhev. 'Taken as a prisoner?'

'I don't know what the Unfinished would want with prisoners,' Bratzva replied, 'but I don't fancy finding out first hand.' His eyes tracked up a narrow path that clung to the edge of the pit. 'Looks like our sniffer has a scent. Let's get cracking.'

They followed the tiny creature into the heart of the demon stronghold. The architecture seemed nonsensical. Corridors would bulge and narrow at random points, intersections led to dead ends, entire chambers would be filled with stairways and awkward inclines that lead into each other and away to new corridors. The walls of the keep were grey and glossy, as if covered in lacquer. What was most unerring was the emptiness of it all, as if it had been constructed for its own sake rather than any kind of purpose. It was not only empty of furniture, food, or any signs of normal life, but also curiously empty of demons.

They reached yet another intersection and the plungduggler paused. It lifted its bat-like nose into the air and sniffed hard. Briefly, it looked to the left, but then scampered with renewed surety down the right-hand passage. As the group started to follow, something caught Rhev's attention. He stopped, falling behind the main party. Only his friends waited.

'What is it, Rhev?' asked Sterling. Rhev put a finger to his lips, and strained his ears.

'Talking,' he said, quietly. *'People* talking, down that corridor.'

'But that's the wrong way.'

'If there are prisoners down there, it's the right way. You saw what had happened to that other bloke.' Rhev gripped the sides of his head and crossed his eyes. 'We can't let that happen to any others. *I* won't let it happen.'

He jogged up to the rear of the party ahead, and called for Bratzva by his name. It didn't feel right calling him 'dad', not in front of these people at least. The party stopped and Bratzva walked back to meet him.

'What wrong, lad? Unfinished?'

'No. People. Down the left passage. I heard them talking.'

'Are you sure? This place echoes in strange ways. You

303

weren't hearing us?'

Rhev looked into his father's eyes. For some reason he expected to see a dismissiveness, judgement, scorn even. Instead, he saw a genuine concern.

'I'm certain. There are people down there, prisoners maybe. We should help them if we can.'

His father looked back into his son's eyes, and felt pride rise in his chest. He knew, deep down, that if he had been around to raise the kid, he wouldn't have turned out like this. But here they were, an old dwarf trying to be better, and a young dwarf who already was. He hoped his son knew that about himself.

'Lead the way, Rhev.' His son clenched his jaw and nodded, then turned and began taking them down the other passage.

All was quiet except for the scrape of boots on the dimly reflective floor. Rhev started to doubt what he had heard. *Perhaps it* had *just been echoes?* A new susurration wafted through the air towards him. *No, you were right. Not echoes,* he thought. *Whispers.*

They rounded a corner to find a pitiful sight. Cells constructed of the same calcified dust that surrounded them lined the walls. Stalagmite bars arranged like teeth penned in the withered occupants, like they were trapped in the jaws of a great beast. They scurried to the back of their cells when the party arrived. Fish bones crunched under them as they curled into foetal positions.

'By Ava, look at them.'

The prisoners were all stick thin, almost skeletal. Their clothes hung from them as if they were on a drying rack, and their hair had grown ashen, even on the youngest of them. A prisoner that still clung to a scrap of vitality uncurled herself and scampered to the bars of her cell. A boney hand reached out.

'Please. Please get me out. I want to go home. By the gods, get me-' she coughed wretchedly.

There were no doors to the cells, but some of the stalagmites looked more freshly made than the others. Bratzva directed the strongest in the group to work on breaking them down. The muscular elves rammed against them with their shoulders, while the dwarves swung their pickaxes in an efficient miner's rhythm. Each time they struck the stalagmites, everyone flinched. The sound of metal on rock and the gradual cracking pinged around the space and down the corridor.

'Hurry, hurry!' Bratzva hoped that he wasn't going to have to regret this detour.

Eventually, all the prisoners, those who were still alive at least, were freed. Some slumped at the feet of their saviours, others hugged whoever happened to be closest to them. One stepped out of the crowd towards Beckett.

'Severin?' The man was stooped and as sickly looking as the rest of the incarcerated, but there was no mistaking the physical similarity between him and the cowardly investor.

'Haverley?' Beckett reached out to the man, taking him gently by the shoulders. 'I didn't... I didn't really think I would... you're really here?' Haverely smiled before bursting into tears.

'I'm sorry,' he choked. 'I'm sorry I wasn't there little brother, to look after you.' He embraced Beckett, who had begun to shake.

'It's... it's fine, Haverley. It's okay.'

'But you had Hampton, yes? I thought- I know I wasn't around, but I always thought you'd be fine with Hampton there.'

Beckett didn't say anything, but his hands dug harder into his brother's boney back. Steem interrupted their embrace.

'This is really your brother? The one you told us about?'

Beckett took a hard look at Haverley again, as if to be sure he wasn't a phantom or hallucination, and nodded.

'I have to ask,' Steem continued, speaking to Haverley urgently, 'have you met someone called Leila Vennts? Leila Vennts of Dankvyr? I've asked all the Lost and no-one had, but if Beckett found you, his brother, I mean, what are the chances?' His voice trailed off as he saw Haverley's gaunt face grow sad.

'I have met a Leila Vennts,' he replied, sadly. 'She had been here a very long time. Longer than anyone else still alive in this wretched place. She remained strong for as long as I knew her.' His eyes wandered over to one of the liberated cells, now empty.

'She was a very strong woman. You should know that.'

Without a word, Steem stumbled over the smashed stalagmites and into the cell Haverley had indicated. He fell to his knees. On the wall in front of him was a crude carving of a rose. He took his battered top hat in his hands, and wept.

Mercy knelt beside him. Teardrops dripped from the tips of his moustache. A ragged inhale was followed, after a pause, by a calm breath. He wiped his nose with the back of his hairy hand, and turned to the hardened warrior next to him.

'Make them pay, Mercy.'

She took him by the shoulders.

'Gladly.'

Some of the liberated prisoners, those too weak to walk, let alone fight, were to be taken back through the labyrinth to where Duncan was waiting. The rest of the prisoners, Haverley included, insisted on joining the raid. They were outfitted with what weapons and pieces of armour could be spared.

The architecture of the demon stronghold continued to baffle them. Their path led them up and down so many times that no-one could be certain if they were higher or lower than

306

where they had started. One thing did start to change though; the rooms were no longer empty.

They found crude smithing workshops full of crooked forges and worked metal that looked more like abstract sculpture than armour. They found a library of sorts, but instead of books it held huge tablets covered in indecipherable pits and knobbles that made one dizzy to look at. After that they found an auditorium containing grotesque horns and sinewy instruments. It appeared that, in some twisted way, the Unfinished were attempting to emulate the world above.

Then they came to a room that had no analogue in civilised culture. An elevated walkway traversed a hall full of open topped vats. The liquids inside them were monochromatic, much like everything in the Unterwelt, except for a few. These liquids were a mixture of reds, greens, and browns, all either very dark or very pale. Rhev knelt on the walkway and peered into one of the vats full of a black-greenish liquid. He jumped as a femur bone popped to the surface. There was an exclamation from one of the other dwarves, who was pointing at a massive vice suspended over one of the vats. In its grip was the crushed remains of a human body. There was a splash as someone threw up into a pool.

'I suspected as much,' whispered Haverley. 'They're trying to synthesise colour from our bodies.'

'It's vile!' said Beckett between gags.

'It's desperation,' Harverley replied. 'This place breeds it. The demons have succumbed to it.'

After they had recovered from the initial shock, everyone was keen to get out of the 'squeezing room'. They continued down the stygian corridors of the keep with a renewed vigour. The warriors were keen to punish the Unfinished for their unholy deeds.

***

Erin could see now why the gods trapped in Nigrond were so apathetic. The malaise was insidious. It was as if the place was designed to fog the mind, push out discontent and rebellious thoughts and replace them with melancholy. Or perhaps it was just what happened when a god is separated from the sustaining power of belief.

Her mind wandered back to recent events: something Merky had said, about the gods having to have faith in mortals, like it was a joke. *Was it a joke though? Why couldn't gods have faith? We're not so different really. We have hopes and desires, faults and misgivings.* Infallible *deities, now that was a joke.*

She got up from the cold stone seat and walked over to the other side of the amphitheatre. 'Anteus?'

'Oh hello, Orun. How can I help?'

She smiled sadly and sat next to the ancient god. 'It's Erin actually, but don't worry about that. I'm not very good with names either.'

'Ah yes, my apologies. Erin, god of, erm... those little creatures with the soft bellies and the spikes on their backs, erm... porcupines?'

'Close enough. I just wanted you to know that I believe in you. I believe you're telling that truth when you say that you know how to get out of Nigrond, and I believe that you can remember.'

Anteus looked confused for a moment, then his eyes squinted in a smile. 'That's very kind of you Erin, but I don't think I can remember. I'm not even sure I remember remembering, to be quite honest with you. They always tell me that I don't remember whenever I bring it up.' He gestured to the dour throng on the seats above them. Erin pushed on.

'But you can remember, Anteus! You must have done it once before. I have faith that you can do it again. *I have faith,* Anteus.'

308

There. There it was. The faintest glimmer of a glimmer. Something was returning to his eyes.

'Can you lot be quiet, I'm trying to sleep.' It was Ohm, shifting uncomfortably on the hard stone. 'And stop talking about faith, there's none here. Can't get in, that's the whole point of this place.' He rolled over to face away from them.

'Don't you see?' said Erin, determined that she was onto something. 'We're so used to mortals believing in *us*, we've never bothered to believe in *ourselves*. That's why you're all so… depressed.'

Ohm opened his eyes and looked at Erin with indignation. 'I'm not depressed, I'm tired. Tired of being in a prison for the last thirty years.'

'If you're so tired of being here, why don't you try and do something about it?'

'What are you suggesting? That I worship Anteus here? *Worship another god*? It makes me sick just thinking about it.'

'No, not worship. Just, *have faith*. Have faith in him. Have faith in what he can do.'

Merky was roused by argument and wandered over. 'I believe in Anteus.'

'I believe in you, Anteus.' It was the god of badgers. There were some other murmurs of the same from nearby.

'This is ridiculous,' muttered Pingle from the back of the amphitheatre. 'Look at you all, you've gone mad down here. This isn't how it works. You take the faith, you don't give it out.'

'Why not?' said Erin.

'Well, because. *Because*. Because it just isn't… done.'

'Uh-huh.' Erin turned back to Anteus. 'We believe in you Anteus. You can remember.'

Anteus was blushing hard from all this. He wasn't quite sure what was happening or what he should be doing. All he did know is that somewhere behind his eyes a fire that had long been dormant was being stoked. He thought of temples on distant hilltops, of tall bonfires in the night, of low, harmonic chants. The gods were crowding around him now, some putting their hands on his shoulders, some gently nodding with encouragement. He didn't realise it, but a pure, white light was blossoming from his old eyes.

'I remember.'

There was a silence.

'Did he just say that he remembers?' said Ohm in astonishment. Anteus turned to the three eyed god.

'I am the god of Memories, after all,' he replied with a grin. 'Right, let's get out of this blasted place and give Ava a piece of our minds. First of all, everybody needs to start walking backwards.'

***

Bratzva held up a hand and motioned for everyone to quieten down. Faintly, Rhev could now hear the bassy gurglings of what he assumed were the demons they sought. It was coming from just around the next corner.

'This is it,' said Bratzva, softly but firmly. 'We're about to make contact. Judging by how empty this place has been so far, my guess is that the majority of the creeps are in the next room. We go in, hard and fast. Weapons at the ready.'

He then addressed Mina directly. Sterling had noticed earlier in a moment of doe-eyed fixation that she carried no weapons herself. 'Mina, you know what to do.' The girl grimaced, but understood whatever Bratzva was referring to.

Sterling whispered to her. 'What's he talking about?'

'Don't worry about it. Just don't be scared, okay?'

Bratzva breathed deeply.

'For the Lost.'

He took one last meaningful look at his son.

'Let's make them proud.'

He took off down the corridor, twin blades drawn. They

all followed him.

The inner sanctum of the Unfinished stronghold was colossal. Hundreds of steps dropped steeply away from the entrance of the chamber, spanning the entire quarter mile width of the space. At the foot of these stairs a morass of undulating bodies jostled around speleothem pillars, their attention fixed on a larger specimen of their kind working on a dais. In the centre of the dias lay the box, the infamous demongate. Its new owner, 'Mister Kowloon', in its true gruesome form, lurched about the edge of the dias constructing pylons from the surrounding dust and its own secretions. With a terrible black claw, it carved sigils into their surfaces. Three pylons had already been constructed. They each threw out continuous streams of black lightning that whipped around the surface of the box like groping tentacles. Both Kowloon and its disciples were utterly engrossed in the work. They had yet to notice the warband assembled at the top of the stairs behind them.

'What's it doing?' Rhev asked out of the side of his mouth.

'I think, from what I understand,' stammered Kevin, 'that it's probably stabilising the demongate, locking the exit point of its portal to a specific location.'

The box was visibly writhing in the grip of the black tethers now.

'I'm not sure what would happen to the box if we tried to take it now…'

'As long as we stop these things-' Rhev finally drew his greatsword and was immediately cut off by its echoing battlecry.

'END THAT WHICH SHOULD NOT HAVE BEGUN!'

The phrase rang out over and over as the echoes bounced around the sanctum. As one, the Unfinished turned their blank eyes towards him. So did Rhev's companions.

'Well, you heard the sword!' cried Bratzva.

As one, Rhev and his father lead the charge down the mighty steps into the throng of demons. Tooth met sword, claw met axe, hooks clanged off plate, and tails whipped around stray limbs. The fighting was more fierce than Rhev could have imagined. The only advantage they had against the horde was the high ground of the steps. To his left, one of the dwarven miners fell under the slash of multiple razor claws, his pickaxe thrown wildly across the chamber. Two of the large elves weathered blow after blow, their old plate armour denting with every strike. Standing back to back, they swung their longswords in great arcs, releasing grey bile from the vulnerable spots on the things assailing them. Rhev was surprised by the effectiveness of his oath-hurling greatsword. With each great swing he cleaved through carapace and sinew with a satisfying crunch. He swore his sword was beginning to laugh.

Sterling, Kevin, and Mina were cut off from the rest of the group, and were backing away towards the edge of the room. Like a man possessed the halfling flung knife after knife at the encroaching bodies, never stopping to question how he continued to find fresh weapons about his body. Beside him, Mina was grunting like a wounded animal, but he couldn't see any blood or bruising on her. An Unfinished near her shifted its limbs to pounce, its body momentarily *shlorping* and slurping as it transformed. Seeing his opening, Sterling sank a stiletto into its softened shins.

'Are you okay, Mina? What are you doing?' he said, avoiding another close call as a claw raked the air above his head. She moaned like a cat and sank to all fours. 'Mina?!' He was distracted for a moment too long. The claw that he had just dodged came back around and caught him in the side. He tumbled. Only with a frantic grab from Kevin did he not fall into the slathering clutches of the Unfinished.

With a terrible crunch Mina's petite frame expanded into a

312

bright red horror. Her mouth elongated, needle teeth shooting out from her receded gums. Her arms extended and popped as they gained an extra elbow joint, and membranes of veiny skin stretched from her underarms to her torso. With a violent shriek she descended upon Sterling's attacker and began tearing it apart between her teeth and newly formed claws.

On the other side of the battle, Mercy was screaming like a banshee. Warum moved like an extension of her own body, whirling about her in a single fluid motion. Years of training drilled into her on the frontlines of the east came to the fore. *This is it,* she thought, *this is the worthy enemy.* After her third kill she had perfected the means to dispatch the Unfinished. As she feinted to the left another one of the demons squeezed the tissue on their right flank into a spiked carapace, allowing her to follow the feint through in a figure of eight to attack its fleshy left side. As she became more confident she began to wade in towards the enemy, no longer fighting defensively. She was fighting for the Lost. She was fighting for her world. She was fighting to punish those that hurt the man who took her in all those years ago. She was fighting for herself. She wasn't scared no longer.

At the centre of the steps, Rhev lifted the heavy sword above his head to prepare for another downward strike. The violence of the swing took him backwards, enough for his foot to trip on the step behind. He fell hard on his arse. A sickle-shaped barb descended, aimed at his belly. The barb was caught in the crook of two crossed swords.

'Get up, lad!' shouted Bratzva as he heaved the barb to the side. With the barb out of the way, he thrust both swords point first into the fleshy underside of the demon as it attempted to manifest another barb. He turned and offered a hand. Rhev took it. Bratzva leant his forehead against his son's.

'Together now.'

Father and son fought alongside each other with devastating effect. Every opening Bratzva made with his quick swordsmanship was capitalised by a heavy blow from Rhev's screaming greatsword.

Across the chamber, Kevin and Sterling were struggling. In her monstrous form, Mina was managing to hold off most of the Unfinished surrounding them, but there were tears in her wings and wounds peppering her body. As she harried yet another foe from the air like a demented falcon, a large tentacle shot out from the mob and wrapped itself around her foot. She was now anchored to the ground, her wings flapping in vain. A creature made entirely of gnashing teeth took hold of her other foot. Pinned and desperate, Mina was forced to transform back into her humanoid form, her slim legs slipping from the grip of the teeth and tentacles. She landed near a prone Sterling.

'Kevin,' said the wounded halfling. 'Now really would be a good time to pull a Montefort.'

'I can't! I can't!' The elf was frantically gesturing with his free hand, attempting to conjure every spell he had ever committed to memory. Only sputtering sparks emanated from the tip of his wand. He had resorted to stabbing with it wildly. By luck alone he poked one of the many eyes of an arachnoid demon, pushing it back for just a moment. *Half an ear, half an elf… half a wizard, if that!*

'I've seen you do incredible things before, friend!' yelled Sterling. 'Don't doubt yourself! I don't!'

Kevin felt the most amazing sensation, like air touching one's skin when they have been submerged for a very long time, so long that they had forgotten what it felt like to be dry. Magick was in the air. Magick that he could feel, that he could understand and draw from. Pingle, forty-seventh, or possibly forty-sixth, mightiest of the gods, had returned.

As quickly as elvenly possible, Kevin traced a series of

314

sigils in the air with his slender fingers. Starting at the tip of his index finger, an incredible red glow developed, as if a bright light was being shone through his skin. It passed rapidly through his whole body, culminating at the tip of his wand. A ball of white-hot flame gathered there, its steady expansion forcing Kevin's arm backwards with the effort of controlling it. Just as his best friend was about to be devoured by a hulking demon, he released the ball of fire.

A raging inferno blossomed from his wand and immolated several ranks of the Unfinished surrounding them. Kevin, exhausted by the strain of the spell, slumped next to Sterling to catch his breath.

'I knew you had it in you,' the halfling said, patting his friend weakly on the knee. 'A proper wizard, worthy of the hot pants.'

'I reckon you owe me at least three bottles of wine for saving your life,' Kevin wheezed, sharing a grin with Sterling.

'Oh, my poor, cocksure friend. It's not over yet. I'm certain I can save your life at least once before this is over.' They shared a chuckle. Sterling tasted blood in his mouth.

After the smoke had cleared, it appeared that the Lost had managed to tip the scales in their favour, but for how long, they couldn't be sure. Many of them had already suffered grievous wounds. Some of them had died. One of the knightly elves stood valiantly over the bodies of his comrades, hidden under the rent metal of their armour. The gang of humans fought ferociously, some reduced to using hunting knives or spiked knuckledusters. One of them resembled a swamp creature; her long hair, loosened from its tight braids, slick with black blood.

Among the havok, the two Becketts had taken refuge in the protective circle of the dwarves. Once or twice they were forced to use their knives on Unfinished that broke through the ring, and together they were able to actually slay one of the beasts. Severin felt the heat of the fireball on his face as it decimated the enemies to their flank. For a moment, there was an opening.

'Come on, brother, now!' he shouted in Haverely's ear over the din of battle. 'The time is right, there's a way through. We can take the box for ourselves!'

'Ourselves?! Are you insane, Severin?' In his weakened state, Haverley was beginning to tire. His words can out hoarse and breathless.

'The box is the key, don't you see? We can rise to the top again, envy of Fence Street once more. Beckett and Beckett, a name to be respected, feared even! We'd have the monopoly on an entire world! You and I, brother!'

'Fence Street? Fence Street!' Haverley's eyes were wild with astonishment. He couldn't believe the blind avarice of his brother, still alive and kicking even in a damned place like this. 'Please see the bigger picture here! This isn't about the copper pennies any more.You're thinking small, Severin, like a bloody-' he coughed violently, the outburst draining him, '-accountant!'

Somewhere in the back of Severin Beckett's mind, a final, load-bearing thread snapped. His eye twitched. A hot, angry tear fell from it. Years of failure and humiliation came to a head. He thought of Hampton's betrayal, the sting of his words. 'I have a duty to something bigger than you, sir,' he had said on that beach as that blasted fisherfolk had spluttered back to life. He thought of the sign above his firm's front door. 'Beckett and Becketts'. Two Becketts. He knew that his brother had always thought of him as the second. Time to show them all for the fools they were.

Before Haverley could stop him, his brother made a break for the gap in the horde. Miraculously, his slight frame avoided the swipes of the remaining Unfinished on the right flank. Panting violently, he reached the foot of the dias. The demon artificer, the leader of the pack, was hurriedly carving sigils in what looked to be the final pylon. Distracted by the near completion of its work, it didn't notice Beckett climb the stairs to the top of the platform.

Haverley cried out as loudly as he could manage: 'Please, Severin! I can't lose you again!'

His brother rushed between the bolts of whipping black energy, his shabby frock coat disintegrating where it flapped into the oath of the magickal beams. Before finishing the final sigil, Kowloon turned in time to witness Beckett kneel down and lift the box from its ethereal moorings. An abominable scream of despair escaped the horror's maw. The black ropes of magick surrounding the box scraped at its surface with an awful rubbery sound. They had wrapped tightly around it, each line crossing another and knotting them in place. Beckett tugged. With no slack available, the knotted lines squeezed hard against the box. Intent on releasing his prize from its bonds at any cost, Beckett tugged again with all his might. The box exploded in his hands.

The raw magick contained inside expanded instantly into a terrifying pearlescent vortex. Everyone's eyes, humanoid and Unfinished alike, turned towards the blinding flash of light.

'What has he done?!' asked Kevin, pushing himself up from the ground. 'It's uncontained! All that magick is free!'

'What can we do?' said Sterling weakly.

'I don't know! Once it's out of the box we can't put it back in. I'm not even certain how long the portal will stay there.'

'We can't take it back to the Lost, can we?'

Kevin shook his head. Even as they spoke, the huge vortex was beginning to shrink towards a point at its center.

With a bloodcurdling howl, the Unfinished who had been attempting to control the demongate leapt through into the maelstrom and disappeared.

'Dad! Look!' Rhev pointed towards the dias. 'We're too late. The demons have started to go through.'

'Not on my watch.' Bratzva flourished his swords, flicking streams of black blood onto the floor.

'Nor mine.' Father and son nodded to each other. Between them they started clearing a path through the Unfinished scum.

The battle became even more brutal and confused than before. Seeing that the portal was open but diminishing, many of the demons turned their backs to the warriors in their frantic attempt to get through. The remaining Lost pushed their advantage and harried their escape, planting their blades into the twisted spines of those retreating. A couple of Unfinished managed to follow their leader through the portal, trampling over the unmoving body of Severin Beckett.

Finally, the doughty crew of Steem Vennts' & Co, including Bratzva and Mina, made it through the throng to the foot of the dias. Mina held the almost unconscious body of Sterling in her arms. Mercy was covered in blood, both of the demons and her own. In her furied state, she had hardly noticed the wounds she had suffered. Steem had lost his top hat for good. Kevin's wand steamed from the bolts of fire he had been slinging to cover their advance.

The portal was reducing rapidly. It was now barely the height of a man at its widest point.

'I don't think it will last much longer,' yelled Kevin over the sound of raw magickal energy sparking in front of them. 'I can't stabilise it. If we're going through, it's now or never.'

'What about the rest of the Lost? Back at the camp?' asked Rhev. 'We can't just leave them.'

'Yes you can,' said Bratzva solemnly. 'You heard the wizard. There's nothing more you can do for them now. All that's left is to worry about those souls in the world above. That's the only path left.'

'Bratzva's right. We can do more good up there than down here,' said Mercy.

The portal was shrinking rapidly now.

'Let's finish what we started!' screamed Steem. He dived headlong into the roiling light and disappeared. Mercy followed, then Kevin, pushing Mina through with Sterling in his arms. By the time it was Rhev's turn, the portal was barely larger than a dinner plate.

'Come on dad. Together now.' A look of deep sadness fell across his father's ruddy face. 'Dad?'

Bratzva drew his lips in with the strain of keeping them from wobbling. 'I love you, Rhev. I'm proud of you. But you don't need me now. The Lost do.'

'You just said there's nothing more we can do for them!'

'That *you* can do for them, Rhev. I know you have a good heart, but it isn't your burden to bear, your promise to keep. I told the people here that I would do whatever I could to protect them. I told you I was trying to be better, yes? What am I if I don't keep that promise? I've broken so many promises, son...'

'Please, dad. If this is because... I shouldn't have judged you so harshly. I've made mistakes too, I've-'

'And you learnt from them, right? Each one led you here, guided your hand, helped you make the right choice. Now's your chance to help your friends, help the people of *your* world. Remember the stories I used to tell you before bed? It was never supposed to be me in those stories, Rhev. It was you.'

With an almighty shove, he threw Rhev into the saucer-sized portal behind him. His form funnelled into the bright centre, and both dwarf and portal disappeared with the sound of a thousand matches going out.

Bratzva faced the remaining horde of demons. The slathering mass stood atop his fallen comrades. He grunted in fatalistic determination. Then he noticed one of the ex-prisoners kneeling over the body of the cowardly man in the singed frock coat.

'Oi, mate.' Haverley looked up, tears in his eyes. Bratzva threw one of his swords to the man. He caught it awkwardly. 'Wanna be a hero?'

***

Cal, Dermis, and Aed stared dumbfounded as a host of bedraggled but determined gods strode past the Table chamber. Two familiar faces popped their heads in.

'Erin? Merky? I thought you'd been smote or something?' said Cal.

'No smiting for us,' said Merky, who was unusually happy. 'We were thrown into the pits of Nigrond instead. Turns out anyone who doesn't agree with how things are run around here gets locked away for eternity. You don't even get to wait around for the paperwork to be filed.'

'That sounds quite unreasonable,' said Aed.

'It does, doesn't it? We're all going up now to tell Ava how corrupt her system is and how, as a religious experiment, it's failed entirely.'

'Oh, blimey. I mean, I didn't want to say anything...' Dermis muttered.

'We've got a progenitor with us as well. Want to come along? We've already got most of the prayer stratification department with us. Turns out their job satisfaction rates were pretty low.'

The three gods glanced at each other with looks that suggested that no-one was brave enough to say yes until someone else did.

'It's not like you're going to do anything else on your lunch break,' said Erin.

After much hullabaloo, the renegade gods stood before the doors of Ava's sanctum. Ohm had a squad of Flaw Managers

320

transfixed by the power of his third eye. They graciously moved aside.

'I think you should go first,' said Anteus to Erin. 'This is your little revolution, really. Don't worry, we all believe in you.'

'Look, I get that it's very important to believe in each other,' said Pingle from a few ranks back, 'but do we really have to be so on the nose about it? Can we just sort of do it silently, in our heads? It's getting a bit repetitive.'

There was a general booing from the other gods.

'Fine, *fine*. I believe in you, Erin.'

It was non-committal, but appreciated all the same. Erin steeled herself with a thumbs up from Merky, and opened the tall gilded doors of the sanctum.

The room was not as she had expected. It was large, yes, but unexpectedly cosy. The floors were covered in richly decorated rugs and an abundance of armchairs with accompanying pouffes. At the back of the room stood a grand desk, but instead of being covered in paperwork or writing implements, it was instead covered in an unfinished jigsaw puzzle. As Erin cautiously entered the room, she could see that it was made up of infinitesimally small pieces and depicted a kitten playing with a ball of yarn. The kitten had a bow on its head.

'I didn't think I had any more appointments for at least another seven months.' The newcomer was old, perhaps even older than Anteus. She wore a modest pinny covered in intricately embroidered flowers, and what appeared to be knitting needles in her hair. Over the pinny, quite offsetting the whole outfit, was a shining gold breastplate.

'Ava?'

The god continued over to the desk and sat down in the comfortable wingback chair behind it.

'Hmm?' she asked as she placed a miniscule puzzle piece.

'You're Ava, Almighty Mother, head of this pantheon, right?'

'Yes, dear. Very observant.'

Ava still hadn't noticed the horde of gods jostling at the door to her sanctum. Erin wasn't sure how to proceed. She turned around to see all the gods beaming at her. Merky gave her another thumbs up.

'We are, erm, that is to say, a lot of us, aren't very happy with how things are being run. It's not working. Temples, prayers, magick, it's all not as good as it should be.'

Ava looked up. 'My, my, there are a lot of you, aren't there. I'm sorry to hear you all think that, but my people assure me everything is going splendidly. Lots of prayers coming in and all that. What was it they said, erm, oh yes - peak theological growth with optimum theurgy to providence ratios.'

'I'm sorry to have to say this, but I think those are fancy ways of saying that we're not... actually doing anything.'

'Oh, really?' Ava put the puzzle piece in her hand down on the table. 'But they always say everything is going so well when I ask them and that I wasn't to worry about the complicated running of the whole thing. I'm not very good with the bureaucratic bits, you see. Bit of an old-fashioned sort.'

Erin looked at the god in front of her with a mixture of sternness and sympathy. 'When was the last time you took a look at how things were going down there?'

'Quite a while now, I suppose. I've been very busy with this puzzle.'

The look on Erin's face in response told her all she needed to know.

'Oh dear. That bad, is it? I did have a *little* bit of an inkling, I just didn't want to look the gift horse in the mouth, as I believe the mortal phrase goes. You better sit down and fill me in. No, not there, that one's for your feet.'

***

Rhev couldn't feel any part of his body. His mind, which strangely he *could* feel, told him that he felt very much like a gas. It occurred to him that he might just be dead. His theory was supported by the incredible whiteness all around him. He looked around, which was quite impressive as he couldn't find his eyes. *Where's my dad?* Then he remembered their conversation. *He's left me again.* Sadness swept through his being. Then anger. Hot anger. As the gas of his body began to condense into something more familiar, a new emotion filled him. Pride. Not the pride he had felt for his father growing up. This was a different pride. It had more weight to it. It was real.

Whumpf.

Squawk.

Creak.

Ding-ding-ding.

Rhev felt the wind against his back. Water droplets splattered against his face. A grey sky was all he could see. The grey sky became a grey box. The grey box became smaller and smaller, until Rhev realised with horror that he was falling away from it. No sooner than had he made this realisation did he land with an unexpected softness. He was lying on a hay wagon.

Rhev sat bolt upright, and surveyed his surroundings. Defying all probability, he found himself in Velheim, the city of his birth. The limpet shanties on the walls of the Underport came into view, and he realised he was descending on one of the many goods lifts.

'Rhev, wherever you are, can you help please!'

Kevin's voice echoed around the vast cavern. Rhev looked in the direction of the shout and picked out his companions' standing on one of the largest lifts in the Underport, over

323

three hundred feet away from where Rhev currently sat. Kevin was desperately firing off jagged bolts of lightning in the direction of a gruesome Unfinished and sporadically taking cover behind crates. Nearby, Mina stood over the body of Sterling, brandishing one of his trademark throwing knives and defensively slashing at another demon. Steem, in a surprising feat of what could only be described as 'old man strength', was wrestling with a smaller demon, his cleaver embedded in the planks beside him. At the opposite corner of the platform Mercy duelled the mastermind behind all of this: the true, abominable form of Mister Kowloon.

Rhev's greatsword lay on the hay next to him. He grasped the hilt and used it to push himself up.

'You need to stop the platform!' he yelled. 'If it gets down to the docks all hell will break loose! Go for the pulleys...!'

His voice was drowned out by his own screeching blade.

'UNNATURAL, UNWELCOME, UNFINISHED!'

There was a demon on the same platform as Rhev. It had no head, but instead a drooling, tooth lined maw that took up its entire torso. With an awful popping sound, the maw opened wide. As its jaw unhinged, a black tongue slithered between its teeth, taking flesh from the rapidly inverting body of the Unfinished and adding it to the extending protrusion. The tongue lashed out at Rhev in a sinuous and unpredictable wave that he had no way of blocking. It wrapped around his left arm and then pulled like a ripcord. As the tongue slithered back, Rhev saw that his bicep had been horribly eviscerated. He realised that the tongue, although slick with drool, was covered in thousands of tiny barbs that had ripped through skin and muscle, right down to the bone.

He cried out. Forced to wield the large sword one-handed, he used his whole body to swing it in a horizontal arc, severing the tongue. The demon gurgled and began reforming the rows of teeth into many fingered claws. The momentum of

Rhev's swing was too much to take and the sword flew from his hand, smashing into a crate and releasing a torrent of potatoes. Unarmed, Rhev had no defense to stop the demon's claws from raking his chest and shoulders. Slick with blood and utterly stunned, Rhev tripped on a bucket behind him and sprawled on the planks. A lucky kick from the ground made contact with the Unfinished's single black eye, and it backed off momentarily.

Rhev felt a lump in the small of his back.

'Gi' o'er ya gammy bastard!' said a small, muffled voice.

Rhev felt under him and retrieved a potato.

'Get ya filthy mitts off meh!' it said, although not through any visible mouth.

With mere seconds to spare before the demon would be able to grow another eye, Rhev had an idea.

'You look like you could do with some fibre, ya monster!' he screamed as he hurled the potato at the demon's mouth. It caught it with terrifying agility and gulped it down whole. A wail of indignant reprimands assaulted both their ears as the remaining potatoes witnessed the murder of their brethren. Free from the confines of their crate, there was nothing stopping them from leaping into action. First it was just a few spuds that flung themselves at the demon, bouncing harmlessly from its chitin or skewing themselves on its claws. Then more and more of the tubers hailed down on the confused monster, until an avalanche of would-be chips had buried it completely.

Meanwhile, Kevin had succeeded in halting their lift by growing thick vines out of the wood of the pulley mechanism, which glowed dimly in the half dark of the Underport. The wizard now turned his attention back to the fight. Steem was nowhere to be seen. Kevin panicked.

From somewhere over the lip of the platform came a very muffled cry for help. Kevin skidded over to where he thought

325

he had heard the voice, and looked over the edge. Vertigo kicked in almost immediately, another phobia to add to his list. Far below the platform, on the quayside, lay a large pile of mangled flesh.

Kevin shrieked. 'Steem?!'

To his right he heard the muffled voice again. 'O'er 'ere, 'oo 'ooron.'

Dangling there by the tips of his fingers was Steem, his meat cleaver gripped in his teeth. His eyes were wide and imploring. Kevin could see his fingers slipping on the rain slick wood.

'Hang on!' He crawled over, heart palpitating as he got another look at the drop below him. 'I'm coming!'

He grabbed Steem's hairy mitts and pulled. It was difficult. Kevin cursed himself, realising this was the one time he wished he had taken after his strapping father. Just as he got past the worst of gravity's effects on his boss's body, his boot slipped. Both Kevin and Steem's eyes bulged as together they lunged towards the open air and certain death.

At the last moment, he felt something tug at the hem of his trousers, anchoring him just enough to gain a footing.

'On second thoughts, it's a good thing you haven't got your hot pants yet,' Sterling grimaced, 'because I sure as heck wouldn't want to grab on to those.'

With Kevin and Sterling's strength combined, pitiful though it was, they were able to haul Steem onto the platform. He took the cleaver out of his mouth.

'Good to see you two finally putting in some hard graft,' he wheezed, 'rather than leaving it up to Mercy.'

Mercy was struggling. The wounds that she had shrugged off through sheer adrenaline were slowly overcoming her. She parried blow after blow from Kowloon's savage claws. The creature had transformed into a true stygian nightmare now. At least twelve feet tall, its eyes set vertically in a tapered

326

head, its six arms equipped with a terrifying array of natural weaponry.

The shock of a final valiant parry knocked the power from her sword arm. Kowloon could see all too well that she was near to defeat. Its face deformed into that of the old man's guise he had adopted in Little Mosshill, with the exception of the vertically slit eyes in its forehead. There was a bubbling sound as the demon formed humanoid vocal cords somewhere in its throat.

'Why would you deny us this realm?' it asked, its voice a strange dual tone of bass and wheezy tenor. 'We were forgotten, forsaken by the gods.' A huge, eagle-like foot pinned Mercy to the floor. 'Did we deserve to be denied the colour of life?'

With great effort, Mercy replied: 'After all the senseless violence and torture, I'd say so.'

Kowloon gurgled out a laugh. 'Oh, that came after we were condemned. It's amazing what horrors someone will commit when you take the sky away from them.'

'There's… no… excuse.'

'Is that so, warrior? *Killer*? I can see in your eyes the violence you've committed. For lesser reasons, I suspect. Unjust and petty wars, no doubt. The least you could have done to redeem yourself is share this world with my kind. Alas, it now seems I have but one avenue left to me. I shall rage.'

Kowloon shifted its full weight onto its foot, crushing Mercy beneath it. Her chainmail grinded, cutting into her skin. She cursed in pain.

'Hands off my employee!'

A meat cleaver cut through Kowloon's leg at the ankle, severing myriad tendons and digging into bone. It stuck fast. The demon screamed as he was forced to take weight off the foot. Kevin, Sterling, and Mina dragged Mercy out from under

327

it. Steem was thrown away violently and landed limply against a crate. Kevin, his hands shaking from stress, hastily conjured a jet of flame that streamed towards the lord of the Unfinished. In reaction, the creature manifested a thick membrane between three of its arms to use as a shield. The pale flesh bubbled under the heat of the fire, but Kevin couldn't hold the spell for long. As the red hot wash subsided, he could see that the majority of the damage had been absorbed. His wand steamed as cold rain continued to fall, and without warning it cracked along its length.

Rhev dragged his sword along the ground. He was losing a lot of blood. His vision was becoming blurred. He saw his friends far away, battling a huge demon that was growing bigger second by second. Then he realised that for the first time since the battle started, his sword had grown silent. With difficulty, he looked down at it. *I must be close to death,* he thought, *I'm hallucinating.* A multicoloured light was pulsating in intervals from the sword's hilt and down to the tip of the blade. *This is definitely more what I would call 'magick sword' territory, but I'm not sure if a light show is going to help.*

RHEV

The voice was inside his head. Its tones were strong, resolute, female.

IN THIS HOUR OF NEED, I GRANT YOU AN IOTA OF MY POWER

His vision began to regain focus. He felt his injured arm twinge, and saw the blood that he had left behind him slither up the blade, over his body, and down into the wound. He clenched his muscle, and found it was functional again.

WIELD THE CHAMPION'S SWORD RIGHTEOUSLY

Well I never, I've got to go buy old Hoskin a drink or three if I ever get out of this.

BLESSINGS OF AVA UPON YOU

Ava? AVA? Is this some sort of... godsword?

328

...YES

Pretty convenient if you ask me. Could have done with knowing this sooner. This feels like a bit of a cop out now.

YOU STILL HAVE TO SWING THE BLOODY THING

Rhev felt the divine presence leave his mind, but the sword continued to glow. Each time the light pulsed down the fuller it illuminated the lettering there: *Onur.*

Okay, maybe just one drink for my illiterate friend.

He looked to the final combat. Mercy was standing over Steem, her bastard sword grasped in both hands, her shoulders slumped with fatigue. Sterling was weakly flinging knives at Kowloon from a supine position. Kevin crouched by his friend, frantically hitting his wand in an attempt to get it working again. Mina was trying desperately to distract the demon, darting this way and that but with no chance of landing a strike.

Rhev counted silently in his head. He reckoned he was about the length of ten lifts away from their fight. A well-timed, clean run was all he needed, lift to lift. He cast his mind back to the last time he had attempted something like this. *You got very lucky*, he thought. *If you get the timing wrong again, you're more than likely a skidmark on the cobbles. We're trying not to be reckless, right?*

Then again, it all depends on why *you're doing it.*

Rhev brandished the holy greatsword above his head, and charged. The blade left a faint rainbow trail above his head as he ran across the lifts. Forward one, then left, hard right, little jump. He kept his momentum. Every lift lined up exactly as he wanted it to. Anothing little jump, then another. A pang of doubt hit him. He couldn't quite see, but he realised that he might be too high. *No time.* He reached the tenth lift. *Keep going.* Almost at the edge. *Bugger.*

A single nail jutting up from the final plank tripped him, and he fell. The scene below unfolded before him. Kowloon

329

was over twenty feet tall now and had developed a carapace over its entire body, in a parody of a knight's plate. One of its arms had solidified into a single blade, raised to strike Mercy, who now kneeled over Steem. Its head was bare, as if it had removed its helmet to better appreciate its conquest.

Rhev sensed a blossoming of light behind him. His friends looked up, and witnessed a pair of incredible luminescent wings sprouting forth from the dwarf's back. In truth, he looked quite ridiculous. Rhev himself couldn't see this, and had no idea what was happening. All he could think of, in what he was certain were his final moments, was that he wanted to be able to sink his mighty sword into the demon's head before he died. Miraculously, he did.

The blessed sword split Kowloon's crown with an almighty crack. The entirety of the Underport was illuminated in blinding white light. Thunder echoed throughout the cavern. In the middle of it all, Rhev floated.

The Unfinished toppled to the floor, the force of which broke the vines holding the platform in place. Slowly, it descended to the docks, and so did Rhev. His wings disappeared.

Cliff Guardsman Feculent, also known as Buttmug, watched dumbstruck as his old rival Rhev Culluggan lowered into view. The dwarf stood astride the corpse of a huge monster, his hands still holding the hilt of a greatsword embedded in the creature's skull.

Feculent blew his whistle. 'Guards! Guards!' A squad of watchmen jogged around the corner. The orc sergeant led them up onto the goods lift. 'Slap this no-good, dirty, stinking shortarse in irons!' he ordered.

'Oh bugger off, Buttmug, really not the time,' said Rhev as he tugged at the sword. 'I'm pretty sure we've just done your job for you.'

A sucking sound preceded the sword being drawn from

the skull. Then there was a flash, and the entire sword disintegrated in Rhev's hands.

'Trust a shoddy excuse like you to have an equally shoddy excuse for a weapon,' the orc smirked. 'Playing pretend with a pretend sword; classic little Rhev. Where you been all this time, eh? Hiding your face? Couldn't hack Velheim anymore?'

'You know what, Feculent, you're right. I couldn't hack Velheim any more. It was bringing me down. Not enough opportunities for adventure. Not enough opportunities to be who I wanted to be.'

'Oh yeah, what's that then? A big ol' la-dee-dah hero?'

Rhev looked pointedly at the giant monster corpse next to him, and grinned. 'Well, I know I'm not the villain.'

'Bah! Well, maybe it will shock you to know, *dwarf*, that people around here still remember the truth about ol' Rhev Culluggan. A soft touch, britches-wetting, *loser* who ain't getting no respect from any Velheimnian who matters. Especially after all this mess you've just caused, and mark my words, you'll be paying for the cleaning.'

Rhev just smiled in reply, as he realised, with all his heart, that he truly didn't care. He knew what he had done and who he was, and that's all that mattered now.

The unexpected lack of retort perturbed Feculent. Frustrated, he gestured to his comrades. Two guardsmen grabbed the battle-weary dwarf from behind and held his hands fast behind his back.

'Woah, woah, hang on lads. I know the law. On what grounds are you arresting me?'

'Disturbing the peace.' Feculent spat at Rhev's feet, and ordered the men to drag him away. Too tired to resist, Rhev simply slumped and dragged his feet along the ground, determined not to make their job easy. He saw his friends, still on the platform, growing further and further away. He was pleased to see that they all seemed to be alive, more or less.

331

Wearily, they each held a fist to their breast in salute. Rhev felt a warmth inside of him.

'Don't worry about me,' he called to them. 'They can't hold me for long!'

***

'What are the chances that he had one of Ava's old swords, eh?' said Merky, as he tucked into a supersized bowl of ambrosia. 'Bit convenient if you ask me.'

'I don't know, a little bit of predestination never hurt. It's stuff like that this world needs a little more of. I'd take convenient holy artifacts over mass produced Missus Milton's Marvelous Honey, "Now Church Approved!"'

Erin dove into the bowl of ambrosia with a spoon of her own and came up with a healthy dollop. 'What do you think you'll do now?' she said through a mouthful.

'They're going to need someone with experience in oaths and agreements to help sort out this new pantheon. Nothing too draconian, mind you, we're going to keep it loose, like it used to be. Just a few sensible covenants here and there. What about you?'

'Back to the hedgehogs for me. I really do miss them.'

'Really? You were the leader of a divine revolution! You changed things, Erin!'

'Don't get me wrong, I'm glad I did. But after talking to Ava, who is actually very sweet by the way, I know that I don't want what she had. Success made her blind, Merky. It complicated things for her, left her open to exploitation. I don't need that. I already know what makes me happy.'

She took another scoop of the ambrosia and savoured it, her eyes closed in contentment.

'How can you say "no" to happiness?'

***

Rhev knew every inch of the jail, both inside and outside the cells. An hour or so later, when Feculent had finally had

332

enough of gloating, Rhev deftly picked the lock with a chicken bone he had hidden behind a brick many years ago, and snuck out the back door.

The jail hadn't been far from his own hovel, deep in the slums of the Underport. Without conscious thought, Rhev's feet took him back there now. They even managed to trip over Steve the harbour cat. An urchin stuck their fingers up at him. All was very much the same, except for how it felt. Instead of the comforting feeling he had expected, there was now a hollowness. The city around him was like a used up husk, and the cavernous roof of the Underport brought back unwanted reminiscences of the Unterwelt's endless ceiling. He trudged on.

Josephine had kept her word and fixed Rhev's front door. She had even gone as far to add a crude lock, which surprised him. Of course, Rhev didn't have the key, which would mean a necessary encounter with Josephine herself. He braced himself, and knocked on her door. The knock was answered with violent coughing sounds for several seconds before the door actually opened.

'You came back?' she exclaimed, not in the tone of indignant surprise that Rhev had expected, but in relief. Before Rhev had time to answer, the plague-ridden old woman embraced him in a boney and slightly wet hug. It was as pleasant as it was unexpected.

'Thanks for fixing the door,' Rhev wheezed when she finally let him go. 'I was hoping to get the key.'

Ignoring his question, Josephine continued in a hushed voice, 'Did you find Ava, Rhev?'

Rhev paused, then chuckled. 'I suppose you could say Ava found me.'

Josephine frowned. 'Oh dear. I see what the outside world has done to you. Inflated that wicked head of yours. Too good to go looking for Ava, eh? Decided you'd just wait around and

333

let her do the hard graft? Blasphemy!'

She rifled through her shift and fished out a key, which she thrust roughly into Rhev's palm.

'Begone with you! Go back to the heathens you call friends,' she screeched. 'And don't bother paying me for the door, I don't want your dirty money.'

Taking no heed of her ravings, Rhev continued calmly, 'Please Josephine, I have to give you something.'

'No, no. I did it out of respect for your old mum. She tried her best to raise you, she really did. A real hero, that woman. *A real hero*. Always doing her best for others. Such a shame you only think about yourself, Rhev Culluggan!'

With that, she slammed the door in his face. As Rhev unlocked his door and sat down in the stale, empty hovel, he thought on her words. He took no offense to them, he knew the old bat was as mad as they came, but there was truth to them nonetheless. He couldn't believe how blind he had been. His mum *was* a hero, more so than his dad even. He understood that now. True heroism was doing something not because you wanted to do it for yourself, but because you wanted to do it for others. It was selflessness, not thrill-seeking. It was something that his dad hadn't fully learnt until too late in his life, but now, thinking back, Rhev realised that some seed of it *had* been there, and he had tried his best to pass to his son to grow. As Rhev thought back to the stories his father had told, all the more vivid now that he was sitting in his childhood home, he realised he had been focusing on the wrong parts. He remembered his favourite tale, of the brave warrior and the thieving dragon deep in its fiery mountain lair. As a child, he had been fixated on the death defying deeds and wondrous treasure, but had forgotten about why the warrior had been there in the first place: he was there to win back the stolen property of the townsfolk, and return it to them safely. He was doing it for *them*.

Rhev dragged the old locker out from under his bed, and retrieved the last item of any real value left in the old hovel: his mum's snuffbox. He tucked it safely into his jerkin, then locked up his old home, and slipped the key under Josephine's door. He had no intention of ever returning.

Tired of not seeing the sky, he went straight for the surface-bound goods lift. The lift had already been cleaned of demonflesh, the residents of Velheim being notorious scavengers. After reaching topside, Rhev headed straight to The Jolly Foreigner. Bensen McKrath welcomed him as if he had never been gone, and took great delight in showing off the sponge that had recently replaced his hook. Apparently it made it a lot easier to clean the tankards, and had prevented a lot of injuries he would have otherwise suffered when trying to scratch his nose.

'Oh, and before I forget, a sorry lot of ruffians hired out the smoking room earlier. Said they were expecting you.'

With a flash of deja vu, Rhev ventured through the curtain into the back room. Everyone was laid out on the cushions, except for Mina, who was roughly re-applying a bandage to the head of a protesting Sterling. When Mercy saw Rhev enter, she got up and gripped him in a tight, one-armed hug.

'You could have pulled that stunt a bit earlier.'

'Tell me about it,' Rhev replied. 'If I knew I could fly I would never have signed up to be stuck with you lot. I'd be making a living catching birds or something.'

'Really?' said Kevin, rubbing the two halves of his wand together absently. 'Out of all the things you could do with the power of flight, you'd use it to *catch birds*? You could, well I don't know, hunt dragons or something?'

'Just because I can fly doesn't mean I'm suicidal, Kev. There's plenty of piratical folk in Velheim who lose their parrots. Alas, now that my sword is gone, I reckon my flying days are over.'

Batting Mina's hand away, Sterling piped up. 'Bugger the sword! It was *you* who slayed the beast!'

'Mercy and I softened it up a bit,' croaked Steem. 'Don't let it go to the lad's head.' He winked.

They spent the rest of the evening recuperating in the smokey den. Last orders came and the crew took some rooms upstairs. Rhev went out like a light, and dreamt of hedgehogs.

He followed the scent of a full Velheimnian breakfast downstairs the next morning. Steem was already seated, tucking into a particularly large hash brown.

'So, did I pass my probation?' asked Rhev as he took a seat opposite. Steem chuckled.

'Aye, that you have. Unfortunately, without a means to transport any cargo, there won't be an awful lot of work going around.'

'You're not thinking of breaking up the company, are you?'

'My days on the road are done, lad. I'm done looking.' He smiled sadly. 'Time to see what I have in the bank and settle down. Perhaps I'll be a butcher, eh? I felt pretty handy with that cleaver.'

'What's all this about settling down?' said Mercy. She sat down next to Rhev and began slowly cutting a sausage with one hand, the other hanging bandaged at her side.

'Just telling young Rhev here that he ought to set up his own group of mercenaries, or should I say "adventurers"?'

Rhev's cheeks flushed.

'I'm game,' replied Mercy, to his surprise.

'Adventurers, is it?' Sterling hobbled over to the bench with Mina's help and climbed on. 'I suppose you'll be needing some marketing?'

'Ah, yes, the archetypal heroes of old: the warrior, the wizard, and the marketer.' Kevin slumped down next to Steem. 'And whatever Mina is. No offense, Mina.'

She flashed some fangs and the elf shivered.

'You're actually interested? Adventuring for a living?' asked Rhev.

'It's a job,' winked Mercy.

'And we've got the experience now.' said Sterling. 'Easier to be a hero if you've done it once before. Plus, we know what pitfalls to avoid. Dodgy contracts, weird old men, that sort of thing. What do you reckon, Mina?'

'My entire life has been spent either in a castle full of monsters or the underworld. I think you *need* me.' She laughed, and Sterling swooned. It really was quite disgusting.

'Kevin?' asked Rhev.

The elf played with his food uneasily. 'Sterling still owes me five ducats from our last game of Stacks.'

'Looks like we have a full squad,' said Mercy.

'Not quite,' replied Rhev. 'I've got a couple of friends in mind. Good at nabbing, can take a beating, surprisingly handy in a tight spot. Plus, I owe them. Fingers crossed, we'll find them in Krovania.'

'Sounds like you've got yourselves a plan,' said Steem. 'You know what they say: every good adventure starts in a tavern.'

THE END